PHANTASMAGORIA

JANE MOBLEY has taught at the University of Kansas and at SUNY-Binghamton.

PHANTASMAGORIA
Tales of Fantasy
and the Supernatural

Edited with an Introduction by
JANE MOBLEY

ANCHOR BOOKS
Anchor Press/Doubleday
Garden City, New York

The Anchor Books edition is the first publication of *Phantasmagoria: Tales of Fantasy and the Supernatural.*

Anchor Books edition: 1977

Library of Congress Cataloging in Publication Data
Main entry under title:
Phantasmagoria: tales of fantasy and the supernatural.
CONTENTS: The wondrous fair: Anonymous. Arthur and Gorlagon. MacDonald, G. The golden key. Lord Dunsany. The fortress unvanquishable save for Sacnoth. Sturgeon, T. The silken swift. Bloch, R. The dark isle. Borges, J. L. The rejected sorcerer. Gray, N. S. According to tradition. Norton, A. The gifts of Asti. Le Guin, U. K. The rule of names. Warner, S. T. Winged creatures. Beagle, P. S. Sia. [etc.]
1. Fantastic fiction, English. 2. Fantastic fiction, American. I. Mobley, Jane.
PZ1.P4574   1977 [PR1309.F3]   823'.0876
ISBN 0-385-12329-9
Library of Congress Catalog Card Number 76-52007

ACKNOWLEDGMENTS

"The Golden Key" by George MacDonald. Reprinted by permission of Ballantine Books.

"The Fortress Unvanquishable Save for Sacnoth" by Lord Dunsany. Reprinted by permission of John Cushman Associates, Inc.

"The Dark Isle" by Robert Bloch. Copyright 1939 by *Weird Tales.* Copyright renewed © 1965 by Robert Bloch. Reprinted by permission of the author and the author's agents, Scott Meredith Literary Agency, Inc., 845 Third Ave., New York, N.Y. 10022.

"The Rejected Sorcerer" by Jorge Luis Borges. Copyright © 1960 by Great American Publications Inc.

"The Gifts of Asti" by Andre Norton. Copyright 1949 by Andre Norton. Reprinted by permission of the author and the author's agent, Larry Sternig Literary Agency.

ACKNOWLEDGMENTS

I am grateful to my students at the University of Kansas and the State University of New York at Binghamton who talked with me about fantasy and made suggestions about stories to use in this collection. For help in finding the stories, I am indebted to the staffs of the Watson Library Inter-library Loan Department and the Spencer Library at the University of Kansas. To Ann Hyde of Spencer Library, my special thanks; she offered endless patience, good humor, and encouragement in addition to her professional expertise. Thank you also to Professor Thomas Clareson, John Nizalowski, and Howard Devore for assistance in locating stories.

Like many books, I suspect, mine could never have been done without help from friends and family. To each of you who listened to me so tolerantly, thank you.

This book belongs in large part to Phillip Hofstra who believes in magic and in me.

*For Aaroncha,
best of good fairies,
in partial payment against an old debt*

CONTENTS

The Good are attracted by Men's perceptions,
And think not for themselves;
Till Experience teaches them to catch
And to cage the Fairies and Elves.

And then the Knave begins to snarl
And the Hypocrite to howl;
And all his good Friends shew their private ends,
And the Eagle is known from the Owl.

William Blake

Motto to the *Songs of Innocence and Experience*

PREFACE

This collection of stories grew out of an abiding love for fairy stories and tales of the supernatural which neither age nor schooling has managed to shake. When I was younger I spent long hours searching under the garden foliage for elves, and one afternoon I repeatedly climbed atop a chest of drawers and jumped resolutely off, sure in both body and heart that any moment I would fly, revealing at last to the world that I was the fairy changeling I believed myself to be. Bruised and dejected, I finally gave up. The requirements of adulthood have taken away the time to sit patiently peering into the throats of snapdragons, and all evidence points to the fact that I am human, too human to fly and too cautious now to risk the attempt. But still I am drawn to the magical, the supernatural, the "long ago and far away" of Faërie.[1]

---

[1] The realm of Faërie is difficult to describe or define. Dictionaries do not do well with it, nor for the most part do scholars. J. R. R. Tolkien (writing about it less as a scholar than as a frequent traveler in the perilous Realm) offers the only definition I know that seems adequate:

> . . . Faërie, the realm or state in which fairies have their being. Faërie contains many things besides elves and fays, and besides dwarfs, witches, trolls, giants, or dragons: it holds the seas, the sun, the moon, the sky; and the earth and all things that are in it: tree and bird, water and stone, wine and bread, and ourselves, mortal men, when we are enchanted. . . . I will not attempt to

How I yearn with Tolkien when he says, "I desired dragons with a profound desire."[2] Because I have not yet seen a dragon, nor for that matter an elf or—far more ordinary—a ghost, I satisfy my longing with fiction.

I am in good company. Fantastic stories have held listeners spellbound for as long as we have record of stories being told. Though tales of the wonderful and supernatural have taken many shapes since marvelous stories first were shared in leaping firelight, they have always been in answer to the same deep desire: the human craving to be carried or enchanted to worlds beyond the one we know, or to have revealed to us here in this world some glimpse of the Other, some understanding or experience wholly different from what we normally perceive or consider possible.

Fantastic literature—stories of magic and the supernatural—takes as its province a reality which is unverifiable but is nonetheless real because of the impact it has on us. These stories offer us either impossible worlds—Secondary Worlds which operate by laws outside the range of reason and probability—or the known natural world substantially altered or transfigured by the supernatural. The science fiction writer is concerned with what is probable, if yet unsubstantiated, and science fiction is, disconcertingly enough, often a presage

_____

define [the nature of Faërie], nor to describe it directly. It cannot be done. Faërie cannot be caught in a net of words; for it is one of its qualities to be indescribable, though not imperceptible. It has many ingredients, but analysis will not necessarily discover the secret of the whole . . . Faërie itself may be perhaps most nearly translated by Magic—but it is magic of a peculiar mood and power, at the furthest pole from the vulgar devices of the laborious, scientific, magician.

The most important idea here, the truth which makes a definition of Faërie impossible, is that mortals may be in Faërie "when we are enchanted." In that magical state feeling is first, and we have little use for definitions: once there, we know where we are. (From Tolkien, "On Fairy-stories" in The Tolkien Reader (New York: Ballantine Books, 1966), pp. 9–10.)

[2] J. R. R. Tolkien, Tree and Leaf (New York: Houghton Mifflin Co., 1965), p. 40.

of scientific discovery. But the fantasist, or the occult writer, is concerned with experience that remains forever beyond the grasp of empirical method and rationality and carries its truth in intuition and feeling. The purpose of fantastic fiction is the evoking of wonder, the confrontation with the mysterious. The response may range from a kind of gawking astonishment to profound awe, and to be sure, the fiction itself ranges from stories which are simply pleasant sleight-of-hand brushes with parlor magic to those which reveal some inexpressible "meaning-in-the-mysterious" which can leave a reader touched and changed. In any case, the Real Life of this fiction is not in fact but in feeling.

The fantastic is often derided as "escapist" literature, the release of frustrated readers. And escape it is—escape from a technological world where life seems all too frequently to be programed and manipulated by technophiles. Fantastic fiction is not a means of evading reality, but of contesting it. The escape is to an "ever-ever land" of fundamental questions and needs, a world where Imagination, Will, and Belief are still viable and the importance of Investigation, Hypothesis, and Confirmed Data recedes.

There has been in Western society a post-Enlightenment bias against literature which appears excessively whimsical or fanciful; tales of magic and the supernatural have often suffered the neglect of readers. Certainly the attitude of literary critics toward most fantasy and supernatural fiction remains largely the sneering contempt of highbrows for hacks, though steadily more critics are beginning to recognize this fiction as better than a pulp genre. As Ursula Le Guin pointed out in her National Book Award acceptance speech (in 1972 for *The Farthest Shore*):

> We who hobnob with hobbits and tell tales about little green men are quite used to being dismissed as mere entertainers, or sternly disapproved of as escapists. But I think that perhaps the categories are changing, like the times. Sophisticated readers are accepting the fact that an improbable and unmanageable world is going to produce a hypothetical and improbable art. At this point,

realism is perhaps the least adequate means of understanding or portraying the incredible realities of our
existence.[8]

Certainly fantastic literature is enjoying a tremendous revival of interest from readers and writers. This collection is
meant to aid that interest by offering stories which are generally hard to come by for most readers—the lone fantasy or
weird tale buried in a collection of other kinds of stories, stories out of print or printed originally in small magazines, as
well as stories which are in print but in places to which many
readers might not have access.

The shape of the collection—half magical and half supernatural stories—is not an arbitrary lumping on the theory
that readers who like hobbits will like haunters. It comes instead from the fact that these two kinds of stories are closely
bound in their heritage and in the kind of story-telling they
presuppose. They are closer to their folk-tale heritage than
any other genre of short fiction being written today. Whereas
most short fiction has followed other pursuits—experimenta-
tion with forms and techniques; "bits o' life" approaches
that are nearer to reportage than tale telling; or the evocation
of mood at the expense of action—wonder tales and supernatural tales are alike in that they preserve and use both the
form and feeling of the folk tale.

Fantasy stories are wonder tales and many are true fairy
tales (though that does not mean that fairies must appear in
the story, only that it evoke the mysterious realm of Faërie);
they depend on the same motifs, characters, and marvelous adventures that oral wonder tales have used since time
out of mind. Supernatural tales are legends with the same
conventions and trappings of legends that are current in a
specific community and shared there orally. Additionally, fantasy and supernatural writers attempt the same kind of entertainment an oral folk-tale teller hopes to achieve; that is, the
tale teller tries to make his listeners acutely aware of what is

---

[8] Ursula K. Le Guin, "National Book Award Acceptance Speech"
in *Dreams Must Explain Themselves* (New York: Algol Press,
1975), p. 29.

just outside the circle of firelight, what lives at the edges and in the shadows of our normal perception. With the wonder tale, the teller makes us aware that another world exists in the place where light and darkness meet, and then takes us there. In a supernatural tale, he tells us that unnameable things lurk in the shadow waiting to creep in upon us. What chiefly differentiates wonder and supernatural tales from other kinds of stories is the irreducible, inexplicable reality of the magical, the impossible, or the supernatural.

All the following tales share this characteristic, but as you will see they differ enormously from one another in subject, style, and tone. They range from the sprightly, even satirical, to the macabre and dolorous. They treat subjects as specific as the unicorn and as general as the universe, and their language, like their landscapes, runs from spare and starkly suggestive to ornamented and elaborately detailed.

Though wonder tales and supernatural stories share the premise that things are as we "know" they are not, this does not mean these two kinds of tales are rigidly separate from other kinds of speculative fiction. Perhaps it is well to think of speculative fiction (which is really any kind of fiction that deals in what *might be* instead of what *is* or *has been*) not as a big box with other little boxes inside (science fiction, fantasy, horror, and so on), but as a continuum stretched until it finally touches in a circle, rather like a shining silver thread with marvelously intricate strung beads along it. The beads may be far apart—as some stories are very different from each other while still clearly speculative fiction—or they may be pushed so close together that two appear to make one joined bead. The thread of the continuum can be said to spin out from mystical fiction, with its intended obscurities and intuitions on the one end, to hard-finish, machine-oriented science fiction on the other, where all speculation is carefully justified in technologically credible terms. In between are magical fantasy, supernatural fiction, weird fiction, and some dream literature. In every instance, one may find stories which exemplify one or the other type, and stories which combine two or more types.

Some of the stories in this collection are exemplary of a particular type, for example, M. R. James's "Oh, Whistle, and I'll Come to You, My Lad," a classic of the ghost-story genre. Some are blends, as is Andre Norton's "The Gifts of Asti" which combines science fiction and magical fantasy. None really needs classification, definition, or explanation. In every story you will find yourself encroached upon by the unknown or enchanted away into it as these tales draw you into the passing strange and wondrous fair.

THE WONDROUS FAIR:
Magical Fantasy

FANTASY IS the ability to envision life situations radically different from anything one has experienced. It is a uniquely human activity, fundamental to human consciousness and an inescapable process in human life. The family beagle may dream of rabbits, but only man can construct imaginative situations wholly different from the realities of his daily life. That man can, in fact, scarcely keep himself from such constructions is becoming more evident as psychological studies of fantasizing increase. Much of our ability to continue coping with the complexities of our everyday world is apparently dependent on the associational flights of imagination that break—intentionally or otherwise—into our patterns of directed, instrumental, or problem-solving thought. Fantasizing allows us not only to recoup our inner forces for struggle with the outer world, it also projects us beyond the moment, granting us release from the time-space continuum which other animals cannot escape. In fantasizing we can concentrate a number of dimensions within our immediate thinking, gathering up the past (and revising it to suit ourselves) or advancing into the future, to bring either or both to bear on our emotional needs. Theologian Harvey Cox calls man *homo fantasia* and says ". . . it was just as much his propensity to dream and fantasize as it was his augers and axes that first set man apart from the beasts."[1]

For all the prominent place of fantasizing in man's mental processes, fantasy in our culture has usually been suspect as

[1] Harvey Cox, *The Feast of Fools* (Cambridge: Harvard University Press, 1969), p. 11.

an unworthy mode of thought. Our concern with naming as
"real" only those elements of our outer waking lives has been
roundly reinforced by a technological society, leading us to
neglect, repress, or ignore whenever possible the reality of our
"dreaming" lives. Western civilization since the Enlightenment has continually emphasized active, willed, reasoned
thought, and fantasy has been in disgrace in our increasingly
fact-obsessed world. In the last few years, however, more and
more inquiries—popular, aesthetic, academic, and clinical—
have been made into the worlds of inner experience, and fantasy as a process and as an artistic expression has received a
goodly share of the attention.

Rational and technological explanations of man's environment and his place in it have not sufficed to allow him to be
at home in this world; science neither allays our deepest fears
nor expresses fully our wonder and joy. In modern times, science has encouraged us to unlearn metaphysical terror, but in
dreams and fantasies our dormant fears and awes wake and
stretch. Fantasy fiction is the literary expression of this kind
of dream. Any fiction is closely linked to man's desire and
need to fantasize, but fantasy fiction is perhaps closer than
any other to the free-floating process where time and space
and probability are overcome in the play of imagination.

Fantasy fiction is a challenging form to write and to read.
Serious adult fantasy attempts to confront and question not
only what is real but our perceptions of reality as well. To
admit fantasy's premise—that things are as we "know" they
are not—demands from the reader an altered perception
from his everyday mind set. Symbolically, this fiction is about
consciousness and the major themes of fantasy—change,
power, and endurance—act out stories about the reach and
flex of consciousness and imagination. More than other
genre of fiction, fantasy can confront the confusing, incon-
gruous, and grotesque as well as the beautiful and mysterious
—all elements of changes of mind, all demands on imagination and will—because it presents life situations which would
be absolutely impossible if the world were merely as we know
it to be on a daily basis. Fantasy suggests it may well be

more. It is fiction in a subjunctive mood, beginning always with the premise "if it were so that. . . ."

To be sure, all fiction to some extent presents life as different from our own immediate experiences, but fiction is "fantastic" when it distorts the ordinary and offers marvels, incongruities, and impossibilities, in short, any deviation from the daily understanding we have of our world and its limits. Fantastic, mystic, and speculative fiction all share the same focus: they reveal more than most people usually believe is there to be seen. Fantasy differs from other kinds of fiction in that it grounds this focus specifically in concepts of magic, a concentration of forces which cannot be scientifically established or measured but which can still be part of our direct experience. These forces include fates, divinations, chthonic powers, spells, mystic powers, sacred realities, and the potencies of prayer, will, and passion; in other words, the realm of the daemonic. Within the narrative there is no attempt to explain where the magic comes from; it simply *is*, and it informs the places, the people, and the situations in a fantasy story. More than that, the narrative itself is in a sense magical. It enchants the reader, drawing him into the world of the fiction so that he neither demands nor expects explanations as to how he got there. Fantasy is evocative, not explanatory, and the world evoked is magical. Like the workings of magic itself, the Secondary World must be accepted and understood intuitively. We cannot apply explanations (nor do we want to if the story is good enough to be really enchanting) be they those of dreams, psychosis, physical nature, or science.

In fantasy fiction we must accept the reality of the world within the narrative as independent of normal frames. The story takes the reader into a Secondary World, as does most fiction; narratives are necessarily created worlds no matter how accurately they reflect this one. But in fantasy there is no attempt to connect the Secondary World to our world, the Primary World, by any bridge of explanation. We are simply dropped into the Secondary World which is self-sustaining, made up and governed according to its own rules. Often the main character of the story is also a visitor to a strange world and his predicament and discovery are analogous to the reader's own as the story unfolds.

Even other speculative fiction requires a "real life" norm from which some or all meaning may be drawn. For example, dream literature offers the touchstone of waking. If, say, we are too distressed at Alice's troubles in Wonderland, we can reassure ourselves that she is merely sleeping. Likewise, fantasies which are psychological constructs on the part of the narrator in the story, or one of the characters, let the reader choose whether to believe the fantastic element or not. We can always choose to believe that the narrator is crazy, so that the world he thinks up is not one we have to take too seriously. Science fiction offers the assurance of scientific jargon, machines, or explanations about time warps and holes in the universe. In all these the reader has a methodology or reasoning drawn from daily experience to help him deal with the "reality" of the Other World. But in fantasy no explanations are offered which make the supernatural or the fantastic element seem possible in ordinary terms. The laws of fantasy are not those of discursive reasoning or rationality or empirical probability. They are laws of imagination. When magic is the heart of the matter, reason is of no use, and the enigmas of fantasy can only be felt into being.

Perhaps most mysterious and yet most necessary to fantasy is the elemental force of magic which underlies the tales. Magic may be simply the given creative force in the Secondary World, what we would ordinarily call nature. By this natural magic forests are enchanted, beanstalks grow to the clouds, stones grant wishes, and the like. It may also be a force which imposes itself on man capriciously (or is imposed by spirits or divine beings) or it may be a power which is controlled and induced by man for his purposes. In the first forms, natural magic works in human affairs largely by chance; the hero (or the landscape or other characters and creatures) may be cursed or blessed by magic according to luck rather than worth or skill. In the other form, personal or directed magic is a power called out by a gifted one, a mage or wizard, an initiate in the art of magic usage. His skill is the end of study, not luck, and he has a special role in the community as wizards, shamans, sorcerers, and seers always must. In either instance, magic is a reservoir of power and its brilliant potency illumines the entire story.

As fantasy is so dependent upon and concerned with this wonderful force, the right use or reckless misuse of magic becomes a frequent dilemma in the stories. In this collection, the theme of power and its exercise is treated directly in Jorge Luis Borges' "The Rejected Sorcerer," Ursula Le Guin's "The Rule of Names," and Sylvia Townsend Warner's "Winged Creatures."

It is one of the functions of magical power to transform— to change the shapes of things though their essence or meaning remains the same. Hence the recurrence in fantasy of shape-shifters, skin-changers, familiars (animal shapes in which a human spirit may travel), as well as all the changes in natural environment, in the energies of heat, light, and sound, and in the forces we perceive as weight, form, and color. None of these changes are alien to human life, since humans are always involved in what might be called bio-psychic transformations of one kind or another. Physical forms change and consciousness changes throughout a person's life; these changes correspond to others in nature, in animal life and the seasons. But in fantasy these changes can be caused by the workings of magic. They are not tricks or illusions, like rabbits produced from a hat. Instead, these changes are revelations of the interrelatedness of created nature and the forces of the universe. To the consciousness which holds a magical view of the universe, all the multiplicities of design and the shifting shapes of life assume a balance, an underlying unity. A were-creature is no shock, since man and beast share common origins and energies. In fantasy (as in myth and fairy tale) this unity is stressed instead of repressed. All the world is regarded as if it had life and potential consciousness, so trees may well speak, frog skins can easily house princes, forests may cause some people to lose their ways while others are allowed to pass freely.

To understand fantasy it is important that the reader accept this view of the world, at least for the space of the narrative, and that he find it comfortable and necessary. The element of magic in a tale must be irreducible, not explained away or simply gratuitous. And in the course of the story the reader must be made to feel familiar with the magical element, at home in the Secondary World. Here fantasy differs sharply from supernatural or horror fiction in which the supernatural element is always alien to human life and both characters and readers are uncomfortable with it. In fantasy, the transformations of magic seem as wonderful and natural as the fact that caterpillars become butterflies.

Once upon a time you would not have had to read fantasy to find this kind of thinking about the world; you would have shared it with almost everybody else as the way to look at the universe. Until the Enlightenment thinking was not grounded in what we call "rational" modes. Man once saw the world as a pulsing whole, potentially alive in all its forms. The thunder had a voice, dragons coursed sea and sky, and one might have conceivably run across a fairy or fallen down a hole into an enchanted realm beneath the earth. For example, the story "Arthur and Gorlagon" dates from the fourteenth century, and the sense of shared belief is easy to see in the tale. The point of the story is not really the were-wolf; his plight and deliverance are so taken for granted that they form only a vehicle for the story's real point—something far more mysterious than a were-creature—the nature of woman. To audiences contemporary with this story, such things as were-creatures were possible—that is, people shared a belief in their likelihood; to find the reality of a castle in the clouds did not cancel or threaten the reality of a home on earth.

As the Renaissance gathered momentum, men began to make distinctions which severed the connection of this world and others. Rational thinking (from *ratio*—to divide) approaches its subject by making categories, dividing that which is to be thought into relationships of cause and effect and then treating the whole as a sum of these parts. This approach altered man's way of looking at his world. Where once he saw a vital whole, alive in all its connected parts, man began to make distinctions that separated self from surroundings, and then divided the surroundings still further into groups, then sub-groups, each steadily more alien from the human sense of increasingly isolated self. No wonder we have lost the belief in animal speech. If man and animal are so separate, whatever could they have to say to each other? We order by patterns and systems we devise for distinction's sake, whereas once man did not devise patterns but sought to recognize the pattern in the whole, a pattern which unified rather than fragmented. The growth of science isolated physical from metaphysical, natural from supernatural, and reason from belief.

While philosophers and scientists were turning to this divided view of reality, the folk were still telling wonder tales and belief in marvels continued. But even the currency of the stories lessened in time since such belief requires sharing to survive. "The sheep ate up the fairies" is a folk expression which speaks to the decline of such belief and the lessening of wonder lore in the face of growing economic concern, first with the rise of individually farmed land (since lore tended to flourish when the land was held in common and the community was a tighter unit, and to fade when laws were passed which allowed common land to be fenced by individuals for pasture) and then, of course, with increasing industrialization. In time, stories that once would have earned a wide, if not universal, credibility in the community were viewed not just as extraordinary, but as impossible: they became fantasy where before they had been accounts of believable marvels.

In a way fantasy is retrospective because it requires the reader to regain this lost credulity. Fantasy returns us to a kind of thinking which does not demand too many distinctions. This means familiar categories are nullified or transformed. Fantasy does not force us to make distinctions between the Real and Not-Real on the basis of empirical evidence which may not have validity in the realm of feeling. We must approach these stories intuitively, for they offer a world not sharply divided into spirit and matter, but a world that is whole, all things integrally participant in it.

Fantasy is also deliberately retrospective in more than its focus or mind set. In its form, too, it returns to the old tales of marvels and wonders. The history of fantasy goes back beyond the history of written fiction to the oral fiction of the people: the folk tale.

By strictest definition folk tales are traditional narratives passed down through the years by word of mouth. These orally transmitted stories are important to an understanding of literary fantasy because very often the contemporary fantasy writer serves a similar function to the figure called "story catcher" in American Indian myths, a narrator who preserves the tradition, reconstructing old stories for use in the present age. Contemporary fantasy bears striking similarities to the folk wonder tale, both in theme and structure. It often appears to be trying to create in written narrative the effect of the orally related tale, recapturing the immediacy of excitement and drama and the feeling of "living history" common to such tales but frequently lacking in other contemporary fiction with more sophisticated narrative techniques.

Although the relationship of contemporary fantasy to the traditional folk tale is an important one, that is not to say that one is the other. Fantasy is not folk tale inasmuch as it is written narrative with known authorship; these fictions do not have their primary life in oral circulation among the people, as do true folk tales. However, fantasy grows directly out of the folk tale and preserves distinct likenesses to the folk form from which it comes.

While not all fantasists turn to the folk tale as a model for their fiction, some consciously do. Book-length fantasies which directly use folk tales include Fletcher Pratt and L. Sprague DeCamp's *Land of Unreason*, which uses the story of Frederick Barbarossa; Evangeline Walton's tetralogy (*The Island of the Mighty*, *The Children of Llyr*, *The Song of Rhiannon*, and *The Prince of Annawn*) which retells the Mabinogian, and Poul Anderson's *The Broken Sword* and *Hrolf Kraki's Saga* which are directly indebted to Icelandic saga, to name only a few. Andre Norton in "On Writing Fantasy" goes so far as to suggest that the writer of fantasy keep to hand Stith Thompson's study *The Folktale*. However, more fantasists than not use folk-tale traditions unobtrusively, perhaps sometimes even unwittingly. A likely expla-

nation is that the body of traditional lore is so familiar and
deals so explicitly with many of the themes modern fantasists
want to use that the stories are retold the way folk tales
themselves often were, with little sense of where the original
story came from or exactly how it went. Instead, the teller is
working out of a body of tradition which yields up certain
recurrent schema, and, combined, these patterns produce stories essentially similar regardless of their place and time and
mode of telling.

In "On Fairy Stories," J. R. R. Tolkien suggests for this
process the image of a soup pot, which he calls "the Caul-
dron of Story,"[2] in which all the bits and pieces of stories
have been boiled through time with any given story emerging
as a dish served up by a particular teller. Perhaps this is only
another way of saying there are really no new stories but only
myriad ways of telling the old ones. The process this suggests
is subtle yet persistent in the human community and it has
to do with the indestructible nature of some patterns and in-
terests in human life. Traditions blossom while others wither,
but these do not die; they only become latent. The germs of
some stories remain a living, if dormant, part of the community's imaginative life and when a need for those stories arises
they are told again. Wonder tales are a deep-rooted tradition
in Western culture, and such stories easily grow afresh.

We have long ago passed the time when one tale teller, or
one tale, could answer the needs of even a group, much less
the community at large. Fantasy fiction cannot hope to have
the validity in the community that the folk tale had for cul-
tures less complex than ours, but fantasists find that the folk
tale has shared themes and images which speak to their own
needs as writers and to the needs of many readers. These
forms and motifs are so much a part of our cultural heritage
that sometimes neither writer nor audience is aware that the
patterns are borrowed from the folk tale. Instead, the characters and the situations seem new but have the delicious appeal of stories forgotten and rediscovered, simultaneously familiar and strange.

[2] Tolkien, "On Fairy Stories" in *The Tolkien Reader* (New York:
Ballantine Books, 1966), p. 26.

The oral narrative served more wide-ranging functions in the preliterate society than fiction can in a literate one. But at an individual rather than a community level, some of the needs served are similar. Primary among these is the entertainment value of the tale. Even in sophisticated societies where leisure activities are far more numerous than anyone has leisure enough to explore, wonder tales provide an entertainment that other activities cannot afford. Folk tales have always allowed listeners to participate vicariously in experiences otherwise denied them in daily life, and fantasy fiction accomplishes the same purpose for the contemporary reader. In an age which is noticeably antiheroic for most people, fantasy provides the opportunity for heroism, for swashbuckling action and derring-do. It replaces the ordinary frustrations and daily difficulties with glittering adventures unavailable to the reader in any form except imaginary. Certainly, such entertainment is readily found now in many forms other than fantasy fiction; other types of fiction, as well as films and television can offer the contemporary adventure-seeker this release. The point is that fantasy fiction and the folk tale entertain the reader with virtually the same stories. The very heroes, ladies, and dragons that excited, amused, and awed people uncounted years ago still have the power to wake a similar response in readers today.

Another appeal that folk tale and fantasy share is the fulfillment of curiosity about the past. For the simple individual the folk tale often revealed to him all he knew about the history of his people. That function is no longer necessary to us, but what does remain is a desire to identify with a heroic and splendid past. This identification is complicated for the fantasy reader, as it was not for the folk-tale listener, in that we now know that in all probability the "far away and long ago" of the stories is not the least bit historically accurate. Yet the question of whether the material is true historically becomes immaterial when we read as long as it is true to our imaginative conception of the past. A recent film account of the life of Judge Roy Bean introduced itself with "This is a story of the Old West. If this isn't how it was, then it's how it ought to have been." Both folk tale and fantasy give the ordinary individual a past in which he can take pride. In terms of his imaginative satisfaction, whether the past "happened" that way or not is irrelevant.

Other kinds of fiction have moved far from the folk forms, and if some elements of the folk stories have surfaced again here and there, most contemporary fiction has addressed itself to other purposes and other structures than the fairly strict ones of folk narrative. Fantasy fiction, on the other hand, maintains the spirit of folk tale in the kind of entertainment it seeks to provide, and preserves as well the form of the wonder tale—episodic, filled with marvels, concentrated on action, a place where gods and heroes mingle freely with ordinary men, set in a chimerical, magical world that never was but certainly ought to have been.

Contemporary fantasy follows two basic directions, both derived from the folk tale. One might be termed the "literary fairy tale" which grows out of the *Märchen* or wonder tale. The other, known to readers as Sword-and-Sorcery, is a descendant of the hero tale.

The wonder tale is a story which offers a series of episodes in which a variety of characters may have prominent parts (the hero isn't the only important character though he may be the most noticeable one). It moves in a world which has only a vaguely defined locale and is filled with the marvelous. Throughout the tale the element of wonder is important and motifs such as supernatural adversaries or helpers, supernatural husbands or wives, supernatural tasks, supernatural objects, and magical knowledge or power are central to the tale. Generally the tale involves a quest, journey, or search on the part of the main character, and at the completion of the major adventure (sometimes following a series of lesser adventures) the hero is rewarded with either material treasure, a marriage partner, power, or with some combination of these. In this collection, Lord Dunsany's "The Fortress Unvanquishable Save for Sacnoth" and George MacDonald's "The Golden Key" are fairy tales of this kind, and Nicholas Stuart Gray's "According to Tradition" is a gentle parody of this form.

This kind of folk tale has a rich literary lineage and has

often been used by writers in a variety of ways. Some writers have lifted the tales directly out of tradition; Chaucer did so, as did the poet of *Gawain and the Green Knight*. Other writers have taken the form and materials of folk tales and turned them to their own uses, crafting imaginative, flexible narratives which have allowed the writers escape from literary conventions in the periods in which they write as well as escape from the mundane world. French and German Romantic writers used fairy tales in this way, reacting against Enlightenment literature, and in the Victorian period in England the works of William Morris and George Mac-Donald began a fantasy tradition in English letters decidedly counter to most mainstream fiction. From the time of Morris and MacDonald, the literary fairy tale has evolved steadily; early in this century fantasists such as Lord Dunsany, E. R. R. Eddison, and James Branch Cabell developed the ornate, highly stylized, yet vigorously imaginative fantasy which still serves as a delight to readers and as a model to younger fantasists.

Sword-and-Sorcery, or heroic fantasy, is a great-grandchild of the folk form called the hero tale. The hero tale recounts a series of adventures of the same hero, and heroic fantasy recounts the adventures of a single super-hero. The hero tale is a cluster of the exploits of a single hero who provides the focal point of the story and whose heroism does not need to be developed or proven but only displayed. In fantasy fiction, Sword-and-Sorcery stories describe the adventures of an indomitable warrior in a barbaric world where landscape and characters all provide challenges to the hero. He battles monsters, demons, and entire invading armies in a world of towering peaks, thundering cataracts, and threatening forests. In these stories action and adventure are both means and end; the plot is a series of adventures and the theme of the tale is the value of heroic action. This sub-genre of fantasy owes its growth to the cheap, popular magazines called "pulps." These magazines, which began to proliferate in the 1920s, were outgrowths of the "dime novel" and "penny dreadful," and they encouraged a fantasy much less sophisticated than the literary fairy tales of Morris and MacDonald and their successors. The magazine serials had in common with other fantasy devices such as the Secondary World, as well as magical elements, but the serials emphasized heroic adventure to the subordination of all other dimensions of the stories. This sea-change worked in fantasy during the pulp era caused fantasy to prosper as a popular fiction and to reach a wider readership than ever before. These were pure adventure stories, fast-paced, easy-reading, exciting, that appealed to a readership which would have been impatient with the epic proportions of Eddison's work, the poetic prose of Morris or Dunsany, or Cabell's dry wit. Heroic fantasy made fantasy fiction a popular phenomenon; it continues to attract fans today to the resurrected works of Robert E. Howard, whose Conan books serve as a model for much Sword-and-Sorcery, and to the works of a legion of Howard imitators and embellishers. In this collection, Robert Bloch's "The Dark Isle" is a fine piece of heroic fantasy, set in a historical framework, but with all the necessary magic and adventure.

Although the literary fairy tale and Sword-and-Sorcery seem to be the gemini of fantasy—one artsy and delicate and the other athletic and rough-and-tumble—that is too simplistic a separation. In the best fantasy fiction the fairy tradition and the heroic lore combine to give the reader heroic values —camaraderie, commitment, bravery, endurance—in a phantasmagorical world of shape-shifters and marvels.

No matter what shape fantasy assumes—fairy tale or heroic adventure or some combination of these—and no matter what skin-changers and wonders appear there, the true center of fantasy is man. However, it is not man utterly alone as much of modern literature has shown him. Fantasy shows man in a magic circle, ever-widening in what it can encompass, yet strong and sure in its encirclement, girding all creation in an unbroken round. Man is forever in relation, and fantasy explores the multifold possibilities of this relatedness. It stresses above all man's integration into a dynamic whole, his place in all that is, his integrity within that place, his communion with all else in the circle.

These are old values, and fantasy, like the myths and tales of which it is a modern exponent, reaches to the time of Beginnings to bring to life the old concerns, the old stories, for solace and strength in the present age. It does not deny the present; instead it bends the linear view we take of our lives and draws us once again into the age-old circle. Past, Present, and Future are a full cycle, with all that man is and ever shall be informed by all that he has been. To reveal this, the old stories are necessary; but so are new ones, and fantasy fiction is telling them, crafting primal values, dreams, and dreads into myths for our times.

That is not to say that contemporary fantasy is merely Grimm's for grownups, old stories retold. Though they share in the conventions and traditions of the folk tale, these are new stories and their creators have by the word brought new worlds into being. While the subjects of the stories are fundamentally shared human desires and concerns, these are acted out in worlds where, as Le Guin says, "no voice has ever spoken before; where the act of speech is the act of creation."[3] To be sure, all writers of fiction give a world life with the power of the word, but the worlds of realistic fiction do have a referent in ordinary experience. Huck Finn's Mississippi is brought to life by Twain, but there is, after all, a Mississippi River, and knowing that river—even if it is only hearsay knowledge—determines to some extent our response to the river in Huck's world. This kind of fiction exists with its subject in a direct map/territory relation: the fictional work is a design drawn from actual, physical reality. The design might be a distortion of the actual territory, but it does represent it in a recognizable way. In fantasy, the map/territory relation that language creates is more complex since the design (the story) maps a territory which itself is only a design in the mind of the writer/map maker. The map of Hyperborea, of Babbulkund, or Sattins Island is a map in the mind of the writer; our only referent to it is the word.

Thus the language of fantasy is in the most basic sense informational; it describes or imparts knowledge, but it also informs, or calls up shapes which make real the subject of the narrative. The fantasist is, then, not only a dealer in the

3 Le Guin, *From Elfland to Poughkeepsie* (Portland, Oregon: Pendragon Press, 1973), p. 23.

symbolic—that is, the images of things not actually present or the imagining of one thing through another—he is also an informer, granting shape and substance to things which are not even actual in ordinary terms.

The skillful fantasist is the true wizard. Through the magic of naming he makes real, he calls things into being. As namer, the wonder-story teller is a poet, and his is the oldest form of poetry: incantation, the making of magic through words. The connection between storytelling and magic is as old as both and listeners have always recognized it. Thus the Indian "story-catcher" was the shaman of the tribe, and often a mage or wizard took the guise of a bard to make his travels less conspicuous. For incantation is not just the power vested in the Word itself—the power to create and make real —it is also the power the Word's user has over other men through the spoken charm. Tolkien notes "Small wonder that 'spell' means both a story told, and a formula of power over living men."[4] And so the fantasist, in a process unique in fiction, works a pervasive magic, at once summoning the shapes of another reality and enchanting his readers to believe in them. In each of the following stories, this ensorcellment will steal you as a changeling, a human child taken up to Faërie, and will carry you beyond time and reason to magic inexplicable and wondrous fair.

[4] Tolkien, "On Fairy Stories," p. 31.

ARTHUR AND GORLAGON

By Anonymous*

AT CAERLEON, King Arthur was keeping the festival of Pentecost and he had invited there the great men and nobles and their ladies of the whole of his kingdom. When the solemn ceremonies were over, he bade them all come into the great hall to a banquet laid so richly and so generously that even the nobles who had been before to Arthur's celebrations were dazzled. It is said that on this occasion twenty thousand knights sat at the board and with them twenty thousand ladies. Every man sat with a woman, even he who had no wife sat with a sister or friend, and that was a sign of great courtesy. The hall was loud with the sound of voices and the music of minstrels and Arthur was so joyous at the sight of all the nobility and beauty of his kingdom gathered before him that in the excess of his happiness, he threw his arms around his queen, seated beside him at the head of the great table, and kissed her affectionately before all the on-lookers. The queen was amazed at his conduct and, pulling away from his embrace, blushing deeply, she demanded to know why he had kissed her so at such an unusual time and place.

"Because," cried the King, flushed with wine and the glory of his kingship, "of all my riches none are so pleasing and of all my delights none are so fair as you."

The queen's dignity was as disarrayed as her gown and she responded, "Well, if, as you say, you love me so much, you must think you know well my heart and my affection."

Arthur was taken aback by her sharpness but he soon said gallantly, "I do not doubt that your heart is given only to

* Adapted from the original by Jane Mobley

me, my queen, and I certainly think your affection is absolutely known to me."

The queen's temper was still ruffled. "Arthur, perhaps you are misled. Now acknowledge that you have never yet understood either the nature or the heart of a woman."

It was clearly a challenge, though had it been made in the privacy of the royal chambers it might well have been met with joking and kisses. Here, where certainly the highest nobles of the land had been witness to it, the challenge would have to be met more formally. After a moment's hesitation, and a furtive glance at the knights who sat nearest him and even now paused with goblets halfway to their lips, awaiting the king's answer, Arthur said, "I call heaven as my witness, that if up to now these have been hidden from me, I will seek them out, and sparing no difficulty, I will never taste food until by fortune I fathom them."

If she had meant her spur to prick more lightly than that, the queen gave no sign, and bent her head demurely to the rest of her dinner. The nobles drank, and looked over the rims of their goblets with approval at their king. It would not have been well to leave such a challenge unmet. The ladies glowed at the queen. It had been a point worth raising.

When the feast was ended, Arthur called to his server Kay and said, "Kay, you and my nephew Gawain will mount your horses and accompany me on the business to which I have pledged myself. Let the rest remain and entertain my guests until I am returned." Though it meant their journey must begin in darkness, Arthur took Kay and Gawain and they mounted their horses to ride to a neighboring country ruled by a king famed for his wisdom, a certain Gargol. Gold and jewels decorated the saddles, and golden bits were in the horses' mouths, yet the travelers took not even the provisions of peasants with them on account of Arthur's promise; they took food for the horses only.

Two days and two nights they rode without stopping and on the third day they reached a valley and there they stopped to rest, quite exhausted, for they had not eaten or slept on their journey. Now just beyond on the far side of the valley was a high mountain, covered at the foot by a pleasant forest, and through the trees and here and there above them was visible a strong fortress of polished stone, built against the mountain fastness. When he saw the glint of stone through the trees, Arthur ordered Kay to ride on before and bring back to him word of the town and to whom it belonged. Kay rode with all speed and entered the town, let to pass by the sentries for so rich was his dress and the trappings of his horse that he could only be the emissary of a king. When he left the fortress again, he met Arthur and Gawain riding toward it, and told them that the town was indeed that of King Gargol to whom they had been making their way with such haste.

As it happened, King Gargol had just sat down at his table to dinner when Arthur came into his presence on horseback and saluted most courteously the king and those who were seated with him. King Gargol said with some astonishment, "Who are you? and from whence do you come? and why have you entered our presence so urgently?"

"I am Arthur," he replied, riding nearer to King Gargol, "the King of Britain, and I have come to learn from you what are the heart, the nature, and the ways of women, for I have often heard that you are wise in matters of this kind." "Well," answered Gargol, still surprised at the abrupt entrance of his visitor, "yours is a weighty question, Arthur, and few are those who know how to answer it. But come now, take this advice, dismount and eat with me. Rest today, for I can see your tiring journey has made you overwrought. Tomorrow I will tell you what I know of these matters."

But Arthur denied that he was overwrought, and insisted he would honor his pledge not to eat until he had learned the answer for which he searched. At last, however, he was so pressed by the king and the company gathered there with him to eat with them that he assented, and, dismounting, took the seat that was brought for him and placed opposite the king. Kay and Gawain ate too, glad to be relieved of the pledge of fasting. The question Arthur had come to ask met no mention again in the feasting and afterward Arthur passed a troubled night. As soon as it was dawn, he went to King Gargol to claim the promise that had been made to him and said, "Oh my dear king, make known to me now that which you promised yesterday you would tell me today."

Gargol said, "It is folly you are showing now, Arthur. Until this I had always believed you a wise man. As to the heart, the nature, and the ways of woman, no one ever had a conception of what they are, and I do not think I can give you any information on the subject. Still, I have a brother, King Gorleil, whose kingdom borders my own. He is older than I and wiser too. Indeed, if any there are who may be skilled in this matter that disturbs you, Gorleil will know of him. Seek out my brother, and petition him on my account to tell you what he knows of it."

So, Arthur bade Gargol a friendly farewell and departed riding hard on the continuance of his journey. After four days' ride, he came to King Gorleil's country and castle and, as it happened, he found the king at dinner. Arthur exchanged greetings with Gorleil, answering the king's questions about his name and purpose, "I am Arthur, King of Britain, sent to you by your brother King Gargol that you might explain to me a matter my ignorance of which has sent me on this journey and obliged me to approach your royal presence."

"Well, what is that?" inquired Gorleil.

"I have pledged to investigate the heart, the nature, and the ways of women and have not been able to find anyone to tell what they are. I would have you, to whom I have been sent by your brother who praises your wisdom, instruct me in these matters, and if the answers are known to you, I beg you will not keep them from me."

"Indeed," said Gorleil, anxious to return to his dinner, "yours is a weighty question, Arthur, and few there are who know how to answer it. But come, now is not the time to discuss such matters. Dismount and eat with me and rest today, tomorrow I will tell you what I know of these things."

"I shall eat enough in time," insisted Arthur, pledged again to his fast, "and by my faith, I will not eat until I have learned the answers for which I search." Finally, however, he was so pressed by the king and the company gathered there with him, that he reluctantly dismounted, took the seat placed for him opposite the king, and ate with them. But in the morning he hurried to Gorleil's chambers and began to ask for what he had been promised.

"Ah, Arthur," Gorleil said sadly, "it is folly to pursue this matter. And I had heard that you were a wise man. But if you are so bent upon it then go to my brother, King Gorlagon, for he is older than I am and wiser too, and I have no doubt that he has knowledge of that which you pursue. If anyone can know these things, it will be Gorlagon."

So Arthur took his leave of Gorleil and hastened on to the kingdom of Gorlagon, reaching it after two days' journey. As it happened, he found King Gorlagon at dinner, just as he had found the others.

Arthur announced himself boldly, for he felt certain his search must be near an end, and made known why he had come. But as Arthur kept pressing for the information on the matters which had brought him there, King Gorlagon said, "Yours is a weighty question, Arthur. Do dismount and eat with me now and tomorrow I will tell you what you wish to know."

But Arthur would not do so, and when Gorlagon urged him again to dismount, Arthur swore he would not until he learned what he had come for. This time Arthur would not be persuaded to break his pledged fast. King Gorlagon could see his entreaties were of little use, so he said, "Arthur, since you persist in your resolve to take no food until you know the answers to your questions, I will tell you a tale, though the trouble of telling it will be great, and it will bring you little peace. Still I will relate to you what happened to a certain king and from that tale you will be able to test the heart, the nature, and the ways of woman. But Arthur, do dismount and eat, I beg you. Yours is a weighty question, and few there are who know how to answer it. When I have told my tale you will be but little wiser."

"Say on as you propose," insisted Arthur, "and do not ask me again to eat."

"Very well," replied Gorlagon, who had pity on those who rode with the determined king, "let your companions eat."

"Very well," said Arthur, "let them do so." And all three

dismounted, Kay and Gawain glad to sit at the table, though Arthur himself still would not eat.

When all were seated, King Gorlagon said, "Arthur, since you are so eager to hear this tale, listen carefully and remember well what I am about to say to you.

"Once there was a king whom I knew well, noble, accomplished, rich, and widely famed for his justice and love of truth. He had caused to be made for him a garden more beautiful than any others, and in it he had made to be sown all manner of trees and fruits, flowers and spices of all sorts. Among the other trees which grew in this garden was one tree he had not directed to be planted there; it was a lovely sapling of exactly the same height as the king himself, which broke forth from the ground and began to grow on the night and at the hour the king was born. Now by fate it had been decreed that whoever should cut this sapling down and, striking his head with the slenderest part of it, should cry 'Be a wolf and have the understanding of a wolf,' would at once be a wolf and have the understanding of a wolf. This ordinance of fate had been made known to the king and for this reason he watched the sapling with great care and diligence for he had no doubt that his own safety rested upon it. He surrounded the garden with a strong, high wall made of stones, and allowed in it no one but the guardian who was a trusted friend of his. The king made it his custom to visit the sapling four or five times a day, and to take no food until he had visited it, even though it meant sometimes he would fast until evening. He alone knew the great importance of the tree.

"The king had a beautiful wife, but though she was fair without and lovely to look upon, she did not prove chaste, and her beauty was the cause of her woe. It happened that she loved a youth, the son of a pagan king, and preferring his love to that of her lord, she took great pains to put her lord in danger so that she and the youth might enjoy the embraces for which they longed. Observing the king enter the garden so many times a day, she thought to question him on the subject, but never had the courage to do so.

"One day the king returned from his hunting later than

usual and went into the garden alone, and the queen was unable to endure any longer her desire to know what it was he
did there (as it is customary for a woman to want to know
everything). So when her husband had come in from the
royal garden and was seated to dinner, she asked him with a
deceiving smile why it was that he went to his garden so
many times a day, why even before taking food he went
there. The king answered that it was a matter which did not
concern her, and she then flew into a rage—though certainly
it was feigned—and guessed he must be consorting with an
adulteress in his garden. 'May all the gods of heaven witness
that I will never eat with you again until you tell me the
reason you go into your wretched garden,' she cried, and she
rose suddenly from the table and went to her bedchamber
where for three days she cunningly pretended sickness and
would take no food.

"On the third day, the king, seeing that she was intent
upon her fast and fearing that her life might be endangered
by her obstinacy, began to beg her with kind words to rise
and eat, telling her that the thing she wished to know was a
secret he could reveal to no one, and promising her that he
met no woman in his garden. 'You ought not to have secrets
from your wife,' she sulked, 'and you should know that I
would rather die than live thinking I am so little loved by
you that you can keep secrets from me.' She would not be
persuaded to eat. At last, afraid for his wife and misled by his
affection for her, the king's resolve weakened and he explained to her the secret of the sapling. But first he made her
promise never to betray the secret to anyone and to guard the
tree as carefully as she would her own life.

"The queen had gotten from him the information she
needed for her faithless purpose, and even while she held
him in her arms, whispering of devotion and love, she began
to plan the way in which she might bring about his downfall
as she had so long wished to do. When the king went the
next day to hunt, she took an ax, and, sneaking into the garden, she cut down the tree and hurried toward her chambers.
However, the king returned more quickly than she had expected, and when she heard him approaching, she hid the

sapling in her gown's long sleeve which hung all loose, and she went to meet him, appearing gay and welcoming to hide her deed. She leaned close as though to kiss him and then suddenly drew the sapling from within her sleeve and struck him about the head with it, one blow and then another, crying, 'Be a wolf, be a wolf!' and in her agitation though she meant to add 'and have the understanding of a wolf' said instead 'and have the understanding of a man.' Immediately, it occurred just as she had spoken it and the king was a great wolf at her feet. But his human understanding remained unimpaired, and the eyes of the wolf were the eyes of the king, staring up at her in outrage and betrayal. She set the palace hounds upon him and wolf-king fled to the woods.

"So Arthur, in that you may perceive in part the heart, the nature, and the ways of woman. Come now and eat, and afterward I will go on with my tale. For yours is a weighty question, and few are those who know how to answer it. Indeed, when I have told you all you will be but little wiser."

Arthur still would not eat, and he urged, "The tale goes very well and pleases me to hear. Please follow what you have begun."

Gorlagon said, "Then listen well to what follows.

"When the queen had set to flight her own husband, she called to her the young man of whom I spoke earlier and made him the head of government and lay with him as his wife, and in time they had two sons. The wolf roamed in the deep of the woods near the palace, and there he allied himself with a she-wolf and begot on her two cubs. But he remembered the wrong done him by his wife, for his understanding was yet that of a man, and he questioned himself everyday how he could take revenge upon her. One evening the wolf-king took his mate and cubs and rushed savagely into the town. There, playing beside a tower with no one to guard them, were the two little boys his wife had born to the young man who had replaced him as king, and the wolf-king attacked them and killed them, tearing them cruelly limb from limb as his mate and cubs stood by. As the wolves fled, a great clamor arose at what they had done, but all four escaped in safety. The queen was overwhelmed with sorrow at the loss of her sons and she ordered her retainers to keep careful watch against the wolves' return. Before long, the wolf-king thought his revenge had not been enough and he again went to the town with his mate and cubs, and he found at the palace gates two counts who were brothers to the queen. He killed them viciously, tearing out their bowels with his great fangs. Hearing the growls and screams, the servants rushed to the place, and by shutting the gates, captured the cubs and there they hanged them. The she-wolf they ran through with a sword. But the wolf-king was stronger and more cunning and pulled free from whose who held him and escaped without hurt.

"The wolf was desperate with grief at the loss of his cubs and his companion and, driven mad with the enormity of his sorrow, he made nightly forays to the pens and pastures of the country and caused such great slaughter in the flocks and herds that the peasants gathered together with hounds and weapons to hunt for him daily. The danger vexed the wolf and he made for a neighboring country where he continued his ravages. But there the inhabitants banded together also and he was chased to still a third country where in his rage he attacked not only animals but human beings as well. Now it happened that the king of that country was young in years and mild in disposition, but both wise and industrious. When the destruction the wolf made was reported to him he appointed a day on which he would set out to hunt the wolf and gathered a large force of hunters and hounds to go with him. Such great fear had the wolf raised in the land that none dared go out in the day and at night households found little rest as all shared sleepless watch against the wolf.

"One night the wolf had gone to a village, greedy for blood, and had sought the shadow under the eaves of a house, listening to a conversation going on within. So it happened that he heard a man tell of the king's proposal to seek the wolf beginning the next morning. Everyone in the room spoke of the kindness and clemency of the king and wondered at the outcome of the hunt. Trembling, the wolf returned to the woods. That night he did not kill anything but remained deep in the recesses of the wood deliberating what would be the best course for him to follow.

"In the morning, the long, low notes of horns came to the wolf and soon the woods rang with the clamor of the king's retinue and the baying of an enormous pack of hounds. The king himself, accompanied by two of his nearest friends, rode behind the others. The wolf hid himself carefully by the road where the king would pass and when all others had gone by the wolf saw one approaching whom he judged by his countenance and rich clothing to be the king. The wolf dropped his head and ran close beside the king until he could reach up with his paws to the king's right foot like a supplicant begging mercy and he groaned as piteously as he was able. The two noblemen guarding the king had never seen a wolf of such size and they cried out in terror, 'Lord, here is the wolf we seek! Slay him! Slay him!' But the wolf did not flinch before their cries or run away as they charged him. He followed close to the king, gently licking at his boot. The king was wonderfully moved, for it was clear that there was no fierceness in the wolf and that he came as one who craved pardon. Greatly astonished, he commanded that none of his men should harm the wolf, for the animal showed signs of human understanding, and, putting down his hand, the merciful king stroked the wolf and scratched his ears. Then he leaned from his saddle and tried to lift the wolf up to him, but the wolf, perceiving the king's intent, leapt up joyfully before him and sat upon the neck of the charger in front of the king.

"The king called his followers and ordered that they should drive the raging hounds away from him and the wolf and ride on before, and together the wolf and the king rode toward the castle. Suddenly a great stag appeared in a forest meadow and paused with his head thrown up and his great antlers gleaming in the sun. The king said, 'Here is a chance to see if there is worth and strength in my wolf and if he can obey my commands.' And he set the wolf upon the stag thrusting him away from the charger. Great was the wolf's skill with such prey, and quickly he pursued and killed the stag and laid it dead before the king. The king called the wolf to him and said, 'Truly you must be kept alive and not killed, for you know how to show us such service.' And he returned home taking the wolf with him.

"So the wolf stayed with the king and was shown great affection by him. Whatever the king commanded, the wolf performed and he never showed fierceness to anyone nor harmed any living creature. When the king sat to eat, the wolf stood by him erect as a man eating from the same bread and drinking from the same cup as the king. At night he slept beside his master's couch and the king never went anywhere without his wolf to accompany him.

"As it happened, the king had to make a long journey to confer with another king. He had to go at once and the journey was to take more than ten days, so he called his queen to him and said, 'As I must leave so quickly and the journey is so long, I give this wolf into your protection and I command you to treat him as I would, if he will stay with you, and to minister to his wants.' But the queen already hated the wolf because of the understanding she sensed in him (and as it is so often true the wife hates what the husband loves), so she said, 'My lord, I fear that when you are gone he will attack me in the night if he sleeps in his usual place and will mangle me there.' The king replied, 'I have no fear of that for I have seen no sign of fierceness in him since he has been with me. But if you will be happier, I will have a chain made and have him fastened to my bedpost.' So the king had made a golden chain and when the wolf had been fastened beside the bed, the king went away on his business.

"Once the king had gone, the queen did not show the wolf the care she ought. He lay always chained though the king had left orders he should be chained at night only. Now the queen loved the king's steward unlawfully, and it was her practice to go to him whenever the king was absent. On the eighth day after the king had left on his journey, the lovers went into the king's chamber at midday and climbed into the bed together, paying no attention to the wolf chained there. When the wolf saw them rushing to each other's embraces he blazed with fury, his eyes red and the hair on his neck standing up, and would have attacked them, but held by the chain he could only rage at them at the end of it. When he saw they had no intention of ceasing their adulterous play, he gnashed his teeth and dug at the floor with his claws and howled most awfully, throwing himself against the tight chain so violently that it finally broke in two. Then he leaped to the bed and threw the steward from it and tore at him so savagely that he left the man half dead. To the queen he did no harm but only looked at her with hatred and growled deep in his chest. Hearing the screams of the steward, the servants tore down the bolted door and rushed in. The cunning queen had ready a lying story, and she told the servants that the wolf had devoured her little son and had attacked the steward who was trying to rescue the child from death, and that the wolf would have torn her too had they not arrived to save her. So the steward was carried half dead to the guest chamber. And while the servants were busy with that, the queen, fearing the king would discover the truth of the matter, took the child and shut him up with his nurse in an underground room far removed from the rest of the castle, leaving everyone to believe he had indeed been devoured. Then she considered how she might take revenge on the wolf who waited still in the bedchamber where none dared approach him.

"News came to the queen that the king was returning sooner than expected. So the woman, in her deceit and cunning, further tore her hair and scratched her own cheeks and disarranged her clothing and ran forward to meet the king, her garments splashed with blood. When she saw him she cried out 'Alas! Alas! My lord, you cannot know the loss I have suffered in your absence!' The dumbfounded king asked what was the matter and she replied, sobbing falsely, 'That wretched wolf of yours—the one I have justly suspected all along—has devoured your son, snatching him from my lap; and when your steward tried to rescue him the beast mangled and nearly killed the man and would have treated me the same way had not the servants broken in to save me. See, here is the blood of our child splashed on my garments. Here is evidence of this awful thing!'

"Hardly had she finished her accusations when the wolf, hearing the king approach, sprang from the bedchamber and leaped into the king's arms, leaping and gamboling joyfully as though he deserved to have his welcome well received. The king was distracted by the conflicting appearances of his wife's welcome and the wolf's. He reflected that his wife would not lie about such a matter, yet surely if the wolf had done this hideous crime he would not have dared meet his master with such joyful bounds.

"He dismissed his raving wife to her chambers and went to consider the matter, refusing to eat, even though his journey had been hard. As the king sat pondering, his mind driven first here then there by the appearances of what had taken place in his absence, the wolf came close beside him and touched his boot gently with one paw, then took the border of the king's cloak in his mouth and tugged on it as though he wished to be followed. It was a customary signal of the wolf to the king, and without hesitation the king followed his wolf through the passages of the castle until they reached the underground room where the child had been locked away. Finding the door bolted, the wolf scratched at it with his paw as if to ask that it might be opened. But there was some delay in finding a key, for the queen had hidden it. Unable to wait any longer, the wolf drew back and gathered his formidable strength, and hurling himself at the door with his claws outstretched, smashed it to the floor broken and shattered. Running into the room, the wolf lifted up the infant from the cradle and in his shaggy arms carried the child to the king, holding it up before him as if offering it for a kiss.

"The king was now more confused than ever, and sending the child away to its chambers with his nurse, the king said to the wolf, 'There is something beyond all this which is not clear to me.' Thereupon the wolf again took up the king's cloak and led him away to the guest chamber where the dying steward was laid. There the king was amazed at the sudden fury of the wolf and he could scarcely keep him from rushing upon the dying man. The king sat beside the steward's bed and questioned him closely, but the only tale he could get from the steward about his wounds was that in rescuing the boy from the wolf, the wolf had turned upon him;

he called for the queen to be witness to his story. Then some things began to be clear to the king and he drew himself up very tall beside the steward's bed and said in a voice edged like a sword, 'You are evidently lying. My son lives. He was not devoured at all, and now that I have found him I accuse you and the queen of treachery to me, of forging lies, and I suspect that more may be false also. I know the reason why my wolf attacked you so savagely though savagery is contrary to his habits here: he was furious at my disgrace. Confess to me now the truth of this matter, or I swear by heaven, I will give you to the flames to be burned.' Then the wolf pressed close to the steward, his great jaws open on the man's throat, and he would have torn it out had he not been held back by the king.

"Why go on at length? When the king had insisted with threats and coaxing the steward at last confessed his crime and prayed for forgiveness. But the wrath of the king was uncontrollable then, and he gave the steward over to be kept in prison and immediately called his council of nobles and through them tried this great crime. They passed sentence. The steward was flayed alive and hanged. The queen was torn limb from limb by horses and then cast into balls of flame.

"After these terrible events, the king brooded long on the extraordinary sagacity and persistence of the wolf, and he discussed the subject with the kingdom's wisest men. He said to them that a creature who showed such great intelligence must surely have the understanding of a man, 'For no beast surely would have such great wisdom or show to anyone such wonderful devotion as the wolf has shown me. He understands perfectly whatever is said to him; he does what he is ordered. He stands by me waiting to serve me; he rejoices when I rejoice, and sorrows with me when I sorrow. In short, none of my retainers shows me more service and sympathy than does this wolf. Anyone who could avenge the wrong done me as this wolf has done must have had great sagacity and ability. I can only think that this is a wise and courageous man who has assumed the form of a wolf under some spell or incantation.'

"At these words, the wolf, who was in his customary place beside the king, shivered all over with great joy and licking the king's hands and feet, he pressed close beside him. In every gesture of his body and in the expression of his eyes the wolf showed the king he had spoken the truth.

"Then the king said to his counselors, 'See, he shows I have spoken truly. From this unmistakable sign there can be no further doubt in the matter, and now I must seek the means to free him. Would that the power be given me to know if by some act or device I might restore him to his former state. I would do this at the cost of my kingdom, yea, even at the risk of my own life.' Finally, after long deliberation, it was agreed that the wolf should be sent off to go before the king and to take any direction he pleased by land or sea. 'Perhaps,' the king thought, 'if we could reach the country he came from, we might know what happened to him and find some remedy for it.'

"So the wolf set out to go where he would, and the king and his counselors followed after. The wolf made at once for the sea and dashed again and again into the waves looking back imploringly at the king. The wolf's own country was separated from that region on one side by the sea, though in another direction it could be reached by land, but the route was much longer. Seeing that the wolf wished to cross over, the king gave orders that the fleet should be called out and the army should assemble.

"Having ordered his ships and equipped his army, the king set out sailing before a great force. For three days they sailed, the wolf standing high in the prow of the king's ship sniffing eagerly into the wind. On the third day they reached the shore and the wolf was the first to leap from the ship. He ran wildly up and down the beach and signified to them by his elation that this was indeed his country. The king took a small force and, leaving the remainder of his army at anchor, he hastened in secret to a small city near the shore. He had scarcely entered the city and heard the conversations of but a few persons when the situation became clear. For all the citizens of that province, both nobles and peasants, were groaning under the tyranny of the one who had taken the wolf-king's throne, and with one voice they mourned their rightful master and grieved over the craft and subtlety of his wife who had changed him into a wolf. Her perfidy was widely known. All recalled sadly how wise and gentle their true master had been.

"The king had found what he wanted to know, and pausing only to inquire where the king of that country was living, he returned with all speed to his ship, marched out his troops, and attacked the king so suddenly that all his defenders were slain or put to flight, and the false king and queen were captured.

"In the very hour of his victory, the king assembled a council of the chief men of the kingdom and from one of them who had been the guardian of the royal garden before it had been violated by the wicked queen he learned of the wolf-king's sapling and the queen's theft of it, for this man had guessed the means by which the king had been made into a wolf. Then the king who had befriended the wolf called the queen and sat her in the sight of them all and said, 'O most perfidious and evil woman! What madness led you to plot such treachery against your husband? But I have no interest in bandying words with one who is not worthy of community with anyone. Answer this question I put to you at once, or surely I will cause you to die by hunger and thirst and exquisite tortures, unless you show me straight away where the sapling with which you transformed your lord into a wolf lies hidden. Perhaps with it the human shape you caused him to lose can be restored.' But the queen swore she did not know where the sapling was, insisting that it had been broken up and burned. As she would not confess, the king gave her over to tormentors, who tortured her daily and exhausted her with punishment until at last she weakened and revealed where the sapling was hidden. Though she was bruised and wounded, they led her to the place and she gave the sapling to the king.

"Then the king took it from her and brought the wolf into their midst. With a hopeful heart, he took the sapling and struck the wolf with the thicker part of it, once and then again about the head, crying, 'Be a man and have the under-

standing of a man!' No sooner were the words spoken than
the wolf became a man as he had been before, though he was
now even more comely, possessed of the wild grace and
strength of a creature of the woods. Anyone could see he was
a man of great nobility. The king, seeing such a man standing before him, metamorphosed from a wolf, was filled with
pity at the wrong he had suffered, and ran to him and took
him in his arms, embracing him and shedding tears. As they
embraced each other with sighs of love and joy, all the multitude standing around were moved to weep. The one repeated
his grateful thanks at the kindnesses shown him; the other
protested and lamented that he had shown less consideration
than he ought, sorrowful that he had caused such a one to
sleep on the floor and be held in chains. What more is there
to say? Extraordinary rejoicing was there in all the kingdom,
and the king accepted the submission of his principal nobles
and at once regained his sovereignty. Then the adulterer and
adulteress were brought into his presence and he consulted
his council as to what should be done with them. The pagan
king he condemned to death, but though the council
suggested otherwise, he only divorced the queen and of his
inborn mercy he spared her life, though richly she deserved
to lose it. The other king, honored and weighted down with
costly gifts, set sail for his own kingdom.

"Now then, Arthur, you have learned what the heart, the
nature, and the ways of woman are. Have a care for yourself
and see if you are any the wiser for it. Come now and eat, for
we both have earned this meal, I for the tale I have told and
you for listening to it."

"No," said Arthur, "I still cannot eat until you answer one
more question I would ask you."

"What is that?" asked Gorlagon.

"Who is that woman sitting opposite you of such sad
countenance, who holds before her on a platter a human
head bespattered with blood, and who weeps when you smile
and who kisses the bloody head whenever you have kissed
your wife during the telling of this tale?"

Gorlagon sighed heavily. Then he replied, "If this were
known to me alone, Arthur, I would not tell you. But as it is

well known to all those at this table, I am not ashamed that you should know as well. That woman sitting opposite me is she who, as I have just told you, wrought so great a crime against her husband and king, that is to say against myself. In me you see the wolf who as you have heard was first transformed from a man into a wolf, and then from a wolf into a man again. When I became a wolf, it was the kingdom of my brother Gorleil to which I went first. And the king who took such great pains to care for me is, as you must be guessing, no other than my youngest brother, Gargol, to whom you rode first at the beginning of your journey. The blood-stained head which that woman holds in front of her in the dish is the head of the youth for the love of whom she planned her crime. When I returned to my rightful shape again, I subjected her to this one penalty only, that she should have always the head of her paramour before her, and that when I kissed the wife I married after her, she should kiss him for whom she committed her crime. I had the head embalmed to keep it from rotting away, for I knew no punishment could be more grievous than that she must make a perpetual display of her wickedness in the sight of all the world.

"So, Arthur, eat if you will. For I have invited you, and if you will not, then I shall eat without you and you may remain as you are."

So Arthur ate with the king, and on the following day he set out for home, a nine days' journey. He marveled greatly at what he had heard, though, in truth, as Gorlagon had foretold, Arthur was little the wiser for it.

THE GOLDEN KEY

By George MacDonald

THERE WAS a boy who used to sit in the twilight and listen to his great-aunt's stories.

She told him that if he could reach the place where the end of the rainbow stands he would find there a golden key.

"And what is the key for?" the boy would ask. "What is it the key of? What will it open?"

"That nobody knows," his aunt would reply. "He has to find that out."

"I suppose, being gold," the boy once said thoughtfully, "that I could get a good deal of money for it if I sold it."

"Better never find it than sell it," returned his aunt.

And then the boy went to bed and dreamed about the golden key.

Now all that his great-aunt told the boy about the golden key would have been nonsense, had it not been that their little house stood on the borders of Fairyland. For it is perfectly well known that out of Fairyland nobody ever can find where the rainbow stands. The creature takes such good care of its golden key, always flitting from place to place, lest any one should find it! But in Fairyland it is quite different. Things that look real in this country look very thin indeed in Fairyland, while some of the things that here cannot stand still for a moment, will not move there. So it was not in the least absurd of the old lady to tell her nephew such things about the golden key.

"Did you ever know anybody to find it?" he asked, one evening.

"Yes. Your father, I believe, found it."

"And what did he do with it, can you tell me?"

"He never told me."

"What was it like?"

"He never showed it to me."

"How does a new key come there always?"

"I don't know. There it is."

"Perhaps it is the rainbow's egg."

"Perhaps it is. You will be a happy boy if you find the nest."

"Perhaps it comes tumbling down the rainbow from the sky."

"Perhaps it does."

One evening, in summer, he went into his own room, and stood at the lattice-window, and gazed into the forest which fringed the outskirts of Fairyland. It came close up to his great-aunt's garden, and, indeed, sent some straggling trees into it. The forest lay to the east, and the sun, which was setting behind the cottage, looked straight into the dark wood with his level red eye. The trees were all old, and had few branches below, so that the sun could see a great way into the forest; and the boy, being keen-sighted, could see almost as far as the sun. The trunks stood like rows of red columns in the shine of the red sun, and he could see down aisle after aisle in the vanishing distance. And as he gazed into the forest he began to feel as if the trees were all waiting for him, and had something they could not go on with till he came to them. But he was hungry and wanted his supper. So he lingered.

Suddenly, far among the trees, as far as the sun could shine, he saw a glorious thing. It was the end of a rainbow, large and brilliant. He could count all seven colours, and could see shade after shade beyond the violet; while before the red stood a colour more gorgeous and mysterious still. It was a colour he had never seen before. Only the spring of the rainbow-arch was visible. He could see nothing of it above the trees.

"The golden key!" he said to himself, and darted out of the house, and into the wood.

He had not gone far before the sun set. But the rainbow only glowed the brighter. For the rainbow of Fairyland is not dependent upon the sun as ours is. The trees welcomed him. The bushes made way for him. The rainbow grew larger and brighter; and at length he found himself within two trees of it.

It was a grand sight, burning away there in silence, with its gorgeous, its lovely, its delicate colours, each distinct, all combining. He could now see a great deal more of it. It rose high into the blue heavens, but bent so little that he could not tell how high the crown of the arch must reach. It was still only a small portion of a huge bow.

He stood gazing at it till he forgot himself with delight— even forgot the key which he had come to seek. And as he stood it grew more wonderful still. For in each of the colours, which was as large as the column of a church, he could faintly see beautiful forms slowly ascending as if by the steps of a winding stair. The forms appeared irregularly—now one, now many, now several, now none—men and women and children—all different, all beautiful.

He drew nearer to the rainbow. It vanished. He started back a step in dismay. It was there again, as beautiful as ever. So he contented himself with standing as near it as he might, and watching the forms that ascended the glorious colours towards the unknown height of the arch, which did not end abruptly but faded away in the blue air, so gradually that he could not say where it ceased.

When the thought of the golden key returned, the boy very wisely proceeded to mark out in his mind the space covered by the foundation of the rainbow, in order that he might know where to search, should the rainbow disappear. It was based chiefly upon a bed of moss.

Meantime it had grown quite dark in the wood. The rainbow alone was visible by its own light. But the moment the moon rose the rainbow vanished. Nor could any change of place restore the vision to the boy's eyes. So he threw himself down upon the mossy bed, to wait till the sunlight would give him a chance of finding the key. There he fell fast asleep.

When he woke in the morning the sun was looking straight into his eyes. He turned away from it, and the same moment saw a brilliant little thing lying on the moss within a foot of his face. It was the golden key. The pipe of it was of plain gold, as bright as gold could be. The handle was curiously wrought and set with sapphires. In a terror of delight he put out his hand and took it, and had it.

He lay for a while, turning it over and over, and feeding his eyes upon its beauty. Then he jumped to his feet, remembering that the pretty thing was of no use to him yet. Where was the lock to which the key belonged? It must be somewhere, for how could anybody be so silly as make a key for which there was no lock? Where should he go to look for it? He gazed about him, up into the air, down to the earth, but saw no keyhole in the clouds, in the grass, or in the trees.

Just as he began to grow disconsolate, however, he saw something glimmering in the wood. It was a mere glimmer that he saw, but he took it for a glimmer of rainbow, and went towards it.—And now I will go back to the borders of the forest.

Not far from the house where the boy had lived, there was another house, the owner of which was a merchant, who was much away from home. He had lost his wife some years before, and had only one child, a little girl, whom he left to the charge of two servants, who were very idle and careless. So she was neglected and left untidy, and was sometimes ill-used besides.

Now it is well known that the little creatures commonly called fairies, though there are many different kinds of fairies in Fairyland, have an exceeding dislike to untidiness. Indeed, they are quite spiteful to slovenly people. Being used to all the lovely ways of the trees and flowers, and to the neatness of the birds and all woodland creatures, it makes them feel miserable, even in their deep woods and on their grassy carpets, to think that within the same moonlight lies a dirty, uncomfortable, slovenly house. And this makes them angry with the people that live in it, and they would gladly drive them

out of the world if they could. They want the whole earth
nice and clean. So they pinch the maids black and blue, and
play them all manner of uncomfortable tricks.

But this house was quite a shame, and the fairies in the
forest could not endure it. They tried everything on the
maids without effect, and at last resolved upon making a
clean riddance, beginning with the child. They ought to have
known that it was not her fault, but they have little principle
and much mischief in them, and they thought that if they
got rid of her the maids would be sure to be turned away.

So one evening, the poor little girl having been put to bed
early, before the sun was down, the servants went off to the
village, locking the door behind them. The child did not
know she was alone, and lay contentedly looking out of her
window towards the forest, of which, however, she could not
see much, because of the ivy and other creeping plants which
had straggled across her window. All at once she saw an ape
making faces at her out of the mirror, and the heads carved
upon a great old wardrobe grinning fearfully. Then two old
spider-legged chairs came forward into the middle of the
room, and began to dance a queer, old-fashioned dance. This
set her laughing, and she forgot the ape and the grinning
heads. So the fairies saw they had made a mistake, and sent
the chairs back to their places. But they knew that she had
been reading the story of Silverhair all day. So the next moment she heard the voices of the three bears upon the stair,
big voice, middle voice, and little voice, and she heard their
soft, heavy tread, as if they had had stockings over their
boots, coming nearer and nearer to the door of her room, till
she could bear it no longer. She did just as Silverhair did, and
as the fairies wanted her to do: she darted to the window,
pulled it open, got upon the ivy, and so scrambled to the
ground. She then fled to the forest as fast as she could run.

Now, although she did not know it, this was the very best
way she could have gone; for nothing is ever so mischievous
in its own place as it is out of it; and, besides, these mischievous creatures were only the children of Fairyland, as it were,
and there are many other beings there as well; and if a wan-

derer gets in among them, the good ones will always help him more than the evil ones will be able to hurt him.

The sun was now set, and the darkness coming on, but the child thought of no danger but the bears behind her. If she had looked round, however, she would have seen that she was followed by a very different creature from a bear. It was a curious creature, made like a fish, but covered, instead of scales, with feathers of all colours, sparkling like those of a hummingbird. It had fins, not wings, and swam through the air as a fish does through the water. Its head was like the head of a small owl.

After running a long way, and as the last of the light was disappearing, she passed under a tree with drooping branches. It dropped its branches to the ground all about her, and caught her as in a trap. She struggled to get out, but the branches pressed her closer and closer to the trunk. She was in great terror and distress, when the air-fish, swimming into the thicket of branches, began tearing them with its beak. They loosened their hold at once, and the creature went on attacking them, till at length they let the child go. Then the air-fish came from behind her, and swam on in front, glittering and sparkling all lovely colours; and she followed.

It led her gently along till all at once it swam in at a cottage-door. The child followed still. There was a bright fire in the middle of the floor, upon which stood a pot without a lid, full of water that boiled and bubbled furiously. The air-fish swam straight to the pot and into the boiling water, where it lay quiet. A beautiful woman rose from the opposite side of the fire and came to meet the girl. She took her up in her arms, and said,—

"Ah, you are come at last! I have been looking for you a long time."

She sat down with her on her lap, and there the girl sat staring at her. She had never seen anything so beautiful. She was tall and strong, with white arms and neck, and a delicate flush on her face. The child could not tell what was the colour of her hair, but could not help thinking it had a tinge of dark green. She had not one ornament upon her, but she looked as if she had just put off quantities of diamonds and emeralds. Yet here she was in the simplest, poorest little cottage, where she was evidently at home. She was dressed in shining green.

The girl looked at the lady, and the lady looked at the girl.

"What is your name?" asked the lady.

"The servants always called me Tangle."

"Ah, that was because your hair was so untidy. But that was their fault, the naughty women! Still it is a pretty name, and I will call you Tangle too. You must not mind my asking you questions, for you may ask me the same questions, every one of them, and any others that you like. How old are you?"

"Ten," answered Tangle.

"You don't look like it," said the lady.

"How old are you, please?" returned Tangle.

"Thousands of years old," answered the lady.

"You don't look like it," said Tangle.

"Don't I? I think I do. Don't you see how beautiful I am!"

And her great blue eyes looked down on the little Tangle, as if all the stars in the sky were melted in them to make their brightness.

"Ah! but," said Tangle, "when people live long they grow old. At least I always thought so."

"I have not time to grow old," said the lady. "I am too busy for that. It is very idle to grow old.—But I cannot have my little girl so untidy. Do you know I can't find a clean spot on your face to kiss!"

"Perhaps," suggested Tangle, feeling ashamed, but not too much so to say a word for herself—"perhaps that is because the tree made me cry so."

"My poor darling!" said the lady, looking now as if the moon were melted in her eyes, and kissing her little face, dirty as it was, "the naughty tree must suffer for making a girl cry."

"And what is your name, please?" asked Tangle.

"Grandmother," answered the lady.

"Is it really?"

"Yes, indeed. I never tell stories, even in fun."

"How good of you!"

"I couldn't if I tried. It would come true if I said it, and then I should be punished enough."

And she smiled like the sun through a summer-shower.

"But now," she went on, "I must get you washed and dressed, and then we shall have some supper."

"Oh! I had supper long ago," said Tangle.

"Yes, indeed you had," answered the lady—"three years ago. You don't know that it is three years since you ran away from the bears. You are thirteen and more now."

Tangle could only stare. She felt quite sure it was true.

"You will not be afraid of anything I do with you—will you?" said the lady.

"I will try very hard not to be; but I can't be certain, you know," replied Tangle.

"I like your saying so, and I shall be quite satisfied," answered the lady.

She took off the girl's night-gown, rose with her in her arms, and going to the wall of the cottage, opened a door. Then Tangle saw a deep tank, the sides of which were filled with green plants, which had flowers of all colours. There was a roof over it like the roof of the cottage. It was filled with beautiful clear water, in which swam a multitude of such fishes as the one that had led her to the cottage. It was the light their colours gave that showed the place in which they were.

The lady spoke some words Tangle could not understand, and threw her into the tank.

The fishes came crowding about her. Two or three of them got under her head and kept it up. The rest of them rubbed themselves all over her, and with their wet feathers washed her quite clean. Then the lady, who had been looking on all the time, spoke again; whereupon some thirty or forty of the fishes rose out of the water underneath Tangle, and so bore her up to the arms the lady held out to take her. She carried her back to the fire, and, having dried her well, opened a chest, and taking out the finest linen garments, smelling of grass and lavender, put them upon her, and over all a green dress, just like her own, shining like hers, and soft like hers, and going into just such lovely folds from the waist, where it was tied with a brown cord, to her bare feet.

"Won't you give me a pair of shoes too, grandmother?" said Tangle.

"No, my dear, no shoes. Look here. I wear no shoes."

So saying she lifted her dress a little, and there were the loveliest white feet, but no shoes. Then Tangle was content to go without shoes too. And the lady sat down with her again, and combed her hair, and brushed it, and then left it to dry while she got the supper.

First she got bread out of one hole in the wall; then milk out of another; then several kinds of fruit out a third; and then she went to the pot on the fire, and took out the fish, now nicely cooked, and, as soon as she had pulled off its feathered skin, ready to be eaten.

"But," exclaimed Tangle. And she stared at the fish, and could say no more.

"I know what you mean," returned the lady. "You do not like to eat the messenger that brought you home. But it is the kindest return you can make. The creature was afraid to go until it saw me put the pot on, and heard me promise it should be boiled the moment it returned with you. Then it darted out of the door at once. You saw it go into the pot of itself the moment it entered, did you not?"

"I did," answered Tangle, "and I thought it very strange; but then I saw you, and forgot all about the fish."

"In Fairyland," resumed the lady, as they sat down to the table, "the ambition of the animals is to be eaten by the people; for that is their highest end in that condition. But they are not therefore destroyed. Out of that pot comes something more than the dead fish, you will see."

Tangle now remarked that the lid was on the pot. But the lady took no further notice of it till they had eaten the fish, which Tangle found nicer than any fish she had ever tasted before. It was as white as snow, and as delicate as cream. And the moment she had swallowed a mouthful of it, a change she could not describe began to take place in her. She heard a murmuring all about her, which became more and more articulate, and at length, as she went on eating, grew intelligible. By the time she had finished her share, the sounds of all the animals in the forest came crowding through the door to her ears; for the door still stood wide open, though it was pitch-dark outside; and they were no longer sounds only; they were speech, and speech that she could understand. She could tell what the insects in the cottage were saying to each other too. She had even a suspicion that the trees and flowers all about the cottage were holding midnight communications with each other; but what they said she could not hear.

As soon as the fish was eaten, the lady went to the fire and took the lid off the pot. A lovely little creature in human shape, with large white wings, rose out of it, and flew round and round the roof of the cottage; then dropped, fluttering, and nestled in the lap of the lady. She spoke to it some strange words, carried it to the door, and threw it out into the darkness. Tangle heard the flapping of its wings die away in the distance.

"Now have we done the fish any harm?" she said, returning.

"No," answered Tangle, "I do not think we have. I should not mind eating one every day."

"They must wait their time, like you and me too, my little Tangle."

And she smiled a smile made more lovely by the sadness in it.

"But," she continued, "I think we may have one for supper tomorrow."

So saying she went to the door of the tank, and spoke; and now Tangle understood her perfectly.

"I want one of you," she said,—"the wisest."

Thereupon the fishes got together in the middle of the tank, with their heads forming a circle above the water, and their tails a larger circle beneath it. They were holding a council, in which their relative wisdom should be determined. At length one of them flew up into the lady's hand, looking lively and ready.

"You know where the rainbow stands?" she asked.

"Yes, mother, quite well," answered the fish.

"Bring home a young man you will find there, who does not know where to go."

The fish was out of the door in a moment. Then the lady told Tangle it was time to go to bed; and, opening another door in the side of the cottage, showed her a little arbour, cool and green, with a bed of purple heath growing in it, upon which she threw a large wrapper made of the feathered skins of the wise fishes, shining gorgeous in the firelight. Tangle was soon lost in the strangest, loveliest dreams. And the beautiful lady was in every one of her dreams.

In the morning she woke to the rustling of leaves over her head, and the sound of running water. But, to her surprise, she could find no door—nothing but the moss-grown wall of the cottage. So she crept through an opening in the arbour, and stood in the forest. Then she bathed in a stream that ran merrily through the trees, and felt happier; for having once been in her grandmother's pond, she must be clean and tidy ever after; and, having put on her green dress, felt like a lady.

She spent that day in the wood, listening to the birds and beasts and creeping things. She understood all that they said, though she could not repeat a word of it; and every kind had a different language, while there was a common though more limited understanding between all the inhabitants of the forest. She saw nothing of the beautiful lady, but she felt that she was near her all the time; and she took care not to go out of sight of the cottage. It was round, like a snow-hut or a wigwam; and she could see neither door nor window in it. The fact was, it had no windows; and though it was full of doors, they all opened from the inside, and could not even be seen from the outside.

She was standing at the foot of a tree in the twilight, listening to a quarrel between a mole and a squirrel, in which the mole told the squirrel that the tail was the best of him, and the squirrel called the mole Spade-fists, when, the darkness having deepened around her, she became aware of something shining in her face, and looking round, saw that the door of the cottage was open, and the red light of the fire flowing from it like a river through the darkness. She left Mole and Squirrel to settle matters as they might, and darted off to the cottage. Entering, she found the pot boiling on the fire, and the grand, lovely lady sitting on the other side of it.

"I've been watching you all day," said the lady. "You shall have something to eat by-and-by, but we must wait till our supper comes home."

She took Tangle on her knee, and began to sing to her—such songs as made her wish she could listen to them for ever. But at length in rushed the shining fish, and snuggled down in the pot. It was followed by a youth who had out-grown his worn garments. His face was ruddy with health, and in his hand he carried a little jewel, which sparkled in the firelight.

The first words the lady said were,—

"What is that in your hand, Mossy?"

Now Mossy was the name his companions had given him, because he had a favourite stone covered with moss, on which he used to sit whole days reading; and they said the moss had begun to grow upon him too.

Mossy held out his hand. The moment the lady saw that it was the golden key, she rose from her chair, kissed Mossy on the forehead, made him sit down on her seat, and stood be-fore him like a servant. Mossy could not bear this, and rose at once. But the lady begged him, with tears in her beautiful eyes, to sit, and let her wait on him.

"But you are a great, splendid, beautiful lady," said Mossy.

"Yes, I am. But I work all day long—that is my pleasure; and you will have to leave me so soon!"

"How do you know that, if you please, madam?" asked Mossy.

"Because you have got the golden key."

"But I don't know what it is for. I can't find the key-hole. Will you tell me what to do?"

"You must look for the key-hole. That is your work. I can-not help you. I can only tell you that if you look for it you will find it."

"What kind of box will it open? What is there inside?"

"I do not know. I dream about it, but I know nothing."

"Must I go at once?"

"You may stop here to-night, and have some of my supper.

But you must go in the morning. All I can do for you is to
give you clothes. Here is a girl called Tangle, whom you must
take with you."

"That *will* be nice," said Mossy.

"No, no!" said Tangle. "I don't want to leave you, please,
grandmother."

"You must go with him, Tangle. I am sorry to lose you,
but it will be the best thing for you. Even the fishes, you see,
have to go into the pot, and then out into the dark. If you
fall in with the Old Man of the Sea, mind you ask him
whether he has not got some more fishes ready for me. My
tank is getting thin."

So saying, she took the fish from the pot, and put the lid
on as before. They sat down and ate the fish, and then the
winged creature rose from the pot, circled the roof, and settled on the lady's lap. She talked to it, carried it to the door,
and threw it out into the dark. They heard the flap of its
wings die away in the distance.

The lady then showed Mossy into just such another chamber as that of Tangle; and in the morning he found a suit of
clothes laid beside him. He looked very handsome in them.
But the wearer of Grandmother's clothes never thinks about
how he or she looks, but thinks always how handsome other
people are.

Tangle was very unwilling to go.

"Why should I leave you? I don't know the young man,"
she said to the lady.

"I am never allowed to keep my children long. You need
not go with him except you please, but you must go some
day; and I should like you to go with him, for he has the
golden key. No girl need be afraid to go with a youth that
has the golden key. You will take care of her, Mossy, will you
not?"

"That I will," said Mossy.

And Tangle cast a glance at him, and thought she should
like to go with him.

"And," said the lady, "If you should lose each other as you
go through the—the—I never can remember the name of
that country,—do not be afraid, but go on and on."

She kissed Tangle on the mouth and Mossy on the forehead, led them to the door, and waved her hand eastward. Mossy and Tangle took each other's hand and walked away into the depth of the forest. In his right hand Mossy held the golden key.

They wandered thus a long way, with endless amusement from the talk of the animals. They soon learned enough of their language to ask them necessary questions. The squirrels were always friendly, and gave them nuts out of their own hoards; but the bees were selfish and rude, justifying themselves on the ground that Tangle and Mossy were not subjects of their queen, and charity must begin at home, though indeed they had not one drone in their poorhouse at the time. Even the blinking moles would fetch them an earth-nut or a truffle now and then, talking as if their mouths, as well as their eyes and ears, were full of cotton wool, or their own velvety fur. By the time they got out of the forest they were very fond of each other, and Tangle was not in the least sorry that her grandmother had sent her away with Mossy.

At length the trees grew smaller, and stood farther apart, and the ground began to rise, and it got more and more steep, till the trees were all left behind, and the two were climbing a narrow path with rocks on each side. Suddenly they came upon a rude doorway, by which they entered a narrow gallery cut in the rock. It grew darker and darker, till it was pitch-dark, and they had to feel their way. At length the light began to return, and at last they came out upon a narrow path on the face of a lofty precipice. This path went winding down the rock to a wide plain, circular in shape, and surrounded on all sides by mountains. Those opposite to them were a great way off, and towered to an awful height, shooting up sharp, blue, ice-enamelled pinnacles. An utter silence reigned where they stood. Not even the sound of water reached them.

Looking down, they could not tell whether the valley below was a grassy plain or a great still lake. They had never seen any place look like it. The way to it was difficult and dangerous, but down the narrow path they went, and reached the bottom in safety. They found it composed of smooth, light-coloured sandstone, undulating in parts, but mostly level. It was no wonder to them now that they had not been able to tell what it was, for this surface was everywhere crowded with shadows. It was a sea of shadows. The mass was chiefly made up of the shadows of leaves innumerable, of all lovely and imaginative forms, waving to and fro, floating and quivering in the breath of a breeze whose motion was unfelt, whose sound was unheard. No forests clothed the mountain-sides, no trees were anywhere to be seen, and yet the shadows of the leaves, branches, and stems of all various trees covered the valley as far as their eyes could reach. They soon spied the shadows of flowers mingled with those of the leaves, and now and then the shadow of a bird with open beak, and throat distended with song. At times would appear the forms of strange, graceful creatures, running up and down the shadow-boles and along the branches, to disappear in the wind-tossed foliage. As they walked they waded knee-deep in the lovely lake. For the shadows were not merely lying on the surface of the ground, but heaped up above it like substantial forms of darkness, as if they had been cast upon a thousand different planes of the air. Tangle and Mossy often lifted their heads and gazed upwards to descry whence the shadows came; but they could see nothing more than a bright mist spread above them, higher than the tops of the mountains, which stood clear against it. No forests, no leaves, no birds were visible.

After a while, they reached more open spaces, where the shadows were thinner; and came even to portions over which shadows only flitted, leaving them clear for such as might follow. Now a wonderful form, half bird-like half human, would float across on outspread sailing pinions. Anon an exquisite shadow group of gambolling children would be followed by the loveliest female form, and that again by the grand stride of a Titanic shape, each disappearing in the surrounding press of shadowy foliage. Sometimes a profile of unspeakable beauty or grandeur would appear for a moment and vanish. Sometimes they seemed lovers that passed linked arm in arm, sometimes father and son, sometimes brothers in loving contest, sometimes sisters entwined in gracefullest community of complex form. Sometimes wild horses would tear across, free, or bestrode by noble shadows of ruling men. But some of the things which pleased them most they never knew how to describe.

About the middle of the plain they sat down to rest in the heart of a heap of shadows. After sitting for a while, each, looking up, saw the other in tears: they were each longing after the country whence the shadows fell.

"We *must* find the country from which the shadows come," said Mossy.

"We must, dear Mossy," responded Tangle. "What if your golden key should be the key to *it?*"

"Ah! that would be grand," returned Mossy.—"But we must rest here for a little, and then we shall be able to cross the plain before night."

So he lay down on the ground, and about him on every side, and over his head, was the constant play of the wonderful shadows. He could look through them, and see the one behind the other, till they mixed in a mass of darkness. Tangle, too, lay admiring, and wondering, and longing after the country whence the shadows came. When they were rested they rose and pursued their journey.

How long they were in crossing this plain I cannot tell; but before night Mossy's hair was streaked with grey, and Tangle had got wrinkles on her forehead.

As evening drew on, the shadows fell deeper and rose higher. At length they reached a place where they rose above their heads, and made all dark around them. Then they took hold of each other's hand, and walked on in silence and in some dismay. They felt the gathering darkness, and something strangely solemn besides, and the beauty of the shadows ceased to delight them. All at once Tangle found that she had not a hold of Mossy's hand, though when she lost it she could not tell.

"Mossy, Mossy!" she cried aloud in terror.

But no Mossy replied.

A moment after, the shadows sank to her feet, and down under her feet, and the mountains rose before her. She turned towards the gloomy region she had left, and called once more upon Mossy. There the gloom lay tossing and heaving, a dark stormy, foamless sea of shadows, but no Mossy rose out of it, or came climbing up the hill on which she stood. She threw herself down and wept in despair.

Suddenly she remembered that the beautiful lady had told them, if they lost each other in a country of which she could not remember the name, they were not to be afraid, but to go straight on.

"And besides," she said to herself, "Mossy has the golden key, and so no harm will come to him, I do believe."

She rose from the ground, and went on.

Before long she arrived at a precipice, in the face of which a stair was cut. When she had ascended half-way, the stair ceased, and the path led straight into the mountain. She was afraid to enter, and turning again towards the stair, grew giddy at sight of the depth beneath her, and was forced to throw herself down in the mouth of the cave.

When she opened her eyes, she saw a beautiful little creature with wings standing beside her, waiting.

"I know you," said Tangle. "You are my fish."

"Yes. But I am a fish no longer. I am an aëranth now."

"What is that?" asked Tangle.

"What you see I am," answered the shape. "And I am come to lead you through the mountain."

"Oh! thank you, dear fish—aëranth, I mean," returned Tangle, rising.

Thereupon the aëranth took to his wings, and flew on through the long, narrow passage, reminding Tangle very much of the way he had swum on before her when he was a fish. And the moment his white wings moved, they began to throw off a continuous shower of sparks of all colours, which lighted up the passage before them.—All at once he vanished, and Tangle heard a low, sweet sound, quite different from the rush and crackle of his wings. Before her was an open arch, and through it came light, mixed with the sound of sea-waves.

She hurried out, and fell, tired and happy, upon the yellow sand of the shore. There she lay, half asleep with weariness and rest, listening to the low plash and retreat of the tiny waves, which seemed ever enticing the land to leave off being land, and become sea. And as she lay, her eyes were fixed upon the foot of a great rainbow standing far away against the sky on the other side of the sea. At length she fell fast asleep.

When she awoke, she saw an old man with long white hair down to his shoulders, leaning upon a stick covered with green buds, and so bending over her.

"What do you want here, beautiful woman?" he said.

"Am I beautiful? I am so glad!" answered Tangle, rising. "My grandmother is beautiful."

"Yes. But what do you want?" he repeated, kindly.

"I think I want you. Are not you the Old Man of the Sea?"

"I am."

"Then grandmother says, have you any more fishes ready for her?"

"We will go and see, my dear," answered the old man, speaking yet more kindly than before. "And I can do something for you, can I not?"

"Yes—show me the way up to the country from which the shadows fall," said Tangle.

For there she hoped to find Mossy again.

"Ah! indeed, that would be worth doing," said the old man. "But I cannot, for I do not know the way myself. But I will send you to the Old Man of the Earth. Perhaps he can tell you. He is much older than I am."

Leaning on his staff, he conducted her along the shore to a steep rock, that looked like a petrified ship turned upside down. The door of it was the rudder of a great vessel, ages ago at the bottom of the sea. Immediately within the door was a stair in the rock, down which the old man went, and Tangle followed. At the bottom the old man had his house, and there he lived.

As soon as she entered it, Tangle heard a strange noise, unlike anything she had ever heard before. She soon found that it was the fishes talking. She tried to understand what they said; but their speech was so old-fashioned, and rude, and undefined, that she could not make much of it.

"I will go and see about those fishes for my daughter," said the Old Man of the Sea.

And moving a slide in the wall of his house, he first looked out, and then tapped upon a thick piece of crystal that filled the round opening. Tangle came up behind him, and peeping through the window into the heart of the great deep green ocean, saw the most curious creatures, some very ugly, all very odd, and with especially queer mouths, swimming about everywhere, above and below, but all coming towards the window in answer to the tap of the Old Man of the Sea. Only a few could get their mouths against the glass; but those who were floating miles away yet turned their heads towards it. The Old Man looked through the whole flock carefully for some minutes, and then turning to Tangle, said,—

"I am sorry I have not got one ready yet. I want more time than she does. But I will send some as soon as I can."

He then shut the slide.

Presently a great noise arose in the sea. The old man opened the slide again, and tapped on the glass, whereupon the fishes were all as still as sleep.

"They were only talking about you," he said. "And they do speak such nonsense!—To-morrow," he continued, "I must show you the way to the Old Man of the Earth. He lives a long way from here."

"Do let me go at once," said Tangle.

"No. That is not possible. You must come this way first."

He led her to a hole in the wall, which she had not observed before. It was covered with the green leaves and white blossoms of a creeping plant.

"Only white-blossoming plants can grow under the sea," said the old man. "In there you will find a bath, in which you must lie till I call you."

Tangle went in, and found a smaller room or cave, in the further corner of which was a great basin hollowed out of a rock, and half full of the clearest sea-water. Little streams were constantly running into it from cracks in the wall of the cavern. It was polished quite smooth inside, and had a carpet of yellow sand in the bottom of it. Large green leaves and white flowers of various plants crowded up and over it, draping and covering it almost entirely.

No sooner was she undressed and lying in the bath, than she began to feel as if the water were sinking into her, and she was receiving all the good of sleep without undergoing its forgetfulness. She felt the good coming all the time. And she grew happier and more hopeful than she had been since she lost Mossy. But she could not help thinking how very sad it was for a poor old man to live there all alone, and have to take care of a whole seaful of stupid and riotous fishes.

After about an hour, as she thought, she heard his voice calling her, and rose out of the bath. All the fatigue and aching of her long journey had vanished. She was as whole, and strong, and well as if she had slept for seven days.

Returning to the opening that led into the other part of the house, she started back with amazement, for through it she saw the form of a grand man, with a majestic and beautiful face, waiting for her.

"Come," he said; "I see you are ready."

She entered with reverence.

"Where is the Old Man of the Sea?" she asked, humbly.

"There is no one here but me," he answered, smiling. "Some people call me the Old Man of the Sea. Others have another name for me, and are terribly frightened when they meet me taking a walk by the shore. Therefore I avoid being seen by them, for they are so afraid, that they never see what I really am. You see me now.—But I must show you the way to the Old Man of the Earth."

He led her into the cave where the bath was, and there she saw, in the opposite corner, a second opening in the rock.

"Go down that stair, and it will bring you to him," said the Old Man of the Sea.

With humble thanks Tangle took her leave. She went down the winding-stair, till she began to fear there was no end to it. Still down and down it went, rough and broken, with springs of water bursting out of the rocks and running down the steps beside her. It was quite dark about her, and yet she could see. For after being in that bath, people's eyes always give out a light they can see by. There were no creeping things in the way. All was safe and pleasant though so dark and damp and deep.

At last there was not one step more, and she found herself in a glimmering cave. On a stone in the middle of it sat a figure with its back towards her—the figure of an old man bent double with age. From behind she could see his white beard spread out on the rocky floor in front of him. He did not move as she entered, so she passed round that she might stand before him and speak to him. The moment she looked in his face, she saw that he was a youth of marvellous beauty. He sat entranced with the delight of what he beheld in a mirror of something like silver, which lay on the floor at his feet, and which from behind she had taken for his white beard. He sat on, heedless of her presence, pale with the joy of his vision. She stood and watched him. At length, all trembling, she spoke. But her voice made no sound. Yet the youth lifted up his head. He showed no surprise, however, at seeing her—only smiled a welcome.

"Are you the Old Man of the Earth?" Tangle had said.

And the youth answered, and Tangle heard him, though not with her ears:—

"I am. What can I do for you?"

"Tell me the way to the country whence the shadows fall."

"Ah! that I do not know. I only dream about it myself. I see its shadows sometimes in my mirror: the way to it I do not know. But I think the Old Man of the Fire must know. He is much older than I am. He is the oldest man of all."

"Where does he live?"

"I will show you the way to his place. I never saw him myself."

So saying, the young man rose, and then stood for a while gazing at Tangle.

"I wish I could see that country too," he said. "But I must mind my work."

He led her to the side of the cave, and told her to lay her ear against the wall.

"What do you hear?" he asked.

"I hear," answered Tangle, "the sound of a great water running inside the rock."

"That river runs down to the dwelling of the oldest man of all—the Old Man of the Fire. I wish I could go to see him. But I must mind my work. That river is the only way to him."

Then the Old Man of the Earth stooped over the floor of the cave, raised a huge stone from it, and left it leaning. It disclosed a great hole that went plumb-down.

"That is the way," he said.

"But there are no stairs."

"You must throw yourself in. There is no other way."

She turned and looked him full in the face—stood so for a whole minute, as she thought: it was a whole year—then threw herself headlong into the hole.

When she came to herself, she found herself gliding down fast and deep. Her head was under water, but that did not signify, for, when she thought about it, she could not remember that she had breathed once since her bath in the cave of the Old Man of the Sea. When she lifted up her head a sudden and fierce heat struck her, and she sank it again instantly, and went sweeping on.

Gradually the stream grew shallower. At length she could hardly keep her head under. Then the water could carry her no farther. She rose from the channel, and went step for step down the burning descent. The water ceased altogether. The heat was terrible. She felt scorched to the bone, but it did not touch her strength. It grew hotter and hotter. She said, "I can bear it no longer." Yet she went on.

At the long last, the stair ended at a rude archway in an all but glowing rock. Through this archway Tangle fell exhausted into a cool mossy cave. The floor and walls were covered with moss—green, soft, and damp. A little stream spouted from a rent in the rock and fell into a basin of moss. She plunged her face into it and drank. Then she lifted her head and looked around. Then she rose and looked again. She saw no one in the cave. But the moment she stood upright she had a marvellous sense that she was in the secret of

the earth and all its ways. Everything she had seen, or
learned from books; all that her grandmother had said or
sung to her; all the talk of the beasts, birds, and fishes; all
that had happened to her on her journey with Mossy, and
since then in the heart of the earth with the Old man and
the Older man—all was plain: she understood it all, and saw
that everything meant the same thing, though she could not
have put it into words again.

The next moment she descried, in a corner of the cave, a
little naked child, sitting on the moss. He was playing with
balls of various colours and sizes, which he disposed in
strange figures upon the floor beside him. And now Tangle
felt that there was something in her knowledge which was
not in her understanding. For she knew there must be an
infinite meaning in the change and sequence and individual
forms of the figures into which the child arranged the balls,
as well as in the varied harmonies of their colours, but what
it all meant she could not tell.* He went on busily, tirelessly,
playing his solitary game, without looking up, or seeming to
know that there was a stranger in his deep-withdrawn cell.
Diligently as a lace-maker shifts her bobbins, he shifted and
arranged his balls. Flashes of meaning would now pass from
them to Tangle, and now again all would be not merely obscure, but utterly dark. She stood looking for a long time, for
there was fascination in the sight; and the longer she looked
the more an indescribable vague intelligence went on rousing
itself in her mind. For seven years she had stood there
watching the naked child with his coloured balls, and it
seemed to her like seven hours, when all at once the shape
the balls took, she knew not why, reminded her of the Valley
of Shadows, and she spoke:—

"Where is the Old Man of the Fire?" she said.

"Here I am," answered the child, rising and leaving his
balls on the moss. "What can I do for you?"

There was such an awfulness of absolute repose on the face
of the child that Tangle stood dumb before him. He had no
smile, but the love in his large grey eyes was deep as the

* I think I must be indebted to Novalis for these geometrical figures.

centre. And with the repose there lay on his face a shimmer as of moonlight, which seemed as if any moment it might break into such a ravishing smile as would cause the beholder to weep himself to death. But the smile never came, and the moonlight lay there unbroken. For the heart of the child was too deep for any smile to reach from it to his face.

"Are you the oldest man of all?" Tangle at length, although filled with awe, ventured to ask.

"Yes, I am. I am very, very old. I am able to help you, I know. I can help everybody."

And the child drew near and looked up in her face so that she burst into tears.

"Can you tell me the way to the country the shadows fall from?" she sobbed.

"Yes. I know the way quite well. I go there myself sometimes. But you could not go my way; you are not old enough. I will show you how you can go."

"Do not send me out into the great heat again," prayed Tangle.

"I will not," answered the child.

And he reached up, and put his little cool hand on her heart.

"Now," he said, "you can go. The fire will not burn you. Come."

He led her from the cave, and following him through another archway, she found herself in a vast desert of sand and rock. The sky of it was of rock, lowering over them like solid thunderclouds; and the whole place was so hot that she saw, in bright rivulets, the yellow gold and white silver and red copper trickling molten from the rocks. But the heat never came near her.

When they had gone some distance, the child turned up a great stone, and took something like an egg from under it. He next drew a long curved line in the sand with his finger, and laid the egg in it. He then spoke something Tangle could not understand. The egg broke, a small snake came out, and, lying in the line in the sand, grew and grew till he filled it. The moment he was thus full-grown, he began to glide away, undulating like a sea-wave.

"Follow that serpent," said the child. "He will lead you the right way."

Tangle followed the serpent. But she could not go far without looking back at the marvellous Child. He stood alone in the midst of the glowing desert, beside a fountain of red flame that had burst forth at his feet, his naked whiteness glimmering a pale rosy red in the torrid fire. There he stood, looking after her, till, from the lengthening distance, she could see him no more. The serpent went straight on, turning neither to the right nor left.

Meantime Mossy had got out of the lake of shadows, and, following his mournful, lonely way, had reached the sea-shore. It was a dark, stormy evening. The sun had set. The wind was blowing from the sea. The waves had surrounded the rock within which lay the Old Man's house. A deep water rolled between it and the shore, upon which a majestic figure was walking alone.

Mossy went up to him and said,—

"Will you tell me where to find the Old Man of the Sea?"

"I am the Old Man of the Sea," the figure answered.

"I see a strong kingly man of middle age," returned Mossy.

Then the Old Man looked at him more intently, and said,—

"Your sight, young man, is better than that of most who take this way. The night is stormy: come to my house and tell me what I can do for you."

Mossy followed him. The waves flew from before the footsteps of the Old Man of the Sea, and Mossy followed upon dry sand.

When they had reached the cave, they sat down and gazed at each other.

Now Mossy was an old man by this time. He looked much older than the Old Man of the Sea, and his feet were very weary.

After looking at him for a moment, the Old Man took him by the hand and led him into his inner cave. There he helped him to undress, and laid him in the bath. And he saw that one of his hands Mossy did not open.

"What have you in that hand?" he asked.

Mossy opened his hand, and there lay the golden key.

"Ah!" said the Old Man, "that accounts for your knowing me. And I know the way you have to go."

"I want to find the country whence the shadows fall," said Mossy.

"I dare say you do. So do I. But meantime, one thing is certain.—What is that key for, do you think?"

"For a keyhole somewhere. But I don't know why I keep it. I never could find the keyhole. And I have lived a good while, I believe," said Mossy, sadly. "I'm not sure that I'm not old. I know my feet ache."

"Do they?" said the Old Man, as if he really meant to ask the question; and Mossy, who was still lying in the bath, watched his feet for a moment before he replied,

"No, they do not," he answered. "Perhaps I am not old either."

"Get up and look at yourself in the water."

He rose and looked at himself in the water, and there was not a grey hair on his head or a wrinkle on his skin.

"You have tasted of death now," said the Old Man. "Is it good?"

"It is good," said Mossy. "It is better than life."

"No," said the Old Man: "it is only more life.—Your feet will make no holes in the water now."

"What do you mean?"

"I will show you that presently."

They returned to the outer cave, and sat and talked together for a long time. At length the Old Man of the Sea rose, and said to Mossy,—

"Follow me."

He let him up the stair again, and opened another door. They stood on the level of the raging sea, looking towards the east. Across the waste of waters, against the bosom of a fierce black cloud, stood the foot of a rainbow, glowing in the dark.

"This indeed is my way," said Mossy, as soon as he saw the rainbow, and stepped out upon the sea. His feet made no holes in the water. He fought the wind, and clomb the waves, and went on towards the rainbow.

The storm died away. A lovely day and a lovelier night followed. A cool wind blew over the wide plain of the quiet ocean. And still Mossy journeyed eastward. But the rainbow had vanished with the storm.

Day after day he held on, and he thought he had no guide. He did not see how a shining fish under the waters directed his steps. He crossed the sea, and came to a great precipice of rock, up which he could discover but one path. Nor did this lead him farther than half-way up the rock, where it ended on a platform. Here he stood and pondered.—It could not be that the way stopped here, else what was the path for? It was a rough path, not very plain, yet certainly a path.—He examined the face of the rock. It was smooth as glass. But as his eyes kept roving hopelessly over it, something glittered, and he caught sight of a row of small sapphires. They bordered a little hole in the rock.

"The keyhole!" he cried.

He tried the key. It fitted. It turned. A great clang and clash, as of iron bolts on huge brazen caldrons, echoed thunderously within. He drew out the key. The rock in front of him began to fall. He retreated from it as far as the breadth of the platform would allow. A great slab fell at his feet. In front was still the solid rock, with this one slab fallen forward out of it. But the moment he stepped upon it, a second fell, just short of the edge of the first, making the next step of a stair, which thus kept dropping itself before him as he ascended into the heart of the precipice. It led him into a hall fit for such an approach—irregular and rude in formation, but floor, sides, pillars, and vaulted roof, all one mass of shining stones of every colour that light can show. In the centre stood seven columns, ranged from red to violet. And on the pedestal of one of them sat a woman, motionless, with her face bowed upon her knees. Seven years had she sat there waiting. She lifted her head as Mossy drew near. It was Tangle. Her hair had grown to her feet, and was rippled like the windless sea on broad sands. Her face was beautiful, like her grandmother's, and as still and peaceful as that of the Old Man of the Fire. Her form was tall and noble. Yet Mossy knew her at once.

"How beautiful you are, Tangle!" he said, in delight and astonishment.

"Am I?" she returned. "Oh, I have waited for you so long! But you, you are the Old Man of the Sea. No. You are like the Old Man of the Earth. No, no. You are like the oldest man of all. You are like them all. And yet you are my own old Mossy! How did you come here? What did you do after I lost you? Did you find the keyhole? Have you got the key still?"

She had a hundred questions to ask him, and he a hundred more to ask her. They told each other all their adventures, and were as happy as man and woman could be. For they were younger and better, and stronger and wiser, than they had ever been before.

It began to grow dark. And they wanted more than ever to reach the country whence the shadows fall. So they looked about them for a way out of the cave. The door by which Mossy entered had closed again, and there was half a mile of rock between them and the sea. Neither could Tangle find the opening in the floor by which the serpent had led her thither. They searched till it grew so dark that they could see nothing, and gave it up.

After a while, however, the cave began to glimmer again. The light came from the moon, but it did not look like moonlight, for it gleamed through those seven pillars in the middle, and filled the place with all colours. And now Mossy saw that there was a pillar beside the red one, which he had not observed before. And it was of the same new colour that he had seen in the rainbow when he saw it first in the fairy forest. And on it he saw a sparkle of blue. It was the sapphires round the keyhole.

He took his key. It turned in the lock to the sounds of Æolian music. A door opened upon slow hinges, and disclosed a winding stair within. The key vanished from his fingers. Tangle went up. Mossy followed. The door closed behind them. They climbed out of the earth; and, still climbing, rose above it. They were in the rainbow. Far abroad, over ocean and land, they could see through its transparent walls the earth beneath their feet. Stairs beside stairs wound up together, and beautiful beings of all ages climbed along with them.

They knew that they were going up to the country whence the shadows fall.

And by this time I think they must have got there.

THE FORTRESS UNVANQUISHABLE SAVE FOR SACNOTH

By Edward J. M. D. Plunkett, Lord Dunsany

In a wood older than record, a foster brother of the hills, stood the village of Allathurion; and there was peace between the people of that village and all the folk who walked in the dark ways of the wood, whether they were human or of the tribes of the beasts or of the race of the fairies and the elves and the little sacred spirits of trees and streams. Moreover, the village people had peace among themselves and between them and their lord, Lorendiac. In front of the village was a wide and grassy space, and beyond this the great wood again, but at the back the trees came right up to the houses, which, with their great beams and wooden framework and thatched roofs, green with moss, seemed almost to be a part of the forest.

Now in the time I tell of, there was trouble in Allathurion, for of an evening fell dreams were wont to come slipping through the tree trunks and into the peaceful village; and they assumed dominion of men's minds and led them in watches of the night through the cindery plains of Hell. Then the magician of that village made spells against those fell dreams; yet still the dreams came flitting through the trees as soon as the dark had fallen, and led men's minds by night into terrible places and caused them to praise Satan openly with their lips.

And men grew afraid of sleep in Allathurion. And they grew worn and pale, some through the want of rest, and others from fear of the things they saw on the cindery plains of Hell.

Then the magician of the village went up into the tower of his house, and all night long those whom fear kept awake could see his window high up in the night glowing softly alone. The next day, when the twilight was far gone and night was gathering fast, the magician went away to the forest's edge, and uttered there the spell that he had made. And the spell was a compulsive, terrible thing, having a power over evil dreams and over spirits of ill; for it was a verse of forty lines in many languages, both living and dead, and had in it the word wherewith the people of the plains are wont to curse their camels, and the shout wherewith the whalers of the north lure the whales shoreward to be killed, and a word that causes elephants to trumpet; and every one of the forty lines closed with a rhyme for "wasp."

And still the dreams came flitting through the forest, and led men's souls into the plains of Hell. Then the magician knew that the dreams were from Gaznak. Therefore he gathered the people of the village, and told them that he had uttered his mightiest spell—a spell having power over all that were human or of the tribes of the beasts; and that since it had not availed the dreams must come from Gaznak, the greatest magician among the spaces of the stars. And he read to the people out of the Book of Magicians, which tells the comings of the comet and foretells his coming again. And he told them how Gaznak rides upon the comet, and how he visits Earth once in every two hundred and thirty years, and makes for himself a vast, invincible fortress and sends out dreams to feed on the minds of men, and may never be vanquished but by the sword Sacnoth.

And a cold fear fell on the hearts of the villagers when they found that their magician had failed them.

Then spake Leothric, son of the Lord Lorendiac, and twenty years old was he: "Good Master, what of the sword Sacnoth?"

And the village magician answered: "Fair Lord, no such sword as yet is wrought, for it lies as yet in the hide of Tharagavverug, protecting his spine."

Then said Leothric: "Who is Tharagavverug, and where may he be encountered?"

And the magician of Allathurion answered: "He is the dragon-crocodile who haunts the Northern marshes and ravages the homesteads by their marge. And the hide of his back is of steel, and his under parts are of iron; but along the midst of his back, over his spine, there lies a narrow strip of unearthly steel. This strip of steel is Sacnoth, and it may be neither cleft nor molten, and there is nothing in the world that may avail to break it, nor even leave a scratch upon its surface. It is of the length of a good sword, and of the breadth thereof. Shouldst thou prevail against Tharagavverug, his hide may be melted away from Sacnoth in a furnace; but there is only one thing that may sharpen Sacnoth's edge, and this is one of Tharagavverug's own steel eyes; and the other eye thou must fasten to Sacnoth's hilt, and it will watch for thee. But it is a hard task to vanquish Tharagavverug, for no sword can pierce his hide; his back cannot be broken, and he can neither burn nor drown. In one way only can Tharagavverug die, and that is by starving."

Then sorrow fell upon Leothric, but the magician spoke on:

"If a man drive Tharagavverug away from his food with a stick for three days, he will starve on the third day at sunset. And though he is not vulnerable, yet in one spot he may take hurt, for his nose is only of lead. A sword would merely lay bare the uncleavable bronze beneath, but if his nose be smitten constantly with a stick he will always recoil from the pain, and thus may Tharagavverug, to left and right, be driven away from his food."

Then Leothric said: "What is Tharagavverug's food?"

And the magician of Allathurion said: "His food is men."

But Leothric went straightway thence, and cut a great staff from a hazel tree, and slept early that evening. But the next morning, awaking from troubled dreams, he arose before the dawn, and, taking with him provisions for five days, set out through the forest northwards towards the marshes. For some hours he moved through the gloom of the forest, and when he emerged from it the sun was above the horizon shining on pools of water in the waste land. Presently he saw the claw-marks of Tharagavverug deep in the soil, and the track of his tail between them like a furrow in a field. Then Leothric followed the tracks till he heard the bronze heart of Tharagavverug before him, booming like a bell.

And Tharagavverug, it being the hour when he took the first meal of the day, was moving toward a village with his heart tolling. And all the people of the village were come out to meet him, as it was their wont to do; for they abode not the suspense of awaiting Tharagavverug and of hearing him sniffing brazenly as he went from door to door, pondering slowly in his metal mind what habitant he should choose. And none dared to flee, for in the days when the villagers fled from Tharagavverug, he, having chosen his victim, would track him tirelessly, like a doom. Nothing availed them against Tharagavverug. Once they climbed the trees when he came, but Tharagavverug went up to one, arching his back and leaning over slightly, and rasped against the trunk until it fell. And when Leothric came near, Tharagavverug saw him out of one of his small steel eyes and came towards him leisurely, and the echoes of his heart swirled up through his open mouth. And Leothric stepped sideways from his onset, and came between him and the village and smote him on the nose, and the blow of the stick made a dint in the soft lead. And Tharagavverug swung clumsily away, uttering one fearful cry like the sound of a great church bell that had become possessed of a soul that uttered upward from the tombs at night—an evil soul, giving the bell a voice. Then he attacked Leothric, snarling, and again Leothric leapt aside, and smote him on the nose with his stick. Tharagavverug uttered like a bell howling. And whenever the dragon-crocodile attacked him, or turned towards the village, Leothric smote him again.

So all day long Leothric drove the monster with a stick and he drove him farther and farther from his prey, with his heart tolling angrily and his voice crying out for pain.

Towards evening Tharagavverug ceased to snap at Leothric, but ran before him to avoid the stick, for his nose was sore and shining; and in the gloaming the villagers came out and danced to cymbal and psaltery. When Tharagavverug heard the cymbal and psaltery, hunger and anger came upon him, and he felt as some lord might feel who was held by force from the banquet in his own castle and heard the creaking spit go round and round and the good meat crackling on it. And all that night he attacked Leothric fiercely, and ofttimes nearly caught him in the darkness; for his gleaming eyes of steel could see as well by night as by day. And Leothric gave ground slowly till the dawn, and when the light came they were near the village again; yet not so near to it as they had been when they encountered, for Leothric drove Tharagavverug farther in the day than Tharagavverug had forced him back in the night. Then Leothric drove him again with his stick till the hour came when it was the custom of the dragon-crocodile to find his man. One third of his man he would eat at the time he found him, and the rest at noon and evening. But when the hour came for finding his man a great fierceness came on Tharagavverug, and he grabbed rapidly at Leothric, but could not seize him, and for a long while neither of them would retire. But at last the pain of the stick on his leaden nose overcame the hunger of the dragon-crocodile, and he turned from it howling. From that moment Tharagavverug weakened. All that day Leothric drove him with his stick, and at night both held their ground; and when the dawn of the third day was come the heart of Tharagavverug beat slower and fainter. It was as though a tired man was ringing a bell. Once Tharagaverrug nearly seized a frog, but Leothric snatched it away just in time. Towards noon the dragon-crocodile lay still for a long while, and Leothric stood near him and leaned on his trusty stick. He was very tired and sleepless, but had more leisure now for eating his provisions. With Tharagavverug the end was coming fast, and in the afternoon his breath came hoarsely, rasping in his throat. It was as the sound of many huntsmen blowing blasts on horns, and towards evening his breath came faster but fainter, like the sound of a hunt going furious to the distance and dying away, and he made desperate rushes towards the village; but Leothric still leapt about him, battering his leaden nose. Scarce audible now at all was the sound of his heart: it was like a church bell tolling beyond hills for the death of some one unknown and far away. Then the sun set and flamed in the village windows, and a chill went over the world, and in some small garden a woman sang; and Tharagavverug lifted up his head and starved, and his life went from his invulnerable body, and Leothric lay down beside him and slept. And later in the starlight the villagers came out and carried Leothric, sleeping, to the village, all praising him in whispers as they went. They laid him down upon a couch in a house, and danced outside in silence, without psaltery or cymbal. And the next day, rejoicing, to Allathurion they hauled the dragon-crocodile. And Leothric went with them, holding his battered staff; and a tall, broad man, who was smith of Allathurion, made a great furnace, and melted Tharagavverug away till only Sacnoth was left, gleaming among the ashes. Then he took one of the small eyes that had been chiselled out, and filed an edge on Sacnoth, and gradually the steel eye wore away facet by facet, but ere it was quite gone it had sharpened redoubtably Sacnoth. But the other eye they set in the butt of the hilt, and it gleamed there bluely.

And that night Leothric arose in the dark and took the sword, and went westwards to find Gaznak; and he went through the dark forest till the dawn, and all the morning and till the afternoon. But in the afternoon he came into the open and saw in the midst of The Land Where No Man Goeth the fortress of Gaznak, mountainous before him, little more than a mile away.

And Leothric saw that the land was marsh and desolate. And the fortress went up all white out of it, with many buttresses, and was broad below but narrowed higher up, and was full of gleaming windows with the light upon them. And near the top of it a few white clouds were floating, but above them some of its pinnacles reappeared. Then Leothric advanced into the marshes, and the eye of Tharagavverug looked out warily from the hilt of Sacnoth; for Tharagavverug had known the marshes well, and the sword nudged Leothric to the right or pulled him to the left away from the dangerous places, and so brought him safely to the fortress walls.

And in the wall stood doors like precipices of steel, all studded with boulders of iron, and above every window were terrible gargoyles of stone; and the name of the fortress shone on the wall, writ large in letters of brass: "The Fortress Unvanquishable, Save for Sacnoth."

Then Leothric drew and revealed Sacnoth, and all the gargoyles grinned, and the grin went flickering from face to face right up into the cloud-abiding gables.

And when Sacnoth was revealed and all the gargoyles grinned, it was like the moonlight emerging from a cloud to look for the first time upon a field of blood, and passing swiftly over the wet faces of the slain that lie together in the horrible night. Then Leothric advanced towards a door, and it was mightier than the marble quarry, Sacremona, from which of old men cut enormous slabs to build the Abbey of the Holy Tears. Day after day they wrenched out the very ribs of the hill until the Abbey was builded, and it was more beautiful than anything in stone. Then the priests blessed Sacremona, and it had rest, and no more stone was ever taken from it to build the houses of men. And the hill stood looking southwards lonely in the sunlight, defaced by that mighty scar. So vast was the door of steel. And the name of the door was The Porte Resonant, the Way of Egress for War.

Then Leothric smote upon the Porte Resonant with Sacnoth, and the echo of Sacnoth went ringing through the halls, and all the dragons in the fortress barked. And when the baying of the remotest dragon had faintly joined in the tumult, a window opened far up among the clouds below the twilit gables, and a woman screamed, and far away in Hell her father heard her and knew that her doom was come.

And Leothric went on smiting terribly with Sacnoth, and the grey steel of the Porte Resonant, the Way of Egress for War, that was tempered to resist the swords of the world, came away in ringing slices.

Then Leothric, holding Sacnoth in his hand, went in through the hole that he had hewn in the door, and came into the unlit, cavernous hall.

An elephant fled trumpeting. And Leothric stood still, holding Sacnoth. When the sound of the feet of the elephant had died away in the remoter corridors, nothing more stirred, and the cavernous hall was still.

Presently the darkness of the distant halls became musical with the sound of bells, all coming nearer and nearer.

Still Leothric waited in the dark, and the bells rang louder and louder, echoing through the halls, and there appeared a procession of men on camels riding two by two from the interior of the fortress, and they were armed with scimitars of Assyrian make and were all clad with mail, and chain-mail hung from their helmets about their faces, and flapped as the camels moved. And they all halted before Leothric in the cavernous hall, and the camel bells clanged and stopped. And the leader said to Leothric:

"The Lord Gaznak has desired to see you die before him. Be pleased to come with us, and we can discourse by the way of the manner in which the Lord Gaznak has desired to see you die."

And as he said this he unwound a chain of iron that was coiled upon his saddle, and Leothric answered:

"I would fain go with you, for I am come to slay Gaznak."

Then all the camel-guard of Gaznak laughed hideously, disturbing the vampires that were asleep in the measureless vault of the roof. And the leader said:

"The Lord Gaznak is immortal, save for Sacnoth, and weareth armour that is proof even against Sacnoth himself, and hath a sword the second most terrible in the world."

Then Leothric said: "I am the Lord of the sword Sacnoth."

And he advanced towards the camel-guard of Gaznak, and Sacnoth lifted up and down in his hand as though stirred by an exultant pulse. Then the camel-guard of Gaznak fled, and the riders leaned foward and smote their camels with whips, and they went away with a great clamour of bells through colonnades and corridors and vaulted halls, and scattered into the inner darknesses of the fortress. When the last sound of them had died away, Leothric was in doubt which way to go, for the camel-guard was dispersed in many directions, so he went straight on till he came to a great stairway in the midst of the hall. Then Leothric set his foot in the middle of a

wide step, and climbed steadily up the stairway for five minutes. Little light was there in the great hall through which
Leothric ascended, for it only entered through arrow slits
here and there, and in the world outside evening was waning
fast. The stairway led up to two folding doors, and they stood
a little ajar, and through the crack Leothric entered and tried
to continue straight on, but could get no farther, for the
whole room seemed to be full of festoons of ropes which
swung from wall to wall and were looped and draped from
the ceiling. The whole chamber was thick and black with
them. They were soft and light to the touch, like fine silk,
but Leothric was unable to break any one of them, and
though they swung away from him as he pressed forward, yet
by the time he had gone three yards they were all about him
like a heavy cloak. Then Leothric stepped back and drew
Sacnoth, and Sacnoth divided the ropes without a sound, and
without a sound the severed pieces fell to the floor. Leothric
went forward slowly, moving Sacnoth in front of him up and
down as he went. When he was come into the middle of
the chamber, suddenly, as he parted with Sacnoth a great
hammock of strands, he saw a spider before him that was
larger than a ram, and the spider looked at him with eyes
that were little, but in which there was much sin, and said:

"Who are you that spoil the labour of years all done to the
honour of Satan?"

And Leothric answered: "I am Leothric, son of Lorendiac."

And the spider said: "I will make a rope at once to hang
you with."

Then Leothric parted another bunch of strands, and came
nearer to the spider as he sat making his rope, and the spider,
looking up from his work, said: "What is that sword which
is able to sever my ropes?"

And Leothric said: "It is Sacnoth."

Thereat the black hair that hung over the face of the spider parted to left and right, and the spider frowned: then the
hair fell back into its place, and hid everything except the sin
of the little eyes which went on gleaming lustfully in the
dark. But before Leothric could reach him, he climbed away

with his hands, going up by one of his ropes to a lofty rafter, and there sat, growling. But clearing his way with Sacnoth, Leothric passed through the chamber, and came to the farther door; and the door being shut, and the handle far up out of his reach, he hewed his way through it with Sacnoth in the same way as he had through the Porte Resonant, the Way of Egress for War. And so Leothric came into a well-lit chamber, where Queens and Princes were banqueting together, all at a great table; and thousands of candles were glowing all about, and their light shone in the wine that the Princes drank and on the huge gold candelabra, and the royal faces were irradiant with the glow, and the white table-cloth and the silver plates and the jewels in the hair of the Queens, each jewel having a historian all to itself, who wrote no other chronicles all his days. Between the table and the door there stood two hundred footmen in two rows of one hundred facing one another. Nobody looked at Leothric as he entered through the hole in the door, but one of the Princes asked a question of a footman, and the question was passed from mouth to mouth by all the hundred footmen till it came to the last one nearest Leothric; and he said to Leothric, without looking at him:

"What do you seek here?"

And Leothric answered: "I seek to slay Gaznak."

And footman to footman repeated all the way to the table: "He seeks to slay Gaznak."

And another question came down the line of footmen: "What is your name?"

And the line that stood opposite took his answer back.

Then one of the Princes said: "Take him away where we shall not hear his screams."

And footman repeated it to footman till it came to the last two, and they advanced to seize Leothric.

Then Leothric showed to them his sword, saying, "This is Sacnoth," and both of them said to the man nearest: "It is Sacnoth," then screamed and fled away.

And two by two, all up the double line, footman to footman repeated, "It is Sacnoth," then screamed and fled, till the last two gave the message to the table, and all the rest had gone. Hurriedly then arose the Queens and Princes, and fled out of the chamber. And the goodly table, when they were all gone, looked small and disorderly and awry. And to Leothric, pondering in the desolate chamber by what door he should pass onwards, there came from far away the sounds of music, and he knew that it was the magical musicians playing to Gaznak while he slept.

Then Leothric, walking towards the distant music, passed out by the door opposite to the one through which he had cloven his entrance, and so passed into a chamber vast as the other, in which were many women, weirdly beautiful. And they all asked him of his quest, and when they heard that it was to slay Gaznak, they all besought him to tarry among them, saying that Gaznak was immortal, save for Sacnoth, and also that they had need of a knight to protect them from the wolves that rushed round and round the wainscot all the night and sometimes broke in upon them through the mouldering oak. Perhaps Leothric had been tempted to tarry had they been human women, for theirs was a strange beauty, but he perceived that instead of eyes they had little flames that flickered in their sockets, and knew them to be the fevered dreams of Gaznak. Therefore he said:

"I have a business with Gaznak and with Sacnoth," and passed on through the chamber.

And at the name of Sacnoth those women screamed, and the flames of their eyes sank low and dwindled to sparks.

And Leothric left them, and, hewing with Sacnoth, passed through the farther door.

Outside he felt the night air on his face, and found that he stood upon a narrow way between two abysses. To left and right of him, as far as he could see, the walls of the fortress ended in a profound precipice, though the roof still stretched above him; and before him lay the two abysses full of stars, for they cut their way through the whole Earth and revealed the under sky; and threading its course between them went the way, and it sloped upward and its sides were sheer. And beyond the abysses, where the way led up to the farther chambers of the fortress, Leothric heard the musicians playing their magical tune. So he stepped on to the way, which was scarcely a stride in width, and moved along it holding Sacnoth naked. And to and fro beneath him in each abyss whirred the wings of vampires passing up and down, all giving praise to Satan as they flew. Presently he perceived the dragon Thok lying upon the way, pretending to sleep, and his tail hung down into one of the abysses.

And Leothric went towards him, and when he was quite close Thok rushed at Leothric.

And he smote deep with Sacnoth, and Thok tumbled into the abyss, screaming, and his limbs made a whirring in the darkness as he fell, and he fell till his scream sounded no louder than a whistle and then could be heard no more. Once or twice Leothric saw a star blink for an instant and reappear again, and this momentary eclipse of a few stars was all that remained in the world of the body of Thok. And Lunk, the brother of Thok, who had lain a little behind him, saw that this must be Sacnoth and fled lumbering away. And all the while that he walked between the abysses, the mighty vault of the roof of the fortress still stretched over Leothric's head, all filled with gloom. Now, when the farther side of the abyss came into view, Leothric saw a chamber that opened with innumerable arches upon the twin abysses, and the pillars of the arches went away into the distance and vanished in the gloom to left and right.

Far down the dim precipice on which the pillars stood he could see windows small and closely barred, and between the bars there showed at moments, and disappeared again, things that I shall not speak of.

There was no light here except for the great Southern stars that shone below the abysses, and here and there in the chamber through the arches lights that moved furtively without the sound of footfall.

Then Leothric stepped from the way, and entered the great chamber.

Even to himself he seemed but a tiny dwarf as he walked under one of those colossal arches.

The last faint light of evening flickered through a window painted in sombre colours commemorating the achievements of Satan upon Earth. High up in the wall the window stood, and the streaming lights of candles lower down moved stealthily away.

Other light there was none, save for a faint blue glow from the steel eye of Tharagavverug that peered restlessly about it from the hilt of Sacnoth. Heavily in the chamber hung the clammy odour of a large and deadly beast.

Leothric moved forward slowly with the blade of Sacnoth in front of him feeling for a foe, and the eye of the hilt of it looking out behind.

Nothing stirred.

If anything lurked behind the pillars of the colonnade that held aloft the roof, it neither breathed nor moved.

The music of the magical musicians sounded from very near.

Suddenly the great doors on the far side of the chamber opened to left and right. For some moments Leothric saw nothing move, and waited clutching Sacnoth. Then Wong Bongerok came towards him, breathing.

This was the last and faithfullest guard of Gaznak, and came from slobbering just now his master's hand.

More as a child than a dragon was Gaznak wont to treat him, giving him often in his fingers tender pieces of man all smoking from his table.

Long and low was Wong Bongerok, and subtle about the eyes, and he came breathing malice against Leothric out of his faithful breast, and behind him roared the armoury of his tail, as when sailors drag the cable of the anchor all rattling down the deck.

And well Wong Bongerok knew that he now faced Sacnoth, for it had been his wont to prophesy quietly to himself for many years as he lay curled at the feet of Gaznak.

And Leothric stepped forward into the blast of his breath, and lifted Sacnoth to strike.

But when Sacnoth was lifted up, the eye of Tharagavverug in the butt of the hilt beheld the dragon and perceived his subtlety.

For he opened his mouth wide, and revealed to Leothric the ranks of his sabre teeth, and his leather gums flapped upward. But while Leothric made to smite at his head, he shot forward scorpion-wise over his head the length of his armoured tail. All this the eye perceived in the hilt of Sacnoth, who smote suddenly sideways. Not with the edge smote Sacnoth, for, had he done so, the severed end of the tail had still come hurtling on, as some pine tree that the avalanche has hurled point foremost from the cliff right through the broad breast of some mountaineer. So had Leothric been transfixed; but Sacnoth smote sideways with the flat of his blade, and sent the tail whizzing over Leothric's left shoulder; and it rasped upon his armour as it went, and left a groove upon it. Sideways then at Leothric smote the foiled tail of Wong Bongerok, and Sacnoth parried, and the tail went shrieking up the blade and over Leothric's head. Then Leothric and Wong Bongerok fought sword to tooth, and the sword smote as only Sacnoth can, and the evil faithful life of Wong Bongerok the dragon went out through the wide wound.

Then Leothric walked on past that dead monster, and the armoured body still quivered a little. And for a while it was like all the ploughshares in a county working together in one field behind tired and struggling horses; then the quivering ceased, and Wong Bongerok lay still to rust.

And Leothric went on to the open gates, and Sacnoth dripped quietly along the floor.

By the open gates through which Wong Bongerok had entered, Leothric came into a corridor echoing with music. This was the first place from which Leothric could see anything above his head, for hitherto the roof had ascended to mountainous heights and had stretched indistinct in the gloom. But along the narrow corridor hung huge bells low and near to his head, and the width of each brazen bell was from wall to wall, and they were one behind the other. And as he passed under each the bell uttered, and its voice was mournful and deep, like to the voice of a bell speaking to a man for the last time when he is newly dead. Each bell uttered once as Leothric came under it, and their voices sounded solemnly and wide apart at ceremonious intervals. For if he walked slow, these bells came closer together, and when he walked swiftly they moved farther apart. And the echoes of each bell tolling above his head went on before him whispering to the others. Once when he stopped they all jangled angrily till he went on again.

Between these slow and boding notes came the sound of the magical musicians. They were playing a dirge now very mournfully.

And at last Leothric came to the end of the Corridor of the Bells, and beheld there a small black door. And all the corridor behind him was full of the echoes of the tolling, and they all muttered to one another about the ceremony; and the dirge of the musicians came floating slowly through them like a procession of foreign elaborate guests, and all of them boded ill to Leothric.

The black door opened at once to the hand of Leothric, and he found himself in the open air in a wide court paved with marble. High over it shone the moon, summoned there by the hand of Gaznak.

There Gaznak slept, and around him sat his magical musicians, all playing upon strings. And, even sleeping, Gaznak was clad in armour, and only his wrists and face and neck were bare.

But the marvel of that place was the dreams of Gaznak; for beyond the wide court slept a dark abyss, and into the abyss there poured a white cascade of marble stairways, and widened out below into terraces and balconies with fair white statues on them, and descended again in a wide stairway, and came to lower terraces in the dark, where swart uncertain shapes went to and fro. All these were the dreams of Gaznak, and issued from his mind, and, becoming gleaming marble, passed over the edge of the abyss as the musicians played. And all the while out of the mind of Gaznak, lulled by that strange music, went spires and pinnacles beautiful and slender, ever ascending skywards. And the marble dreams moved slow in time to the music. When the bells tolled and the musicians played their dirge, ugly gargoyles came out suddenly all over the spires and pinnacles, and great shadows passed swiftly down the steps and terraces, and there was hurried whispering in the abyss.

When Leothric stepped from the black door, Gaznak

opened his eyes. He looked neither to left nor right, but stood up at once facing Leothric.

Then the magicians played a deathspell on their strings, and there arose a humming along the blade of Sacnoth as he turned the spell aside. When Leothric dropped not down, and they heard the humming of Sacnoth, the magicians arose and fled, all wailing, as they went, upon their strings.

Then Gaznak drew out screaming from its sheath the sword that was the mightiest in the world except for Sacnoth, and slowly walked towards Leothric; and he smiled as he walked, although his own dreams had foretold his doom. And when Leothric and Gaznak came together, each looked at each, and neither spoke a word; but they smote both at once, and their swords met, and each sword knew the other and from whence he came. And whenever the sword of Gaznak smote on the blade of Sacnoth it rebounded gleaming, as hail from off slated roofs; but whenever it fell upon the armour of Leothric, it stripped it off in sheets. And upon Gaznak's armour Sacnoth fell oft and furiously, but ever he came back snarling, leaving no mark behind, and as Gaznak fought he held his left hand hovering close over his head. Presently Leothric smote fair and fiercely at his enemy's neck, but Gaznak, clutching his own head by the hair, lifted it high aloft, and Sacnoth went cleaving through an empty space. Then Gaznak replaced his head upon his neck, and all the while fought nimbly with his sword; and again and again Leothric swept with Sacnoth at Gaznak's bearded neck, and ever the left hand of Gaznak was quicker than the stroke, and the head went up and the sword rushed vainly under it.

And the ringing fight went on till Leothric's armour lay all round him on the floor and the marble was splashed with his blood, and the sword of Gaznak was notched like a saw from meeting the blade of Sacnoth. Still Gaznak stood unwounded and smiling still.

At last Leothric looked at the throat of Gaznak and aimed with Sacnoth, and again Gaznak lifted his head by the hair; but not at his throat flew Sacnoth, for Leothric struck instead at the lifted hand, and through the wrist of it went Sacnoth whirring, as a scythe goes through the stem of a single flower.

And bleeding, the severed hand fell to the floor; and at once blood spurted from the shoulders of Gaznak and dripped from the fallen head, and the tall pinnacles went down into the earth, and the wide fair terraces all rolled away, and the court was gone like the dew, and a wind came and the colonnades drifted thence, and all the colossal halls of Gaznak fell. And the abysses closed up suddenly as the mouth of a man who, having told a tale, will for ever speak no more.

Then Leothric looked around him in the marshes where the night mist was passing away, and there was no fortress nor sound of dragon or mortal, only beside him lay an old man, wizened and evil and dead, whose head and hand were severed from his body.

And gradually over the wide lands the dawn was coming up, and ever growing in beauty as it came, like to the peal of an organ played by a master's hand, growing louder and lovelier as the soul of the master warms, and at last giving praise with all its mighty voice.

Then the birds sang, and Leothric went homeward, and left the marshes and came to the dark wood, and the light of the dawn ascending lit him upon his way. And into Allathurion he came ere noon, and with him brought the evil wizened head, and the people rejoiced, and their nights of trouble ceased.

.   .   .   .

This is the tale of the vanquishing of The Fortress Unvanquishable, Save For Sacnoth, and of its passing away, as it is told and believed by those who love the mystic days of old.

Others have said, and vainly claim to prove, that a fever came to Allathurion, and went away; and that this same fever drove Leothric into the marshes by night, and made him dream there and act violently with a sword.

And others again say that there hath been no town of Allathurion, and that Leothric never lived.

Peace to them. The gardener hath gathered up this autumn's leaves. Who shall see them again, or who wot of them? And who shall say what hath befallen in the days of long ago?

THE SILKEN SWIFT . . .

By Theodore Sturgeon

THERE'S A village by the Bogs, and in the village is a Great House. In the Great House lived a squire who had land and treasures and, for a daughter, Rita.

In the village lived Del, whose voice was a thunder in the inn when he drank there; whose corded, cabled body was golden-skinned, and whose hair flung challenges back to the sun.

Deep in the Bogs, which were brackish, there was a pool of purest water, shaded by willows and wide-wondering aspen, cupped by banks of a moss most marvellously blue. Here grew mandrake, and there were strange pipings in midsummer. No one ever heard them but a quiet girl whose beauty was so very contained that none of it showed. Her name was Barbara.

There was a green evening, breathless with growth, when Del took his usual way down the lane beside the manor and saw a white shadow adrift inside the tall iron pickets. He stopped, and the shadow approached, and became Rita. "Slip around to the gate," she said, "and I'll open it for you."

She wore a gown like a cloud and a silver circlet round her head. Night was caught in her hair, moonlight in her face, and in her great eyes, secrets swam.

Del said, "I have no business with the squire."

"He's gone," she said. "I've sent the servants away. Come to the gate."

"I need no gate." He leaped and caught the top bar of the fence, and in a continuous fluid motion went high and across and down beside her. She looked at his arms, one, the other; then up at his hair. She pressed her small hands tight together and made a little laugh, and then she was gone through the tailored trees, lightly, swiftly, not looking back. He followed, one step for three of hers, keeping pace with a new pounding in the sides of his neck. They crossed a flower bed and a wide marble terrace. There was an open door, and when he passed through it he stopped, for she was nowhere in sight. Then the door clicked shut behind him and he whirled. She was there, her back to the panel, laughing up at him in the dimness. He thought she would come to him then, but instead she twisted by, close, her eyes on his. She smelt of violets and sandalwood. He followed her into a great hall, quite dark but full of the subdued lights of polished wood, cloisonné, tooled leather and gold-threaded tapestry. She flung open another door, and they were in a small room with a carpet made of rosy silences, and a candle-lit table. Two places were set, each with five different crystal glasses and old silver as prodigally used as the iron pickets outside. Six teakwood steps rose to a great oval window. "The moon," she said, "will rise for us there."

She motioned him to a chair and crossed to a sideboard, where there was a rack of decanters—ruby wine and white; one with a strange brown bead; pink, and amber. She took down the first and poured. Then she lifted the silver domes from the salvers on the table, and a magic of fragrance filled the air. There were smoking sweets and savories, rare seafood and slivers of fowl, and morsels of strange meat wrapped in flower petals, spitted with foreign fruits and tiny soft sea-shells. All about were spices, each like a separate voice in the distant murmur of a crowd: saffron and sesame, cumin and marjoram and mace.

And all the while Del watched her in wonder, seeing how the candles left the moonlight in her face, and how completely she trusted her hands, which did such deftnesses without supervision—so composed she was, for all the silent secret laughter that tugged at her lips, for all the bright dark mysteries that swirled and swam within her.

They ate, and the oval window yellowed and darkened

while the candlelight grew bright. She poured another wine, and another, and with the courses of the meal they were as May to the crocus and as frost to the apple.

Del knew it was alchemy and he yielded to it without question. That which was purposely over-sweet would be piquantly cut; this induced thirst would, with exquisite timing, be quenched. He knew she was watching him; he knew she was aware of the heat in his cheeks and the tingle at his fingertips. His wonder grew, but he was not afraid.

In all this time she spoke hardly a word; but at last the feast was over and they rose. She touched a silken rope on the wall, and panelling slid aside. The table rolled silently into some ingenious recess and the panel returned. She waved him to an L-shaped couch in one corner, and as he sat close to her, she turned and took down the lute which hung on the wall behind her. He had his moment of confusion; his arms were ready for her, but not for the instrument as well. Her eyes sparkled, but her composure was unshaken.

Now she spoke, while her fingers strolled and danced on the lute, and her words marched and wandered in and about the music. She had a thousand voices, so that he wondered which of them was truly hers. Sometimes she sang; sometimes it was a wordless crooning. She seemed at times remote from him, puzzled at the turn the music was taking, and at other times she seemed to hear the pulsing roar in his eardrums, and she played laughing syncopations to it. She sang words which he almost understood:

> Bee to blossom, honey dew,
> Claw to mouse, and rain to tree,
> Moon to midnight, I to you;
> Sun to starlight, you to me . . .

and she sang something wordless:

> Ake ya rundefle, rundefle fye,
> Orel ya rundefle kown,
> En yea, en yea, ya bunderbee bye
> En sor, en see, en sown.

which he also almost understood.

In still another voice she told him the story of a great hairy spider and a little pink girl who found it between the leaves of a half-open book; and at first he was all fright and pity for the girl, but then she went on to tell of what the spider suffered, with his home disrupted by this yawping giant, and so vividly did she tell of it that at the end he was laughing at himself and all but crying for the poor spider.

So the hours slipped by, and suddenly, between songs, she was in his arms; and in the instant she had twisted up and away from him, leaving him gasping. She said, in still a new voice, sober and low, "No, Del. We must wait for the moon."

His thighs ached and he realized that he had half-risen, arms out, hands clutching and feeling the extraordinary fabric of her gown though it was gone from them; and he sank back to the couch with an odd, faint sound that was wrong for the room. He flexed his fingers and, reluctantly, the sensation of white gossamer left them. At last he looked across at her and she laughed and leapt high lightly, and it was as if she stopped in midair to stretch for a moment before she alighted beside him, bent and kissed his mouth, and leapt away.

The roaring in his ears was greater, and at this it seemed to acquire a tangible weight. His head bowed; he tucked his knuckles into the upper curve of his eye sockets and rested his elbows on his knees. He could hear the sweet susurrus of Rita's gown as she moved about the room; he could sense the violets and sandalwood. She was dancing, immersed in the joy of movement and of his nearness. She made her own music, humming, sometimes whispering to the melodies in her mind.

And at length he became aware that she had stopped; he could hear nothing, though he knew she was still near. Heavily he raised his head. She was in the center of the room, balanced like a huge white moth, her eyes quite dark now with their secrets quiet. She was staring at the window, poised, waiting.

He followed her gaze. The big oval was black no longer, but dusted over with silver light. Del rose slowly. The dust was a mist, a loom, and then, at one edge, there was a shard of the moon itself creeping and growing.

Because Del stopped breathing, he could hear her breath; it was rapid and so deep it faintly strummed her versatile vocal cords.

"Rita . . ."

Without answering she ran to the sideboard and filled two small glasses. She gave him one, then, "Wait," she breathed, "oh, wait!"

Spellbound, he waited while the white stain crept across the window. He understood suddenly that he must be still until the great oval was completely filled with direct moonlight, and this helped him, because it set a foreseeable limit to his waiting; and it hurt him, because nothing in life, he thought, had ever moved so slowly. He had a moment of rebellion, in which he damned himself for falling in with her complex pacing; but with it he realized that now the darker silver was wasting away, now it was a finger's breadth, and now a thread, and now, and *now*—.

She made a brittle feline cry and sprang up the dark steps to the window. So bright was the light that her body was a jet cameo against it. So delicately wrought was her gown that he could see the epaulettes of silver light the moon gave her. She was so beautiful his eyes stung.

"Drink," she whispered. "Drink with me, darling, darling . . ."

For an instant he did not understand her at all, and only gradually did he become aware of the little glass he held. He raised it toward her and drank. And of all the twists and titillations of taste he had had this night, this was the most startling; for it had no taste at all, almost no substance, and a temperature almost exactly that of blood. He looked stupidly down at the glass and back up at the girl. He thought that she had turned about and was watching him, though he could not be sure, since her silhouette was the same.

And then he had his second of unbearable shock, for the light went out.

The moon was gone, the window, the room, Rita was gone. For a stunned instant he stood tautly, stretching his eyes wide. He made a sound that was not a word. He dropped the glass, and pressed his palms to his eyes, feeling them blink, feeling the stiff silk of his lashes against them. Then he snatched the hands away, and it was still dark, and more than dark; this was not a blackness. This was like trying to see with an elbow or with a tongue; it was not black, it was *Nothingness.*

He fell to his knees.

Rita laughed.

An odd, alert part of his mind seized on the laugh and understood it, and horror and fury spread through his whole being; for this was the laugh which had been tugging at her lips all evening, and it was a hard, cruel, self-assured laugh. And at the same time, because of the anger or in spite of it, desire exploded whitely within him. He moved toward the sound, groping, mouthing. There was a quick, faint series of rustling sounds from the steps, and then a light, strong web fell around him. He struck out at it, and recognized it for the unforgettable thing it was—her robe. He caught at it, ripped it, stamped upon it. He heard her bare feet run lightly down and past him, and lunged, and caught nothing. He stood gasping painfully.

She laughed again.

"I'm blind," he said hoarsely. "Rita, I'm blind!"

"I know," she said coolly, close beside him. And again she laughed.

"What have you done to me?"

"I've watched you be a dirty animal of a man," she said.

He grunted and lunged again. His knees struck something —a chair, a cabinet—and he fell heavily. He thought he touched her foot.

"Here, lover, here!" she taunted.

He fumbled about for the thing which had tripped him, found it, used it to help him upright again. He peered uselessly about.

"Here, lover!"

He leaped, and crashed into the door jamb: cheekbone, collarbone, hip-bone, ankle were one straight blaze of pain. He clung to the polished wood.

After a time he said, in agony, "Why?"

"No man has ever touched me and none ever will," she sang. Her breath was on his cheek. He reached and touched nothing, and then he heard her leap from her perch on a statue's pedestal by the door, where she had stood high and leaned over to speak.

No pain, no blindness, not even the understanding that it was her witch's brew working in him could quell the wild desire he felt at her nearness. Nothing could tame the fury that shook him as she laughed. He staggered after her, bellowing.

She danced around him, laughing. Once she pushed him into a clattering rack of fire-irons. Once she caught his elbow from behind and spun him. And once, incredibly, she sprang past him and, in midair, kissed him again on the mouth.

He descended into Hell, surrounded by the small, sure patter of bare feet and sweet cool laughter. He rushed and crashed, he crouched and bled and whimpered like a hound. His roaring and blundering took an echo, and that must have been the great hall. Then there were walls that seemed more than unyielding; they struck back. And there were panels to lean against, gasping, which became opening doors as he leaned. And always the black nothingness, the writhing temptation of the pat-pat of firm flesh on smooth stones, and the ravening fury.

It was cooler, and there was no echo. He became aware of the whisper of the wind through trees. The balcony, he thought; and then, right in his ear, so that he felt her warm breath, "Come, lover . . ." and he sprang. He sprang and missed, and instead of sprawling on the terrace, there was nothing, and nothing, and nothing, and then, when he least expected it, a shower of cruel thumps as he rolled down the marble steps.

He must have had a shred of consciousness left, for he was vaguely aware of the approach of her bare feet, and of the small, cautious hand that touched his shoulder and moved to his mouth, and then his chest. Then it was withdrawn, and either she laughed or the sound was still in his mind.

Deep in the Bogs, which were brackish, there was a pool of

purest water, shaded by willows and wide-wondering aspens, cupped by banks of a moss most marvellously blue. Here grew mandrake, and there were strange pipings in mid-summer. No one ever heard them but a quiet girl whose beauty was so very contained that none of it showed. Her name was Barbara.

No one noticed Barbara, no one lived with her, no one cared. And Barbara's life was very full, for she was born to receive. Others are born wishing to receive, so they wear bright masks and make attractive sounds like cicadas and operettas, so others will be forced, one way or another, to give to them. But Barbara's receptors were wide open, and always had been, so that she needed no substitute for sunlight through a tulip petal, or the sound of morning-glories climbing, or the tangy sweet smell of formic acid which is the only death cry possible to an ant, or any other of the thousand things overlooked by folk who can only wish to receive. Barbara had a garden and an orchard, and took things in to market when she cared to, and the rest of the time she spent in taking what was given. Weeds grew in her garden, but since they were welcomed, they grew only where they could keep the watermelons from being sunburned. The rabbits were welcome, so they kept to the two rows of carrots, the one of lettuce, and the one of tomato vines which were planted for them, and they left the rest alone. Goldenrod shot up beside the bean hills to lend a hand upward, and the birds ate only the figs and peaches from the waviest top branches, and in return patrolled the lower ones for caterpillars and egg-laying flies. And if a fruit stayed green for two weeks longer until Barbara had time to go to market, or if a mole could channel moisture to the roots of the corn, why it was the least they could do.

For a brace of years Barbara had wandered more and more, impelled by a thing she could not name—if indeed she was aware of it at all. She knew only that over-the-rise was a strange and friendly place, and that it was a fine thing on arriving there to find another rise to go over. It may very well be that she now needed someone to love, for loving is a most receiving thing, as anyone can attest who has been loved without returning it. It is the one who is loved who must give and give. And she found her love, not in her wandering, but at the market. The shape of her love, his colors and sounds, were so much with her that when she saw him first it was without surprise; and thereafter, for a very long while, it was quite enough that he lived. He gave to her by being alive, by setting the air athrum with his mighty voice, by his stride, which was, for a man afoot, the exact analog of what the horseman calls a "perfect seat."

After seeing him, of course, she received twice and twice again as much as ever before. A tree was straight and tall for the magnificent sake of being straight and tall, but wasn't straightness a part of him, and being tall? The oriole gave more now than song, and the hawk more than walking the wind, for had they not hearts like his, warm blood and his same striving to keep it so for tomorrow? And more and more, over-the-rise was the place for her, for only there could there be more and still more things like him.

But when she found the pure pool in the brackish Bogs, there was no more over-the-rise for her. It was a place without hardness or hate, where the aspens trembled only for wonder, and where all contentment was rewarded. Every single rabbit there was *the* champion nose-twinkler, and every waterbird could stand on one leg the longest, and proud of it. Shelf-fungi hung to the willow-trunks, making that certain, single purple of which the sunset is incapable, and a tanager and a cardinal gravely granted one another his definition of "red."

Here Barbara brought a heart light with happiness, large with love, and set it down on the blue moss. And since the loving heart can receive more than anything else, so it is most needed, and Barbara took the best bird songs, and the richest colors, and the deepest peace, and all the other things which are most worth giving. The chipmunks brought her nuts when she was hungry and the prettiest stones when she was not. A green snake explained to her, in pantomime, how a river of jewels may flow uphill, and three mad otters described how a bundle of joy may slip and slide down and down and be all the more joyful for it. And there was the magic moment when a midge hovered, and then a honeybee, and then a bumblebee, and at last a hummingbird; and there they hung, playing a chord in A sharp minor.

Then one day the pool fell silent, and Barbara learned why the water was pure.

The aspens stopped trembling.

The rabbits all came out of the thicket and clustered on the blue bank, backs straight, ears up, and all their noses as still as coral.

The waterbirds stepped backwards, like courtiers, and stopped on the brink with their heads turned sidewise, one eye closed, the better to see with the other.

The chipmunks respectfully emptied their cheek pouches, scrubbed their paws together and tucked them out of sight; then stood still as tent pegs.

The pressure of growth around the pool ceased: the very grass waited.

The last sound of all to be heard—and by then it was very quiet—was the soft *whick!* of an owl's eyelids as it awoke to watch.

He came like a cloud, the earth cupping itself to take each of his golden hooves. He stopped on the bank and lowered his head, and for a brief moment his eyes met Barbara's, and she looked into a second universe of wisdom and compassion. Then there was the arch of the magnificent neck, the blinding flash of his golden horn.

And he drank, and he was gone. Everyone knows the water is pure, where the unicorn drinks.

How long had he been there? How long gone? Did time wait too, like the grass?

"And couldn't he stay?" she wept. "Couldn't he stay?"

To have seen the unicorn is a sad thing; one might never see him more. But then—to have seen the unicorn!

She began to make a song.

It was late when Barbara came in from the Bogs, so late the moon was bleached with cold and fleeing to the horizon. She struck the highroad just below the Great House and turned to pass it and go out to her garden house.

Near the locked main gate an animal was barking. A sick animal, a big animal. . . .

Barbara could see in the dark better than most, and soon saw the creature clinging to the gate, climbing, uttering that coughing moan as it went. At the top it slipped, fell outward, dangled; then there was a ripping sound, and it fell heavily to the ground and lay still and quiet.

She ran to it, and it began to make the sound again. It was a man, and he was weeping.

It was her love, her love, who was tall and straight and so very alive—her love, battered and bleeding, puffy, broken, his clothes torn, crying.

Now of all times was the time for a lover to receive, to take from the loved one his pain, his trouble, his fear. "Oh, hush, hush," she whispered, her hands touching his bruised face like swift feathers. "It's all over now. It's all over."

She turned him over on his back and knelt to bring him up sitting. She lifted one of his thick arms around her shoulder. He was very heavy, but she was very strong. When he was upright, gasping weakly, she looked up and down the road in the waning moonlight. Nothing, no one. The Great House was dark. Across the road, though, was a meadow with high hedgerows which might break the wind a little.

"Come, my love, my dear love," she whispered. He trembled violently.

All but carrying him, she got him across the road, over the shallow ditch, and through a gap in the hedge. She almost fell with him there. She gritted her teeth and set him down gently. She let him lean against the hedge, and then ran and swept up great armfuls of sweet broom. She made a tight springy bundle of it and set it on the ground beside him, and put a corner of her cloak over it, and gently lowered his head until it was pillowed. She folded the rest of the cloak about him. He was very cold.

There was no water near, and she dared not leave him. With her kerchief she cleaned some of the blood from his face. He was still very cold. He said, "You devil. You rotten little devil."

"Shh." She crept in beside him and cradled his head. "You'll be warm in a minute."

"Stand still," he growled. "Keep running away."

"I won't run away," she whispered. "Oh, my darling, you've been hurt, so hurt. I won't leave you. I promise I won't leave you."

He lay very still. He made the growling sound again.

"I'll tell you a lovely thing," she said softly. "Listen to me, think about the lovely thing," she crooned.

"There's a place in the bog, a pool of pure water, where the trees live beautifully, willow and aspen and birch, where everything is peaceful, my darling, and the flowers grow without tearing their petals. The moss is blue and the water is like diamonds."

"You tell me stories in a thousand voices," he muttered.

"Shh. Listen, my darling. This isn't a story, it's a real place. Four miles north and a little west, and you can see the trees from the ridge with the two dwarf oaks. And I know why the water is pure!" she cried gladly. "I know why!"

He said nothing. He took a deep breath and it hurt him, for he shuddered painfully.

"The unicorn drinks there," she whispered. "I *saw* him!"

Still he said nothing. She said, "I made a song about it. Listen, this is the song I made:

And He—suddenly gleamed! My dazzled eyes
Coming from outer sunshine to this green
And secret gloaming, met without surprise
The vision. Only after, when the sheen
And splendor of his going fled away,
I knew amazement, wonder and despair,
That he should come—and pass—and would not stay,
The Silken-swift—the gloriously Fair!
That he should come—and pass—and would not stay.
So that, forever after, I must go,
Take the long road that mounts against the day,
Travelling in the hope that I shall know
Again that lifted moment, high and sweet,

Somewhere—on purple moor or windy hill—
Remembering still his wild and delicate feet,
The magic and the dream—remembering still!

His breathing was more regular. She said, "I truly saw him!"

"I'm blind," he said. "Blind, I'm blind."

"Oh, my dear . . ."

He fumbled for her hand, found it. For a long moment he held it. Then, slowly, he brought up his other hand and with them both he felt her hand, turned it about, squeezed it. Suddenly he grunted, half sitting. "You're here!"

"Of course, darling. Of course I'm here."

"Why?" he shouted. "Why? *Why?* Why all of this? Why blind me?" He sat up, mouthing, and put his great hand on her throat. "Why do all that if . . ." The words ran together into an animal noise. Wine and witchery, anger and agony boiled in his veins.

Once she cried out.

Once she sobbed.

"Now," he said, "you'll catch no unicorns. Get away from me." He cuffed her.

"You're mad. You're sick," she cried.

"Get away," he said ominously.

Terrified, she rose. He took the cloak and hurled it after her. It almost toppled her as she ran away, crying silently.

After a long time, from behind the hedge, the sick, coughing sobs began again.

Three weeks later Rita was in the market when a hard hand took her upper arm and pressed her into the angle of a cottage wall. She did not start. She flashed her eyes upward and recognized him, and then said composedly, "Don't touch me."

"I need you to tell me something," he said. "And tell me you *will!*" His voice was as hard as his hand.

"I'll tell you anything you like," she said. "But don't touch me."

He hesitated, then released her. She turned to him casually. "What is it?" Her gaze darted across his face and its almost-healed scars. The small smile tugged at one corner of her mouth.

His eyes were slits. "I have to know this: why did you make up all that . . . prettiness, that food, that poison . . . just for me? You could have had me for less."

She smiled. "Just for you? It was your turn, that's all."

He was genuinely surprised. "It's happened before?"

She nodded. "Whenever it's the full of the moon—and the squire's away."

"You're lying!"

"You forget yourself!" she said sharply. Then, smiling, "It is the truth, though."

"I'd've heard talk—"

"Would you now? And tell me—how many of your friends know about your humiliating adventure?"

He hung his head.

She nodded. "You see? They go away until they're healed, and they come back and say nothing. And they always will."

"You're a devil . . . why do you do it? Why?"

"I told you," she said openly. "I'm a woman and I act like a woman in my own way. No man will ever touch me, though. I am virgin and shall remain so."

"You're *what*?" he roared.

She held up a restraining, ladylike glove. "Please," she said, pained.

"Listen," he said, quietly now, but with such intensity that for once she stepped back a pace. He closed his eyes, thinking hard. "You told me—the pool, the pool of the unicorn, and a song, wait. 'The Silken-swift, the gloriously Fair . . .' Remember? And then I—I saw to it that *you'd* never catch a unicorn!"

She shook her head, complete candor in her face. "I like that, 'the Silken-swift.' Pretty. But believe me—no! That isn't mine."

He put his face close to hers, and though it was barely a whisper, it came out like bullets. "Liar! Liar! I couldn't forget. I was sick, I was hurt, I was poisoned, but I know what I did!" He turned on his heel and strode away.

She put the thumb of her glove against her upper teeth for a second, then ran after him. "Del!"

He stopped but, rudely, would not turn. She rounded him, faced him. "I'll not have you believing that of me—it's the one thing I have left," she said tremulously.

He made no attempt to conceal his surprise. She controlled her expression with a visible effort, and said, "Please. Tell me a little more—just about the pool, the song, whatever it was."

"You don't remember?"

"I don't *know!*" she flashed. She was deeply agitated.

He said, with mock patience, "You told me of a unicorn pool out on the Bogs. You said you had seen *him* drink there. You made a song about it. And then I—"

"Where? Where was this?"

"You forget so soon?"

"Where? Where did it happen?"

"In the meadow, across the road from your gate, where you followed me," he said. "Where my sight came back to me, when the sun came up."

She looked at him blankly, and slowly her face changed. First the imprisoned smile struggling to be free, and then— she was herself again, and she laughed. She laughed a great ringing peal of the laughter that had plagued him so, and she did not stop until he put one hand behind his back, then the other, and she saw his shoulders swell with the effort to keep from striking her dead.

"You animal!" she said, goodhumoredly. "Do you know what you've done? Oh, you . . . you *animal!*" She glanced around to see that there were no ears to hear her. "I left you at the foot of the terrace steps," she told him. Her eyes sparkled. "Inside the gates, you understand? And you . . ."

"Don't laugh," he said quietly.

She did not laugh. "That was someone else out there. Who, I can't imagine. But it wasn't I."

He paled. "You followed me out."

"On my soul I did not," she said soberly. Then she quelled another laugh.

"That can't be," he said. "I couldn't have . . ."

"But you were blind, blind and crazy, Del-my-lover!"

"Squire's daughter, take care," he hissed. Then he pulled his big hand through his hair. "It can't be. It's three weeks; I'd have been accused . . ."

"There are those who wouldn't," she smiled. "Or—perhaps she will, in time."

"There has never been a woman so foul," he said evenly, looking her straight in the eye. "You're lying—you know you're lying."

"What must I do to prove it—aside from that which I'll have no man do?"

His lip curled. "Catch the unicorn," he said.

"If I did, you'd believe I was virgin?"

"I must," he admitted. He turned away, then said, over his shoulder, "But—*you?*"

She watched him thoughtfully until he left the marketplace. Her eyes sparkled; then she walked briskly to the goldsmith's, where she ordered a bridle of woven gold.

If the unicorn pool lay in the Bogs nearby, Rita reasoned, someone who was familiar with that brackish wasteland must know of it. And when she made a list in her mind of those few who travelled the Bogs, she knew whom to ask. With that, the other deduction came readily. Her laughter drew stares as she moved through the marketplace.

By the vegetable stall she stopped. The girl looked up patiently.

Rita stood swinging one expensive glove against the other wrist, half-smiling. "So you're the one." She studied the plain, inward-turning, peaceful face until Barbara had to turn her eyes away. Rita said, without further preamble, "I want you to show me the unicorn pool in two weeks."

Barbara looked up again, and now it was Rita who dropped her eyes. Rita said, "I can have someone else find it, of course. If you'd rather not." She spoke very clearly, and people turned to listen. They looked from Barbara to Rita and back again, and they waited.

"I don't mind," said Barbara faintly. As soon as Rita had

left, smiling, she packed up her things and went silently back
to her house.

The goldsmith, of course, made no secret of such an extraordinary commission; and that, plus the gossips who had
overheard Rita talking to Barbara, made the expedition into a
cavalcade. The whole village turned out to see; the boys kept
firmly in check so that Rita might lead the way; the young
bloods ranged behind her (some a little less carefree than
they might be) and others snickering behind their hands.
Behind them the girls, one or two a little pale, others eager as
cats to see the squire's daughter fail, and perhaps even . . .
but then, only she had the golden bridle.

She carried it casually, but casualness could not hide it, for
it was not wrapped, and it swung and blazed in the sun. She
wore a flowing white robe, trimmed a little short so that she
might negotiate the rough bogland; she had on a golden girdle and little gold sandals, and a gold chain bound her head
and hair like a coronet.

Barbara walked quietly a little behind Rita, closed in with
her own thoughts. Not once did she look at Del, who strode
somberly by himself.

Rita halted a moment and let Barbara catch up, then
walked beside her. "Tell me," she said quietly, "why did you
come? It needn't have been you."

"I'm his friend," Barbara said. She quickly touched the bridle with her finger. "The unicorn."

"Oh," said Rita. "The unicorn." She looked archly at the
other girl. "You wouldn't betray all your friends, would
you?"

Barbara looked at her thoughtfully, without anger. "If—
when you catch the unicorn," she said carefully, "what will
you do with him?"

"What an amazing question! I shall keep him, of course!"

"I thought I might persuade you to let him go."

Rita smiled, and hung the bridle on her other arm. "You
could never do that."

"I know," said Barbara. "But I thought I might, so that's

why I came." And before Rita could answer, she dropped behind again.

The last ridge, the one which overlooked the unicorn pool, saw a series of gasps as the ranks of villagers topped it, one after the other, and saw what lay below; and it was indeed beautiful.

Surprisingly, it was Del who took it upon himself to call out, in his great voice, "Everyone wait here!" And everyone did; the top of the ridge filled slowly, from one side to the other, with craning, murmuring people. And then Del bounded after Rita and Barbara.

Barbara said, "I'll stop here."

"Wait," said Rita, imperiously. Of Del she demanded, "What are you coming for?"

"To see fair play," he growled. "The little I know of witch-craft makes me like none of it."

"Very well," she said calmly. Then she smiled her very own smile. "Since you insist, I'd rather enjoy Barbara's company too."

Barbara hesitated. "Come, he won't hurt you, girl," said Rita. "He doesn't know you exist."

"Oh," said Barbara, wonderingly.

Del said gruffly, "I do so. She has the vegetable stall."

Rita smiled at Barbara, the secrets bright in her eyes. Barbara said nothing, but came with them.

"You should go back, you know," Rita said silkily to Del, when she could. "Haven't you been humiliated enough yet?"

He did not answer.

She said, "Stubborn animal! Do you think I'd have come this far if I weren't sure?"

"Yes," said Del, "I think perhaps you would."

They reached the blue moss. Rita shuffled it about with her feet and then sank gracefully down to it. Barbara stood alone in the shadows of the willow grove. Del thumped gently at an aspen with his fist. Rita, smiling, arranged the bridle to cast, and laid it across her lap.

The rabbits stayed hid. There was an uneasiness about the grove. Barbara sank to her knees, and put out her hand. A chipmunk ran to nestle in it.

This time there was a difference. This time it was not the slow silencing of living things that warned of his approach, but a sudden babble from the people on the ridge.

Rita gathered her legs under her like a sprinter, and held the bridle poised. Her eyes were round and bright, and the tip of her tongue showed between her white teeth. Barbara was a statue. Del put his back against his tree, and became as still as Barbara.

Then from the ridge came a single, simultaneous intake of breath, and silence. One knew without looking that some stared speechless, that some buried their faces or threw an arm over their eyes.

He came.

He came slowly this time, his golden hooves choosing his paces like so many embroidery needles. He held his splendid head high. He regarded the three on the bank gravely, and then turned to look at the ridge for a moment. At last he turned, and came round the pond by the willow grove. Just on the blue moss, he stopped to look down into the pond. It seemed that he drew one deep clear breath. He bent his head then, and drank, and lifted his head to shake away the shining drops.

He turned toward the three spellbound humans and looked at them each in turn. And it was not Rita he went to, at last, nor Barbara. He came to Del, and he drank of Del's eyes with his own just as he had partaken of the pool—deeply and at leisure. The beauty and wisdom were there, and the compassion, and what looked like a bright white point of anger. Del knew that the creature had read everything then, and that he knew all three of them in ways unknown to human beings.

There was a majestic sadness in the way he turned then, and dropped his shining head, and stepped daintily to Rita. She sighed, and rose up a little, lifting the bridle. The unicorn lowered his horn to receive it—

—and tossed his head, tore the bridle out of her grasp, sent the golden thing high in the air. It turned there in the sun, and fell into the pond.

And the instant it touched the water, the pond was a bog

and the birds rose mourning from the trees. The unicorn looked up at them, and shook himself. Then he trotted to Barbara and knelt, and put his smooth, stainless head in her lap.

Barbara's hands stayed on the ground by her sides. Her gaze roved over the warm white beauty, up to the tip of the golden horn and back.

The scream was frightening. Rita's hands were up like claws, and she had bitten her tongue; there was blood on her mouth. She screamed again. She threw herself off the now withered moss toward the unicorn and Barbara. "She can't be!" Rita shrieked. She collided with Del's broad right hand. "It's wrong, I tell you, she, you, I. . . ."

"I'm satisfied," said Del, low in his throat. "Keep away, squire's daughter."

She recoiled from him, made as if to try to circle him. He stepped forward. She ground her chin into one shoulder, then the other, in a gesture of sheer frustration, turned suddenly and ran toward the ridge. "It's mine, it's mine," she screamed. "I tell you, it can't be hers, don't you understand? I never once, I never did, but she, but she—"

She slowed and stopped, then, and fell silent at the sound that rose from the ridge. It began like the first patter of rain on oak leaves, and it gathered voice until it was a rumble and then a roar. She stood looking up, her face working, the sound washing over her. She shrank from it.

It was laughter.

She turned once, a pleading just beginning to form on her face. Del regarded her stonily. She faced the ridge then, and squared her shoulders, and walked up the hill, to go into the laughter, to go through it, to have it follow her all the way home and all the days of her life.

Del turned to Barbara just as she bent over the beautiful head. She said, "Silken-swift . . . go free."

The unicorn raised its head and looked up at Del. Del's mouth opened. He took a clumsy step forward, stopped again. "*You!*"

Barbara's face was wet. "You weren't to know," she

choked. "You weren't ever to know . . . I was so glad you
were blind, because I thought you'd never know."

He fell on his knees beside her. And when he did, the unicorn touched her face with his satin nose, and all the girl's
pent-up beauty flooded outward. The unicorn rose from his
kneeling, and whickered softly. Del looked at her, and only
the unicorn was more beautiful. He put out his hand to the
shining neck, and for a moment felt the incredible silk of the
mane flowing across his fingers. The unicorn reared then, and
wheeled, and in a great leap was across the bog, and in two
more was on the crest of the farther ridge. He paused there
briefly, with the sun on him, and then was gone.

Barbara said, "For us, he lost his pool, his beautiful pool."

And Del said, "He will get another. He must." With
difficulty he added, "He couldn't be . . . punished . . . for
being so gloriously Fair."

THE DARK ISLE

By Robert Bloch

I

THE CELTS knew it as Mona; the Britons called it Anglesey; but the Welsh spoke truly when they named the shunned spot "Ynys Dywyll"—the Dark Isle.

But all the peoples of Britain feared it for its dwellers. Here were the oaken temples of the Druids, the caves and caverns of the forest people, and the strange altars reared to dread gods. In these times the Clan of Mabon ruled, and heavy was its hold upon the lands. Erin knew the furtive, bearded priests that stalked through the forests seeking stealthy counsel with voices that moaned in the night. The Britons paid their tribute, turning over the criminally condemned for unspeakable sacrifice before the menhirs of the Druids in groves of oak. The Welsh feared these silent wizards and wonder-workers who appeared at clan gatherings to dispense law and justice throughout the land. They feared what they knew of these men, but greater still was the fear of what they *suspected*.

It was said that the Druids first came from Greece, and before that, from lost Atlantis; that they ruled in Gaul and crossed the seas in boats of stone. It was whispered that they were gifted with curious magics, that they could control the winds and waves and elemental fires. Certainly they were a sect of priests and sorcerers possessing powers before which the savage, blue-painted Britons quailed; black wisdom to quell the wild clans of Erin. They made the laws of the land, and they prophesied before the tribal kings. And ever they took their toll of prisoners for altar rites, their tribute of maidens and young men rich in blooded life.

There were certain dark groves in isolated forests where the boldest huntsmen did not venture, and there were great domed hills bearing curious stones and dolmens where voices cried in the night—voices good folk did not care to hear. In glades of oak the priestcraft dwelt, and what they did there was not a thing to be rashly spoken of.

For this was an age of demons and monsters, when dragons slumbered in the seas, and coiling creatures slithered through burrows beneath the hills; the time of Little Folk, and swamp kelpies, of sirens and enchanters. All these the Druids controlled, and it was not good to stir their wrath. They kept their peace, and their island stronghold of Anglesey was inviolate to other men.

But Rome knew no master. Caesar came, and the legions thundered into bloody battle with the stout kings of Britain. Emperor Claudius followed later, and the Eagle Standards were planted ever farther in the land. Then crafty Nero held the throne afar, and he sent Seutonius Paulinus to ravage Wales. And so it was that one black night, Vincius looked on Anglesey—the Dark Isle of the Druids.

II

Vincius the Reaper gazed on Anglesey with bold black eyes; wise, unblinking eyes that had seen much that was beautiful, and strange, and dreadful. These eyes had seen Imperial Rome, they had beheld the Sphinx, they had visioned the dark forests of the Rhine, the templed columns of ancient Greece.

They had witnessed blood and battle; fierce fighting, scenes of pain, anguish, barbaric torture.

Yet now they stared in a manner previously unknown; behind the dark pupils crept an unfamiliar tinge of fear. For the great dark island rising out of the sea was reputed a dreadful place. During the long sea-voyage to Britain, the fleet had buzzed with wild tales of the Druids; tales of their dire magic and hideous blood-thirst in the presence of enemies.

Vincius' friends—grizzled veterans of the legions—had known comrades serving against the Druids in Gaul. Some of these comrades had returned with horrific stories of almost unbelievable sorceries they had seen; of voices that cried out in the night, and of sentries found with mangled throats in the morning. They had whispered, these comrades, of how the beasts of the forest fought side by side with the blue barbarians; how packs of wolves and boars were summoned by wizard priests who piped. And these returning comrades of Vincius had been haggard, their laughter hushed, as though dark memories precluded all thoughts of gaiety again. Then too, many of Vincius' comrades had not returned at all. The tales of their dying were singularly unnerving—Druid killing and torture and sacrifice employed ghastly magics.

All through the voyage, rumours and hintings spread from vessel to vessel. For once the invincible might of the Roman standard was questioned; arms were not invulnerable to wizardry. And everyone knew that the fleet sailed to Anglesey —the great sullen island stronghold of the chief Druid clans. It had been a disturbing passage, through the dismal green seas of the North.

Now, anchored offshore, the fleet awaited morning to land and attack.

And Vincius, sleepless, took the deck and stared out across the brooding waters towards the black bulk of the island.

His lean, lantern-jawed face, browned by Syrian sun in the last campaign, was set in a scowl of puzzled bewilderment. Vincius was a veteran, and there were many things about this night which past experiences warned him of.

For one thing, the great island was too dark, too silent. Usually on the eve of battle the barbarian peoples gathered for war-dances about great fires. They would shriek and prance to the thunder of drums, give frenzied sacrifice to the gods for victory. But here all was dark and still; and the darkness and the stillness hinted of secret thoughts and plottings.

Again, Vincius' trained senses told him that the fleet was being watched. Although they had anchored under the cover of a foggy dusk, he felt that their movements had been observed; nay, expected. And now eyes peered across the silent waters.

The old soldier scowled, and stroked an ancient scar which whitely slashed the bronze of his forehead. A restless uneasiness kept him from sleep; some inner intuition told him to wait out the night and the silence.

The silence—it was too silent! The sullen lapping of waters against the sides of the vessel had seemingly ceased. Instinctively, the Reaper's eyes turned towards the helm, where a sentry stood peering and still. In the murky torchlight Vincius saw that his eyes were open, but glazed. He had turned, so that his back was to the rail.

And now, in the soundless hush, Vincius stared at the rail —stared at the two blue talons that slowly crept above it and clutched for support.

Two *blue* talons!

And two blue arms—long, emaciated arms, leprous and phosphorescent in the night—writhed above the rail. A great shaggy head appeared over the side of the ship, a terrible head, haloed by a tumbling mass of matted white hair. It framed a face shaped in Hell; a gaunt, thin face with cadaverous cheeks, hollowed eye-sockets, and a snarling mouth opened to reveal animal fangs. Two burning yellow eyes blazed under corpse-lids.

The face was blue.

Vincius the Reaper stared transfixed, and gaped as the bony body slithered over the rail, dropped noiselessly to the deck and stood erect; a figure clad in animal skins; a figure whose moist and dripping skin was deep, unearthly blue—a burning blue no dye could produce.

The withered old man crept slowly towards the glassy-eyed sentry. His hands stretched out, and taloned claws sought a windpipe. Then Vincius moved.

A flash of reason bade him still the cry which instinctively rose to his lips. The enormity of this: a naked barbarian boarding a ship of the fleet and killing a sentry at will—it would be shocking and shameful were this fact revealed to the legions on the eve of battle. Better to keep silent; better to draw one's sword, leap silently across the deck, press the blade into the neck of the ancient horror.

Vincius did so. The old man dropped the sentry's body without a sound. As the lean claws released their hold, a muffled burbling came from the dying throat of the strangled soldier. Then the strange blue creature turned and stared.

Vincius held him, pinioning his arms with one hand and holding his sword with the other. His flesh crawled at the feel of the slimy wet flesh that seemed unnaturally cold, and dreadfully soft.

Still, his grip never relaxed as with his free arm he drew the naked sword-blade in an arc under the throat of the ancient horror that gazed at him unblinking and impassive. Looking deep into the empty yellow eyes, the Reaper shuddered. On the wrinkled forehead he now discerned the almost imperceptible outline of a coiled serpent set in raised weals against the terrible bluish flesh.

"A Druid priest!" The exclamation escaped him in a whisper. At the sound of the words his captive smiled.

"Aye." A croaking voice wheezed out, as though the effort of speech were painful and the Latin tongue difficult.

"Aye," said the blue man. "Druid am I. Mark ye, Roman —I came to slay, but ye thwarted me in that; else there would be a dozen sentries dead, and as many ships at the mercy of my peoples.

"I came to slay, but I remain to warn. Tell this to your commander, oh blasphemer! On the morrow ye come to attack the shrines of our people; this we know. And we are ready. Aye! It will be a warm welcome—by Primal Nodens, know that we of the Druids can conjure magics for your confoundment. Tell your commander to turn back lest he and all his cursed hordes perish dreadfully before the children of Mabon. Tell him, fool."

The old man croaked out his words slowly, in deep gutturals which unnerved Vincius more than he durst admit even to himself. Impulse prompted him to drive his sword home and destroy this creature whose weird blue skin was somehow utterly unnatural.

Still, reason told him to wait. This old priest evidently knew the plans of the enemy. Threats might force him to talk, or else torture might be employed as a last resort.

Accordingly, the Reaper whispered.

"Speak of these plans, dog, or my sword will prompt your tongue." The blade bit into the neck.

And the old man lifted his blue and ghastly face in a horrid smile. Retching mirth burst in cackles from his corded throat.

"Eeeeeeeh! The fool—the heathen fool threatens me with death. The jest is rich. Eeeeeeeh!"

Mad laughter, though Vincius shook the withered body in rage. Then the terrible eyes slitted, and the fretted mouth gaped again.

"Look at me," hissed the ancient Druid. "Did ye not mark the blue pallor of my flesh? Think ye the Druids are fools to send a common priest on a desperate errand such as this? No!"

Vincius guessed, with a thrill of horror, the next words.

"Look at me," droned the croaking voice. "No paint, no dye empurples the flesh to my hue. Yet ye think to threaten me with death! Know then, fool, that I *am* dead—dead and drowned these three years past!"

With a sort of madness, Vincius lunged his blade out at the laughing corpse-head, slashed at the bony yellow eyes set in flabby, bluing skin. The sword sheared the grinning face, and laughter ceased. The body fell, and like a pricked bladder, collapsed. No blood flowed forth, yet the form dwindled and shrank upon the deck. There was an instant of terrible coagulation as the flesh fused, and then the planks were drenched with a wave of gelatinous ichor. Where the twice-dead body had crumpled there was now only a greenish-black pool of slime that flowed bubbling over the deck towards the rail.

Vincius the Reaper turned and ran cursing from the spot.

III

Trumpets sounded the dawn. The boats set out, laden with cargoes of living steel. Armoured, and corseletted men glared shoreward through the mists. Sword, lance, spear, bow, shield, helmet, breastplate—these were thousandfold duplicated jewels to glitter against the rising sun. These were thousandfold instruments to clash in martial symphony. These were thousandfold symbols of the might that was Mother Rome. The boats rode shoreward.

Vincius stared again at Anglesey as it loomed near. He had not spoken of the night to anyone. The ichor had vanished almost instantly from the deck when he returned after arousing another sentry to stand watch.

Wisdom had kept him from going to Paulinus, the commander, with any fantastic tale of a dead Druid who came to slay and warn. Not only was such a story difficult to credit, but even belief meant only disaster—for such a fearful warning might dishearten the leaders. As it was, Vincius noticed that there had been no report on the auguries taken this morning; no word that favourable omens had been observed before battle. It was a bad sign when the gods did not prophesy victory for the arms of Rome. The soldier's smile was grimly echoed by his comrades.

Now the boats were beached. The phalanx formed along the sandy shore as the leaders gathered under the Eagles. Britons and scouts delegated by the Army of Occupation were scurrying off into the deep woods offshore. They sought the Druid hordes in the woods.

Formations stood in silence; then signals flashed in swordpoints against the sun. Bugles blared, and kettle-drums set up a martial clangour. The long lines swept on. If the Druids chose to keep silent and lurk in the woods, they would be hunted out—beaten from cover.

Armoured ranks swept across the rocky beach towards the still green depths. Clank of weapons set against the utter silence from beyond.

And then, soundlessly, a thousand serpents flew straight

against the sun. A thousand barbed, feathered serpents, rigid and unswerving, dipped towards the legion rows.

Arrows!

From the seemingly deserted woods they poured, and found their marks. Men dropped.

Another cloud followed very swiftly. Screaming and cursing, the phalanx formations burst into a charge. More arrows met their advance, and hundreds fell. Each dart, wherever it struck, produced a hideous result. Within a moment after the wound was inflicted, the unfortunate victim was writhing on the ground, froth bubbling from shrieking lips. A moment later and the man was dead—dead and decaying!

Indeed, the Druids employed strange magic. Invisible, they poured poisoned arrows into the finest men of Rome.

The broken front ranks entered the outskirts of the woods. Arrows hummed about them as they sought foemen behind tree-trunk and buried boulder. They found only death—swift, writhing death.

Officers swore, bugles bleated vain commands, men shouted in confusion, fear, sudden agony. The dark woods closed about the legions—the bold legions that planned to swoop in unbroken lines straight across the barbarian island.

And still, no foes appeared.

Men cursed and died there in the green dark, as swarming arrows struck again and again—yet never a face of the enemy.

Vincius was in the van. Perhaps a hundred had managed to penetrate the wood to any extent; behind them came the confused murmur which bore the shameful tale of an army in flight. The legion was retreating back down the beach!

Vincius' companions turned to follow, arrows pursuing. And then there were shrill whistlings and pipings all about them, and from beyond further trees robed figures appeared —blue faced, bearded men screaming in wild triumph as they closed in on the fleeing band. Now stone clubs whizzed about helmeted heads. To the commands conveyed by the pipings, little groups were creeping around to head off the escaping men. Stones catapulted into the running bodies. Arrows found screaming targets.

Vincius and two companions made for a thicket. The Reaper took the lead, beckoning for the others to follow. He knew that an instant's delay would be fatal, for the forest men had virtually cut off all avenues of escape.

He entered the brush—and five skin-clad savages rose to confront him. Roman swords and stone war-clubs met in blow, thrust, parry. A legion man went down, his face crushed to red pulp. A short dagger tore a bearded throat. The Reaper's sword whirled about in a pendulum-course of death. The blue-skinned men crept under the guard as the second Roman fell, pinned to the ground by a shivered spear. The Reaper fought alone, lopping at arms that brandished bludgeons and crude maces. He fought until a crouching figure sidled to his rear, half turned to meet the blow of his enemy; then sank to the ground as red fire drowned his senses.

IV

Vincius opened his eyes. He lay where he had fallen, in the shadow of a large rock.

He stirred tentatively, then sat up and rubbed his aching head where the glancing blow of the stone club had left its painful bruise. Satisfied that he had suffered no permanent or seriously incapacitating injury, the Roman glanced about.

The glade was very still, and there were no noises audible from the beach. Far out on the water, the galleys still rolled at anchor. But from them rose no martial clangour, no trumpeting of victory. The pennons of triumph did not flutter forth amidst the billowed sails. The Reaper was puzzled—could it be that the attack had failed?

In the glade about him he found the answer with his eyes; the mute answer of arrow-riddled bodies, heaped in gory profusion. The men of the legions lay where they had fallen, and in death they were hideous to see. Some few had fallen by the sword or by the blow of club and axe, and these had made a peaceful passing compared to the greater number that lay slain by Druid arrows. For the latter were lying in twisted and contorted attitudes of agony. Their hands clutched at the sod in torture, their faces bore the mark of

delirium. And their bodies—their writhing, convulsed bodies
—were blue! Swollen, puffed, bloated with evil poison from
the wounds, they had died in an instant; an instant that
brought them madness. It was an awesome spectacle, and one
which caused the soldier to shudder. Never before had he
seen Romans in a death like this. It hinted of sorcery, of the
dark magic prophesied by the Druid priest.

Vincius the Reaper rose to his feet slowly, his thoughts a
confused jumble of pity for his companions, awe at their de-
feat, and furtive fear at the manner of their passing. But in a
moment a much more personal note of concern obtruded.

For even as he rose, a hand fell upon his shoulder. Cat-like
the Roman wheeled and faced—a Druid warrior!

Short, squat, his moon-face painted blue in ghastly simula-
tion of the dead, the Druid confronted him. Vincius raised
his sword.

The Druid held up his hand hastily and spoke; spoke in
Latin—not as the old priest had spoken, hesitantly—but as
though it were his native tongue.

"Wait, soldier," the short man gasped. "I'm Roman, not a
savage."

Half expectant of some treachery, though he now saw that
the fellow was unarmed, Vincius lowered his blade.

"Who are you?" he growled. "And if you're a Roman,
what means this heathen garb?"

"I can explain," babbled the little man, hastily. "Lupus,
my nickname is. I served on the triremes—at the oars, you
know. Galley slave for bad debts. The ship foundered off this
cursed coast three months ago, and I swam ashore. They captured me, the priests did, and gave me my choice: service or
death. Well, I'd no mind to die; so since then I've lived with
these blasted barbarians."

"What do you seek now?" asked the Reaper, suspiciously.

The little man's face was pale beneath the woad-stains.
He peered up at the tall soldier earnestly.

"Believe me in this," he murmured. "When I heard the attack today I sought the shore hoping to escape; even the galleys are better than life among such godless swine. But more
than that, I had hoped to find someone whom I could warn.

The attack failed; I could not pass through the fray and make myself known in time. I've been skulking about in the bushes ever since, hoping to find some survivor to give my message to."

"Well, speak up, man," grunted the Reaper.

Lupus nodded gravely before continuing.

"My message is this," he said. "I've heard in their black council last night that these heathens mean to sink the fleet tomorrow."

"Sink the fleet?" echoed the Roman, incredulously. "Why, that's impossible! They've no boats, and besides they fight on land behind the trees like the cowards they are."

"So?" said Lupus. His voice was mocking, but his manner gravely earnest. "Did not the attack fail? Look around you and tell me what you see." With a wave of his hand he indicated the blue and swollen bodies of the dead.

"I tell you that they spoke truly. If they vowed to sink the fleet they'll do it. Not with boats, or men, but with their cursed magics. It was magic that defeated us today, and it will be magic that brings doom on the morrow. I know. I've seen their devilish ways before. They control land, air, fire, water—and *things that dwell in them*. What demons they mean to conjure up for the deed I cannot say, but be warned. We must get news to the ships."

The Reaper scowled.

"How are we to do this?" he questioned. "We're marooned, practically prisoners here. There are no boats available, and the shore is probably guarded well."

"I have a plan," said Lupus, slowly. "We can't get through to the beach without being observed. If we move inland we are equally liable to capture. But tonight there will be a big ceremony and sacrifice in the biggest temple grove."

"I understand," nodded the Reaper. "We shall wait until then, and make for the beach."

"Not so fast, friend," returned the other, with a sad smile. "It isn't as simple as that, by any means. The Druids are cunning. They keep guard everywhere along the shore, by night as well as by day. Only on the sea-wall is there no sentinel. And it is a thousand-foot drop of sheer rock."

"Then what do you propose?" countered the Reaper.

"This." Lupus lowered his voice to a confidential whisper. "In my days here I have had occasion to observe many things. I watched, and I learned. There is one altar in the big glade that has a hollow base. Beneath it is a tunnel of some sort that runs under the island to an opening on the base of the sea-wall. This the priests have spoken of, and with my own eyes I have seen certain of them go and come by means of this tunnel below the altar. Methinks I can find that altar and learn the secret of its pivot."

"But what is the purpose of this passage?" asked the soldier, a trifle incredulously. Lupus looked grave.

"That I do not know," he answered. "What the priests do down there I cannot say. Perhaps they commune with their black heathen gods. They are strange men. We may encounter peril below, but it is better than certain death above, say I."

"Your plan?" persisted the Roman.

"Simply this. In the evening they will gather by the oak glade and perform some damnable rite or other. That I know. Then the woods between there and the beach-sentries will be free, and we can approach the spot. After their ceremonies will come some revel or feast. At any rate, the grove will be deserted for the rest of the night. We can enter then, find the altar-stone and the passage beneath it, and take our chances on making the shore by morning. From there we shall swim out to the ship, the gods willing."

"Umm." The Roman grunted. Then he placed his hand on the little man's shoulder. "A pact it is, friend," he said.

Until twilight they remained crouching in the concealment of the boulders. Lupus kept up a steady stream of conversation in a soft voice, narrating his story of captivity among the oak-men. He told the soldier of the Druid ways, and the strange faith of the nature-gods these people worshipped. He spoke of their black powers, and how their magic had driven back even the Roman might this afternoon.

Night fell, and as the moon crept across the sky, the two ventured forth from their place of concealment. The Roman was hungry. Down the path lay a body—that of a huge German mercenary, in full regalia. The Reaper, spying the provision pouch at the dead man's belt, stooped down and tugged it free. His eyes grew wide with loathing at the sight of that blue, contorted face, those blackened, swollen limbs that bore mute testimony to the strange power of Druid poison. With an oath, he tossed the pouch aside and followed his companion down the path that led into the woods.

They walked slowly, in wary silence. The trees about them rustled in the stillness, and Lupus started nervously upon several occasions.

How far they proceeded it was difficult to judge, but the moon rode high in the heavens when first the sound of voices was audible from somewhere ahead.

Soon faint flickers of light filtered through the twisting trees. Lupus leading, they warily circled the path and crept close through the untracked woodland. In a short time they were nearing the open space in the forest from which the light and sound proceeded.

The Reaper scowled at the spectacle before him. A throng of triumphant Druids moved about the grove, clustering before stone altars on which reposed the limp bodies of sheep and cattle. Blood bubbled redly on the slabs in the light of the torches flaring at the sides of the clearing; blood stained the robes and limbs of the celebrants.

Gongs clashed, horns blared, men and women moved and gestured, but the whole gathering maintained an attitude of expectancy.

Lupus gestured the Reaper to come forward, and together they took their station behind a thick cluster of underbrush.

Vincius saw the priests foregather about the central altar and heard the throbbing drums boom out in a subtle, augmented rhythm that steadily mounted to a delirious crescendo. Something was about to happen!

Drums beating, and the shadows on the trees. . . . For the first time the two men noticed that tree-bordered background and discerned what stood against it.

It seemed as though there were great, shadowy shapes weaving and hovering over the heads of the multitude; great shapes moving in rhythm with the surging drums; nightmare shamblers, tall as the tree-tops. The drums boomed madly. More torches flared.

"Look!" cried Lupus. His fingers dug into the Reaper's wrist as with his free hand he gestured excitedly towards the clearing ahead.

The Reaper gazed, and for all his stoicism he could not repress an involuntary shudder. For in the torchlight he discerned the outlines of the great, shadowy figures; saw that they were green and moving; saw that these giants were like trees in the shape of men. And they were forty feet tall!

V

Crouching in the bushes, Vincius the Reaper stared in fascinated horror at the cyclopean shapes looming before him. Gigantic human trees? That was not possible. What then?

Lupus placed his mouth against the Reaper's ear as he whispered an explanation.

"It's the sacrifice," he murmured. "The Druids are disposing of the prisoners. I've heard tales of this: Caesar's men spoke of it in Rome. The devils build great wicker frames and place branches around them; these they shape into a series of cages until they construct the figure of a man. Then they fill these cages with prisoners and condemned and burn the tree-idol in honour of their heathen gods."

The Reaper looked again and saw that his companion spoke truly. For ringed in a semi-circle stood six great green figures made in a horrid mockery of human form. Their lower limbs were trees, their arms vast pruned branches formed from whole trunks, stripped white in ghastly semblance of flesh.

Evil, painted faces were surmounted by leafy hair, so that each giant stood like a green ogre in the forest—a green ogre whose monstrous wicker belly was filled with living men!

Sweat beaded the Reaper's brow as he gazed at the gargantuan paunches that bulged forth in a wicker framework from those huge and dreadful simulacra. Through lattice and leafy interstice, through knotted rope and wicker vine he saw that each idol's body was in reality a vast cage, a cage packed with the huddled bodies of Roman soldiers and mercenaries.

Stifled, half suffocated by the density of their crowding together, they clawed vainly at the bars of their prison, or stared down in white-faced horror at the dancing throng below.

Vincius caught the flash of armour through the green trellises, heard the moaning wails of frightened men as they huddled together awaiting an undreamt-of fate.

Nor was that fate long in coming. For even now the bearded priests had stepped forth from the throng, and, torches in hand, they approached the white columns of the giant feet. The torches flared, then quickly kindled the dry wood. The limbs of the moving monster-shapes burst into livid flame.

Others had climbed to adjoining trees, the Reaper noticed. Now, leaning out on the branches, they flung their brands into the bushy green hair of the gigantic images so that each painted brow now wore a flaming crown.

A scream of animal ecstasy rose exultant from the crowd below. It was echoed by a shriek of horror from the imprisoned men, as they strained at the iron bellies of the monsters that held them.

Vincius stifled an oath, and his hand leaped instinctively to his scabbard. But Lupus pulled him back into the concealment of the shrubbery.

"Don't be a fool, man!" he growled. "One man can't help them. An army couldn't, now."

It was true. The flames were eating into oaken arms and rising to girdle the wooden waists. Suddenly, with a grotesqueness utterly terrifying in its sheer unexpected horror, the six painted faces of the burning monsters were contorted as if with hideous pain. Great eyes rolled in anguish-torn sockets, and red lips writhed back to reveal clenched white teeth. Deep, droning bellows rose from the burning wooden throats.

The Reaper trembled. The voices of the tortured gods! Then common sense told him that the faces were hinged so that they could be manipulated, with ropes by the priests below. Horns and bladders of air in the hollow necks produced the terrifying sounds. But the reality was dreadful, for the fiery images moved flaming arms as if in torment, and crumbling legs twisted in agony. The howling worshippers danced and bowed in adoration, their faces ever turned upward, for now the flames were reaching the bound bellies from both ends of the tree-monsters' burning bodies. The flames were licking at the wicker prisons, and the captives were wheezing and choking in the swirling smoke.

Tongues of fire licked between the oil-soaked bars. A man cried out terribly in a scream that rose even above the roar of the fire as he was consumed by the blast. Others within the prison beat at their flaming hair. The fire spread, until all six of the colossal shapes were merely great pillars of glowing flame; flame that glowed more redly as it sucked fresh nourishment from the burning bellies.

Then, one after another, the giants pitched forward, still burning. Showers of sparks singed the bodies of the fleeing crowd; the images fell with thunderous crashings and disintegrated into ashy embers or smoking dust. The fire still ate away at the skeleton bellies and a few awful shapes still writhed and twisted in the red furnaces.

But the priests and devotees had gone, back into the forest groves. From far away came the thudding thunder of their drums.

"It's over," Lupus whispered. "No one will disturb this spot till morning now. You see, the whole rite is connected with the religion; it is symbolic. The tree-images are those of Mabon and their other devil-gods. The prisoners are placed in the bellies to signify that the gods have devoured their enemies. The fire is a purification of the gods after their contamination by enemies. Now that the rite is accomplished the gods sleep appeased, and the Druids—curse their black entrails!—may celebrate their triumph undisturbed by wrathful eyes. They will not return here to wake the divine spirits."

Vincius grunted. The sonorous speech of his companion annoyed him. A man of action, he wanted only to escape. Consequently it was he who led the way into the clearing. Lupus followed, stepping gingerly to avoid the rosy ashes and still smoking embers that littered their path.

Soon they reached a spot untouched by the flames, for the bare, hard-packed earth did not allow the fire to spread. Then Lupus resumed his place as leader, and guided the soldier to a shadowy corner of the grotto. Here loomed an altar, grey against the darkness.

"This is the one," the little man whispered. "Give me your sword."

Vincius complied; then, frowning, he watched his guide thrust the tempered blade amidst the small rocks at the altar's base.

"I'll find the pivot," grunted Lupus, as he poked away. "Damnably clever, these barbarians."

The metal rang. Lupus tugged at the hilt of the weapon as he twisted it into some invisible niche. With a little click the stone tilted forward.

"Wrath of Jupiter!" the Reaper swore. Leaning forward, he stared down into a black chasm slanting deep into the earth beneath the altar-base. A series of stone steps was dimly discernible in the darkness.

"I was right, as I told you," said Lupus, calmly, as he relinquished the sword to his companion. The soldier shoved it back into its scabbard with a sigh of satisfaction. But he knitted black brows as he gazed again at the cryptically yawning mouth of that mysterious pit.

"I don't like the looks of this," he declared. "Such crawling about in the dark is not to my liking. And if there be such things below as you hint of—"

The other held up his hand in a gesture of despair that served to silence the Roman.

"It's our only chance," he whispered. "We can't skulk about in those heathen-infested woods, and when the morning comes we'll be taken surely. I do not like the passages myself, but I like still less the usage accorded those in the wicker cages." With a wry grimace, Lupus indicated the smudging remains of the fire-giants.

"What we may encounter there below I dare not say, but I would rather risk my skin with a chance of reaching the beach and escaping than stay behind. They'll kill you, but I shall assuredly be tortured." Lupus subsided, awaiting a reply.

The Reaper smiled dourly. "Come on, then," he said, pushing his companion before him. "We'll chance the caverns. But I'm not blundering through darkness."

So saying he stooped and picked up a burning branch from one of the tree images. It made an admirable torch.

Steps led down. Torchlight flickered on stone stairs, low rock walls of a narrow passage. The Reaper turned, and drew the altar-base down over their heads. His muscles tautened with effort, and his face contorted.

Lupus's countenance was likewise contorted, but it expressed fear rather than exertion.

"There's no turning back now," he whispered, eyeing the now immovable stone barrier above their heads. "We'll have to risk whatever lies ahead, and I've little stomach for Druid magic this night."

The Reaper smiled grimly.

"It's your decision," he declared, "and we must abide by it. Let's be off."

Torch in hand, he padded down the stairs, Lupus following with obvious reluctance as he stared at the carved-out walls of the tunnel. The stairs turned, then abruptly gave way to a slanting stretch of stone that wound off into deep darkness. It was a hot, unhealthy darkness; as they walked, the rocky floor became damp. Moisture dripped from the walls and the low ceiling. Moss and lichens were green-coiled on wet walls beaded with a diamond sweat in the firelight. They walked on in silence, into still blacker abysses ahead.

Now the footing became precarious, as they toiled through the rocky under-earth. Occasionally side-passages pitted the walls, sometimes singly and sometimes in pairs like the eyeless sockets of some strange stone monsters. The silence and damp heat were more oppressive as time went on. Stolidly, the Reaper plodded ahead; Lupus glanced about with increasing nervousness.

The little man grasped Vincius by the sword-arm, halting his stolid stride. He whispered shrilly in the soldier's ear.

"I've a feeling we're being observed. Quick—your torch."

Grasping the beacon, he flashed it suddenly towards the nearest opening in the wall just ahead. Was it fancy, or did the light indeed glint upon two staring eyes in the darkness? Neither man could say, for in a moment the half-fancied flash of reflection had disappeared. The flame disclosed only the silent blackness welling from the orifice mouth.

"Hurry," mumbled Lupus.

Their feet quickened as they half ran along the rocky floor of the burrow. The Reaper was almost flung against the wall when with a sudden sharp turning the tunnel twisted still deeper into the earth.

Now the damp silence exuded tangible menace. As they gazed down the long corridor ahead, their pace slackened to a halt. They stared into the gloomy shaft, its sides so ominously slitted with grinning cavern mouths.

And then from afar rose the sound of a strange piping—a faint, eerie cascade of sweetness. Its import was unmistakable; only a combination of reed and lips could produce that high stabbing wail that held within its weird beauty a hint of summoning and dark command.

It came from one of the side-burrows ahead, and welled forth to echo through the stillness of the caves. The unseen piper played, and Lupus half turned as if to flee.

"We can't go back, you fool," the Reaper muttered. "The altar-stone is replaced."

"Druid magic," whimpered the other. "We—"

"Come on." Vincius half dragged his cowering companion along the path. "There's a man playing that pipe, and I've something here to change the scoundrel's tune."

His sword flashed silver as he thrust the torch into Lupus's trembling hands.

They advanced down the corridor, and still that high-pitched music swelled, luring and calling.

Abruptly another sound was superimposed upon the shrillness; a deep whispering, a rustling noise that gathered rhythmic volume. It came from the pit mouths, and slithered forth as though answering the music's summons.

The Reaper's eyes scanned each pitted opening in turn,

seeking the source of the shrilling pipes. Then the strange
rustling crawled, and the Reaper, glancing downward, saw
coiled horror.

The path before him was filled with serpents. Weaving,
writhing, hissing in dreadful rhythm to the sound of the far-
off flute, they swayed and undulated forth from each pit until
the floor of the shaft ahead was a wriggling mass of moving
emerald menace. Snakes of every size and shape glided across
the gelid stones.

For a moment Vincius recoiled. Lupus crouched behind
him in sudden terror. His mumbled prayers were faint against
the eery wailing, the rustle and hissing. The great living wave
advanced.

Steeling himself, the Reaper met the attack. His sword
rose, descended to shear the heads of a dozen wriggling foes.
And still the serpentine sea moved forward, choking the narrow passage and rising knee-deep in living, writhing dread.
The Roman slashed again, and again. Hissing in pain, a score
twisted severed coils, but those behind swept on, commanded
by the wild whistling of the unseen pipes.

The great mass bore down upon the two, a twisting torrent
studded with opal eyes that flamed malignantly in the dusk.
The Reaper scanned the choked path before him, then
turned hastily to his cringing companion.

"Get ready to follow me," he whispered. Lupus nodded,
lips working in his white face.

Vincius stepped forward, both hands gripping the hilt of
his weapon as he brought it down in a sweeping arc. Again
and again it rose and fell, slashing, slicing, shearing at the
shapes that now pressed his very legs. He felt the slimy
wetness of cold bodies, smelt the sickening reek of their
foulness. He hacked a pathway through, only to see it obliterated by fresh hordes from further pits. And the piping
mocked from afar.

The writhing blob swept him back. The green strands of
Medusa's locks were coiling about his waist and thighs, dragging him down to fanged kisses and choking caresses.

"Follow," he yelled, glancing at Lupus over his shoulder.

Wheeling he dashed back a few paces along the corridor,

with Lupus at his heels. Then he turned and again confronted the reptile army. He ran forward, swinging his blade.
To Lupus's startled eyes it looked as though he were running
directly into the mass that crawled before him.

But as he reached the spot he leaped. His jump carried
him over the heads of the foremost serpents. Lupus closed
his eyes and followed suit. His feet left the ground, he sailed
into space. His feet landed on a treacherous wriggling heap.
He leaped again, seeing the Reaper ahead of him. The
Roman was alternately leaping and landing. So sudden were
his movements that the reptiles had no time to prepare themselves for striking, and each time he came down the sword
swooped.

Within a few breathless minutes the two stood clear of the
blocked corridor.

Vincius forced a wry smile.

"Much more of that," he observed, "and we'll never live to
deliver our little message of warning before daybreak."

It was quite evident from his frightened face that the little
man agreed only too well with this statement. When the soldier started forward once more, Lupus restrained him.

"Don't go on," he begged. "They know we're here. The
priests—the high priests—must be down here tonight. And
I've a feeling that they are summoning up their Powers for
the morrow."

"What's this?" the Roman queried.

"This must be the Place of Mysteries they speak of,"
Lupus went on. "The place where the Arch-Druids and the
inner circle come to seek aid of their gods for magic. Tonight
they have to do with the wrecking of the fleet. We'd best
turn back. Those devils would never let us through alive, and
if we were to encounter what they may have summoned to
aid them—"

"We must go on," pronounced the Reaper, shortly. "You
know there's no turning back. And hurry."

"It's death."

"Death for the fleet if we don't get through," Vincius
reminded. "We'll have to try."

Turning, he hurried down the gloomy incline. Lupus

dogged his heels, turning his head quickly from side to side
and eyeing each burrow he passed as though expecting the
worst.

Winding, twisting, writhing into darkness, deeper and
deeper into the tunnelled maze they plunged. A hundred
turnings, each with a thousand branch burrows, were passed
at almost running speed. There were no further evidences of
hostility, but both men still felt that peculiar sensation of
being under scrutiny of alien eyes—wise, evil eyes that
waited.

Then they took that final turning that led into the
cyclopean chamber where the red torches flared interminably
from rocky niches in the vaulted walls. They saw the piper
waiting before them—a tall, white-robed Druid, with the
shaven head of a Vate, and a bearded face alight with gloating expectancy. In one slim hand he bore the slender reed of
his piping, and in the other he held a coiling viper that
fawned up at him even as it hissed. And from out of the
chamber's stone sides stepped other Druids, armed and ready
for combat.

They were silent, and the Reaper did not speak as he
reached again for his sword. But he was speechless not at the
sight of them, but at the vision of what lay behind them. For
he saw that which they guarded.

There was a pool in the centre of the cavern—a great
murky pool of gelid water that rose subterraneously from
some hidden spring below. It was black, unmoving. Beside its
ringed orbit stood a flat stone and on it lay something huge
and red and swollen—something that bled horribly, yet wob-
bled as though still pulsing with life. It was monstrous, gigantic, yet unmistakable—a swollen, severed *tongue*.

Vincius could not tear his eyes away from the tremendous
ruby organ that lolled palpitant upon the stones. Imagination
quailed before the thought of a beast so enormous as to possess a tongue of this incredible size. Lupus cowered behind
him.

Then the slender, shaven-headed piper raised his head so
that his gaze challenged and commanded attention. The

other Druids grouped behind him in the red torchlight, standing upon the brink of the black chasm of water at their back.

The mocking Vate smiled, stepped forward.

"Who interrupts the Council of the Crescent?" he purred. "You stupid Roman intruders have troubled our deliberations."

Vincius scowled, but stood silent. His grimness cloaked a fear only too fully manifested by the quaking Lupus at his side. Why did this priest speak? Why not strike? His sneer of mockery seemed to veil a horror greater than anything yet revealed to the Reaper—and the Roman almost wanted to cast himself forward on the swords of the foe, to die in a red blaze that might drown the uneasy presence of dread which now oppressed him.

Yet the priest continued, sibilantly. "Ye have dared the secret temple of our people, and for that ye shall die. But a few hours and all your kind shall perish. We Druids will never bow before the spawn of Rome. Even as today the Dragon's tongue venom laid your comrades low, so tomorrow the Dragon shall destroy the cursed ships which brought ye."

Dragon's tongue? Vincius glanced again at the monstrous red thing lying on the stone—glanced at the oozing greenish fluid which dripped on to the floor—and knew the secret of the day's battle. This organ held poison; reptile venom, which, placed on the Druid arrows, had brought swift and dreadful death.

Dragon's tongue? Dragons—those were the terrible creatures of old British legend; great sea-serpents, reptilian monsters supposed to inhabit the subterrene sea-depths. But they were only legends, like the Tritons, and Dagon, and Greek monsters.

Or were they? This great red tongue was real, and the Druids could summon and control all beasts and creatures of the deep. Tomorrow they planned to wreck the fleet, and a Dragon could pull ships down into the sea. Was it possible?

Vincius mused for only a second. Then he realised that the cunning priest had revealed these words to him for that reason alone—so that in a moment's contemplation he would be lost.

Now the other priests had crept up behind, and Lupus screamed. The Reaper wheeled, to see three priests stab at the short man's unprotected throat. Roaring, Vincius slashed out. A head rolled to the floor, to stare up Medusa-like from a pool of serpentinely rilling blood.

Again the sword leaped and fell, parrying a stabbing thrust and coming down on the arm of the second priest. He dropped, howling as he clutched a jerking stump of shoulder.

And then a half-dozen priests were at his back. Vincius leaped, dodged, smote. They pressed forward, while the slim bearded leader urged them on.

"Into the pool!" shouted the Vate. "Food for the Primal One! Take him—by the Three and Thirty Tests, I command ye!"

They fought grimly, though two fell. The Reaper's arm was tiring under the weight of the heavy blade. He all but slipped in a sticky red pool, and was forced to give ground again. Now he was being forced back to the brink of the terrible black chasm where inky water lapped. The Druid swords were everywhere. Vincius tried to round the stone on which the gigantic tongue rested. They pressed him back against it—one blade shot out under the Reaper's waist. His quick duck brought the Druid against him, and they grappled. Locked in deadly embrace, they reeled against the stone.

Then Vincius knew. His sword-arm jerked free. He plunged his weapon to the hilt in the great spongy red mass upon the altar-stone. It gave and something green and wet spurted on to the blade. Vincius tore the sword free and sought the enemy's back. At the first thrust the Druid stiffened and fell.

And Vincius swung. One swordsman after another felt the terrible point, felt the poisoned tip of the steel bite into his veins; fell in writhing death. The Vate piped wildly.

The last man he beheaded completely, then re-thrust his weapon into the envenomed organ. He raced after the fleeing

Vate, who ran frantically back towards the tunnel entrance. The Reaper was swift. His blade was swifter. With a scream of anguish the last Druid priest went down in final agony.

Vincius turned. The black pool loomed. Beyond it was a dark slit in the rock—and poor dead Lupus had said that it led to the sea.

He must still warn the fleet, Dragon or no Dragon. Into the gelid waters, then.

Murky, clinging, slimy depths enfolded him as he leaped, sword tucked into his belt. The dark waves were sticky and warm, as though befouled. Vincius swam quickly, making for the orifice beyond, where he fancied he could detect a faint glimmering of starlight. A few strokes now . . .

Then horror came. From directly ahead the water spouted and inky jets spurted upward. A boiling froth arose, and great waves bubbled from the depths.

Suddenly a head appeared—a gigantic head, born only in a nightmare delirium and the realms of insane myth. Great, green, scaly head, red eyes glaring from behind huge, dripping jaws—and then a thrashing body; reticulated jade, gilled, slitted, winged, with a tremendous lashing tail.

The mad head rose and undulated above the waves on a long barrel-neck; then the great scarlet jaws drew back to disclose scimitar fangs—and a great empty cavern that was red, bleeding, and *tongueless!*

It was the Dragon of Druid lore.

Vincius saw it tower above him in the slimy black water; heard the brazen bellow, and felt the carrion wind that was its breath.

Its tail was curving towards him, its clawing appendages reached out, its neck swooped down so that the cruel, tremendous maw yawned to engulf him.

It was true then. This was the Beast of Myth which the ancient, evil priests had summoned to destroy the fleet upon the morrow. By some magic power they had lured it here, prisoned it in the pool, and ripped out its tongue for venom to use in their archery warfare. Vincius thought this, but felt fear. The enormous horror had seen him. It thrashed towards his puny, swimming form, loomed larger than any ship. From depths of dread it had come, and on the next day it would drag down the armies of Rome to those drowned realms of dread.

Now the mouth rushed on, churning and bubbling as it cut the waves and reached to swallow the struggling man. No use to fight. Or—

Vincius remembered. His sword—the venom upon it! He groped, drew, raised the blade.

The gigantic teeth ground in his face, then raised. Another swoop and he would be drawn between those fangs. He raised up out of the water, threw himself forward.

As the throat opened, he jammed the blade into the bleeding, tongueless maw of the monster. A shrill scream blasted his eardrums as the beast reared back, sword jerking like a silver sliver in the open jaws. Titanic thrashing sent waves surging across the pool. The Dragon roared with pain; a great green body reared out of the black waters, then fell back to squirm in mad, thunderous pulsations of pain.

With a single moan of gigantic, convulsive agony, the hideous head sank beneath the waves, red eyes glazed in death. The nightmare's own poison had destroyed it.

Vincius trod water until the bubbling from below subsided, then stroked for the slit in the stone without glancing back into the chamber of fear. He entered the narrow opening, swimming on.

Ahead he saw starlight, paling into dawn. A few moments brought him out into open water. He swam slowly out towards the nearest vessel; nor did he even turn to gaze at the dark cliff-wall which shielded this side of Anglesey.

His mission was done. Now, with morning, the Romans might land freely; leaderless, the Druids would give way before the legions. They and their cursed barbarian sorceries would be blotted out for ever.

Vincius smiled as he neared the ship's side. Then he frowned at the final memory of the dying dragon, going down with the Reaper's blade wedged in its throat.

"I'll need a new sword for the morning," he growled.

THE REJECTED SORCERER

By Jorge Luis Borges

IN SANTIAGO there once was a dean who had a consuming desire to learn the art of magic. He heard that Don Illan of Toledo was more versed in it than anyone else, so he set out for Toledo to find him.

The day that he arrived he went directly to Don Illan's house and found him reading a book in a room set apart from his home. The latter received him with good will and bade him put aside the motive of his visit until after eating. He showed him to pleasant quarters and told him that he was very pleased by his arrival. After the meal, the dean disclosed to him the reason for his visit and requested that he instruct him in the science of magic. Don Illan told him he had divined that he was a dean, a man of good position and good fortune, but that he feared that afterward he would be forgotten by him. The dean gave his promise and his assurance that he would never forget the favor, and that he would be always at his service. With the matter now arranged, Don Illan explained that the magic arts could be learned only in a remote place, and, taking him by the hand, led him to an adjoining room on the floor of which there was a large iron ring. He then told the servant girl to prepare partridges for supper, but not to put them on to roast until he so requested. Between them the two men pulled up on the iron ring and descended so far along a carved stone stairway that it seemed to the dean that the very river bed of the River Tajo must be over their heads. At the foot of the stairway there was a cell and then a library and then a sort of study containing instruments of magic. They began to go through

the books, and were engaged in this, when two men entered
with a letter for the dean, written by his uncle the bishop,
who made it known to him that he was very sick and that he
should not delay in coming if he wished to find him alive.

This news greatly annoyed the dean, on the one hand because of the suffering of his uncle, and on the other because
it meant interrupting his studies. He chose to write his apolo-
gies which he sent to the bishop. Three days later some men
in mourning arrived, carrying other letters for the dean in
which it was learned that the bishop had died, that a successor was being elected, and that it was hoped through the
grace of God that the dean himself would be elected. They
said also that he should not trouble himself to come, since it
seemed preferable that he be elected *in absentia*.

Ten days later there arrived two pages in rich dress who
threw themselves at his feet and kissed his hand, and greeted
him as bishop. When Don Illan saw these things, he
approached the new prelate with great joy and told him that
he praised God that such good news should have come to his
house. Then he requested the vacant deanship for one of his
sons. The bishop made it known to him that he had reserved
the deanship for his own brother, but that he had decided
still to treat him favorably, and that they should depart together for Santiago.

The three went to Santiago, where they were received with
honors. Six months later the bishop received messengers from
the Pope who was offering him the archbishopric of Tolosa,
leaving in his hands the naming of his successor. When Don
Illan heard of this, he reminded him of the former promise
and requested the title for his son. The archbishop made it
known to him that he had reserved the bishopric for his own
uncle, his father's brother, but that he had decided still to
treat him favorably and that they should depart together for
Tolosa. Don Illan had no choice but to accept.

The three went to Tolosa where they were received with
honors and masses. Two years later, the archbishop received
messengers from the Pope who was offering him the office of
cardinal, leaving in his hands the naming of his successor.
When Don Illan heard of this, he reminded him of the for-

mer promise and requested the title for his son. The Cardinal made it known to him that he had reserved the archbishopric for his own uncle, his mother's brother, but that he had decided still to treat him favorably and that they should depart together for Rome. The three went to Rome where they were received with honors, masses, and processions. Four years later the Pope died and our cardinal was elected to the papacy by the others. When Don Illan heard of this he kissed the feet of His Holiness, reminded him of the former promise and requested the cardinalship for his son. The Pope threatened him with imprisonment, saying to him that he knew quite well that he was nothing more than a sorcerer and that in Toledo he had been a professor of magic arts. The unhappy Don Illan said that he was going to return to Spain, and he asked him for something to eat along the road. The Pope refused the request. Then Don Illan (whose face strangely had become younger) said in a firm voice:

"Well, then, I'll have to eat the partridges I ordered for tonight."

The servant girl appeared and Don Illan told her to put them on to roast. With these words, the Pope found himself in the subterranean cell in Toledo, nothing more than dean of Santiago, and so ashamed of his ingratitude that he tried not even to apologize. Don Illan said that this trial was sufficient, denied him his share in the partridges and accompanied him to the street where he wished him a pleasant trip and dismissed him with great courtesy.

ACCORDING TO TRADITION

By Nicholas Stuart Gray

ONCE, NOT so long ago, there lived a king who had two sons. He was devoted to both but seemed always to favor the elder. To those who knew them, it was odd of him.

Christopher was all that a younger son should be—gentle and kind, fair, handsome, and in every way charming. He was no trouble to anyone. But his elder brother, Blaise, was impossible.

The queen made no obvious favorite of either. Yet one day she said to her husband with quiet determination, "My dear, you are being unfair to them both. You find fault with poor Christopher, where there is none to find. You give him small praise, when there is so much deserved. And Blaise knows too well that he can do no wrong in your eyes and takes full advantage of the fact. You are making it hard for the one to be reliable, and too easy—much too easy—for the other to be bad."

"My dear," said the king, "I know all that. And you know that I know it. And you know my reason for what I do. All my life I have studied the old tales and legends and traditions that make up the wisdom of humanity; and from these it is perfectly clear that the younger son is favored by destiny. Though he may seem to suffer misfortune, yet ultimately he will always win his heart's desire and the approbation of men. And, equally certainly and traditionally, the elder son must fail. Is this true, or is it not?"

Slowly nodding her head, the queen agreed that so the legends maintained.

"Had Blaise been different," said her husband, "had he

been a sterling sort of character, good-natured, honorable, obedient—I might have thought he could rise above his fate, escape the pitfalls and snares that will be set for him by destiny. The king gave a sudden sigh. "But, dear lady, you know as well as I do . . ."

The queen said she did indeed, and she sighed, too.

"I love them both," said the king, "but I grieve for Blaise and so I seem to favor him. I fear I shall have only a short time in which to do it."

Soon after this a frantic messenger came across the hills asking for aid. He carried a note from a neighboring kingdom that explained how its princess had been taken by enchantment from her father's house, deep into the heart of a forest where no one dared to follow. Jacynth was the only child, the heiress; and her hand and kingdom were offered to the prince who could bring her safely home.

The king sent for his sons.

Christopher came at once. And Blaise sent word that he was busy and would come when he could. He kept his father waiting an hour or so and then ambled in, smiling vaguely. The king told them what had happened.

"Oh, poor little Jacynth," said Christopher, who had never met the lady.

"Silly girl," said Blaise, who had.

"I'll go and see what I can do," said Christopher. "She must be so frightened."

"Serve her right," said Blaise.

Christopher bowed to his father, and ran off to get his cloak and his sword and his horse. The king, smiling, watched him go and then turned to explain the whole thing again to Blaise who seemed to have missed the point.

"The joining of these kingdoms would mean peace for all time. Besides, the princess is young and beautiful. Besides, it is your plain duty. Besides, I *order* you to go!"

"How do you know she's so beautiful, Father? *You* haven't seen her."

"*All* ladies in distress are beautiful," said the king firmly. "You should read more. Get along with you."

Blaise shot him a derisive look and strolled away. The king sighed with relief and worried about him a great deal.

The forest was generally understood to be extensive, enchanted, and highly unsafe. Christopher had ridden steadily and directly to where the only path through the trees began; and his horse had just set its hooves on the moss when another, lighter, wilder, more gaily caparisoned horse surged past and reared and slithered to a halt in an uproar of snorting and jingling.

"Why, Christopher!" shouted Blaise. "Fancy meeting you! Lost something? Looking for princesses?"

He pulled his horse back into a calmer pace, alongside his younger brother, and laughed. Blaise had already lost his cap, and his red hair was darkened by the streaming rain. It whipped across his face in long strands. He had forgotten to bring a cloak, and his shoulders were soaking wet already. Christopher gave him a worried look. He thought Blaise was asking to catch a serious cold.

Then there was an old woman standing at the pathside, in the shadow of the trees, shivering in thin rags and bare feet. Blaise nearly ran her down.

"Look out, you stupid hag!" he shouted, as his horse shied.

He pulled up with some difficulty. Christopher stopped, too. He lifted his cap. The old woman surveyed them both, quite unmoved. She spoke in a clear, cold voice that rang above the noise of hooves and harness and wind and rain.

"I am cold. I am old. I live in this forest of sorcery."

"You look all of it," said Blaise through a mouthful of his own hair. "You are the personification of a witch."

"Hush!" said Christopher.

The woman stared with her bright eyes into the equally bright ones of Blaise. There was an appreciable pause.

"Er—" said Christopher.

He was remembering some incidents in legends that he knew. He felt a cold qualm of fear for his brother. He unslung his cloak.

"Madam, take this," he said placatingly. "Forgive us if we

startled you. Any hasty words must be forgiven, too, for we also were startled."

He gave his cloak into her outstretched hands, and noticed as he did so, how slim and fine they were. He smiled down at her. And she smiled back, and her eyes were kind.

"I shall remember, Christopher," said she.

Then she turned on the other, and her eyes flashed green fires at him.

"Blaise," cried she. "Remember me!"

She vanished without another sound into the shadows.

The princes rode on.

"Wasn't she quaint?" said Blaise.

The wind rose. He began to shiver a little in his wet clothes. He shook his reins, and the horse sprang into a canter as he went racing ahead along the root-barred track under the dripping trees.

"He'll come such a tumble," thought Christopher in alarm.

He rode faster, to catch up with his brother, though still he went with care, not wishing to risk his horse's knees in a fall.

"I must try to keep him out of trouble," he thought.

It was a thought he had spent a lot of his life in thinking. But when he did come up with his brother, the trouble had got there first.

On the very edge of a clearing Christopher stopped and stared, open-eyed and -mouthed, at what he saw. The newly risen moon threw a pool of light into the treeless space and showed only too clearly what stood there. A white lion, enormous, black-maned, and silver-clawed. Its eyes were like flames of gold, one paw was lifted, and its jaws were wrinkled in a snarl of rage. Blaise sat his horse, who was objecting with rears and plunges and wild screams, and, to his brother's horror, he lifted his whip and lashed at the lion.

"Oh, no!" moaned Christopher to himself.

He saw the lion's muscles bunch. He shouted aloud and galloped forward. But he was too late. He heard the roar. He saw the leap. And Blaise lay on the ground under the claws of the beast.

Christopher jumped from his horse and drew his sword. The lion lifted a lip sideways at him.

"Keep out of this, Christopher, my boy," it said.

It held the struggling Blaise without apparent effort, and the younger prince said rather helplessly, "Do let him go, *please*."

"Why?" said the lion. "He won't be the slightest use in this quest you're on. In fact, he'll be a drawback to you. Put you in constant danger. You run along and leave him to me."

"No, I—I do beg you not to hurt him."

The lion looked down at Blaise.

"And you?" it said. "Will you beg for mercy?"

Christopher bit his lip. His gentle gray eyes were full of worry and fear. All he could see of his brother was one shoulder, with the doublet torn from it by a claw, though his skin appeared unharmed—so far—and his mud-streaked face that glared back at the lion.

"Beg!" said Blaise breathlessly. "I *demand* that you let me go! You ugly monster!"

He struggled again, without success, to free himself. The lion put its head on one side and eyed his efforts calmly. Then its muzzle wrinkled a little and it said, "I might release you for the moonstone ring you wear."

"You shan't have it!" cried Blaise.

The lion tightened its claws on him a little. Christopher gave a cry of horror and dragged a ring from his own hand.

"This is the counterpart of his!" he said eagerly. "Take it and set him free."

He held out the moonstone on the palm of his hand, and it vanished. Christopher stared at his empty hand, and his jaw dropped.

"I shall remember, Christopher," rumbled the lion.

It sprang away from the elder prince, and its tail swished across his face.

"Blaise, remember me!" the great beast growled.

And it, too, vanished.

Blaise caught his horse, climbed rather stiffly into the saddle, and rode on at his brother's side, but without comment and without looking at him. He did not seem quelled, however, merely cross.

The wind had gained force and was threshing among the tree branches until they groaned. The rain was cold and fierce.

Christopher was, as usual, worried. He wondered just where this path was leading. The missing princess was somewhere in the heart of the forest, but just where, or in what sort of prison, guarded by what magic was all impossible to guess. These thoughts were far from pleasant, but his chief anxiety was for his brother. He wished Blaise would behave properly for once and succeed in this quest. It would be so nice if he could marry the pretty princess—Christopher had no doubts at all about her beauty—and join the two kingdoms. Gentle and affectionate Christopher had never been jealous of his brother, and it did not occur to him now that he himself had more chance of success because of Blaise's nature.

He watched his elder brother on his black horse and wondered if he ever truly wanted to succeed at anything, and he would have ridden past the girl without seeing her, had her voice not reached his ear.

"Help me . . . help me . . ." came the words, faint through the rushing wind.

Christopher pulled up and looked back.

A little way back from the path was a girl—narrow, shining eyes and slender hands and swaying in the air three feet above the ground.

"Wait—wait, Blaise!" he cried after the other.

He saw the black horse halt and turn.

"Oh, help me," wailed the girl.

Christopher took off his cap and bowed to her.

"What shall I do?" he said.

And his brother's light, amused voice cut in:

"What seems to be troubling *her*?"

Blaise laughed.

"Do you think me funny?" screamed the girl.

Her eyes were blazing with the danger light that is the measure of magic.

"Er," said Christopher hurriedly, "tell us, madam, what we can do to help you."

"It's her hair," chuckled Blaise. "All tangled in the branch. Silly little thing!"

Her hair was indeed tangled. Long, pale green hair, glistening with rain, was wound in a tight knot among the twigs high above her head. Stray strands were whipping among the leaves and across her face and body. She must have been as light as a shadow, for there was no visible strain on the hair at all. But she could not free herself.

"Unwind it from the branch," she moaned.

Blaise drew his sword, with a thin swish of the steel, and the girl's eyes opened wide. She gave a piercing scream.

"No! No! It must not be cut! It must never be cut!"

"I've no time to play at cat's-cradle!" said Blaise.

There was a twang, like the snapping of a fiddle string, and the girl swept upward in a rush of rain, to hover in the air with the short ends of her once-flowing hair standing out around her furious face. She looked at Christopher sideways and her expression softened. She said, "Kind Christopher—I will remember."

She turned to his brother, and green sparks glittered in her gaze. She said, "Foolhardy Blaise—remember me!"

And she vanished.

"Tiresome girl," said Blaise.

Time went by, and the wind blew, and the rain fell. Once or twice, between fast-scudding clouds, came glints and glimmers of moonlight and stars. But it was in utter darkness that the next thing happened.

Christopher's horse, which had taken the lead on a very narrow stretch of track, stopped suddenly and gave a wild whicker. There, on the path facing them, was a man on a huge white charger. It was only too easy to see all the details of his and his steed's appearance, for both were glowing with light. A collar around the man's shoulders, a bracelet, a ring, and all the fine harness of the animal seemed sprinkled with pinpoints of fire and snow. Yet this brightness did not draw attention as did the face of the man. It was beautiful, in an eerie fashion, and hung about with straight and shining green hair. It had eyes that slanted like a cat's. They were green like some cats' eyes—but colder, weirder, more unfathomable. For the rest, the stranger had massive shoulders, and thin, strong hands and was quite unmistakably a wizard.

Christopher blinked nervously. He would have spoken, to say something polite and agreeable—he would have made some attempt to set everyone at his ease—but it was impossible to speak through the ensuing turmoil. For Blaise's horse had finally decided it had had enough. It wanted to go home. It plunged and kicked and squealed, behaving as though it had never been tamed or trained or ridden before. It flung itself all over the narrow track. It was trying either to throw Blaise or to brush him off against a tree or both. It was wild with panic. And Blaise fought with it, yelling. It was a shocking display of bad temper all around.

Christopher watched helplessly. There was nothing he could do. So he rubbed his hand across his eyes and then raised his cap to the wizard and smiled ingratiatingly. At any moment his brother and the horse would cannon into the gleaming stranger, and Christopher quailed at the thought of the probable consequences.

The wizard gave him a kindly smile and turned his demon eyes back to the elder prince. Blaise was slowly winning his battle with the horse. He forced its head around and shouted, "You there! Clear the path, or I'll ride you down!"

"Blaise!" said Christopher.

But no one heard him. The wizard sat unmoving. And Blaise dug his heels into his horse's smoking flanks and set it straight at the great white one. Panic-stricken, it jumped. But before its hooves had left the ground, the path before them was empty.

Only a voice drifted down the wind: "I will remember you, Christopher . . ."

And then, more faintly: "Blaise—remember me . . ."

The princes rode on.

The storm mounted until it was so wild that it quite quelled Christopher. Yet he was shocked when his brother said, "Let's go home."

"What?"

"Home. It's too wet."

"But the princess . . ."

"A plague on the princess. I'm cold."

"Well, yes, so am I, but even so . . ."

Both horses went back on their haunches, as the old woman came from the trees and stood glowing in the dark. She said, "I have remembered, Christopher. You shall not be cold. Here is your cloak again."

She tossed it up to the young man's hands. Before he could say anything, it unrolled of its own accord and wrapped itself around him; and all his clothes were suddenly warm and dry. And the old woman was gone.

"You're wetter than I. You take it," said Christopher to his brother. But when he tried to remove it the cloak would not come off. It clung firmly to him. And Blaise went cantering away down the path.

"I wish he'd wait for me. I must look after him," thought the younger man dismally.

He hurried as best he could. But all he overtook at last was a riderless black horse on its way home. Christopher caught the reins, and it stopped unwillingly.

"Blaise!" shouted his brother. "Where are you?"

There was no answer. Only a rope fell around him from a branch overhead, and he was dragged to the ground, where the fall knocked the breath out of him. The rope tightened and was wrapped around his arms and knees, until he could move no muscle. He heard voices, laughter. He saw torches that burned steadily in the howling wind. In their light he saw the speakers, the laughers.

The men of the forest were tall. Their long green hair fell smoothly about their pale faces and blazing eyes. Their clothes were a flutter of rags and tatters, many-colored and sprinkled all over with the glint of jewels and golden ornaments. Jewels shone about their throats, their hands and arms. They set Christopher on his feet, quite gently, and he looked about him for his brother. There was no sign of him.

"Good evening," he said to the men with the jewels and torches.

They laughed.

"Is it?" said they.

"Er . . . please let me go. I've done you no harm."

"Well, no. How could you?" said one.

"But you've trespassed in the forest. We do not care for humans," said others.

"It—it's because of the Princess Jacynth . . ."

"Oh, her!"

The green-haired men laughed even louder and more wildly.

"If you don't like humans," said Christopher reasonably, "why steal her? She's human."

All the time he was peering through the trees, in the shifting torchlight, for a glimpse of his brother. He could hear a good deal of laughing and shouting from farther off in the forest, and wondered if Blaise was among it.

"It wasn't our idea to take the lady," said one of the men beside him, chuckling amusedly. "It was our witch-king's."

"Why would he—?"

"Don't ask us! He must be mad."

"Well if you'd kindly let me go—and my brother, too, if you've got him—I will try to take the princess away. Then you'll be free of humans."

"How kind," giggled his captors.

And then they said, "But we'll never release you without a ransom."

"What sort of ransom?"

The laughter died instantly. There was absolute silence. The strange people regarded him with fixed and concentrated attention.

"Your heart," they said, "your heart forever—or a moonstone ring."

Christopher caught his breath. He no longer had a moonstone ring.

Then, in the middle of them, there was a white lion. And the ring lay at his feet.

"Let him go!" roared the beast.

The forest men snatched up the moonstone with cries of excitement and wild laughter. They cast the rope from Christopher, so that he stood free. And all the torches disappeared dancing, among the trees.

"Er . . . Blaise?" said the young prince doubtfully.

"They've released him."

The lion wrinkled its nose in a sort of laugh and vanished.

In a glimmer of moonlight, out of the forest came Blaise. His clothes were in rags, but he walked with his head in the air. His eyes were glinting. And on his hand he still wore his moonstone ring.

Christopher did not like to question him, and Blaise made no attempt to tell his younger brother what had happened. They rode on in silence.

And they came, in the wind and rain, to a wall across the path. It towered up so high that the top was lost in the tree-tops. It stretched so far on either side that no one could guess its length. And it glowed in the night.

"Oh, this must be the heart of the forest!" said Christopher in wonder.

"It's just a wall."

"Surrounding the lair of the witch-king—the prison of the princess."

"Bound to be."

The younger prince looked to his right, and he looked to his left, and the trees had linked their branches in such en-tanglements that there was no way through them. It was over the wall or back the way they'd come. He looked over his shoulder. The trees had joined across the path. There was no way back.

Blaise began to sing softly to himself. And he went on sing-ing, even when the pale, slender shape of the girl appeared in the air beside them. She smiled at Christopher from under her flying short hair. She said sweetly, "I remember, Christopher. And I'll help you, now."

She frowned and glared at Blaise.

"Stop making that noise!" she snapped.

He went on singing.

"You're most kind, madam," said Christopher loudly, "and I assure you, we are grateful."

The girl came swaying nearer. She unwound a long strand

of pale green hair from her waist, and she flung it high over the wall. It stretched up and up, moving like water, until it reached the top. Then it turned into a ladder.

"It goes down the other side, too," said the girl. "It will bear you safely, Christopher."

The young prince dismounted and went over to set his foot on the bottom rung. It was firm and steady. He went up a step or two and then turned to look at his brother.

Blaise was making no attempt to follow. He was sitting on his horse singing to himself and smiling. In the light that shone from the wall he seemed almost a stranger. The girl was glaring at him in fury.

"You may not climb that ladder!" she cried. "You can never cross the wall, Prince Blaise—not unless I carry you in my arms. And that I will not do. Not unless you kiss me. And if you kiss me, you will never kiss a mortal woman, and so I tell you."

Christopher made a sound of protest and started to go back to them. But the ladder moved, carrying him upward so swiftly that he had no time to jump off. Before he knew what had happened, he was over the wall, in the garden of the witch-king.

But Blaise was there before him, still humming his tune.

They walked on soft moss under trees that were full of singing birds. And the song was that of spring. Yet outside in the forest was autumn and the first breath of winter. Here, apple trees were in blossom, and there was fruit on the branches, too. Daffodils swayed in the grass, which was short and thick, and there were snowdrops and poppies as well. Christopher put out his hand and brushed the trumpet of a summer lily, and with the other hand he touched a cluster of red rowanberries. He turned to speak to Blaise, but he did not speak.

There was no wind here, no rain. Only moonlight. And, in that light, his brother's face was rapt and calm-eyed as no one had ever seen him look before. He had a rose in his hand and was gazing at the castle of the witch-king.

So they went in silence up moss-covered steps, through a

towering stone doorway, into the sort of place that could only have existence in an enchanted world.

On a stool below a dais, at the far end of the hall, sat the princess. Christopher stopped dead in his tracks and stared. She was far lovelier than he had imagined in his courteous mind. And she was sweet, as well. She had dark hair and was looking at him with wide dark eyes. She had the smallest round beauty spot of a mole on her left cheek. And Christopher fell in love.

It was some minutes before he noticed the witch-king. Then he caught the glint of those green eyes that studied the newcomers, and he gave a little at the knees. They belonged to the rider on the white horse.

Blaise had gone forward without hesitation, during all this and now he stood facing the wizard. There was a spine-chilling silence.

It occurred vaguely to Christopher that he had better do something—say something—set everyone at his ease.

"Er . . ." he said.

The wizard smiled slightly.

"You have come for Jacynth?" said he.

"Well . . . yes, please . . ."

"Which of you intends to rescue her?"

"My brother is the elder," said Christopher. "May he?"

"No, he may not," said the witch-king.

"Oh, but sir . . ."

"She is yours, boy, and fairly won. Take her safely home to her father and rule your lands in peace when the time comes."

Christopher gulped. The princess, who had been regarding him very carefully, now gave him a shy smile and rose and placed her hand in his. He tried to speak and failed. He looked dazedly at her. But he kept her hand.

Slowly it came to him then that the hall was full of people. The men of the forest and glowing, green-eyed girls and white hounds and pet deer with jeweled garlands wound about their antlers. There was a sound of music and a sound of laughter. Nothing that was obviously frightening, yet

Christopher felt himself tremble. And the hand of the princess was shaking in his.

"Your horses are outside the door," said the wizard. "Jacynth shall ride the one that belonged to Blaise, and it shall walk gently. Go in safety. The rain has stopped."

"Thank you, sir—oh!"

Christopher began to stammer an incoherent protest. "Ride the horse that belonged to Blaise? Oh, but—no!" He fell silent at last, under the witch-king's amused gaze.

"Blaise will not be going with you," said the wizard.

"He must! What do you mean? Oh, this is impossible!"

The young prince shook off the fear that had descended on him, and he ran to his brother's side. Blaise had neither moved nor spoken. He just stood quite still, with the rose in his hand.

"Blaise," said Christopher urgently, "come along, do! Because, if you don't, I must stay here with you."

The other shook his head very slightly. The wizard leaned forward and said, "All is well, Christopher. Off you go, boy. Your father will understand when you tell him everything that has taken place. No one will blame you. You have done well. You've done all that was expected of you."

"But what about my brother?"

The witch-king gazed thoughtfully at each of the princes in turn. Then he sighed, and said, "Most people can be dealt with, one way or another, by human beings. And quite often without damage on either side, given a little goodwill all around. Yet sometimes one comes who is outside the range of ordinary dealing. And then his only hope is that he may be taken in charge by something other than human care. Your brother could never be at home among mortal men. But here, Christopher, he will be safe."

"I—how can he? I thought you disliked all humans here?"

He watched the glow brighten in the green eyes as the witch-king replied, "But Blaise is no longer human. He is now our kind. I brought the Princess Jacynth here—treating her with every courtesy and consideration, by the way—in order to lure your brother to my castle. It was planned, Christopher. I knew always that he belonged to us. The people of the forest left him his moonstone, for he gave them his heart instead. He kissed the witch-girl. There is no place for him in mortal earth. He is out of danger here."

"Oh . . . I think I begin to see . . ."

Christopher looked at his brother, and caught the half smile and the calmness of his eyes. He touched his hand. And then he turned and went away with the little princess, out to the horses at the door.

They left behind the enchantment, the old legendary wisdom of the many worlds.

THE GIFTS OF ASTI

By Andre Norton

EVEN HERE, on the black terrace before the forgotten mountain retreat of Asti, it was possible to smell the dank stench of burning Memphir, to imagine that the dawn wind bore upward from the pillaged city the faint tortured cries of those whom the barbarians of Klem hunted to their prolonged death. Indeed it was time to leave.

Varta, last of the virgin Maidens of Asti, shivered. The scaled and wattled creature who crouched beside her thigh turned his reptilian head so that golden eyes met the aquamarine ones set slantingly at a faintly provocative angle in her smooth ivory face.

"We go—?"

She nodded in answer to that unvoiced question Lur had set into her brain, and turned toward the dark cavern which was the mouth of Asti's last dwelling place. Once, more than a thousand years before when the walls of Memphir were young, Asti had lived among men below. But in the richness and softness which was trading Memphir, empire of empires, Asti found no place. So He and those who served Him had withdrawn to this mountain outcrop. And she, Varta, was the last, the very last to bow knee at Asti's shrine and raise her voice in the dawn hymn—for Lur, as were all his race, was mute.

Even the loot of Memphir would not sate the shaggy headed warriors who had stormed her gates this day. The stairway to Asti's Temple was plain enough to see and there would be those to essay the steep climb hoping to find a treasure which did not exist. For Asti was an austere God, delighting in plain walls and bare altars. His last priest had lain in the grave niches these three years, there would be none to hold that gate against intruders.

Varta passed between tall, uncarved pillars, Lur padding beside her, his spine mane erect, the talons on his forefeet clicking on the stone in steady rhythm. So they came into the innermost shrine of Asti and there Varta made graceful obeisance to the great cowled and robed figure which sat enthroned, its hidden eyes focused upon its own outstretched hand.

And above the flattened palm of that wide hand hung suspended in space the round orange-red sun ball which was twin to the sun that lighted Erb. Around the miniature sun swung in their orbits the four worlds of the system, each obeying the laws of space, even as did the planets they represented.

"Memphir has fallen," Varta's voice sounded rusty in her own ears. She had spoken so seldom during the last lonely months. "Evil has risen to overwhelm our world, even as it was prophesied in Your Revelations, O, Ruler of Worlds and Maker of Destiny. Therefore, obeying the order given of old, I would depart from this, Thy house. Suffer me now to fulfill the Law—"

Three times she prostrated her slim body on the stones at the foot of Asti's judgment chair. Then she arose and, with the confidence of a child in its father, she laid her hand palm upward upon the outstretched hand of Asti. Beneath her flesh the stone was not cold and hard, but seemed to have an inner heat, even as might a human hand. For a long moment she stood so and then she raised her hand slowly, carefully, as if within its slight hollow she cupped something precious.

And, as she drew her hand away from the grasp of Asti, the tiny sun and its planets followed, spinning now above her palm as they had above the statue's. But out of the cowled figure some virtue had departed with the going of the miniature solar system, it was now but a carving of stone. And Varta did not look at it again as she passed behind its bulk to seek a certain place in the temple wall, known to her from much reading of the old records.

Having found the stone she sought, she moved her hand in a certain pattern before it so that the faint radiance streaming from the tiny sun, gleamed on the grayness of the wall. There was a grating, as from metal long unused, and a block fell back, opening a narrow door to them.

Before she stepped within, the priestess lifted her hand above her head and when she withdrew it, the sun and planets remained to form a diadem just above the intricate braiding of her dull red hair. As she moved into the secret way, the five orbs swung with her, and in the darkness there the sun glowed richly, sending out a light to guide their feet.

They were at the top of a stairway and the hollow clang of the stone as it moved back into place behind them echoed through a gulf which seemed endless. But that too was as the chronicles had said and Varta knew no fear.

How long they journeyed down into the maw of the mountain and, beyond that, into the womb of Erb itself, Varta never knew. But, when feet were weary and she knew the bite of real hunger, they came into a passageway which ended in a room hollowed of solid rock. And there, preserved in the chest in which men born in the youth of Memphir had laid them, Varta found that which would keep her safe on the path she must take. She put aside the fine silks, the jeweled cincture, which had been the badge of Asti's service and drew on over her naked body a suit of scaled skin, gemmed and glistening in the rays of the small sun. There was a hood to cover the entire head, taloned gloves for the hands, webbed, clawed coverings for the feet—as of the skin of a giant, man-like lizard had been tanned and fashioned into this suit. And Varta suspected that that might be so—the world of Erb had not always been held by the human-kind alone.

There were supplies here too, lying untouched in ageless containers within a lizard-skin pouch. Varta touched her tongue without fear to a powdered restorative, sharing it with Lur, whose own mailed skin would protect him through the dangers to come.

She folded the regalia she had stripped off and laid it in the chest, smoothing it regretfully before she dropped the lid upon its shimmering color. Never again would Asti's servant wear the soft stuff of His Livery. But she was resolute enough when she picked up the food pouch and strode forward, passing out of the robing chamber into a narrow way which was a natural fault in the rock unsmoothed by the tools of man.

But when this rocky road ended upon the lip of a gorge, Varta hesitated, plucking at the throat latch of her hood-like helmet. Through the unclouded crystal of its eye-holes she could see the sprouts of yellow vapor which puffed from crannies in the rock wall down which she must climb. If the records of the Temple spoke true, these curls of gas were death to all lunged creatures of the upper world. She could only trust that the cunning of the scaled hood would not fail her.

The long talons fitted to the finger tips of the gloves, the claws of the webbed foot coverings clamped fast to every hand and foot hold, but the way down was long and she caught a message of weariness from Lur before they reached the piled rocks at the foot of the cliff. The puffs of steamy gas had become a fog through which they groped their way slowly, following a trace of path along the base of the cliff.

Time did not exist in the underworld of Erb. Varta did not know whether it was still today, or whether she had passed into tomorrow when they came to a cross roads. She felt Lur press against her, forcing her back against a rock.

"There is a thing coming—" his message was clear.

And in a moment she too saw a dark hulk nosing through the vapor. It moved slowly, seeming to balance at each step as if travel was a painful act. But it bore steadily to the meeting of the two paths.

"It is no enemy—" But she did not need that reassurance from Lur. Unearthly as the thing looked it had no menace.

With a last twist of ungainly body the creature squatted on a rock and clawed the clumsy covering it wore about its bone-thin shoulders and domed-skull head. The visage it revealed was long and gray, with dark pits for eyes and a gaping, fang-studded, lipless mouth.

"Who are you who dare to tread the forgotten ways and rouse from slumber the Guardian of the Chasms?"

The question was a shrill whine in her brain, her hands half arose to cover her ears.

"I am Varta, Maiden of Asti. Memphir has fallen to the barbarians of the Outer Lands and now I go, as Asti once ordered—"

The Guardian considered her answer gravely. In one skeleton claw it fumbled a rod and with this it now traced certain symbols in the dust before Varta's webbed feet. When it had done, the girl stooped and altered two of the lines with a swift stroke from one of her talons. The creature of the Chasms nodded its misshapen head.

"Asti does not rule here. But long, and long, and long ago there was a pact made with us in His Name. Pass free from us, woman of the Light. There are two paths before you—"

The Guardian paused for so long that Varta dared to prompt it.

"Where do they lead, Guardian of the Dark?"

"This will take you down into my country," it jerked the rod to the right. "And that way is death for creatures from the surface world. The other—in our old legends it is said to bring a traveler out into the upper world. Of the truth of that I have no proof."

"But that one I must take," she made slight obeisance to the huddle of bones and dank cloak on the rock and it inclined its head in grave courtesy.

With Lur pushing a little ahead, she took the road which ran straight into the flume-veiled darkness. Nor did she turn to look again at the Thing from the Chasm world.

They began to climb again, across the slimed rock where there were evil trails of other things which lived in this haunted darkness. But the sun of Asti lighted their way and perhaps some virtue in the rays from it kept away the makers of such trails.

When they pulled themselves up onto a wide ledge the talons on Varta's gloves were worn to splintered stubs and there was a bright girdle of pain about her aching body. Lur lay panting beside her, his red-forked tongue protruding from his foam ringed mouth.

"We walk again the ways of men," Lur was the first to note the tool marks on the stone where they lay. "By the Will of Asti, we may win out of this maze after all."

Since there were no signs of the deadly steam Varta dared to push off her hood and share with her companion the sustaining power she carried in her pouch. There was a freshness to the air they breathed, damp and cold though it was, which hinted of the upper world.

The ledge sloped upward, at a steep angle at first, and then more gently. Lur slipped past her and thrust head and shoulders through a break in the rock. Grasping his neck spines she allowed him to pull her through that narrow slit into the soft blackness of a surface night. They tumbled down together, Varta's head pillowed on Lur's smooth side, and so slept as the sun and worlds of Asti whirled protectingly above them.

A whir of wings in the air above her head awakened Varta. One of the small, jewel bright flying lizard creatures of the deep jungle poised and dipped to investigate more closely the worlds of Asti. But at Varta's upflung arm it uttered a rasping cry and planed down into the mass of vegetation below. By the glint of sunlight on the stone around them the day was already well advanced. Varta tugged at Lur's mane until he roused.

There was a regularity to the rocks piled about their sleeping place which hinted that they had lain among the ruins left by man. But of this side of the mountains both were ignorant, for Memphir's rule had not run here.

"Many dead things in times past," Lur's scarlet nostril pits were extended to their widest. "But that was long ago. This land is no longer held by men."

Varta laughed cheerfully. "If here there are no men, then there will rise no barbarian hordes to dispute over rule. Asti has led us to safety. Let us see more of the land He gives us."

There was a road leading down from the ruins, a road still to be followed in spite of the lash of landslip and the crack of time. And it brought them into a cup of green fertility where the lavishness of Asti's sowing was unchecked by man. Varta seized eagerly upon globes of blood red fruit which she recognized as delicacies which had been cultivated in the Temple gardens, while Lur went hunting into the fringes of the jungle, there dining on prey so easily caught as to be judged devoid of fear.

The jungle-choked highway curved and they were suddenly fronted by a desert of sere desolation, a desert floored by glassy slag which sent back the sun beams in a furnace glare. Varta shaded her eyes and tried to see the end of this, but, if there was a distant rim of green beyond, the heat distortions in the air concealed it.

Lur put out a front paw to test the slag but withdrew it instantly.

"It cooks the flesh, we can not walk here," was his verdict.

Varta pointed with her chin to the left where, some distance away, the mountain wall paralleled their course.

"Then let us keep to the jungle over there and see if it does not bring us around to the far side. But what made this—?" She leaned out over the glassy stuff, not daring to touch the slick surface.

"War." Lur's tongue shot out to impale a questing beetle. "These forgotten people fought with fearsome weapons."

"But what weapon could do this? Memphir knew not such—"

"Memphir was old. But mayhap there were those who raised cities on Erb before the first hut of Memphir squatted on tidal mud. Men forget knowledge in time. Even in Memphir the lords of the last days forgot the wisdom of their earlier sages—they fell before the barbarians easily enough."

"If ever men had wisdom to produce this—it was not of Asti's giving," she edged away from the glare. "Let us go."

But now they had to fight their way through jungle and it was hard—until they reached a ridge of rock running out from the mountain as a tongue thrust into the blasted valley. And along this they picked their slow way.

"There is water near—" Lur's thought answered the girl's desire. She licked her dry lips longingly. "This way—" her companion's sudden turn was to the left and Varta was quick to follow him down a slide of rock.

Lur's instinct was right, as it ever was. There was water before them, a small lake of it. But even as he dipped his fanged muzzle toward that inviting surface, Lur's spined head jerked erect again. Varta snatched back the hand she had put out, staring at Lur's strange actions. His nostrils expanded to their widest, his long neck outstretched, he was swinging his head back and forth across the limpid shallows.

"What is it—?"

"This is no water such as we know," the scaled one answered flatly. "It has life within it."

Varta laughed. "Fish, water snakes, your own distant kin, Lur. It is the scent of them which you catch—"

"No. It is the water itself which lives—and yet does not live—" His thought trailed away from her as he struggled with some problem. No human brain could follow his unless he willed it so.

Varta squatted back on her heels and began to look at the water and then at the banks with more care. For the first time she noted the odd patches of brilliant color which floated just below the surface of the liquid. Blue, green, yellow, crimson, they drifted slowly with the tiny waves which lapped the shore. But they were not alive, she was almost sure of that, they appeared more a part of the water itself.

Watching the voyage of one patch of green she caught sight of the branch. It was a drooping shoot of the turbi, the same tree vine which produced the fruit she had relished less than an hour before. Above the water dangled a cluster of the fruit, dead ripe with the sweet pulp stretching its skin. But below the surface of the water. . . .

Varta's breath hissed between her teeth and Lur's head snapped around as he caught her thought.

The branch below the water bore a perfect circle of green flowers close to its tip, the flowers which the turbi had born naturally seven months before and which should long ago have turned into just such sweetness as hung above.

With Lur at her heels the girl edged around to pull cautiously at the branch. It yielded at once to touch, swinging its tip out of the lake. She sniffed—there was a languid perfume in the air, the perfume of the blooming turbi. She examined the flowers closely, to all appearances they were perfect and natural.

"It preserves," Lur settled back on his haunches and waved one front paw at the quiet water. "What goes into it remains as it was just at the moment of entrance."

"But if this is seven months old—"

"It may be seven years old," corrected Lur. "How can you tell when that branch first dipped into the lake? Yet the flowers do not fade even when withdrawn from the water. This is indeed a mystery!"

"Of which I would know more!" Varta dropped the turbi and started on around the edge of the lake.

Twice more they found similar evidence of preservation in flower or leaf, wherever it was covered by the opaline water.

The lake itself was a long and narrow slash with one end cutting into the desert of glass while the other wet the foot of the mountain. And it was there on the slope of the mountain that they found the greatest wonder of all, Lur scenting it before they sighted the remains among the stones.

"Man-made," he cautioned, "but very, very old."

And truly the wreckage they came upon must have been old, perhaps even older than Memphir. For the part which rested above the water was almost gone, rusty red stains on the rocks outlining where it had lain. But under water was a smooth silver hull, shining and untouched by the years.

Varta laid her hand upon a ruddy scrap between two rocks and it became a drift of powdery dust. And yet—there a few feet below was strong metal!

Lur padded along the scrap of shore surveying the thing.

"It was a machine in which men traveled," his thoughts arose to her. "But they were not as the men of Memphir. Perhaps not even as the sons of Erb—"

"Not as the sons of Erb!" her astonishment broke into open speech.

Lur's neck twisted as he looked up at her. "Did the men of Erb, even in the old chronicles fight with weapons such as would make a desert of glass? There are other worlds than Erb, mayhap this strange thing was a sky ship from such a world. All things are possible by the Will of Asti."

Varta nodded. "All things are possible by the Will of Asti," she repeated. "But, Lur," her eyes were round with wonder, "perhaps it is Asti's Will which brought us here to find this marvel! Perhaps He has some use for us and it!"

"At least we may discover what lies within it." Lur had his own share of curiosity.

"How? The two of us can not draw that out of the water!"

"No, but we can enter into it!"

Varta fingered the folds of the hood on her shoulders. She knew what Lur meant, the suit which had protected her in the underworld was impervious to everything outside its surface—or to every substance its makers knew—just as Lur's own hide made his flesh impenetrable. But the fashioners of her suit had probably never known of the living lake and what if she had no defense against the strange properties of the water?

She leaned back against a rock. Overhead the worlds and sun of Asti still traveled their appointed paths. The worlds of Asti! If it was His Will which had brought them here, then Asti's power would wrap her round with safety. By His Will she had come out of Memphir over ways no human of Erb had ever trod before. Could she doubt that His Protection was with her now?

It took only a moment to make secure the webbed shoes, to pull on and fasten the hood, to tighten the buckles of her gloves. Then she crept forward, shuddering as the water rose about her ankles. But Lur pushed on before her, his head disappearing fearlessly under the surface as he crawled through the jagged opening in the ship below.

Smashed engines which had no meaning in her eyes occupied most of the broken section of the wreck. None of the metal showed any deterioration beyond that which had occurred at the time of the crash. Under her exploring hands it was firm and whole.

Lur was pulling at a small door half hidden by a mass of twisted wires and plates and, just as Varta crawled around this obstacle to join him, the barrier gave way allowing them to squeeze through into what had once been the living quarters of the ship.

Varta recognized seats, a table, and other bits of strictly utilitarian furniture. But of those who had once been at home there, there remained no trace. Lur, having given one glance to the furnishings, was prowling about the far end of the cabin uncertainly, and now he voiced his uneasiness.

"There is something beyond, something which once had life—"

Varta crowded up to him. To her eyes the wall seemed without line of an opening, and yet Lur was running his broad front paws over it carefully, now and then throwing his weight against the smooth surface.

"There is no door—" she pointed out doubtfully.

"No door—ah—here—" Lur unsheathed formidable fighting claws to their full length for perhaps the first time in his temple-sheltered life, and endeavored to work them into a small crevice. The muscles of his forelegs and quarters stood out in sharp relief under his scales, his fangs were bare as his lips snapped back with effort.

Something gave, a thin black line appeared to mark the edges of a door. Then time, or Lur's strength, broke the ancient locking mechanism. The door gave so suddenly that they were both sent hurtling backward and Lur's breath burst from him in a huge bubble.

The sealed compartment was hardly more than a cupboard but it was full. Spread-eagled against the wall was a four-limbed creature whose form was so smothered in a bulky suit that Varta could only guess that it was akin in shape to her own. Hoops of metal locked it firmly to the wall, but the head had fallen forward so that the face plate in the helmet was hidden.

Slowly the girl breasted the water which filled the cabin and reached her hands toward the bowed helmet of the prisoner. Gingerly, her blunted talons scraping across metal, she pulled it up to her eye level.

The eyes of that which stood within the suit were closed, as if in sleep, but there was a warm, healthy tint to the bronze skin, so different in shade to her own pallid coloring. For the rest, the prisoner had the two eyes, the centered nose, the properly shaped mouth which were common to the men of Erb. Hair grew on his head, black and thick and there was a faint shadow of beard on his jaw line.

"This is a man—" her thought reached Lur.

"Why not? Did you expect a serpent? It is a pity he is dead—"

Varta felt a rich warm tide rising in her throat to answer that teasing half question. There were times when Lur's thought reading was annoying. He had risen to his hind legs so that he too could look into the shell which held their find.

"Yes, a pity," he repeated. "But—"

A vision of the turbi flowers swept through her mind. Had Lur suggested it, or had that wild thought been hers alone? Only this ship was so old—so very old!

Lur's red tongue flicked. "It can do no harm to try—" he suggested slyly and set his claws into the hoop holding the captive's right wrist, testing its strength.

"But the metal on the shore, it crumpled into powder at my touch—" she protested. "What if we carry him out only to have—to have—" Her mind shuddered away from the picture which followed.

"Did the turbi blossom fade when pulled out?" countered Lur. "There is a secret to these fastenings—" He pulled and pried impatiently.

Varta tried to help but even their united strength was useless against the force which held the loops in place. Breathless the girl slumped back against the wall of the cabin while Lur settled down on his haunches. One of the odd patches of color drifted by, its vivid scarlet like a jewel spiraling lazily upward. Varta's eyes followed its drift and so were guided to what she had forgotten, the worlds of Asti.

"Asti!"

Lur was looking up too.

"The power of Asti!"

Varta's hand went up, rested for a long moment under the sun and then drew it down, carefully, slowly, as she had in Memphir's temple. Then she stepped toward the captive. Within her hood a beaded line of moisture outlined her lips, a pulse thundered on her temple. This was a fearsome thing to try.

She held the sun on a line with one of the wrist bonds.

She must avoid the flesh it imprisoned, for Asti's power could kill.

From the sun there shot an orange-red beam to strike full upon the metal. A thin line of red crept across the smooth hoop, crept and widened. Varta raised her hand, sending the sun spinning up and Lur's claws pulled on the metal. It broke like rotten wood in his grasp.

The girl gave a little gasp of half-terrified delight. Then the old legends were true! As Asti's priestess she controlled powers too great to guess. Swiftly she loosed the other hoops and restored the sun and worlds to their place over her head as the captive slumped across the threshold of his cell.

Tugging and straining they brought him out of the broken ship into the sunlight of Erb. Varta threw back her hood and breathed deeply of the air which was not manufactured by the wizardry of the lizard skin and Lur sat panting, his nostril flaps open. It was he who spied the spring on the mountain side above, a spring of water uncontaminated by the strange life of the lake. They both dragged themselves there to drink deeply.

Varta returned to the lake shore reluctantly. Within her heart she believed that the man they had brought from the ship was truly dead. Lur might hold out the promise of the flowers, but this was a man and he had lain in the water for countless ages.

So she went with lagging steps, to find Lur busy. He had solved the mystery of the space suit and had stripped it from the unknown. Now his clawed paw rested lightly on the bared chest and he turned to Varta eagerly.

"There is life—"

Hardly daring to believe that, she dropped down beside Lur and touched their prize. Lur was right, the flesh was warm and she had caught the faint rhythm of shallow breath. Half remembering old tales, she put her hands on the arch of the lower ribs and began to aid that rhythm. The breaths were deeper.

Then the man half turned, his arm moved. Varta and Lur drew back.

For the first time the girl probed gently the sleeping mind before her—even as she had read the minds of those few of Memphir who had ascended to the temple precincts in the last days.

Much of what she read now was confused or so alien to Erb that it had no meaning for her. But she saw a great city plunged into flaming death in an instant and felt the horror and remorse of the man at her feet because of his own part in that act, the horror and remorse which had led him to open rebellion and so to his imprisonment. There was a last dark and frightening memory of a door closing on light and hope.

The spaceman moaned softly and hunched his shoulders as if he struggled vainly to tear loose from bonds.

"He thinks that he is still prisoner," observed Lur. "For him life begins at the very point it ended—even as it did for the turbi flowers. See—now he awakens."

The eyelids rose slowly, as if the man hated to see what he must look upon. Then, as he sighted Varta and Lur, his eyes went wide. He pulled himself up and looked dazedly around, striking out wildly with his fists. Catching sight of the clumsy suit Lur had taken from him he pulled at it, looking at the two before him as if he feared some attack.

Varta turned to Lur for help. She might read minds and use the wordless speech of Lur. But his people knew the art of such communication long before the first priest of Asti had stumbled upon their secret. Let Lur now quiet this outlander.

Delicately Lur sought a way into the other's mind, twisting down paths of thought strange to him. Even Varta could not follow the subtle waves sent forth in the quick examination and reconnoitering, nor could she understand all of the conversation which resulted. For the man from the ancient ship answered in speech aloud, sharp harsh sounds of no meaning. It was only after repeated instruction from Lur that he began to frame his messages in his mind, clumsily and disconnectedly.

Pictures of another world, another solar system, began to grow more clear as the space man became more at home in the new way of communication. He was one of a race who had come to Erb from beyond the stars and discovered it a world without human life. So they had established colonies and built great cities—far different from Memphir—and had lived in peace for centuries of their own time.

Then on the faraway planet of their birth there had begun a great war, which brought flaming death to all that world. The survivors of a last battle in outer space had fled to the colonies on Erb. But among this handful were men driven mad by the death of their world, and these had blasted the cities of Erb, saying that their kind must be wiped out.

The man they had rescued had turned against one such maddened leader and had been imprisoned just before an attack upon the largest of the colony's cities. After that he remembered nothing.

Varta stopped trying to follow the conversation—Lur was only explaining now how they had found the space man and brought him out of the wrecked ship. No human on Erb, this one had said, and yet were there not her own people, the ones who had built Memphir? And what of the barbarians, who, ruthless and cruel as they seemed by the standards of Memphir, were indeed men? Whence had they come then, the men of Memphir and the ancestors of the barbarian hordes? Her hands touched the scaled skin of the suit she still wore and then rubbed across her own smooth flesh. Could one have come from the other, was she of the blood and heritage of Lur?

"Not so!" Lur's mind, as quick as his flickering tongue, had caught that panic-born thought. "You are of the blood of this space wanderer. Men from the riven colonies must have escaped to safety. Look at this man, is he not like the men of Memphir—as they were in the olden days of the city's greatness?"

The stranger was tall, taller than the men of Memphir and there was a certain hardness about him which those city dwellers in ease had never displayed. But Lur must be right, this was a man of her race. She smiled in sudden relief and he answered that smile. Lur's soft laughter rang in both their heads.

"Asti in His Infinite Wisdom can see through Centuries. Memphir has fallen because of its softness and the evildoing of its people and the barbarians will now have their way with the lands of the north. But to me it appears that Asti is not yet done with the pattern He was weaving there. To each of you He granted a second life. Do not disdain the Gifts of Asti, Daughter of Erb!"

Again Varta felt the warm tide of blood rise in her cheeks. But she no longer smiled. Instead she regarded the outlander speculatively.

Not even a Maiden of the Temple could withstand the commands of the All Highest. Gifts from the Hand of Asti dared not be thrown away.

Above the puzzlement of the stranger she heard the chuckling of Lur.

THE RULE OF NAMES

By Ursula K. Le Guin

MR. UNDERHILL came out from under his hill, smiling and breathing hard. Each breath shot out of his nostrils as a double puff of steam, snow-white in the morning sunshine. Mr. Underhill looked up at the bright December sky and smiled wider than ever, showing snow-white teeth. Then he went down to the village.

"Morning, Mr. Underhill," said the villagers as he passed them in the narrow street between houses with conical, overhanging roofs like the fat red caps of toadstools. "Morning, morning!" he replied to each. (It was of course bad luck to wish anyone a *good* morning; a simple statement of the time of day was quite enough, in a place so permeated with Influences as Sattins Island, where a careless adjective might change the weather for a week.) All of them spoke to him, some with affection, some with affectionate disdain. He was all the little island had in the way of a wizard, and so deserved respect—but how could you respect a little fat man of fifty who waddled along with his toes turned in, breathing steam and smiling? His fireworks were fairly elaborate but his elixirs were weak. Warts he charmed off frequently reappeared after three days; tomatoes he enchanted grew no bigger than canteloupes; and those rare times when a strange ship stopped at Sattins harbor, Mr. Underhill always stayed under his hill—for fear, he explained, of the evil eye. He was, in other words, a wizard the way wall-eyed Gan was a carpenter: by default. The villagers made do with badly-hung doors and inefficient spells, for this generation, and relieved their annoyance by treating Mr. Underhill quite familiarly, as a mere fellow-villager. They even asked him to dinner. Once he asked some of them to dinner, and served a splendid repast, with silver, crystal, damask, roast goose, sparkling Andrades '639, and plum pudding with hard sauce; but he was so nervous all through the meal that it took the joy out of it, and besides, everybody was hungry again half an hour afterward. He did not like anyone to visit his cave, not even the anteroom, beyond which in fact nobody had ever got. When he saw people approaching the hill he always came trotting to meet them. "Let's sit out here under the pine trees!" he would say, smiling and waving towards the fir-grove, or if it was raining, "Let's go have a drink at the inn, eh?" though everybody knew he drank nothing stronger than well-water.

Some of the village children, teased by that locked cave, poked and pried and made raids while Mr. Underhill was away; but the small door that led into the inner chamber was spell-shut, and it seemed for once to be an effective spell. Once a couple of boys, thinking the wizard was over on the West Shore curing Mrs. Ruuna's sick donkey, brought a crowbar and a hatchet up there, but at the first whack of the hatchet on the door there came a roar of wrath from inside, and a cloud of purple steam. Mr. Underhill had got home early. The boys fled. He did not come out, and the boys came to no harm, though they said you couldn't believe what a huge hooting howling hissing horrible bellow that little fat man could make unless you'd heard it.

His business in town this day was three dozen fresh eggs and a pound of liver; also a stop at Seacaptain Fogeno's cottage to renew the seeing-charm on the old man's eyes (quite useless when applied to a case of detached retina, but Mr. Underhill kept trying), and finally a chat with old Goody Guld the concertina-maker's widow. Mr. Underhill's friends were mostly old people. He was timid with the strong young men of the village, and the girls were shy of him. "He makes me nervous, he smiles so much," they all said, pouting, twisting silky ringlets round a finger. "Nervous" was a newfangled word, and their mothers all replied grimly, "Nervous my foot, silliness is the word for it. Mr. Underhill is a very respectable wizard!"

After leaving Goody Guld, Mr. Underhill passed by the school, which was being held this day out on the common. Since no one on Sattins Island was literate, there were no books to learn to read from and no desks to carve initials on and no blackboards to erase, and in fact no schoolhouse. On rainy days the children met in the loft of the Communal Barn, and got hay in their pants; on sunny days the school-teacher, Palani, took them anywhere she felt like. Today, surrounded by thirty interested children under twelve and forty uninterested sheep under five, she was teaching an important item on the curriculum: the Rules of Names. Mr. Underhill, smiling shyly, paused to listen and watch. Palani, a plump, pretty girl of twenty, made a charming picture there in the wintry sunlight, sheep and children around her, a leafless oak above her, and behind her the dunes and sea and clear, pale sky. She spoke earnestly, her face flushed pink by wind and words. "Now you know the Rules of Names already, children. There are two, and they're the same on every island in the world. What's one of them?"

"It ain't polite to ask anybody what his name is," shouted a fat, quick boy, interrupted by a little girl shrieking, "You can't never tell your own name to nobody my ma says!"

"Yes, Suba. Yes, Popi dear, don't screech. That's right. You never ask anybody his name. You never tell your own. Now think about that a minute and then tell me why we call our wizard Mr. Underhill." She smiled across the curly heads and the woolly backs at Mr. Underhill, who beamed, and nervously clutched his sack of eggs.

"Cause he lives under a hill!" said half the children.

"But is it his truename?"

"No!" said the fat boy, echoed by little Popi shrieking, "No!"

"How do you know it's not?"

"Cause he came here all alone and so there wasn't anybody knew his truename so they could not tell us, and *he* couldn't—"

"Very good, Suba. Popi, don't shout. That's right. Even a wizard can't tell you his truename. When you children are through school and go through the Passage, you'll leave your child-names behind and keep only your truenames, which you must never ask for and never give away. Why is that the rule?"

The children were silent. The sheep bleated gently. Mr. Underhill answered the question: "Because the name is the thing," he said in his shy, soft, husky voice, "and the truename is the true thing. To speak the name is to control the thing. Am I right, Schoolmistress?"

She smiled and curtseyed, evidently a little embarrassed by his participation. And he trotted off towards his hill, clutching the eggs to his bosom. Somehow the minute spent watching Palani and the children had made him very hungry. He locked his inner door behind him with a hasty incantation, but there must have been a leak or two in the spell, for soon the bare anteroom of the cave was rich with the smell of frying eggs and sizzling liver.

The wind that day was light and fresh out of the west, and on it at noon a little boat came skimming the bright waves into Sattins harbor. Even as it rounded the point a sharp-eyed boy spotted it, and knowing, like every child on the island, every sail and spar of the forty boats of the fishing fleet, he ran down the street calling out, "A foreign boat, a foreign boat!" Very seldom was the lonely isle visited by a boat from some equally lonely isle of the East Reach, or an adventurous trader from the Archipelago. By the time the boat was at the pier half the village was there to greet it, and fishermen were following it homewards, and cowherds and clamdiggers and herb-hunters were puffing up and down all the rocky hills, heading towards the harbor.

But Mr. Underhill's door stayed shut.

There was only one man aboard the boat. Old Seacaptain Fogeno, when they told him that, drew down a bristle of white brows over his unseeing eyes. "There's only one kind of man," he said, "that sails the Outer Reach alone. A wizard, or a warlock, or a Mage . . ."

So the villagers were breathless hoping to see for once in their lives a Mage, one of the mighty White Magicians of the rich, towered, crowded inner islands of the Archipelago. They were disappointed, for the voyager was quite young, a handsome black-bearded fellow who hailed them cheerfully from his boat, and leaped ashore like any sailor glad to have made port. He introduced himself at once as a sea-peddler. But when they told Seacaptain Fogeno that he carried an oaken walking-stick around with him, the old man nodded. "Two wizards in one town," he said. "Bad!" And his mouth snapped shut like an old carp's.

As the stranger could not give them his name, they gave him one right away: Blackbeard. And they gave him plenty of attention. He had a small mixed cargo of cloth and sandals and *piswi* feathers for trimming cloaks and cheap incense and levity stones and fine herbs and great glass beads from Venway—the usual peddler's lot. Everyone on Sattins Island came to look, to chat with the voyager, and perhaps to buy something—"Just to remember him by!" cackled Goody Guld, who like all the women and girls of the village was smitten with Blackbeard's bold good looks. All the boys hung round him too, to hear him tell of his voyages to far, strange islands of the Reach or describe the great rich islands of the Archipelago, the Inner Lanes, the roadsteads white with ships, and the golden roofs of Havnor. The men willingly listened to his tales; but some of them wondered why a trader should sail alone, and kept their eyes thoughtfully upon his oaken staff.

But all this time Mr. Underhill stayed under his hill.

"This is the first island I've ever seen that had no wizard," said Blackbeard one evening to Goody Guld, who had invited him and her nephew and Palani in for a cup of rushwash tea. "What do you do when you get a toothache, or the cow goes dry?"

"Why, we've got Mr. Underhill!" said the old woman.

"For what that's worth," muttered her nephew Birt, and then blushed purple and spilled his tea. Birt was a fisherman, a large, brave, wordless young man. He loved the schoolmistress, but the nearest he had come to telling her of his love was to give baskets of fresh mackerel to her father's cook.

"Oh, you do have a wizard?" Blackbeard asked. "Is he invisible?"

"No, he's just very shy," said Palani. "You've only been

her a week, you know, and we see so few strangers here . . ."
She also blushed a little, but did not spill her tea.

Blackbeard smiled at her. "He's a good Sattinsman, then,
eh?"

"No," said Goody Guld, "no more than you are. Another
cup, nevvy? keep it in the cup this time. No, my dear, he
came in a little bit of a boat, four years ago was it? just a day
after the end of the shad run, I recall, for they was taking up
the nets over in East Creek, and Pondi Cowherd broke his
leg that very morning—five years ago it must be. No, four.
No, five it is, 'twas the year the garlic didn't sprout. So he
sails in on a bit of a sloop loaded full up with great chests
and boxes and says to Seacaptain Fogeno, who wasn't blind
then, though old enough goodness knows to be blind twice
over, 'I hear tell,' he says, 'you've got no wizard nor warlock
at all, might you be wanting one?'—'Indeed, if the magic's
white!' says the Captain, and before you could say cuttlefish
Mr. Underhill had settled down in the cave under the hill
and was charming the mange off Goody Beltow's cat.
Though the fur grew in grey, and 'twas an orange cat.
Queerlooking thing it was after that. It died last winter in
the cold spell. Goody Beltow took on so at that cat's death,
poor thing, worse than when her man was drowned on the
Long Banks, the year of the long herring-runs, when nevvy
Birt here was but a babe in petticoats." Here Birt spilled his
tea again, and Blackbeard grinned, but Goody Guld proceeded undismayed, and talked on till nightfall.

Next day Blackbeard was down at the pier, seeing after the
sprung board in his boat which he seemed to take a long
time fixing, and as usual drawing the taciturn Sattinsmen
into talk. "Now which of these is your wizard's craft?" he
asked. "Or has he got one of those the Mages fold up into a
walnut shell when they're not using it?"

"Nay," said a stolid fisherman. "She's oop in his cave,
under hill."

"He carried the boat he came in up to his cave?"

"Aye. Clear oop. I helped. Heavier as lead she was. Full
oop with great boxes, and they full oop with books o' spells,
he says. Heavier as lead she was." And the stolid fisherman

turned his back, sighing stolidly. Goody Guld's nephew, mending a net nearby, looked up from his work and asked with equal stolidity, "Would ye like to meet Mr. Underhill, maybe?"

Blackbeard returned Birt's look. Clever black eyes met candid blue ones for a long moment; then Blackbeard smiled and said, "Yes. Will you take me up to the hill, Birt?"

"Aye, when I'm done with this," said the fisherman. And when the net was mended, he and the Archipelagan set off up the village street towards the high green hill above it. But as they crossed the common Blackbeard said, "Hold on a while, friend Birt. I have a tale to tell you, before we meet your wizard."

"Tell away," says Birt, sitting down in the shade of a live-oak.

"It's a story that started a hundred years ago, and isn't finished yet—though it soon will be, very soon . . . In the very heart of the Archipelago, where the islands crowd thick as flies on honey, there's a little isle called Pendor. The sealords of Pendor were mighty men, in the old days of war before the League. Loot and ransom and tribute came pouring into Pendor, and they gathered a great treasure there, long ago. Then from somewhere away out in the West Reach, where dragons breed on the lava isles, came one day a very mighty dragon. Not one of those overgrown lizards most of you Outer Reach folk call dragons, but a big, black, winged, wise, cunning monster, full of strength and subtlety, and like all dragons loving gold and precious stones above all things. He killed the Sealord and his soldiers, and the people of Pendor fled in their ships by night. They all fled away and left the dragon coiled up in Pendor Towers. And there he stayed for a hundred years, dragging his scaly belly over the emeralds and sapphires and coins of gold, coming forth only once in a year or two when he must eat. He'd raid nearby islands for his food. You know what dragons eat?"

Birt nodded and said in a whisper, "Maidens."

"Right," said Blackbeard. "Well, that couldn't be endured forever, nor the thought of him sitting on all that treasure. So after the League grew strong, and the Archipelago wasn't

so busy with wars and piracy, it was decided to attack Pendor, drive out the dragon, and get the gold and jewels for the
treasury of the League. They're forever wanting money, the
League is. So a huge fleet gathered from fifty islands, and
seven Mages stood in the prows of the seven strongest ships,
and they sailed towards Pendor . . . They got there. They
landed. Nothing stirred. The houses all stood empty, the
dishes on the tables full of a hundred years' dust. The bones
of the old Sealord and his men lay about in the castle courts
and on the stairs. And the Tower rooms reeked of dragon.
But there was no dragon. And no treasure, not a diamond
the size of a poppyseed, not a single silver bead . . . Knowing
that he couldn't stand up to seven Mages, the dragon had
skipped out. They tracked him, and found he'd flown to a
deserted island up north called Udrath; they followed his
trail there, and what did they find? Bones again. His bones—
the dragon's. But no treasure. A wizard, some unknown wizard from somewhere, must have met him singlehanded, and
defeated him—and then made off with the treasure, right
under the League's nose!"

The fisherman listened, attentive and expressionless.

"Now that must have been a powerful wizard and a clever
one, first to kill a dragon, and second to get off without leaving a trace. The lords and Mages of the Archipelago couldn't
track him at all, neither where he'd come from nor where
he'd made off to. They were about to give up. That was last
spring; I'd been off on a three-year voyage up in the North
Reach, and got back about that time. And they asked me to
help them find the unknown wizard. That was clever of
them. Because I'm not only a wizard myself, as I think some
of the oafs here have guessed, but I am also a descendant of
the Lords of Pendor. That treasure is mine. It's mine, and
knows it's mine. Those fools of the League couldn't find it,
because it's not theirs. It belongs to the House of Pendor,
and the great emerald, the star of the hoard, Inalkil the
Greenstone, knows its master. Behold!" Blackbeard raised his
oaken staff and cried aloud, "Inalkil!" The tip of the staff
began to glow green, a fiery green radiance, a dazzling haze
the color of April grass, and at the same moment the staff

tipped in the wizard's hand, leaning, slanting till it pointed straight at the side of the hill above them.

"It wasn't so bright a glow, far away in Havnor," Blackbeard murmured, "but the staff pointed true. Inalkil answered when I called. The jewel knows its master. And I know the thief, and I shall conquer him. He's a mighty wizard, who could overcome a dragon. But I am mightier. Do you want to know why, oaf? Because I know his name!"

As Blackbeard's tone got more arrogant, Birt had looked duller and duller, blanker and blanker; but at this he gave a twitch, shut his mouth, and stared at the Archipelagan. "How did you . . . learn it?" he asked very slowly.

Blackbeard grinned, and did not answer.

"Black magic?"

"How else?"

Birt looked pale, and said nothing.

"I am the Sealord of Pendor, oaf, and I will have the gold my fathers won, and the jewels my mothers wore, and the Greenstone! For they are mine.—Now, you can tell your village boobies the whole story after I have defeated this wizard and gone. Wait here. Or you can come and watch, if you're not afraid. You'll never get the chance again to see a great wizard in all his power." Blackbeard turned, and without a backward glance strode off up the hill towards the entrance to the cave.

Very slowly, Birt followed. A good distance from the cave he stopped, sat down under a hawthorn tree, and watched. The Archipelagan had stopped; a stiff, dark figure alone on the green swell of the hill before the gaping cave-mouth, he stood perfectly still. All at once he swung his staff up over his head, and the emerald radiance shone about him as he shouted, "Thief, thief of the Hoard of Pendor, come forth!"

There was a crash, as of dropped crockery, from inside the cave, and a lot of dust came spewing out. Scared, Birt ducked. When he looked again he saw Blackbeard still standing motionless, and at the mouth of the cave, dusty and disheveled, stood Mr. Underhill. He looked small and pitiful, with his toes turned in as usual, and his little bowlegs in black tights, and no staff—he never had had one, Birt sud-

denly thought. Mr. Underhill spoke. "Who are you?" he said
in his husky little voice.

"I am the Sealord of Pendor, thief, come to claim my
treasure!"

At that, Mr. Underhill slowly turned pink, as he always did
when people were rude to him. But he then turned something else. He turned yellow. His hair bristled out, he gave a
coughing roar—and was a yellow lion leaping down the hill
at Blackbeard, white fangs gleaming.

But Blackbeard no longer stood there. A gigantic tiger,
color of night and lightning, bounded to meet the lion . . .

The lion was gone. Below the cave all of a sudden stood a
high grove of trees, black in the winter sunshine. The tiger,
checking himself in mid-leap just before he entered the
shadow of the trees, caught fire in the air, became a tongue
of flame lashing out at the dry black branches . . .

But where the trees had stood a sudden cataract leaped
from the hillside, an arch of silvery crashing water, thundering down upon the fire. But the fire was gone . . .

For just a moment before the fisherman's staring eyes two
hills rose—the green one he knew, and a new one, a bare,
brown hillock ready to drink up the rushing waterfall. That
passed so quickly it made Birt blink, and after blinking he
blinked again, and moaned, for what he saw now was a great
deal worse. Where the cataract had been there hovered a
dragon. Black wings darkened all the hill, steel claws reached
groping, and from the dark, scaly, gaping lips fire and steam
shot out.

Beneath the monstrous creature stood Blackbeard, laughing.

"Take any shape you please, little Mr. Underhill!" he
taunted. "I can match you. But the game grows tiresome. I
want to look upon my treasure, upon Inalkil. Now, big
dragon, little wizard, take your true shape. I command you
by the power of your true name—Yevaud!"

Birt could not move at all, not even to blink. He cowered
staring whether he would or not. He saw the black dragon
hang there in the air above Blackbeard. He saw the fire lick
like many tongues from the scaly mouth, the steam jet from

the red nostrils. He saw Blackbeard's face grow white, white as chalk, and the beard-fringed lips trembling.

"Your name is Yevaud!"

"Yes," said a great, husky, hissing voice. "My true name is Yevaud, and my true shape is this shape."

"But the dragon was killed—they found dragon-bones on Udrath Island—"

"That was another dragon," said the dragon, and then stooped like a hawk, talons outstretched. And Birt shut his eyes.

When he opened them the sky was clear, the hillside empty, except for a reddish-blackish, trampled spot, and a few talon-marks in the grass.

Birt the fisherman got to his feet and ran. He ran across the common, scattering sheep to right and left, and straight down the village street to Palani's father's house. Palani was out in the garden weeding the nasturtiums. "Come with me!" Birt gasped. She stared. He grabbed her wrist and dragged her with him. She screeched a little, but did not resist. He ran with her straight to the pier, pushed her into his fishing-sloop the *Queenie*, untied the painter, took up the oars and set off rowing like a demon. The last that Sattins Island saw of him and Palani was the *Queenie*'s sail vanishing in the direction of the nearest island westward.

The villagers thought they would never stop talking about it, how Goody Guld's nephew Birt had lost his mind and sailed off with the schoolmistress on the very same day that the peddler Blackbeard disappeared without a trace, leaving all his feathers and beads behind. But they did stop talking about it, three days later. They had other things to talk about, when Mr. Underhill finally came out of his cave.

Mr. Underhill had decided that since his truename was no longer a secret, he might as well drop his disguise. Walking was a lot harder than flying, and besides, it was a long, long time since he had had a real meal.

WINGED CREATURES

By Sylvia Townsend Warner

WHEN, AFTER many years of blameless widowhood devoted to ornithology, Lady Fidès gave birth to a son, no one in the fairy Kingdom of Bourrasque held it against her. Elfin longevity is counterpoised by elfin infertility, especially in the upper classes, where any addition to good society is welcomed with delight. Naturally, there was a certain curiosity about the father of Fidès' child, and her intimates begged her to reveal his name so that he, too, could be congratulated on the happy event. With the best will in the world, Fidès could not comply. "My wretched memory," she explained. "Do you know, there was one day last week—of course I can't say which—when I had to rack my brains for three-quarters of an hour before I could remember the name 'chiffchaff.' "

The baby's features afforded no clue. It resembled other babies in having large eyes, pursed lips, and a quantity of fine fluff on its head. When the fluff fell out, Lady Fidès had it carefully preserved. It was exactly the shade of brown needed for the mantle of a song thrush she was embroidering at the time. As an acknowledgment, she called the baby Grive. Later on, when a growth of smooth black hair replaced the fluff, she tried to establish the child in its proper category by calling it Bouvreuil. But Grive stuck.

In a more stirring court these incidents would have counted for nothing. Even Fidès' lofty project of decorating a pavilion with a complete record of the indigenous birds of France in needlework, featherwork, and waxwork would have been taken as something which is always there to be exhibited to visitors on a wet day. Bourrasque preferred small events: not too many of them, and not dilated on. The winds blowing over the high plains of the Massif Central provided all the stir, and more, that anyone in his senses could want.

Indeed, Bourrasque originated in a desire for a quiet life. It was founded by an indignant fairy whose virginity had been attempted by a Cyclops. Just when this happened, and why she should have left the sheltering depth of the Margeride Forest for a bare hillside of the Plomb du Cantal, is not known. Apparently, her first intention was to live as a solitary, attended only by a footman and a serving-woman, but this design was frustrated by friends coming to see how she was getting on. Some decided to join her, and a settlement grew up. In course of time, working fairies raised a surrounding wall. A palace accumulated, a kitchen garden was planted, and terraces were set with vines. The vines flourished (it was the epoch of mild European winters); the population grew, and a group of peasants from the northward, disturbed by earthquakes, migrated with their cattle and became feudatories of the Kingdom of Bourrasque. That was its Golden Age. It ended with a total eclipse, which left the sun weak and dispirited, and filled the air with vapours and falling stars, rain and tempests. Late frosts, blights, and mildew fell from the triumphing malignant moon. Fog crawled over the harvest before the crops could be gathered, and from within the fog came the roar and rumble of the winds, like the mustering of a hidden army. Bourrasque dwindled into what it afterward remained—a small, tight, provincial court of an unlegendary antiquity, where people talked a great deal about the weather, wore nightcaps, and never went out without first looking at the weathercock. If it pointed steadfastly to one quarter, they adjusted their errands. If it swung hither and thither like a maniac, they stayed indoors.

It was not really a favorable climate for an ornithologist.

Fairies are celebrated needlewomen, and do a great deal of fancywork. From her youth up, Fidès had filled her tambour frame with a succession of birds in embroidery: birds on twigs, on nests, pecking fruit, searching white satin snow for crumbs. The subjects were conventional, the coloring fanci-

ful, and everybody said how lifelike. On the day of her husband's death (an excellent husband, greatly her senior) Fidès
entered the death chamber for a last look at him. The window had been set open, as is customary after a death; a
feather had blown in and lay on the pillow. She picked it up.
And in an instant her life had a purpose: she must know
about birds.

At first she was almost in despair. There were so many
different birds, and she could be sure of so few of them.
Robin, blackbird, swallow, magpie, dove, cuckoo by note,
the little wren, birds of the poultry yard—no others. The sea-
son helped her. It was May, the nestlings had hatched, the
parent birds were feeding their young. She watched them
flying back and forth, back and forth, discovered that hen
blackbirds are not black, that robins nest in holes. When no
one was looking, she took to her wings like any working fairy
and hovered indecorously to count the fledglings and see how
the nests were lined. As summer advanced she began to walk
afield, and saw a flock of goldfinches take possession of a this-
tle patch. She picked up every feather she saw, carried it
back, compared it with others, sometimes identified it. The
feather on her husband's pillow, the first of her collection,
was the breast feather of a dove.

An eccentricity made a regular thing of ceases to provoke
remark. Public opinion deplored the freckles on Fidès' nose,
but accepted them—together with her solitary rambles, her
unpunctuality, and her growing inattention to what was
going on around her—as a consequence of her widowed state.
Her brother-in-law, her only relative at Court, sometimes
urged her to wear a mask and gloves, but otherwise respected
her sorrow, which did her, and his family, great credit.

As time went on, and the freckles reappeared every summer and the feathers accumulated to such an extent that she
had to have an attic made over to hold them, he lapsed from
respecting her sorrow to admiring her fidelity—which was
just as creditable but less acutely so. When she made him an
uncle he was slightly taken aback. But it was a nice peaceful
baby, and not the first to be born to a bar sinister—which in
some Courts, notably Elfhame in Scotland, is a positive ad-

vantage. With a little revision Fidès was still creditable: to have remembered with so much attachment the comfort of matrimony through so long and disconsolate a widowhood was undeniably to her credit, and his late brother would have taken it as a compliment.

But as a persuasion to Fidès to stay quietly indoors the baby was totally ineffective. She was no sooner out of child-bed than she was out-of-doors, rambling over the countryside with the baby under her arm. "Look, baby. That's a whinchat. Whinchat. Whinchat." A little jerk to enforce the information. Or "Listen, baby. That's a raven. '*Noirâtre*,' he says. '*Noirâtre*.'" The child's vague stare would wander in the direction of her hand. He was a gentle, solemn baby; she was sure he took it all in and that his first word would be a chirp. If her friends questioned her behavior—Wouldn't the child be overexcited? Wouldn't it be happier with a rattle?—she vehemently asserted that she meant Grive to have his birthright. "I grew up without a bird in my life, as if there were nothing in the world but fairies and mortals. I wasn't allowed to fly—flying was vulgar—and to this day I fly abominably. Birds were things to stitch, or things to eat. Larks were things in a pie. But birds are our nearest relatives. They are the nearest things to ourselves. And far more beautiful, and far more interesting. Don't you see?" They saw poor Fidès unhinged by the shock of having a baby that couldn't be accounted for, and turned the subject.

The working fairies, chattering like swifts as they flew about their duties, were more downright. "Taking the child out in all weathers like any gypsy! Asking Rudel if he'll give it flying lessons! Gentry ought to know their place."

Only Gobelet spoke up for his mistress, saying that weather never did a child any harm. Gobelet spoke from experience. He was a changeling, and had lived in the mortal world till he was seven, when Fidès' husband saw him sucking a cow, took a fancy to his roly-poly charm, and had him stolen away, giving him to Fidès (this was in the early days of their marriage) for St. Valentine's Day. Gobelet grew up short-legged and stocky, and inexpugnably mortal. No one particularly liked him. To prove satisfactory a changeling

must be stolen in infancy. Gobelet's seven years as a laborer's
child encrusted him, like dirt in the crevices of an artichoke.
He ate with his fingers. When he had finished a boiled egg
he drove his spoon through the shell. If he saw a single magpie, he crossed himself; if anyone gave him a penny he spat
on it for luck; he killed slowworms. He was afraid of Fidès,
because he knew he was repulsive to her. Yet once he made
her a most exquisite present. She had gone off on one of her
rambles, and he had been sent after her with a message. He
found her on the heath, motionless, and staring at the
ground with an expression of dismay. She was staring at the
body of a dead crow, already maggoty. Forgetting the message, he picked it up and said it must be buried in an anthill.
She had not expected him to show such feeling, and followed
him while he searched for an anthill large enough for his purpose. When it was found he scrabbled a hole and sank the
crow in it. What the maggots had begun, he said, the ants
would finish. Ants were good workmen. Three months later
he brought her the crow's skeleton, wrapped in a burdock
leaf. Every minutest bone was in place, and she had never
seen a bird's skeleton before. In her rapture she forgot to
thank him, and he went away thinking she was displeased.

Grive's first coherent memory was of a northeasterly squall;
a clap of thunder, darkened air, and hailstones bouncing off
the ground. He was in his mother's arms. She was attending
to something overhead. There was a rift of brilliant March-
blue sky, and small cross-shaped birds were playing there, div-
ing in and out of the cloud, circling round each other, gathering and dispersing and gathering again, and singing in shrill
silken voices. The booming wind came between him and the
music. But it persisted; whenever the wind hushed, he heard
it again, the same dizzying net of sound. He struggled out of
his mother's arms, spread his wings, felt the air beneath
them, and flew toward the larks. She watched him, breathless
with triumph, till a gust of wind caught him and dashed him
to the ground. She was so sure he was dead that she did not
stir, till she heard him whimper. Hugging him small and
warm, to her breast, she waited for him to die. He stiffened,

his face contorted, he drew a sharp breath, and burst into a bellow of fury. She had never heard him cry like that before. He had come back to her a stranger.

She told no one of this. She wanted to forget it. She had her hair dressed differently and led an indoor life, playing bilboquet and distilling a perfume from gorse blossoms. By the time the cuckoo had changed its interval, she was walking on the heath. But she walked alone, leaving Grive in the care of Gobelet—an uncouth companion, but wingless.

Gobelet pitied the pretty child who had suddenly fallen out of favor. He cut him a shepherd's pipe of elder wood, taught him to plait rushes, carved him a ship which floated in a foot-bath. By whisking up the water he raised a stormy ocean; the ship tossed and heeled, and its crew of silver buttons fell off and were drowned. On moonlight nights he threw fox and rabbit shadows on the wall. The fox moved stealthily toward the rabbit, snapping its jaws, winking horribly with its narrow gleaming eye; the rabbit ran this way and that, waving its long ears. As the right-hand fox pursued the left-hand rabbit, Grive screamed with the excitement of the chase, and Gobelet said to himself, "I'll make a man of him yet."

When these diversions were outgrown, they invented an interminable saga in which they were the last two people left alive in a world of giants, dragons, and talking animals. Day after day they ran new perils, escaped by stratagems only to face worse dangers, survived with just enough strength for the next day's installment. Sorting and pairing feathers for Fidès for hours on end, they prompted each other to new adventures in their world of fantasy.

But the real world was gaining on them. Gobelet had grown stout. He walked with a limp, and the east wind gave him rheumatism.

The measure of our mortal days is more or less threescore and ten. The lover cries out for a moment to be eternal, the astronomer would like to see a comet over again, but he knows this is foolish, as the lover knows his mistress will outlive her lustrous eyes and die round about the time he does. Our years, long or short, are told on the same plain-faced dial. But by the discrepancy between elfin and mortal longevity, the portion of time which made Grive an adolescent made Gobelet an aging man. Of the two, Gobelet was the less concerned. He had kept some shreds of his mortal wits about him and felt that, taking one thing with another, when the time came he would be well rid of himself. Grive lived in a flutter of disbelief, compunction, and apprehension, and plucked out each of Gobelet's white hairs as soon as it appeared. Elfins feel a particular reprobation of demonstrable old age. Many of them go into retirement rather than affront society with the spectacle of their decay. As for changelings, when they grow old they are got rid of. Grive, being measured for a new suit, thought that before he had worn it out Gobelet would be gone, discarded like a cracked pitcher, left to beg his way through the world and die in a ditch with the crows standing round like mourners, waiting to peck out his eyes.

Grive was being measured for a new suit because the time had come when he must attend the Queen as one of her pages. It was his first step up in the world, and having determined he would not enjoy it he found himself enjoying it a great deal. At the end of his first spell of duty he returned to the family apartment, full of what he would tell Gobelet. Gobelet was gone. As furious as a child, Grive accused Fidès of cruelty, treachery, ingratitude. "He was the only friend I had. I shall find him and bring him back. Which way did he go?"

Fidès put down the blue tit she was feathering. "How should I know? Do you suppose I was there to wave him goodbye? As it was, I kept him long after he should have been got rid of, because I knew you had been fond of him. But one can't keep changelings forever. He had grown quite repulsively old. He had to be got rid of. Be reasonable, dear. And don't rant." She took up the blue tit and added another feather.

"How it must distress you to think of getting rid of the Queen," he said suavely. It was as if for the first time in his life he had shot with a loaded gun.

Queen Alionde had felt no call to go into retirement. She brandished her old age and insisted on having it acknowledged. No one knew how old she was. There had been confidential bowerwomen, Chancellors sworn to secrecy who knew, but they were long since dead. Her faculties remained in her like rats in a ruin. She never slept. She spoke the language of a forgotten epoch, mingling extreme salacity with lofty euphemisms and punctilios of grammar. She was long past being comical, and smelled like bad haddock. Some said she was phosphorescent in the dark. She found life highly entertaining.

When the pestilence broke out among the peasantry, she insisted on having the latest news of it: which villages it had reached, how many had died, how long it took them. She kept a tally of deaths, comparing it with the figures of other pestilences, calculating if this one would beat them, and how soon it would reach Bourrasque. Working fairies were sent out to look for any signs of murrain among cattle. They reported a great influx of kites. Her diamonds flashed as she clapped her hands at the news. And rats? she asked. Few rats, if any, they said. The reflection of her earrings flitted about the room like butterflies as she nodded in satisfaction. Rats are wise animals, they know when to move out; they are not immune to mortal diseases as fairies are. If the pestilence came to the very gates of Bourrasque, if the dying, frantic with pain, leaped over the palace wall, if the dead had to be raked into heaps under their noses, no fairy would be a penny the worse. Her court was glad to think this was so but wished there could be a change of subject.

Exact to the day she foretold it, the pestilence reached Bourrasque. Her officeholders had to wrench compliments on her accuracy out of their unenthusiastic bosoms, and a congratulatory banquet was organized, with loyal addresses and the young people dancing jigs and *bourrées*. Fires blazed on the hearths, there were candles everywhere, and more food than could be eaten. The elder ladies, sitting well away from their Queen's eye, began to knit shawls for the peasantry. By the time the shawls were finished, they were thankful to wrap them round their own shoulders.

Bourrasque, complying with the course of history, had come to depend on its serfs for common necessities. The pestilence did not enter the castle; it laid siege to it. Fewer carcasses were brought to the larderer's wicket, less dairy stuff, no eggs. The great meal chest was not replenished. Fuel dues were not paid. There was no dearth in the land; pigs and cattle, goats and poultry, could be seen scampering over the fields, breaking down fences, trampling the reaped harvest—all of them plump and in prime condition for Martinmas. But the men who herded and slaughtered, the women who milked the cows and thumped in the churns, were too few and too desperate to provide for any but themselves. Others providing for themselves were the working fairies, who made forays beyond the walls, brought back a goose, a brace of rabbits, with luck an eel from under the mud of a cow pond. They cooked and ate in secret, charitably sparing a little goose fat to flavor the cabbage shared among their betters.

On New Year's morning the Queen was served with a stoup of claret and a boiled egg. The egg was bad. She ate it and called a Council. Hearing that they had hoped to spare her the worst, she questioned them with lively interest about their deprivations, and commanded that Bourrasque should be vacated on the morrow. She had not lived so long in order to die of starvation. The whole court must accompany her; she could not descend on her great-great-great-nephew in Berry without a rag of retinue. They would start an hour after sunrise.

Somehow or other, it was managed. There was no planning, no consultation, no bewailing. They worked like plunderers. The first intention had been to take what was precious, like jewelry, or indispensable, like blankets. This was followed by a passion to leave nothing behind. Tusks, antlers, a rhinoceros horn, some rusty swords, two voiceless bugles, a gong, and an effigy of Charlemagne were rescued from the butler's pantry. The east pavilion was stripped of its decorations. They tore down velvet hangings to wrap round a number of old saucepans. Cushions and dirty napkins were rammed into a deed chest, and lidded with astrological charts. By dawn, the ox wagons stood loaded in the forecourt. A few flakes of snow were falling.

The courtiers had gathered at the foot of the main staircase. Many of them had put on nightcaps for the journey. Alionde was brought down, baled in furs, and carried to her litter. Behind its closed screens she could be heard talking and giving orders, like a parrot in its cage. A hubbub of last-minute voices broke out—assurances of what had been done, reassurances that nothing had been overlooked. Grive heard his mother's voice among them: "I don't think I've forgotten anything. Perhaps I'd better have one last look." She brushed past him, stared up the wide staircase, heard herself being told to hurry, turned back, and was gone with the rest. He stood at the window, watching the cavalcade lumber up the hillside, with the piper going ahead and playing a jaunty farewell. A gust of wind swept the noise out of earshot. Nothing was left except the complaining of the weathercock.

He was too famished to know whether he had been left behind or had stayed. Like his throstle name-giver, *Turdus philomelos*, he was shy and a dainty feeder; rather than jostle for a bacon-rind or a bit of turnip, he let himself be elbowed away. Now, though he knew that every hole and corner had been ransacked for provision for the journey, he made a desultory tour of inspection. A smell of sour grease hung about the kitchen quarters. He sickened at it, and went into the cold pleasure-garden, where he ate a little snow. He returned to the saloon which had been so crowded with departures, listened to the weathercock, noticed the direction of the snowflakes, and lay down to die.

Dying was a new experience. It was part of it that he should be sorting feathers, feathers from long-dead birds, and heavy because of that. A wind along the floor blew him away from the feathers. It was part of dying that a dragon came in and curled up on his feet. It seemed kindly intentioned, but being cold-blooded it could not drive away the chill of death. It was also part of dying that Gobelet was rocking him in his arms. Once, he found Gobelet dribbling milk between his jaws. The milk was warm and sent him to sleep. When he woke he could stretch himself and open his eyes. There was Gobelet's hand, tickling his nose with a raisin. So they were both dead.

Even when Grive was on the mend he remained light-headed. Starvation had capsized his wits. If he were left to sleep too long he began to twitch and struggle; wakened, he would stare round him and utter the same cry: "I had that dreadful dream again. I dreamed we were alive."

Gobelet was not distressed at being alive; on the contrary, it seemed to him that his survival did him credit. It had been against considerable odds. It was the lot of changelings to be dismissed on growing old. He had seen it happen to others and taken it for granted; he did so when it was his turn to be packed off to find a death in a world that had no place for him. But he had been a poor man's child, and the remembrance of how to steal, cajole, and make himself useful came to his aid. He was too old for cajolery to apply, but he flattered, and by never staying long in one place he stole undetected. He had forgotten the name of his birthplace till he heard it spoken by a stranger at the inn. Then everything flashed back on him: the forked pear tree, the fern growing beside the wellhead, his mother breaking a pitcher, the faggot thrust into the bread oven. Knowing what name to ask for, he soon found his way there. Everyone he had known was dead or gone, but the breed of sheep was the same. Here he hired himself as a farmhand and for a couple of years lived honest, till the sudden childhood memory of a gentleman on a horse who drew rein and asked how old he was so unsettled him that he knew he must have another look at Bourrasque. By then the pestilence had reached the neighborhood. He hoped to evade it, but it struck him down on the third day of his journey. Shivering and burning, he sweated it out in a dry ditch, listening to the death-owl screeching to the moon. In spite of the owl, he recovered, laid dock-leaf poultices on his sores, and trudged on through the shortening days. He knew he was nearing Bourrasque when he met an old acquaintance, Grimbaud, one of the working fairies, who was setting a snare. From him he heard how the peasants were dying and the palace starving. He inquired after Lady Fidès. Grimbaud tapped his forehead with two fingers. He could say nothing of Grive.

He rose in the air and was gone, lost in the winter dusk.

"Starving, are you?" Gobelet shouted after him. "No worse than I. And you can whisk off on your wings. No limping on a stiff knee for you." He felt a sudden consuming hatred for the whole fairy race. He took a couple of steps, caught his foot in the snare, and fell, wrenching his knee. It was his good knee. He crawled away on all fours, and made a bracken hut, where he spent a miserable week nursing his knee, changing and unchanging his mind, and listening to the kites mewing in the fog. In the end he decided to go forward. There was nothing to be got by it, but not to finish his wasteful journey would be worse waste. To look at Bourrasque and turn away would clear the score.

The fog lifted and there it was—larger than he remembered, and darker. The gates stood open. A long procession was winding up the hillside, the piper going ahead. The Queen must be dead at last! It was odd that so many wagons, loaded with so much baggage, should be part of the funeral train. But no doubt, freed from her tyranny, the court would bury her and go on to being better fed elsewhere. He watched the procession out of sight, stared at the smokeless chimneys, and renounced Bourrasque, which he had come such a long journey to renounce. As he was turning away, it occurred to him that he owed himself a keepsake, and that one of Lady Fidès' birds would do. He limped on, and entered the palace by the familiar gully where the waste water flowed away. The east pavilion was stripped bare. He remembered other things he had admired and went in search of them. Some furniture remained in the emptied rooms— gaunt beds with no hangings, cabinets with doors hanging open. Meeting his reflection in a mirror, he started back as if it accused him of trespassing. He was hurrying away when he saw Grive lying in a corner.

There was time to remember all this during Grive's convalescence, when the excitement of winning him back to life
was over and the triumphs of stealing provisions from the
homes of the dead had dulled into routine. He compared
Grive's lot with his own: no one had tended him in his
ditch, and never for a moment had he supposed it better to
be dead than alive. What succor would a dying Grive have
got from a dead Gobelet? The comparison was sharpened because the living Gobelet was afraid. The survivors outside the
walls railed against the palace people, who had done nothing
for them, feasted while they starved, danced while they were
dying, deserted them. If this angry remnant invaded the
palace—and certainly it would—Grive and he would be done
for.

They got away as smoothly as they did in their serial story.
It was a clear frosty night, a following wind helped them
uphill, and in the morning they took their last look at Bourrasque, where the villagers, small and busy as ants, were dragging corpses to the plague pit.

With that morning Gobelet began the happiest epoch of
his life. As nearly as possible, he became a fairy. He lost all
sense of virtue and responsibility and lived by pleasures—
pell-mell pleasures, contrived, unforeseen: a doubled rainbow,
roasting a hedgehog. And, as if he shared the hardiness and
resilience of those who live for pleasure, he was immune to
cold and weariness, and felt like a man half his age. Grive
had made an instant and unashamed recovery. Most of the
time he was high overhead, circling while Gobelet walked,
sailing on the wind, flying into clouds and reappearing far
above them. From time to time he dived down to report
what he had seen. There was a morass ahead, so Gobelet
must bear to the left. Another storm was coming up, but if
Gobelet hurried he would reach a wood in time to take shelter. He had seen a likely farm where Gobelet could beg a
meal. He had seen a celandine.

A day later there were a thousand celandines. The swallows
would not be long behind them, remarked Gobelet: swallows

resort to celandines to clear their eyesight after spending the winter sunk in ponds; they plunge in, all together, and lie under the mud. All together, they emerge. What proves it is that you never see a swallow till the celandines are in bloom. On the contrary, Grive said, swallows fly south and spend the winter in some warmer climate where they have plenty of flies to prey on. This had been one of Lady Fidès' crazy ideas: no one at Bourrasque credited it, for why should birds fly to a foreign shore and encounter such dangers and hardships on the way when they could winter comfortably in a pond?

Grive and Gobelet were still disputing this when the swallows came back, twirling the net of their shadows over the grass. By then it was hot enough to enjoy shade. They moved away from the uplands, and lived in wooded country, listening to nightingales. Grive had never heard a nightingale. It was like the celandines—the first single nightingale, so near that he saw its eye reflecting the moonlight, and the next day thousands, chorus rivalling chorus; for they sang in bands and, contrary to the poets, by day as well as by night. Fairies, he said, were far inferior to birds. They have no song; nothing comes out of them but words and a few contrived strains of music from professional singers. Birds surpass them in flight, in song, in plumage. They build nests; they rear large families. No fairy drummer could match a woodpecker, no fairy militia maneuver like a flock of lapwings, no fairy comedian mimic like a starling.

He spoke with such ardor that it would not do to contradict him, though privately Gobelet thought that if Grive could not sing like a nightingale he could praise as fluently and with more invention. Grive was as much in love with birds as ever Lady Fidès had been, but without the frenzy which made her throw the lark pie out of the window. Which was fortunate, as there were many days when the choice of a meal lay between pignuts and an unwary quail spatchcocked. He left provisioning to Gobelet; whether it was begged, stolen, caught, Grive found everything delicious, and sauced by eating it with his fingers. In other respects he

was master. It was part of Gobelet's happiness that this was
so.

All this time they were moving eastward. It was in the
Haute-Loire that Grive suddenly became aware of bats. As
the narrow valley—scarcely wider than the river with its
bankside alders—brimmed with dusk, bats were everywhere,
flying so fast and so erratically that it was hard to say
whether there were innumerable bats or the same bats in a
dozen places at once. As birds surpass fairies, he said, bats
surpass birds. They were the magicians of flight. With a flick,
they could turn at any angle, dart zigzag above the stream,
flicker in and out of the trees, be here, be gone, never hesitate, never collide. They were flight itself. Trying to fly
among them he was as clumsy as a goose. They did not trouble to scatter before him; they were already gone.

The valley was cold at night, and stones fell out of the hillside. It seemed to Gobelet that wherever he went a fox was
watching him. If it had not been for Grive's delight in the
bats, he would have been glad to move on. Instead, he set
himself to catch a bat. He had seen it done in his childhood;
it was not difficult. He took the bat to Grive. Daylight had
meekened it. It let itself be examined, its oiled-silk wings
drawn out, its hooked claws scrutinized, its minute weight
poised in the hand. It was, said Grive, exactly like Queen
Alionde—the same crumpled teats, the same pert face. But
verminous, said Gobelet loyally. Grive said that if fairies did
not wash they would be verminous; he had read in a book
that the fairies of Ireland are renowned for the lice in their
long hair.

He looked more closely at the bat, then threw it away. It
staggered and vanished under a bush. As though a spell had
snapped, he said that they must start at once.

He flew ahead, shielding his eyes from the sun to see more
clearly. Circling to allow time for Gobelet to catch up, he
felt an impatient pity for the old man scrambling up hill-
sides, gaining a ridge only to see another ridge before him,
obstinate as a beetle, and as slow. Gobelet thought he was
making fine speed; they had never travelled so fast since the

wind blew them uphill on their first morning. It was not till they sat together on the summit of the last ridge that Grive relaxed and became conversational. They sat above a heat haze. Beneath and far away was the glimmer of a wide river. He heard Grive's wings stir as if he were about to launch himself toward it, but instead he rolled over on the turf and said, "Tonight we will sup on olives." And he told Gobelet that the river was the Rhone, wide and turbulent, but crossed by a bridge built by pigeons. All they had to do now was to follow it, and then bear eastward. "Where to?" asked Gobelet. "To the sea." All Gobelet's happiness in being mastered (it had been a little jolted by that abrupt departure from the bat valley) flowed back. More than ever before he acknowledged the power and charm of a superior mind.

Later on, when they were walking over the great bridge of Saint-Esprit, he remembered Grive's statement. It seemed to his commonsense thinking that not even eagles, let alone pigeons, could have carried those huge stones and bedded them so firmly in the bellowing currents. He had to bellow himself to express his doubts. Grive repeated that pigeons had done it; they were the architects and overseers, though for the heavier work they might have employed mortals.

For the work of provisioning their journey he still employed Gobelet. They were now among Provençal speakers, but the beggar's tune is the same in all languages, theft is speechless, and bargaining can be conducted by signs and grimaces. Gobelet managed pretty well. One evening he begged from a handsome bona roba (light women were always propitious), who laughed at his gibberish, put money in his hand, ogled Grive, and pointed to an inn. They sat down under an awning, the innkeeper brought bread and olives and poured wine into heavy tumblers. Grive had just begun to drink when he leaped up with a scream, dropped the tumbler, and began frantically defending himself with his hands. A sphinx moth had flown into his face and was fluttering about him. The innkeeper came up with a napkin, smacked the moth to the ground, and trod on it. On second thought, he made the sign of the cross over Grive.

Gobelet was ashamed at this exhibition of terror. Grive,

being a fairy, was not. Trying to better things, Gobelet said it
was an alarmingly large moth—as big as a bat. Had Grive
thought it was a bat?

"An omen!" gasped Grive, as soon as he could unclench
his teeth. "An omen!"

That night they slept under a pine tree. The moth hunted
Gobelet from dream to dream; the stir of the tree in the
dawn wind was like the beating of enormous black wings. He
sat up and rubbed his eyes. Grive was sleeping like a child,
and woke in calm high spirits. After his usual morning flight,
when he soared and circled getting his direction, they continued their journey. Of all the regions they had travelled
through, this was the pleasantest, because it was the most
sweet-smelling. Even in the heat of the day (and it was extremely hot, being late August) they were refreshed by wafts
of scent: thyme, wild lavender and marjoram, bay and
juniper. There was no need to beg or steal; figs, olives, and
walnuts were theirs for the picking. Here and there they saw
cities, but they skirted them. Here and there mountains rose
sharply from the plain, but there was no need to climb them;
they appeared, threatened, and were left behind. The only
obstacle they met in these happy days was a fierce torrent,
too deep to ford till they came to a pebble reach, where it
spread into a dozen channels. It was here that Grive had his
adventure with the doves. They were abbatial doves, belong-
ing to a house of monks who lived retired from the world
with the noise of the torrent always in their ears. Grive saw
the doves sitting demurely on the platforms of their dove-
cote. He made a quick twirling flight to entertain them, and
as he alighted waved his hand toward them. They came tumbling out of their apertures and settled on his raised arm. He
stood for a while talking to them, then shook them off. As if
they were attached to him by some elastic tether, they flew
back and settled again. He cast them off, they returned. He
walked on, they rode on him. He flew and they flew after
him, and settled on him when he returned to earth. "Make
yourself invisible," said Gobelet. "That will fox them." He
did so. The doves stayed where they were, placidly roo-coo-

ing. Gobelet clapped his hands, Grive pranced and rolled on the ground; nothing dislodged them, till a bell rang and a monk came out shaking grain in a measure. They looked startled, and flew back to be fed.

Grive was pleased but unastonished. It was natural, he said; a matter of affinity. The doves felt his affection flow toward them and had responded. He tried the experiment again, with plovers, with fieldfares. Sometimes it worked, sometimes it did not. Once he fetched down a kestrel from the height of its tower. It landed on him, screaming with excitement, and drew blood with its talons. Flock after flock of birds streamed overhead, flying high up; but he had no power over these, they were migrants bent on their journey. One morning he came down from his prospecting flight, having caught sight of the sea, lying beyond a territory of marsh and glittering waterways. Travelling east of south they skirted another city, another mountain. There was a change in the quality of the light, and large birds, flying with effortless ease and not going anywhere in particular, swooped over the landscape; and were seagulls.

"When we get to the sea, what shall we do then?" Gobelet hoped the answer would speak of repose, of sitting and looking around them, as they had done in the spring.

"Find a ship going to Africa. And that reminds me, Gobelet, we must have money for the passage." He snuffed the air. "That's the sea. Do you smell it? That's the sea." Gobelet smelled only dust and oleanders and a dead lizard. But he had an uninstructed nose; he had read no books to tell him what the sea smelled like.

Two days later he felt he had never smelled anything but the sea, nor would ever smell anything else, and that the smell of the sea was exactly paralleled by the melancholy squawking cry of the seagulls. He sat on a bollard and rubbed his knee. It pained him as much as it did when he was turned out of Bourrasque. Grive had flown so fast that morning, and paused so impatiently, that he had had to run to keep up with him. The port town was noisy, crowded, and lavish, and ended suddenly in the mournfulness of the quays

and the towering array of ship beside ship. On all his inland
life Gobelet had never seen anything so intimidating. Their
hulls were dark and sodden, their slackened sails hung
gawkily, they sidled and shifted with the stir of the water.
Black and shabby, they were like a row of dead crows
dangling from a farmer's gibbet. At the back of his mind was
another comparison: the degraded blackness of the sphinx
moth after the innkeeper had smacked it down and trodden
on it. In one of these he must be imprisoned and carried to
Africa, where there would be black men, and elephants. Yet
it depended on him whether they went or no, for he must
steal for their passage money. He had never felt less like
stealing in his life. A cold and stealthy sense of power ran
through him. And a moment later he saw Grive coming toward him and knew he had no power at all. Grive had found
a ship which was sailing to Africa tomorrow at midday. He
had talked to her captain; everything was arranged. Presently
they would take a stroll through the town, prospecting likely
places for Gobelet's thieving. But first Gobelet must come
and admire the ship. She was a magnificent ship, the swiftest
vessel on the Inland Sea, and for that reason she was called
the Sea-Swallow.

"The Sea-Swallow, Gobelet. You and your ponds!"

He walked Gobelet along the quays with an arm round his
neck. A swirl of gulls flew up from a heap of fish guts; he
held out his other arm and they settled on it, contesting for
foothold. He waved them off and they came back again and
settled, as determinedly as the doves had done, but not so
peaceably as the doves. They squabbled, edged each other
away, fell off and clawed their way back. The Sea-Swallow
was at the end of the line. The crew was already making
ready for departure, coiling ropes, clearing the decks, experi-
mentally raising the tarred sails. With one arm still around
Gobelet and the other stretched out under its load of gulls,
Grive stood questioning the captain with the arrogant suavity
of one bred to court life. With the expression of someone
quelled against his reason, the captain answered him with
glum civility, and stared at Gobelet. Asserting himself, he
said that anyone happening to die during the voyage must

not look for Christian burial. He would be dropped in the sea, for no sailors would tolerate a corpse on board; it was certain to bring ill luck. Of course, said Grive. What could be more trouble-saving?

He shook off the seagulls, and they went for a stroll through the town. It wasn't promising. The wares were mostly cheap and gaudy, sailor's stuff, and the vendors were beady-eyed and alert. Grive continued to say that a gold chain with detachable links would be the most convenient and practical theft. A begging friar stood at a corner, and a well-dressed woman coming out of church paused, opened her purse, and dropped a gold coin into his tray. Grive vanished, and a moment later the coin vanished too. Gobelet felt himself nudged into a side street, where Grive rematerialized.

They had supper at an inn, eating grandly in an upper room, whence they could watch the shipmasts sidling and the gulls floating in the sky. The wine was strong, and Grive became talkative and slightly drunk. Gobelet forgot his fatigue and disillusionment in the pleasure of listening to Grive's conversation. Much of it was over his head, but he felt he would never forget it, and by thinking it over would understand it later on. The noise of the port died down, voices and footsteps thinned away; the sighing and creaking of the ships took over. They found a garden on the outskirts—garden or little park, it was too dark to tell—and slept there.

The next morning, all that remained was to acquire the gold chain with detachable links. Grive had displayed such natural talents for theft that Gobelet suggested they should go together. But he was sent off by himself; Grive had a headache and wanted to sit quietly under the trees.

The gold chain was so clear in Gobelet's mind that he felt sure of finding it. It would be in one of the side streets, a shop below street level with steps down into it, the shopkeeper an old man. When he had located the chain, he would walk in and ask to be shown some rings. None would quite do, so the shopkeeper would go off to find others. With the chain in his pocket, he would consider, say he would come again, and be gone—walking slowly, for haste looks sus-

picious. In one of the side streets there was just such a shop,
and looking through the lattice he saw gold buttons that
would serve as well or better. But the chain was so impressed
on his mind that he wandered on, and when he began to
grow anxious and went back for the buttons he could not
find the side street. Blinded with anxiety, he hurried up and
down, was caught in a street market, collided with buyers
and sellers. A marketwoman whose basket of pears he
knocked over ran after him demanding to be paid for them.
He dived into the crowd, saw a church before him, rushed in,
and fell panting on his knees. Looking up he saw the very
chain before him, dangling within reach, from the wrist of a
statue. A ceremony was just over, the congregation was leaving, but some still dawdled, and a beadle was going about
with a broom, sweeping officiously round Gobelet's heels.
There hung the chain, with everything hanging on it. There
he knelt, with every minute banging in his heart. When at
last he was alone, he found that the chain was fastened to the
statue; he had to take his teeth to it. He burst through the
knot of women gossiping round the holy-water stoup, and
ran. The usual misfortune of strangers befell him; he was
lost. Sweat poured down his face, his breathing sawed his
lungs. When he emerged on the quay, it was at the farther
end from the Sea-Swallow. He had no breath to shout with,
no strength to run with. His legs ran, not he.

Grive was standing on the quay. The Sea-Swallow had
hoisted anchor and was leaving the port. A rope ladder had
been pulled up, the gap of water between her and the
quayside was widening. Grive shouted to the captain to wait.
The captain spat ceremonially, and the crew guffawed.

Grive leaped into the air. As the sailors scrambled to catch
him and pull him on board he spread his wings and vanished.
A throng of screaming gulls followed him as he flew up to
the crow's nest, and more and more flocked round and settled, and more and more came flying and packed round those
who had settled, all screaming, squalling, lamenting, pecking
each other, pecking at him. Blood ran through their breast
feathers, their beaks were red with blood. The ship was free
of the port, her mainsails were hoisted and shook in the

wind. The exploding canvas could not be heard, nor the
shouts of the sailors, nor the captain's speaking trumpet. The
ship moved silent as a ghost under her crown of beating
wings and incessant furious voices. She caught the land
breeze, staggered under it, heeled over and recovered herself.
The people who stood on the quay watching this unusual departure saw the gulls slip in a mass from the crow's nest and
fly down to the water's face. There they gathered as if on a
raft. Their raft was sucked into the ship's wake and they
dispersed. The onlookers saw the old man who had stood a
stranger among them pull something bright from his pocket,
drop it into the dirty clucking water, and turn weeping away.

SIA

By Peter S. Beagle

*The following story is a chapter from Peter Beagle's forth-
coming novel. The author writes, "Farrell, the hero, has been
living for a few weeks in a house in Berkeley (called Havelock
in the book) with his oldest friend, Ben Kassoy, and Ben's
lover, a woman named Athanasia Sioris—Sia. She is Greek,
dumpy, charming, strange, twice Ben's age—somewhere in
her early sixties—works as a kind of lay analyst or counselor,
and is, as Farrell gradually comes to realize, actually an extremely ancient and dangerous goddess. In this chapter he
has an instant's glimpse of her real being, and of how dangerous she can be when blasphemed against."*

THERE WAS one job open, driving an electric train in the
shape of an alligator around and around the zoo six afternoons a week, lecturing to his passengers about the animals
they were glimpsing. Farrell had hoped for something to do
with gorillas; but it was outdoor work at least, and decently
mindless. He agreed to start on the following Monday, and
left with a copy of the route and the recitation to memorize.
There were five and a half jokes in it, underlined in red.

When he went home to change his clothes, he found the
driveway occupied by a middle-aged yellow Pontiac with the
left front fender mashed into a rusty fist. He parked Madame
Schumann-Heink a block further along Clare and walked
back to the house. There were skid marks behind the Pontiac
where it had spun up the driveway, clipping off two of Ben's
birdhouses and grinding a patch of wild rosemary to rags.
The driver was still sitting behind the wheel, pushing the

radio buttons, but he looked up and opened the door as Farrell approached. "Hi there," he said in a cheerful, rather boyish voice. "Hey, you seen my wife yet?"

He was younger than Farrell, with a round, firm, deeply tanned face under a surfer's helmet of crusty white-blond hair. His sideburns were a shade darker, thick and stubbly; his mustache colorless, almost invisible. Farrell saw that his lower lip had been bleeding.

"I don't think so," Farrell said. The young man got out of the car as he started past it. He was stockily built, Farrell's height but at least twenty pounds heavier. He said, "But you're going to see her."

Farrell stared. The man came closer, smiling. "I mean, if you go in there, into that house, you'll see her. I mean, that's where she works, isn't it?"

"Oh, Suzy," Farrell said without thinking, and immediately wished he hadn't. The young man's friendly expression did not change, but rather became fixed on his face, as though he had died. "Suzy McManus, right, you got it, good old Suzy. Well, I'm Dave McManus. Dave McManus. I'm good old Dave." He caught Farrell's hand and shook it long and gently, looking straight into his eyes all the while. His own hand was cold and wet and hard.

Farrell had seen white drunkenness before, but not often enough to recognize it at sight. He knew the thing itself, however: the freight train rattling and lurching comically from hilarity to slobbering sorrow, picking up speed as it passed through wild, aimless anger straight on into wild sickness; and then, running smoothly and almost silently now, into a dark place of shaking and sweating and crying, and out again with no warning to where a dazzling snowy light made everything very still. McManus neither swayed nor mumbled, and hardly smelled of alcohol at all, but Farrell began to back away from him. McManus's smile widened with each step.

"I won't hurt you," he said. "I just want to see my wife, the same as you do." He patted his windbreaker pocket, and Farrell saw how heavily the fabric shifted and swung. "You take me on in there. In the house."

Farrell took another step backward, trying to angle himself toward a parked car. McManus patted his pocket again and shook his head earnestly. "Come on, there's a dog. I don't want to hurt the dog."

"She's a trained killer," Farrell warned him. "They had her in the Army, she used to give courses." He was trying desperately to assess the chances of Suzy's being in the house that morning. She was a pale, whispering girl, a sophomore at the university, who had come to work for Sia as a part-time housekeeper and ended up as a non-paying client, sometimes staying the night or the weekend. "You can't do anything," Sia had said, "but you are so cute I think I'll keep you." Farrell had known in a vague way that she was separated from her husband, but she never spoke of him, any more than she ever laughed or raised her voice. McManus put his hand in his pocket and whistled two notes, and Farrell walked slowly past him and up the steps of the house.

Briseis met him at the door, whining nervously at the sight of the stranger crowding in behind him. For a moment Farrell entertained a mad vision of scooping the Alsatian up in his arms and hurling, or at least shoving, her against McManus. But the man was too close; and Farrell knew himself just as likely to rupture something important or throw his back out. McManus stopped slightly to scratch Briseis' ears, and Farrell tensed, thinking *This is not happening.* Then Suzy came out of a tiny sewing room into the hallway.

When she saw McManus she caught her breath, started to speak, and then shut her mouth and very carefully set down the broom and dustpan she was carrying, leaning the broom against the wall. "Dave," she said, and stood waiting.

McManus's ragged lower lip started to bleed again. Tears sprang out of his eyes in a sudden dreadful spurt, more like shotgun pellets than drops of water. "Bitch, fucking bitch!" he shouted at her, his light voice splintering into shrill fragments. "Bitch, I love you!" Suzy turned and ran for the living room, and McManus shoved Farrell aside and leaped after her, tugging at his pocket. He promptly tripped over Briseis and fell flat, landing with the gun under him. Briseis, who expected the end of the world at any given moment,

screamed in confirmation of her worst forebodings. She threw
herself on Farrell for comfort, buffeting him so frantically
that he almost fell himself. McManus scrambled to his feet
and ran after Suzy. He had torn his pocket getting the pistol
out.

"Do you come here often?" Farrell asked Briseis. There
was a crash in the living room, and McManus yelled, "Well,
shit, don't blame me for that!" Farrell went into the room in
a crouching waddle, taking cover behind chairs. Suzy was
halfway up the stairs, but as he watched she paused, turned,
and started slowly back down toward McManus, who was
standing over the shards of a stoneware lamp. "No," she said,
astonishingly loudly. "No, why should I run from you?"

McManus, who had been steadying the gun with both
hands, now let it fall to his side. For the first time he suddenly looked drunk. He chewed his bleeding lip and sniffed,
muttering, "All right, then, come on." But Suzy shook her
head, and to Farrell's amazement she smiled.

"No," she said again. "Go home, Dave. I'm not coming
with you, and I'm not running away from you anymore. I
just now realized I don't have to. She showed me."

"Bitch," McManus whispered. "Bitch, bitch." Farrell
could hardly hear him; and indeed the words seemed not to
be addressed to Suzy at all, but to someone remembered or
imagined. "She showed you. Blow her fucking head off, she
showed you." He raised his head and smiled suddenly, coldly
in touch with his drunkenness again. "I love you, Suzy," he
said. "You know I love you. Look, I threw my brother out, I
mean for good, like you wanted. I just said, *Out, man, Suzy's
coming home.*" Something in the little shrug and cavalier flip
of his free hand—like a Chaplin back-kick—with which he
disposed of his brother made Farrell see for a moment what
Suzy might have loved.

"But I'm not coming home," Suzy said gently. She came
all the way down to the last step, which put her on a level
with McManus, and she met his eyes with a frail, compas-
sionate dignity. She said, "Take care of yourself, Dave. I'll be
all right." Abruptly she ducked her head, kissed McManus

on the cheek, and started past him toward the kitchen. "Cleaning," she said. "Floors."

Later Farrell thought that she might have gotten away with it, except for the kiss. McManus blinked after her and seemed to slump into himself, rubbing his jaw and mumbling, actually beginning to turn away. Then his hand brushed the place where Suzy had kissed him, and without a word he turned and swung the gun up at arm's length, pointing it at her back.

Farrell shouted, and Suzy looked back and cried out, "Mother, help me!" The shot sounded like a baseball bat slamming down on the living room floor. Farrell went over the coffee table, but McManus was down before he reached him, clutching his right leg and wailing in a kind of terrible gargle. The room smelled like a storm. Suzy started toward her husband, almost stepping on the pistol as she did so, and then halted, as frozen as a deer in headlights, looking past Farrell. Sia was on the stair.

She was wearing a long flowered dress that hung on her like a tablecloth, and she looked like stone. The air tightened on Farrell as he stared at her, trapping him as though in thrashed, sweated bedsheets. Her face was without expression, her voice small and colorless when she said to McManus, "Stand up. Stand up on your feet." Farrell saw that she had been braiding her hair.

"He can't," Suzy protested. "He's hurt himself, he needs a doctor." She knelt beside the gasping, whimpering McManus, trying to keep his hands from the wound. The small stone voice said, "Stand up," and Farrell felt the two words grind together in his breath and in his belly. McManus stopped crying.

"Stand up," Sia said once more, and McManus climbed upright and stayed there somehow, his open, straining mouth making him look as though he were waiting to belch. The bullet had apparently gone through the calf of his leg; there was comparatively little blood. He moved his lips weakly, saying, "The gun."

"Go away," the voice said. "Never come near this house again. Never come near her again. She is under my protection, and if you trouble her you will die. She is one of mine. Go now."

Again Suzy declared, "Oh, he can't, don't you see he can't walk? We have to call a doctor." But Sia gave no sign of having heard: she moved her disheveled head slightly, and McManus, as though on wires, made a single grotesque, lurching hop toward the door. His face was as white and wet as cheese, and the reek of his pain burned in Farrell's nostrils.

A plump figure appeared in the living room doorway, trailed by a tiptoeing Briesis. Farrell recognized the man as one of Sia's more wistful clients. He said, "The front door was open, so I just," peering at the scene with a ruminant's unfocused near-interest. Nothing in his round, freckled face, puckered thinly like an aging balloon, suggested even momentarily that he smelled gunpowder or saw the smashed lamp, or any blood.

Farrell, Suzy, and McManus gaped silently at him, but Sia nodded calmly, saying in her normal voice, "Hello, Robert, just go on along." She stepped aside to let him by, and he went up the stairs without looking back. No one spoke or moved until the door of Sia's office rattled overhead.

Suzy went to support McManus then, but he pushed her away violently, summoning all his dazed vitality to make himself step toward Sia. Over his shoulder he said to Suzy, "You better go on up there, baby, the man's waiting." Farrell fully expected to see him lunge barehanded up the stairs at Sia: his voice was slow with pain, and with the loneliness of great hatred, and he looked at Sia fearlessly. "One of yours," he said. "One of yours, right. Got it."

The good leg buckled under him—though Farrell saw nothing that could have made him slip—and he crashed to his knees before Sia at the foot of the stair. Sia neither moved nor spoke. Farrell smelled wet earth, wet crushed grass, something like coffee, something like the fur of a dead animal. He heard a whimpering, took it first for Briseis, and then understood that the sound was happening in his own throat. The air had darkened a little.

It was nothing like the reflected image he had seen of the

huge woman with the dog's head. Sia herself was hardly there
at all: she seemed to thin and dwindle almost to transparency
even in Farrell's mind. But for one truly unbearable moment
one instant in which names for things had not yet been invented—he was more aware of her presence than he ever had
been of his own. He felt her breathing in the stairs, and in
the old floor under his feet; she surrounded him with her
walls and her rooms, moving in the stones of the fireplace,
looking at him from the pieces of the broken lamp, speaking
in the sunlight's darting scrawl across the living-room rug. Beyond the house there was only more of her, no least space
from her inside himself, for she was that place too, laughing
in his bones, teasing his atoms to make them rattle in the
dark like dice. However he turned, he fell toward her, terribly
content.

Beside him, McManus crouched lower and lower, his limbs
spraddling as though a great foot were crushing him to earth.
As Farrell watched, the weight seemed to release him, and he
rose slowly and half hopped, half hobbled toward the front
door, drawing in his breath with every step. Suzy started to
follow, but the woman on the stair looked at her and she put
her hands to her mouth and went into the kitchen. Farrell
heard McManus stumbling and cursing wearily under a window, and then the sound of the Pontiac's engine.

"I couldn't see what happened," he said. "With the gun."
Sia smiled at him in mild puzzlement. Farrell said, "She
called you *mother*."

Sia plucked at the front of her dress, the nervous habit of a
heavy woman. "I must go up to poor Robert," she said. "He
will spend half our time now apologizing for coming in without knocking. Such a strange arrogance they have, the timid
ones, how they peep at themselves." She sniffed and rubbed
her nose, having had a cold for two days.

Farrell watched her hoisting herself up the steps one at a
time, pausing on the landing to sigh angrily, as she always
did. Briseis came to shove her muzzle into his hand, and Farrell petted her, saying absently, "It's all right, don't be
scared." But Briseis smelled the gunshot and the blood, and
she simply lay down flat, too overcome by human confusions

even to whine. Farrell said, "Don't think about it, that's all. Just be a dog, that's what I'm doing." He took her outside to sit on the front steps, where she found her favorite ragged beach towel and killed it several times, while he played some of Henry VIII's songs for her.

THE PASSING STRANGE:
Supernatural Fiction

IN FANTASY fiction the reader goes questing for marvels; in supernatural fiction the marvels find the reader at home. Fantasy takes us to a Secondary World; we either accompany the story's characters to another world altogether, or we discover the Other World parallel to our own, reached by stepping through a mirror, stumbling down a secret path, or entering a forest which proves to be enchanted. In supernatural fiction, the world of the story is the world as you and I know it, and the supernatural is an intrusion, usually not a welcome one, into the secure order of everyday life. In both kinds of stories we come away suspecting that there is more to reality than we might have thought: in fantasy that suspicion is a delightful one, in supernatural fiction it is an unnerving surmise wont to make us look carefully in darkened corners and to snap our heads about to bring the periphery of vision into full focus as we try to catch the quick shapes lurking there.

In both kinds of fiction the narrative comes to terms with realities beyond the mundane; both heighten our awareness of mortality and its consequences by trafficking in the immortal. In fantasy, the preternatural, the magical underlies the world of the narrative and becomes a positive force, one which we can accept and feel comfortable with no matter how grand, how awesome, how potent its workings may appear. In supernatural fiction, the forces which underlie the world are the same ones we are accustomed to and the energy of the preternatural is an invasion; it seems a shock, an outrage, an alien energy bent on disrupting the probabilities of cause and effect on which we predicate our daily behavior. In supernatural stories, we are always given the loosening sense of things beyond our control. To some extent this is true in fantasy, but with magic one has the expectation that there is an order there, which, if discovered and abided within, will keep the questor from losing his way altogether. Supernatural fiction reveals breaks in the one order we already are sure of —the daily round. Interestingly enough, the marvels of supernatural fiction pale beside those of fantasy; the disheveled, barely visible specter of a human, often mute, sometimes only a blurred outline, seems puny beside the immense, scaled iridescence of a dragon coiled on the landscape like a mountain with a furnace at its heart. The difference is that to find a dragon we must likely go searching if we are ever to see one at all, whereas a good ghost story reminds us that merely renting a house (as in Sheridan Le Fanu's "An Account of Some Strange Disturbances in Aungier Street"), or doing some other mundane activity, may be an invitation to disaster.

How is it that a ghost story can chill us in a way that even the darkest fantasy cannot? Perhaps the answer is in potentiality. Fantasy fiction is predicated on the impossible: if the world is as we know it to be on a daily basis, then dragons will not accost us on the way to the supermarket. Supernatural fiction is predicated on the merely inexplicable, and worse than that, it edges close to what might be almost explained. Ghosts are much more rationally feasible than dragons; ghosts are what any of us might encounter or become. The suggestion of a human shape barely visible in the night, the faint calling of a voice we think we recognize though that voice should be stilled in death, belong to the realm of what might be. In supernatural fiction, the ordinary world is recurrently separated from the Other World by death, which may be a chasm that neither living nor dead can breech, but may also be a fine line, the merest shimmer of a veil. Since we cannot reasonably know the proximity of this world to that world beyond, the likelihood of a visitation to the quick from the dead requires very little encouragement to seem real. Then, too, the press of mortality is always clearly felt in a ghost story, for even if death does not come as the gaily dancing lady of Peter Beagle's tale, it will come, and the inevitability of that is the witness the dead bear to the living in these stories. Fantasy fiction is transcendent and lifts us to realms where time has little meaning and death a limited dominion. Supernatural fiction gains part of its hold on us by infusing death into life abnormally.

It is the promised end of most ghost and supernatural tales to make the reader uncomfortable. More than any other kind of fiction it is aimed at an immediate emotional result; if the narrative is successful it has its way with us, not we with it. Ghost stories are not meant for exploration and interpretation—though many leave us wondering just how much to believe—they are meant to chill us, to waken foreboding which ranges from nervousness to horror depending on the story. In E. F. Benson's introduction to a collection entitled *The Room in the Tower*, he tells us the stories

> . . . have been written in the hope of giving some pleasant qualms . . . so that, if by chance, anyone may be occupying in their perusal a leisure half-hour before he goes to bed, when the night and the house are still, he may perhaps cast an occasional glance into the corners and dark places of the room where he sits, to make sure that nothing unusual lurks in the shadow. For this is the avowed object of ghost-stories and such tales as deal with the dim, unseen forces which occasionally and perturbingly make themselves manifest. The author therefore fervently wishes his readers a few uncomfortable moments.[1]

Part of the effect a supernatural tale has on its readers derives from its folk-tale heritage. Tales of the supernatural belong to the group of story types called legends, extraordinary events believed to have actually happened. By the time a legend is told the teller may not really believe it, but he tells it as though it were true (wonder tales are not told as true; they are always acknowledged fictions even if their marvels seem believable). To make the tale seem true, the teller will often try to authenticate it by referring to his source,

[1] E. F. Benson, *The Room in the Tower* (London: Mills and Bon, Ltd., 1912), p. vii.

sometimes naming a particular person, and if possible a person known to the listeners. The teller will often grant that the story seems outrageous and then will insist that it is true: "This is a crazy story, I know you're going to say, maybe even impossible, but it happened to a friend of mine who saw it with his own eyes." Also tellers of legends, or belief tales, usually try to place them in a specific locale, in familiar surroundings. For instance, the ghostly hitchhiker story, a staple of slumber parties and fireside tale-telling all over America, has as many versions of the tale as there are towns for it to be set in. The action of the tale[2] is everywhere basically the same, but with every telling it becomes to a degree localized, carefully documenting the exact spot of the occurrence. The power of the belief tale is in its credibility, and naming authorities or locations encourages credence. Even when the tale is long separated from its source, its events and characters live on, strengthened by the fact that they once inspired belief, and it continues to be told as true long past the time when anyone anywhere could verify it.

Many literary ghost stories and supernatural tales are, in fact, legends and belief tales from the European tale body; others are legends or stories an author has heard at some time, and some are, of course, the creations of the author's imagination, but all use the basic motifs common to supernatural stories everywhere. All depend on the same sort of credibility any legend demands: that the tales have some truth to experience, that they happened to someone.

Supernatural tales are of two basic kinds and both are as old as man's fear of the unknown. There are ghost tales which properly and obviously concern themselves with apparitions of some sort, revenants, specters, ghostly messengers, and harbingers of death. And there are weird tales which are stories dependent less on a particular apparition than on the

---

[2] The basic action of the story is usually that a driver picks up a girl hitchhiking on a rainy night and is told she has been in an accident. The driver offers to take her home to her parents and when they arrive there he drops her off, only to discover she has left a wrap in the car. He returns to the parents' house where he is told that their daughter has died some time previously in an accident.

evocation of fear, or dread, as H. P. Lovecraft said, ". . . of contact with unknown spheres and power; a subtle attitude of awed listening, as if for the beating of black wings or the scratching of outside shapes and entities on the known universe's utmost rim."[3] Both kinds are represented in oral tales, and they began to find their ways into literature in Assyria and Egypt; throughout the ancient world the impulse to confront the weird and terrifying, the transcendentally fearful, was close to religious impulse, and these tales are crystallized in sacred script the world over. Greek and Roman literature is full of phantoms, spirits, and presences, and in the Middle Ages the supernatural in literature reveals the general respect and awe of the supernatural in life. In a time when ballads of elfin knights commanded at least some degree of belief, tales told as legends, stories of the return of the dead or of other horrifying spectres, had an unchallenged convincement.

The period of the Reformation and Enlightenment, which caused wonder tales to be regarded more and more as fanciful fiction, had a different effect on the supernatural tale. The first gleams of Enlightenment and the growing urge to rationality did not discredit the supernatural so much as take some areas of it as subject for study. Learned treatises on ghosts and witches appeared. Perhaps the earliest was by Ludwig Lavater of Zurich, who published in 1570 a treatise translated into English in 1572 as *Of Ghosts and Spirites Walking by Nyght and of Strange Noyses, Crackes, and Sundry Forewarnynges*. Since then non-fiction studies of supernatural phenomena have regularly appeared, and today many scientists wrestle with the problem of ghosts, "crackes and sundry forewarnynges." Evidently the more genial wonder tale with its admittedly fictional intent and its exotic wonders and amazements is easy to discredit. Legends portentous and ghastly, ghosts and other things that "go bump in the night" are not.

Ghosts met with popular acclaim in the plays of blood and horror on the Elizabethan and Restoration stage, and in the

[3] H. P. Lovecraft, *Supernatural Horror in Literature* (New York: Dover Publications, Inc., 1973), p. 16.

seventeenth and early eighteenth centuries the conventions
of these plays, together with a revival of Romantic feeling,
combined to bring the supernatural out from beneath the
surface of polite, accepted literature in a new form: the
Gothic novel. In the Gothic novel, the sentimental, the horrible, and the supernatural were combined and the typical
weird tale with which we are familiar today found its literary
expression. The groaning ghosts, sepulchral dungeons, murdered innocents, tortured shades, and mangled visitants
which were stock figures in the Gothics captured the public
imagination, and a great flowering of supernatural fiction occurred in the late eighteenth and in the nineteenth centuries.
Eerie and gruesome romantic novels and tales in magazines
proliferated, and while much of this fiction is dreary and rep-
etitious, out of this period came the semi-Gothic, romantic
tale that is the basic shape of the literary ghost story and
most weird fiction. To this period belongs the work of Mary
Shelley, Sheridan Le Fanu, Wilkie Collins, Conan Doyle,
Edgar Allan Poe, and Robert Louis Stevenson, to name only
a few.

The element of credibility and the demands it places on a
narrative made the fictitious tale of terror a peculiar combination of timeless and timely. While the fear and awe which
ground the tales are basic to sensitive persons in any time, supernatural stories must always make careful contact with the
natural before sweeping the listener or reader into the supernatural. In this way the fiction develops a kind of internal
dating which is evident even when one author is heavily
influenced by an earlier author. Just as orally related legends
root themselves in a locale, so fictional tales of the supernatural tend to root in an era. In order to make the context
of the story seem ordinary to readers, thereby defining what
is extraordinary, the writer must pay attention not only to
place and manner of speech but to social customs of the
time. Supernatural tales generally betray something of the
manners and mores of the audience for which they are intended. For instance, the mid-Victorian interest, even delight, in funereal trappings—in interments and wakes and
sepulchral requirements—is reflected in the ghost stories of

this period, while more recent tales lean to descriptions of other events. In contemporary stories the supernatural often seems to intrude on a holiday, which may well say something of the supernatural speculations of an age enormously concerned with its leisure.

In the early twentieth century the literary ghost tale reached its peak in the stories of M. R. James, Oliver Onions, Algernon Blackwood, and M. P. Shiel. American writers of this period turned more toward weird fiction and horror (Henry James and Edith Wharton are notable exceptions), and in this country the supernatural story became a mainstay of the pulp magazines, and there reached, primarily through *Weird Tales* and its imitators, an increasingly wider readership. During the thirties, forties, and fifties weird fiction enjoyed a heyday, though chiefly in other forms than the ghost tale. While an occasional ghost appeared, most of the weird fiction of the pulp era, and the fiction of writers who grew up with that era, leans toward a vaguely defined horror utilizing what might be called "Lovecraftian" requirements: "atmospheric details . . . impressionistic imagination . . . [and] a malign tensity or psychological verisimilitude."[4]

As much as supernatural tales have differed in subject and style across their history, they all share the same premise: the breakthrough of the supernatural into the normal. Supernatural tales, particularly ghost stories, center on one event—the intrusion of one world into another—and though they also work to establish a mood—which in some cases becomes more pervasive and memorable than the event—still that one climactic event and its ramifications are the center of the story. This does not mean that a ghost can only appear once in a story, of course; the controlling event is that it appears at all and the rest of the story turns on the import of that occurrence. The focus is on action in the story; even when the action has to do with the disintegration of a personality under the pressure of the supernatural, the psychology is so closely connected with the intrusion of the preternatural, that we are really less interested in subtle characterization

[4] Ibid., p. 43.

than in seeing what *happens*. Perhaps this focus on action is a result of the nature of ghosts and other supernatural phenomena: they are phenomena, not persons, even when they assume human shape. We might be made privy to information about what kind of person a ghost was when he was alive, usually to let us know why he deserves to be restlessly wandering about eternity, but to the characters in the story and to us as we read it, the ghost is not a person but an event. Asked about the likelihood of ghosts, Robert Graves replied,

> The common sense view is, I think, that one should accept ghosts very much as one accepts fire—a more common but equally mysterious phenomenon. What is fire? It is not really an element, not a principle of motion, not a living creature—not even a disease though a house can catch fire from its neighbors. It is an event rather than a thing or a creature. Ghosts, similarly, seem to be events rather than things or creatures.[5]

Ghost stories are about these "events" and weird tales recount events whereby the supernatural is made palpable within the natural world. Very rarely do these tales ramble off into philosophizing about whys and wherefores; they report the circumstances and leave the reader to his own conclusions.

The teller of a supernatural tale, much like the teller of an oral legend, conventionally spends some of his narrative establishing the credibility of the tale in the person of an authority, or in the "fact" of a found letter, a diary, journal, or manuscript. The "classic" form of the ghost tale is that of a narrator or main character who establishes his own credentials as a rational person, normally unflinching in the face of even the creepiest situations, the sort of person who would not hesitate to sleep in a cemetery were he not too sensible to be out catching his death of cold. The Professor of Ontography in M. R. James's "Oh, Whistle, and I'll Come to You, My Lad" is such a man. The narrator also frequently

[5] Quoted by Peter Haining in *Ghosts: An Illustrated History* (New York: Macmillan Publishing Co., Inc., 1975), p. 125.

offers some other authority or confirmation: the person who
rented him the haunted house, the recipient of a packet of
letters wherein the horrible tale is told, the neighbors or servants who know of other persons frightened away from the
place. Sometimes, the narrator is a person whose detachment
from the events of the tale is such that he presents himself
as an unbiased observer, merely passing the tale along. Sometimes, he is one whose life has been profoundly altered by
the supernatural (in Doris Betts's story, Benson Watts is
such a narrator though ironically it is his death which is altered). Even if the stories are told from an omniscient point
of view, we are given a center of consciousness, one person
whom we get to know more intimately than the others. In a
sense, we see through that character's eyes even if he is not
actually telling the story. In all supernatural stories, there
must be one character, profoundly affected by the supernatural, with whom we are familiar enough that we can feel
"through" that character the effects of the disruption of the
natural order.

Supernatural stories also establish credibility through a
scrupulous attention to detail, to the stuff of daily life. For
the ghost or supernatural element to seem an encroachment
upon the familiar, we must be given the scope of what is familiar. So the minutiae of life are important to the description in these tales. Detail is equally necessary to fantasy
where the author must make us at home in a Secondary
World, but these may be the details of the marvelous. In a
ghost story, or weird tale, the purpose of detail is to let us
see that we are standing on a regular old everyday rug, and
then to pull that rug out from under our feet. Whereas
fantasy develops its own frame, supernatural fiction is framed
by the ordinary. Lovecraft, in his *Supernatural Horror in Literature*, describes the use of this frame:

> To make a fictional marvel wear the momentary aspect
> of existing fact, we must give it the most elaborate pos-
> sible approach—building up insidiously and gradually
> out of apparently realistic material, realistically handled.
> The time is past when adults can accept marvelous con-
> ditions for granted. Every energy must be bent toward

the weaving of a frame of mind which shall make the
story's single departure from nature seem credible—and
in the weaving of this moon the utmost subtlety and
verisimilitude is required. In every detail except the
chosen marvel, the story should be accurately true to
nature.[6]

This attention to verisimilitude serves a particularly important function in stories about horrors other than ghosts. Psy-
chologists have shown that people and animals most fear
what is similar but discrepant. A chimp is more frightened by
a picture of a chimp with too many legs than by a picture of
an animal with which he has no experience at all, and humans evidently carry a similar unease. So it is in supernatural
fiction that we are most likely to be moved by an event
which is alien to us taking place in normal surroundings, or
by an apparition similar to but discrepant from what we
know as real.

Through a ghost or weird tale, we account carefully for the
elements which are ordinary, looking for the one which is
strange. These stories are close cousins to detective fiction in
a variety of ways, but perhaps most noticeably in the kind of
unraveling which goes on in the tale. Often in a supernatural
story we have no idea what we are pursuing, or even sometimes that we are in an occult situation at all until we are
well into it. In Elizabeth Jane Howard's "Three Miles Up,"
for instance, it is not until the end that we know our journey
into the uncanny has been inexorable throughout the tale;
only after the last page of such a story do we go back through
it looking for clues about where the line between the ordinary and the alien was crossed.

In supernatural stories the reaction of both characters and
readers to the trespass of the Other World is generally that
the situation needs to be remedied and the usual order restored. Fantasy fiction shows an ordered world, even if the
scheme of things is different from the one we know; though
fantasy depends on paradox and incongruity, all is held
within the magic circle, and paradox is drawn out until the

6 Lovecraft quoted by Lin Carter in Lovecraft: A Look Behind the
Cthluhu Mythos (New York: Ballantine Books, 1972), p. xv.

ends meet. A useful emblem for fantasy is the worm Ouroboros, the cosmic serpent which bites its own tail to form a living girdle for the world. In supernatural fiction, on the other hand, the order is split, and as the veil is torn, the commonplace is sometimes rent entirely and irremediably. In a magical tale, there is a knitting up; everything achieves its place, the great capabilities of the hero are realized, and the essence of creatures and characters and their powers are revealed through the magic. In a supernatural tale, essence and capabilities in the natural world are often thwarted or perverted by the intervention of the supernatural. Confronted with a persistently alien element, the characters must accommodate or give up forever the order of their lives. Very often they cannot make this accommodation and are doomed to madness or death as is the writer in Oliver Onions' "The Beckoning Fair One." The only other ending possible in a supernatural tale is the banishing of the ghost, the exorcism of the spirit, or the removal of the living characters to some place where they are again safe from the unwelcome visitation of the dead. The cost of this is often high, as Peter Beagle's fable reveals. A really good ghost or weird tale leaves us with the alarm that the natural order as we understand it is forever susceptible to violation by the supernatural.

The following tales include ones by acknowledged masters of the ghost tale such as James, Onions, and Blackwood, as well as stories by lesser-known writers or writers who dabble only occasionally in the occult or macabre. The classic ghost story is not a fashionable genre these days, though certainly it retains a faithful readership, and one seldom finds contemporary ghost stories as good as some of the older ones. Perhaps now that psychic phenomena have become a nearly respectable field of scientific study producing recordings of ghostly rustles and photographs of spirits, the mystery on which such tales depend is being dispelled. The more recent stories here explore areas of the supernatural other than apparitions. In every story, however, the unnerving sense of the "passing strange" is effectively accomplished, and the reader will find more than a few "uncomfortable moments."

AN ACCOUNT OF SOME
STRANGE DISTURBANCES
IN AUNGIER STREET

By J. Sheridan Le Fanu

IT IS not worth telling, this story of mine—at least, not
worth writing. Told, indeed, as I have sometimes been called
upon to tell it, to a circle of intelligent and eager faces,
lighted up by a good after-dinner fire on a winter's evening,
with a cold wind rising and wailing outside, and all snug and
cosy within, it has gone off—though I say it, who should not
—indifferent well. But it is a venture to do as you would
have me. Pen, ink, and paper are cold vehicles for the marvellous, and a "reader" decidedly a more critical animal than
a "listener." If, however, you can induce your friends to read
it after nightfall, and when the fireside talk has run for a
while on thrilling tales of shapeless terror; in short, if you will
secure me the *mollia tempora fandi*, I will go to my work,
and say my say, with better heart. Well, then, these conditions presupposed, I shall waste no more words, but tell you
simply how it all happened.

My cousin (Tom Ludlow) and I studied medicine together. I think he would have succeeded, had he stuck to the
profession; but he preferred the Church, poor fellow, and
died early, a sacrifice to contagion, contracted in the noble
discharge of his duties. For my present purpose, I say enough
of his character when I mention that he was of a sedate but
frank and cheerful nature; very exact in his observance of
truth, and not by any means like myself—of an excitable or
nervous temperament.

My Uncle Ludlow—Tom's father—while we were attending lectures, purchased three or four old houses in Aungier
Street, one of which was unoccupied. *He* resided in the coun-

try, and Tom proposed that we should take up our abode in the untenanted house, so long as it should continue unlet; a move which would accomplish the double end of settling us nearer alike to our lecture-rooms and to our amusements, and of relieving us from the weekly charge of rent for our lodgings.

Our furniture was very scant—our whole equipage remarkably modest and primitive; and, in short, our arrangements pretty nearly as simple as those of a bivouac. Our new plan was, therefore, executed almost as soon as conceived. The front drawing-room was our sitting-room. I had the bedroom over it, and Tom the back bedroom on the same floor, which nothing could have induced me to occupy.

The house, to begin with, was a very old one. It had been, I believe, newly fronted about fifty years before; but with this exception, it had nothing modern about it. The agent who bought it and looked into the titles for my uncle, told me that it was sold, along with much other forfeited property, at Chichester House, I think, in 1702; and had belonged to Sir Thomas Hacket, who Lord Mayor of Dublin in James II's time. How old it was *then*, I can't say; but, at all events, it had seen years and changes enough to have contracted all that mysterious and saddened air, at once exciting and depressing, which belongs to most old mansions.

There had been very little done in the way of modernising details; and, perhaps, it was better so; for there was something queer and by-gone in the very walls and ceilings—in the shape of doors and windows—in the odd diagonal site of the chimney-pieces—in the beams and ponderous cornices—not to mention the singular solidity of all the woodwork, from the banisters to the window frames, which hopelessly defied disguise, and would have emphatically proclaimed their antiquity through any conceivable amount of modern finery and varnish.

An effort had, indeed, been made, to the extent of papering the drawing-rooms; but, somehow the paper looked raw and out of keeping; and the old woman, who kept a little dirt-pie of a shop in the lane, and whose daughter—a girl of two and fifty—was our solitary handmaid, coming in at sunrise, and chastely receding again as soon as she had made all ready for tea in our state apartment;—this woman, I say, remembered it, when old Judge Horrocks (who, having earned the reputation of a particularly "hanging judge," ended by hanging himself, as the coroner's jury found, under an impulse of "temporary insanity," with a child's skipping-rope, over the massive old banisters) resided there, entertaining good company, with fine venison and rare old port. In those halcyon days, the drawing-rooms were hung with gilded leather, and, I dare say, cut a good figure, for they were really spacious rooms.

The bedrooms were wainscoted, but the front one was not gloomy; and in it the cosiness of antiquity quite overcame its sombre associations. But the back bedroom, with its two queerly-placed melancholy windows, staring vacantly at the foot of the bed, and with the shadowy recess to be found in most old houses in Dublin, like a large ghostly closet, which, from congeniality of temperament, had amalgamated with the bedchamber, and dissolved the partition. At night-time, this "alcove"—as our "maid" was wont to call it—had, in my eyes, a specially sinister and suggestive character. Tom's distant and solitary candle glimmered vainly into its darkness. *There* it was always overlooking him—always itself impenetrable. But this was only part of the effect. The whole room was, I can't tell how, repulsive to me. There was, I suppose, in its proportions and features, a latent discord—a certain mysterious and indescribable relation, which jarred indistinctly upon some secret sense of the fitting and the safe, and raised indefinable suspicions and apprehensions of the imagination. On the whole, as I began by saying, nothing could have induced me to pass a night alone in it.

I had never pretended to conceal from poor Tom my superstitious weakness; and he, on the other hand, most unaffectedly ridiculed my tremors. The sceptic was, however, destined to receive a lesson, as you shall hear.

We had not been very long in occupation of our respective dormitories, when I began to complain of uneasy nights and disturbed sleep. I was, I suppose, the more impatient under this annoyance, as I was usually a sound sleeper, and by no means prone to nightmares. It was now, however, my destiny, instead of enjoying my customary repose, every night to "sup full of horrors." After a preliminary course of disagreeable and frightful dreams, my troubles took a definite form, and the same vision, without an appreciable variation in a single detail, visited me at least (on an average) every second night in the week.

Now, this dream, nightmare, or infernal illusion—which you please—of which I was the miserable sport, was on this wise:—

I saw, or thought I saw, with the most abominable distinctness, although at the time in profound darkness, every article of furniture and accidental arrangement of the chamber in which I lay. This, as you know, is incidental to ordinary nightmare. Well, while in this clairvoyant condition, which seemed but the lighting up of the theatre in which was to be exhibited the monotonous tableau of horror, which made my nights insupportable, my attention invariably became, I know not why, fixed upon the windows opposite the foot of my bed; and, uniformly with the same effect, a sense of dreadful anticipation always took slow but sure possession of me. I became somehow conscious of a sort of horrid but undefined preparation going forward in some unknown quarter, and by some unknown agency, for my torment; and, after an interval, which always seemed to me of the same length, a picture suddenly flew up to the window, where it remained fixed, as if by an electrical attraction, and my discipline of horror then commenced, to last perhaps for hours. The picture thus mysteriously glued to the window-panes, was the portrait of an old man, in a crimson flowered silk dressing-gown, the folds of which I could now describe, with a countenance embodying a strange mixture of intellect, sensuality, and power, but withal sinister and full of malignant omen. His nose was hooked, like the beak of a vulture; his eyes large, grey, and prominent, and lighted up with a more than mortal cruelty and coldness. These features were surmounted by a crimson velvet cap, the hair that peeped from under which was white with age, while the eyebrows retained their original blackness. Well I remember every line, hue, and shadow of that stony countenance, and well I may! The gaze of this hellish visage was fixed upon me, and mine returned it with the inexplicable fascination of nightmare, for what appeared to me to be hours of agony. At last—

> *"The cock he crew, away then flew"*

the fiend who had enslaved me through the awful watches of the night; and, harassed and nervous, I rose to the duties of the day.

I had—I can't say exactly why, but it may have been from the exquisite anguish and profound impressions of unearthly horror, with which this strange phantasmagoria was associated—an insurmountable antipathy to describing the exact nature of my nightly troubles to my friend and comrade. Generally, however, I told him that I was haunted by abominable dreams; and, true to the imputed materialism of medicine, we put our heads together to dispel my horrors, not by exorcism, but by a tonic.

I will do this tonic justice, and frankly admit that the accursed portrait began to intermit its visits under its influence. What of that? Was this singular apparition—as full of character as of terror—therefore the creature of my fancy, or the invention of my poor stomach? Was it, in short, *subjective* (to borrow the technical slang of the day) and not the palpable aggression and intrusion of an external agent? That, good friend, as we will both admit, by no means follows. The evil spirit, who enthralled my senses in the shape of that portrait, may have been just as near me, just as energetic, just as malignant, though I saw him not. What means the whole moral code of revealed religion regarding the due keeping of our own bodies, soberness, temperance, etc.? here is an obvious connexion between the material and the invisible; the healthy tone of the system, and its unimpaired energy, may, for aught we can tell, guard us against influences which would otherwise render life itself terrific. The mesmerist and the electro-biologist will fail upon an average with nine patients out of ten—so may the evil spirit. Special conditions of the corporeal system are indispensable to the production of certain spiritual phenomena. The operation succeeds some-times—sometimes fails—that is all.

I found afterwards that my would-be sceptical companion had his troubles too. But of these I knew nothing yet. One night, for a wonder, I was sleeping soundly, when I was roused by a step on the lobby outside my room, followed by the loud clang of what turned out to be a large brass candle-stick, flung with all his force by poor Tom Ludlow over the banisters, and rattling with a rebound down the second flight of stairs; and almost concurrently with this, Tom burst open my door, and bounced into my room backwards, in a state of extraordinary agitation.

I had jumped out of bed and clutched him by the arm be-fore I had any distinct idea of my own whereabouts. There we were—in our shirts—standing before the open door—star-ing through the great old banister opposite, at the lobby win-dow, through which the sickly light of a clouded moon was gleaming.

"What's the matter, Tom? What's the matter with you? What the devil's the matter with you, Tom?" I demanded, shaking him with nervous impatience.

He took a long breath before he answered me, and then it was not very coherently.

"It's nothing, nothing at all—did I speak?—what did I say?—where's the candle, Richard? It's dark; I—I had a candle!"

"Yes, dark enough," I said, "but what's the matter?—what *is* it?—why don't you speak, Tom?—have you lost your wits? —what is the matter?"

"The matter?—oh, it is all over. It must have been a dream—nothing at all but a dream—don't you think so? It could not be anything more than a dream."

"Of course," said I, feeling uncommonly nervous, "it *was* a dream."

"I thought," he said, "there was a man in my room, and—and I jumped out of bed; and—and—where's the candle?"

"In your room, most likely," I said, "shall I go and bring it?"

"No; stay here—don't go; it's no matter—don't, I tell you;

it was all a dream. Bolt the door, Dick; I'll stay here with you
—I feel nervous. So, Dick, like a good fellow, light your candle and open the window—I am in a *shocking state*."

I did as he asked me, and robing himself like Granuaile in
one of my blankets, he seated himself close beside my bed.

Everybody knows how contagious is fear of all sorts, but
more especially that particular kind of fear under which poor
Tom was at that moment labouring. I would not have heard,
nor I believe would he have recapitulated, just at that moment, for half the world, the details of the hideous vision
which had so unmanned him.

"Don't mind telling me anything about your nonsensical
dream, Tom," said I, affecting contempt, really in a panic;
"let us talk about something else; but it is quite plain that
this dirty old house disagrees with us both, and hang me if I
stay here any longer, to be pestered with indigestion and—
and—bad nights, so we may as well look out for lodgings—
don't you think so?—at once."

Tom agreed, and, after an interval, said—

"I have been thinking, Richard, that it is a long time since
I saw my father, and I have made up my mind to go down
tomorrow and return in a day or two, and you can take rooms
for us in the meantime."

I fancied that this resolution, obviously the result of the vision which had so profoundly scared him, would probably
vanish next morning with the damps and shadows of night.
But I was mistaken. Off went Tom at peep of day to the
country, having agreed that so soon as I had secured suitable
lodgings, I was to recall him by letter from his visit to my
Uncle Ludlow.

Now, anxious as I was to change my quarters, it so happened, owing to a series of petty procrastinations and accidents, that nearly a week elapsed before my bargain was
made and my letter of recall on the wing to Tom; and, in the
meantime, a trifling adventure or two had occurred to your
humble servant, which, absurd as they now appear, di-
minished by distance, did certainly at the time serve to whet
my appetite for change considerably.

A night or two after the departure of my comrade, I was

sitting by my bedroom fire, the door locked, and the ingredients of a tumbler of hot whisky-punch upon the crazy spider-table; for, as the best mode of keeping the

> *"Black spirits and white,*
> *Blue spirits and grey,"*

with which I was environed, at bay, I had adopted the practice recommended by the wisdom of my ancestors, and "kept my spirits up by pouring spirits down." I had thrown aside my volume of Anatomy, and was treating myself by way of a tonic, preparatory to my punch and bed, to half-a-dozen pages of the *Spectator*, when I heard a step on the flight of stairs descending from the attics. It was two o'clock, and the streets were as silent as a churchyard—the sounds were, therefore, perfectly distinct. There was a slow, heavy tread, characterised by the emphasis and deliberation of age, descending by the narrow staircase from above; and, what made the sound more singular, it was plain that the feet which produced it were perfectly bare, measuring the descent with something between a pound and a flop, very ugly to hear.

I knew quite well that my attendant had gone away many hours before, and that nobody but myself had any business in the house. It was quite plain also that the person who was coming downstairs had no intention whatever of concealing his movements; but, on the contrary, appeared disposed to make even more noise, and proceed more deliberately, than was at all necessary. When the step reached the foot of the stairs outside my room, it seemed to stop; and I expected every moment to see my door open spontaneously, and give admission to the original of my detested portrait. I was, however, relieved in a few seconds by hearing the descent renewed, just in the same manner, upon the staircase leading down to the drawing-rooms, and thence, after another pause, down the next flight, and so on to the hall, whence I heard no more.

Now, by the time the sound had ceased, I was wound up, as they say, to a very unpleasant pitch of excitement. I listened, but there was not a stir. I screwed up my courage to a decisive experiment—opened my door, and in a stentorian voice bawled over the banisters, "Who's there?" There was no answer, but the ringing of my own voice through the empty old house,—no renewal of the movement; nothing, in short, to give my unpleasant sensations a definite direction. There is, I think, something most disagreeably disenchanting in the sound of one's own voice under such circumstances, exerted in solitude and in vain. It redoubled my sense of isolation, and my misgivings increased on perceiving that the door, which I certainly thought I had left open, was closed behind me; in a vague alarm, lest my retreat should be cut off, I got again into my room as quickly as I could, where I remained in a state of imaginary blockade, and very uncomfortable indeed, till morning.

Next night brought no return of my barefooted fellow-lodger; but the night following, being in my bed, and in the dark—somewhere, I suppose, about the same hour as before, I distinctly heard the old fellow again descending from the garrets.

This time I had had my punch, and the *morale* of the garrison was consequently excellent. I jumped out of bed, clutched the poker as I passed the expiring fire, and in a moment was upon the lobby. The sound had ceased by this time —the dark and chill were discouraging; and, guess my horror, when I saw, or thought I saw, a black monster, whether in the shape of a man or a bear I could not say, standing, with its back to the wall, on the lobby, facing me, with a pair of great greenish eyes shining dimly out. Now, I must be frank, and confess that the cupboard which displayed our plates and cups stood just there, though at the moment I did not recollect it. At the same time I must honestly say, that making every allowance for an excited imagination, I never could satisfy myself that I was made the dupe of my own fancy in this matter; for this apparition, after one or two shiftings of shape, as if in the act of incipient transformation, began, as it seemed on second thoughts, to advance upon me in its original form. From an instinct of terror rather than of courage, I hurled the poker, with all my force, at its head; and to the music of a horrid crash made my way into my room, and double-locked the door. Then, in a minute more, I heard the horrid bare feet walk down the stairs, till the sound ceased in the hall, as on the former occasion.

If the apparition of the night before was an ocular delusion of my fancy sporting with the dark outlines of our cupboard, and if its horrid eyes were nothing but a pair of inverted teacups, I had, at all events, the satisfaction of having launched the poker with admirable effect, and in true "fancy" phrase, "knocked its two daylights into one," as the commingled fragments of my tea-service testified. I did my best to gather comfort and courage from these evidences; but it would not do. And then what could I say of those horrid bare feet, and the regular tramp, tramp, tramp, which measured the distance of the entire staircase through the solitude of my haunted dwelling, and at an hour when no good influence was stirring? Confound it!—the whole affair was abominable. I was out of spirits, and dreaded the approach of night.

It came, ushered ominously in with a thunder-storm and dull torrents of depressing rain. Earlier than usual the streets grew silent; and by twelve o'clock nothing but the comfortless pattering of the rain was to be heard.

I made myself as snug as I could. I lighted *two* candles instead of one. I forswore bed, and held myself in readiness for a sally, candle in hand; for, *coute qui coute*, I was resolved to *see* the being, if visible at all, who troubled the nightly stillness of my mansion. I was fidgety and nervous and, tried in vain to interest myself with my books. I walked up and down my room, whistling in turn martial and hilarious music, and listening ever and anon for the dreaded noise. I sat down and stared at the square label on the solemn and reserved-looking black bottle, until "FLANAGAN & CO.'S BEST OLD MALT WHISKY" grew into a sort of subdued accompaniment to all the fantastic and horrible speculations which chased one another through my brain.

Silence, meanwhile, grew more silent, and darkness darker. I listened in vain for the rumble of a vehicle, or the dull clamour of a distant row. There was nothing but the sound of a rising wind, which had succeeded the thunder-storm that had travelled over the Dublin mountains quite out of hearing. In the middle of this great city I began to feel myself alone with nature, and Heaven knows what beside. My courage was ebbing. Punch, however, which makes beasts of so many, made a man of me again—just in time to hear with tolerable nerve and firmness the lumpy, flabby, naked feet deliberately descending the stairs again.

I took a candle, not without a tremor. As I crossed the floor I tried to extemporise a prayer, but stopped short to listen, and never finished it. The steps continued. I confess I hesitated for some seconds at the door before I took heart of grace and opened it. When I peeped out the lobby was perfectly empty—there was no monster standing on the staircase; and as the detested sound ceased, I was reassured enough to venture forward nearly to the banisters. Horror of horrors! within a stair or two beneath the spot where I stood the unearthly tread smote the floor. My eye caught something in motion; it was about the size of Goliath's foot—it was grey, heavy, and flapped with a dead weight from one step to another. As I am alive, it was the most monstrous grey rat I ever beheld or imagined.

Shakespeare says—"Some men there are cannot abide a gaping pig, and some that are mad if they behold a cat." I went well-nigh out of my wits when I beheld this *rat*; for, laugh at me as you may, it fixed upon me, I thought, a perfectly human expression of malice; and, as it shuffled about and looked up into my face almost from between my feet, I saw, I could swear it—I felt it then, and know it now, the infernal gaze and the accursed countenance of my old friend in the portrait, transfused into the visage of the bloated vermin before me.

I bounced into my room again with a feeling of loathing and horror I cannot describe, and locked and bolted my door as if a lion had been at the other side. D——n him or *it*; curse the portrait and its original! I felt in my soul that the rat—yes the *rat*, the RAT I had just seen, was that evil being in masquerade and rambling through the house upon some infernal night lark.

Next morning I was early trudging through the miry streets; and, among other transactions, posted a peremptory note recalling Tom. On my return, however, I found a note from my absent "chum," announcing his intended return next day. I was doubly rejoiced at this, because I had succeeded in getting rooms; and because the change of scene and return of my comrade were rendered specially pleasant by the last night's half ridiculous half horrible adventure.

I slept extemporaneously in my new quarters in Digges' Street that night, and next morning returned for breakfast to the haunted mansion, where I was certain Tom would call immediately on his arrival.

I was quite right—he came; and almost his first question referred to the primary object of our change of residence.

"Thank God," he said with genuine fervour, on hearing that all was arranged. "On *your* account I am delighted. As to myself, I assure you that no earthly consideration could have induced me ever again to pass a night in this disastrous old house."

"Confound the house!" I ejaculated, with a genuine mixture of fear and detestation, "we have not had a pleasant hour since we came to live here"; and so I went on, and related incidentally my adventure with the plethoric old rat.

"Well, if that were *all*," said my cousin, affecting to make light of the matter, "I don't think I should have minded it very much."

"Ay, but its eye—it countenance, my dear Tom," urged I; "if you had seen *that*, you would have felt it might be *anything* but what it seemed."

"I am inclined to think the best conjurer in such a case would be an able-bodied cat," he said, with a provoking chuckle.

"But let us hear your own adventure," I said tartly.

At this challenge he looked uneasily round him. I had poked up a very unpleasant recollection.

"You shall hear it, Dick; I'll tell it to you," he said. "Begad, sir, I should feel quite queer, though, telling it *here*, though we are too strong a body for ghosts to meddle with just now."

Though he spoke this like a joke, I think it was serious calculation. Our Hebe was in a corner of the room, packing our cracked delf tea and dinner-services in a basket. She soon suspended operations, and with mouth and eyes wide open became an absorbed listener. Tom's experiences were told nearly in these words:—

"I saw it three times, Dick—three distinct times; and I am perfectly certain it meant me some infernal harm. I was, I say, in danger—in *extreme* danger; for, if nothing else had happened, my reason would most certainly have failed me, unless I had escaped so soon. Thank God. I *did* escape.

"The first night of this hateful disturbance, I was lying in the attitude of sleep, in that lumbering old bed. I hate to think of it. I was really wide awake, though I had put out my candle, and was lying as quietly as if I had been asleep; and although accidentally restless, my thoughts were running in a cheerful and agreeable channel.

"I think it must have been two o'clock at least when I thought I heard a sound in that—that odious dark recess at the far end of the bedroom. It was as if someone was drawing a piece of cord slowly along the floor, lifting it up, and dropping it softly down again in coils. I sat up once or twice in my bed, but could see nothing, so I concluded it must be mice in the wainscot. I felt no emotion graver than curiosity, and after a few minutes ceased to observe it.

"While lying in this state, strange to say; without at first a suspicion of anything supernatural, on a sudden I saw an old man, rather stout and square, in a sort of roan-red dressing-gown, and with a black cap on his head, moving stiffly and slowly in a diagonal direction, from the recess, across the floor of the bedroom, passing my bed at the foot, and entering the lumber-closet at the left. He had something under his arm; his head hung a little at one side; and merciful God! when I saw his face."

Tom stopped for a while, and then said—

"That awful countenance, which living or dying I never can forget, disclosed what he was. Without turning to the right or left, he passed beside me, and entered the closet by the bed's head.

"While this fearful and indescribable type of death and guilt was passing, I felt that I had no more power to speak or stir than if I had been myself a corpse. For hours after it had disappeared, I was too terrified and weak to move. As soon as daylight came, I took courage, and examined the room, and especially the course which the frightful intruder had seemed to take, but there was not a vestige to indicate anybody's having passed there; no sign of any disturbing agency visible among the lumber that strewed the floor of the closet.

"I now began to recover a little. I was fagged and exhausted, and at last, overpowered by a feverish sleep. I came down late; and finding you out of spirits, on account of your dreams about the portrait, whose *original* I am now certain disclosed himself to me, I did not care to talk about the infernal vision. In fact, I was trying to persuade myself that the whole thing was an illusion, and I did not like to revive in their intensity the hated impressions of the past night—or, to risk the constancy of my scepticism, by recounting the tale of my sufferings.

"It required some nerve, I can tell you, to go to my haunted chamber next night, and lie down quietly in the same bed," continued Tom. "I did so with a degree of trepidation, which I am not ashamed to say, a very little matter would have sufficed to stimulate to downright panic. This night, however, passed off quietly enough, as also the next; and so too did two or three more. I grew more confident, and began to fancy that I believed in the theories of spectral illusions, with which I had at first vainly tried to impose upon my convictions.

"The apparition had been, indeed, altogether anomalous. It had crossed the room without any recognition of my presence: I had not disturbed *it*, and *it* had no mission to *me*. What, then, was the imaginable use of its crossing the room in a visible shape at all? Of course it might have *been* in the closet instead of *going* there, as easily as it introduced itself into the recess without entering the chamber in a shape discernible by the senses. Besides, how the deuce *had* I seen it? It was a dark night; I had no candle; there was no fire; and yet I saw it as distinctly, in colouring and outline, as ever I beheld human form! A cataleptic dream would explain it all; and I was determined that a dream it should be.

"One of the most remarkable phenomena connected with the practice of mendacity is the vast number of deliberate lies we tell ourselves, whom, of all persons, we can least expect to deceive. In all this, I need hardly tell you, Dick, I was simply lying to myself, and did not believe one word of the wretched humbug. Yet I went on, as men will do, like persevering charlatans and impostors, who tire people into credulity by the mere force of reiteration; so I hoped to win myself over at last to a comfortable scepticism about the ghost.

"He had not appeared a second time—that certainly was a comfort; and what, after all, did I care for him, and his queer old toggery and strange looks? Not a fig! I was nothing the worse for having seen him, and a good story the better. So I tumbled into bed, put out my candle, and, cheered by a loud drunken quarrel in the back lane, went fast asleep.

"From this deep slumber I awoke with a start. I knew I had had a horrible dream; but what it was I could not remember. My heart was thumping furiously; I felt bewildered and feverish; I sat up in the bed and looked about the room. A broad flood of moonlight came in through the curtainless window; everything was as I had last seen it; and though the domestic squabble in the back lane was, unhappily for me, allayed, I yet could hear a pleasant fellow singing, on his way home, the then popular comic ditty called, 'Murphy Delany.' Taking advantage of this diversion I lay down again, with my face towards the fireplace, and closing my eyes, did my best to think of nothing else but the song, which was every moment growing fainter in the distance:—

'Twas Murphy Delany, so funny and frisky,
  Stept into a shebeen shop to get his skin full;
He reeled out again pretty well lined with whiskey,
  As fresh as a shamrock, as blind as a bull.'

"The singer, whose condition I dare say resembled that of his hero, was soon too far off to regale my ears any more; and, as his music died away, I myself sank into a doze, neither sound nor refreshing. Somehow the song had got into my head, and I went meandering on through the adventures of my respectable fellow-countryman, who, on emerging from the 'shebeen shop,' fell into a river, from which he was fished up to be 'sat upon' by a coroner's jury, who having learned from a 'horse-doctor' that he was 'dead as a door-nail, so there was an end,' returned their verdict accordingly, just as he returned to his senses, when an angry altercation and a pitched battle between the body and the coroner winds up the lay with due spirit and pleasantry.

"Through this ballad I continued with a weary monotony to plod, down to the very last line, and then *da capo*, and so on, in my uncomfortable half-sleep, for how long, I can't conjecture. I found myself at last, however, muttering, '*dead* as a door-nail, so there was an end'; and something like another voice within me, seemed to say, very faintly, but sharply, 'dead! dead! *dead!* and may the Lord have mercy on your soul!' and instantaneously I was wide awake, and staring right before me from the pillow.

"Now—will you believe it, Dick?—I saw the same accursed figure standing full front, and gazing at me with its stony and fiendish countenance, not two yards from the bedside."

Tom stopped here, and wiped the perspiration from his face. I felt very queer. The girl was as pale as Tom; and, assembled as we were in the very scene of these adventures, we were all, I dare say, equally grateful for the clear daylight and the resuming bustle out of doors.

"For about three seconds only I saw it plainly; then it grew indistinct; but, for a long time, there was something like a column of dark vapour where it had been standing between me and the wall; and I felt sure that he was still there. After a good while, this appearance went too. I took my clothes downstairs to the hall, and dressed there, with the door half open; then went out into the street, and walked about the town till morning, when I came back, in a miserable state of nervousness and exhaustion. I was such a fool, Dick, as to be ashamed to tell you how I came to be so upset. I thought you would laugh at me; especially as I had always talked philosophy, and treated *your* ghosts with contempt. I concluded you would give me no quarter; and so kept my tale of horror to myself.

"Now, Dick, you will hardly believe me, when I assure you,

that for many nights after this last experience, I did not go to my room at all. I used to sit up for a while in the drawing-room after you had gone up to your bed; and then steal down softly to the hall-door, let myself out, and sit in the 'Robin Hood' tavern until the last guest went off; and then I got through the night like a sentry, pacing the streets till morning.

"For more than a week I never slept in bed. I sometimes had a snooze on a form in the 'Robin Hood,' and sometimes a nap in a chair during the day; but regular sleep I had absolutely none.

"I was quite resolved that we should get into another house; but I could not bring myself to tell you the reason, and I somehow put it off from day to day, although my life was, during every hour of this procrastination, rendered as miserable as that of a felon with the constables on his track. I was growing absolutely ill from this wretched mode of life.

"One afternoon I determined to enjoy an hour's sleep upon your bed. I hated mine; so that I had never, except in a stealthy visit every day to unmake it, lest Martha should discover the secret of my nightly absence, entered the ill-omened chamber.

"As ill-luck would have it, you had locked your bedroom, and taken away the key. I went into my own to unsettle the bedclothes, as usual, and give the bed the appearance of having been slept in. Now, a variety of circumstances concurred to bring about the dreadful scene through which I was that night to pass. In the first place, I was literally overpowered with fatigue, and longing for sleep; in the next place, the effect of this extreme exhaustion upon my nerves resembled that of a narcotic, and rendered me less susceptible than, perhaps I should in any other condition have been, of the exciting fears which had become habitual to me. Then again, a little bit of the window was open, a pleasant freshness pervaded the room, and, to crown all, the cheerful sun of day was making the room quite pleasant. What was to prevent my enjoying an hour's nap *here*? The whole air was resonant with the cheerful hum of life, and the broad matter-of-fact light of day filled every corner of the room.

"I yielded—stifling my qualms—to the almost overpowering temptation; and merely throwing off my coat, and loosening my cravat, I lay down, limiting myself to *half*-an-hour's doze in the unwonted enjoyment of a feather bed, a coverlet, and a bolster.

"It was horribly insidious; and the demon, no doubt, marked my infatuated preparations. Dolt that I was, I fancied, with mind and body worn out for want of sleep, and an arrear of a full week's rest to my credit, that such measure as *half*-an-hour's sleep, in such a situation, was possible. My sleep was death-like, long, and dreamless.

"Without a start or fearful sensation of any kind, I waked gently, but completely. It was, as you have good reason to remember, long past midnight—I believe, about two o'clock. When sleep has been deep and long enough to satisfy nature thoroughly, one often wakens in this way, suddenly, tranquilly, and completely.

"There was a figure seated in that lumbering, old sofa-chair, near the fireplace. Its back was rather towards me, but I could not be mistaken; it turned slowly round, and, merciful heavens! there was the stony face, with its infernal lineaments of malignity and despair, gloating on me. There was now no doubt as to its consciousness of my presence, and the hellish malice with which it was animated, for it arose, and drew close to the bedside. There was a rope about its neck, and the other end, coiled up, it held stiffly in its hand.

"My good angel nerved me for this horrible crisis. I remained for some seconds transfixed by the gaze of this tremendous phantom. He came close to the bed, and appeared on the point of mounting upon it. The next instant I was upon the floor at the far side, and in a moment more was, I don't know how, upon the lobby.

"But the spell was not yet broken; the valley of the shadow of death was not yet traversed. The abhorred phantom was before me there; it was standing near the banisters, stooping a little, and with one end of the rope round its own neck, was poising a noose at the other, as if to throw over mine; and while engaged in this baleful pantomime, it wore a smile so sensual, so unspeakably dreadful, that my senses were nearly overpowered. I saw and remember nothing more, until I found myself in your room.

"I had a wonderful escape, Dick—there is no disputing *that*—an escape for which, while I live, I shall bless the mercy of heaven. No one can conceive or imagine what it is for flesh and blood to stand in the presence of such a thing, but one who has had the terrific experience. Dick, Dick, a shadow has passed over me—a chill has crossed my blood and marrow, and I will never be the same again—never, Dick —never!"

Our handmaid, a mature girl of two-and-fifty, as I have said, stayed her hand, as Tom's story proceeded, and by little and little drew near to us, with open mouth, and her brows contracted over her little, beady black eyes, till stealing a glance over her shoulder now and then, she established herself close behind us. During the relation, she had made various earnest comments, in an undertone; but these and her ejaculations, for the sake of brevity and simplicity, I have omitted in my narration.

"It's often I heard tell of it," she now said, "but I never believed it rightly till now—though, indeed, why should not I? Does not my mother, down there in the lane, know quare stories, God bless us, beyant telling about it? But you ought not to have slept in the back bedroom. She was loath to let me be going in and out of that room even in the day time, let alone for any Christian to spend the night in it; for sure she says it was his own bedroom."

"*Whose* own bedroom?" we asked, in a breath.

"Why, *his*—the ould Judge's—Judge Horrock's, to be sure, God rest his sowl"; and she looked fearfully round.

"Amen!" I muttered. "But did he die there?"

"Die there! No, not quite *there*," she said. "Shure, was not it over the banisters he hung himself, the ould sinner, God be merciful to us all? and was not it in the alcove they found the handles of the skipping-rope cut off, and the knife where he was settling the cord, God bless us, to hang himself with? It was his housekeeper's daughter owned the rope, my mother often told me, and the child never throve after, and used to be starting up out of her sleep, and screeching in the night time, wid dhrames and frights that cum an her; and they said how it was the speerit of the ould Judge that was tormentin' her; and she used to be roaring and yelling out to hould back the big ould fellow with the crooked neck; and then she'd screech 'Oh, the master! the master! he's stampin' at me, and beckoning to me! Mother, darling, don't let me go!' And so the poor crathure died at last, and the docthers said it was wather on the brain, for it was all they could say."

"How long ago was all this?" I asked.

"Oh, then, how would I know?" she answered. "But it must be a wondherful long time ago, for the housekeeper was an ould woman, with a pipe in her mouth, and not a tooth left, and better nor eighty years ould when my mother was first married; and they said she was a rale buxom, fine-dressed woman when the ould Judge come to his end; an', indeed, my mother's not far from eighty years ould herself this day; and what made it worse for the unnatural ould villain, God rest his soul, to frighten the little girl out of the world the way he did, was what was mostly thought and believed by everyone. My mother says how the poor little crathure was his own child; for he was by all accounts an ould villain every way, an' the hangin'est judge that ever was known in Ireland's ground."

"From what you said about the danger of sleeping in that bedroom," said I, "I suppose there were stories about the ghost having appeared there to others."

"Well, there *was* things said—quare things, surely," she answered, as it seemed, with some reluctance. "And why would not there? Sure it was not up in that same room he slept for more than twenty years? and was it not in the alcove he got the rope ready that done his own business at last, the way he done many a betther man's in his lifetime?—and was not the body lying in the same bed after death, and put in the coffin there, too, and carried out to his grave from it in Pether's churchyard, after the coroner was done? But there was quare stories—my mother has them all—about how one Nicholas Spaight got into trouble on the head of it."

"And what did they say of this Nicholas Spaight?" I asked.

"Oh, for that matther, it's soon told," she answered.

And she certainly did relate a very strange story, which so piqued my curiosity, that I took occasion to visit the ancient lady, her mother, from whom I learned many very curious particulars. Indeed, I am tempted to tell the tale, but my fingers are weary, and I must defer it. But if you wish to hear it another time, I shall do my best.

When we had heard the strange tale I have *not* told you, we put one or two further questions to her about the alleged spectral visitations, to which the house had, ever since the death of the wicked old Judge, been subjected.

"No one ever had luck in it," she told us. "There was always cross accidents, sudden deaths, and short times in it. The first that tuck it was a family—I forget their name—but at any rate there was two young ladies and their papa. He was about sixty, and a stout healthy gentleman as you'd wish to see at that age. Well, he slept in that unlucky back bedroom; and, God between us an' harm! sure enough he was found dead one morning, half out of the bed, with his head as black as a sloe, and swelled like a puddin', hanging down near the floor. It was a fit, they said. He was as dead as a mackerel, and so *he* could not say what it was; but the ould people was all sure that it was nothing at all but the ould Judge, God bless us! that frightened him out of his senses and his life together.

"Some time after there was a rich old maiden lady took the house. I don't know which room *she* slept in, but she lived alone; and at any rate, one morning, the servants going down early to their work, found her sitting on the passage-stairs, shivering and talkin' to herself, quite mad; and never a word more could any of *them* or her friends get from her ever afterwards but, 'Don't ask me to go, for I promised to wait for him.' They never made out from her who it was she meant by *him*, but of course those that knew all about the ould house were at no loss for the meaning of all that happened to her.

"Then afterwards, when the house was let out in lodgings, there was Micky Byrne that took the same room, with his wife and three little children; and sure I heard Mrs. Byrne myself telling how the children used to be lifted up in the bed at night, she could not see by what mains; and how they were starting and screeching every hour, just all as one as the housekeeper's little girl that died, till at last one night poor Micky had a dhrop in him, the way he used now and again; and what do you think in the middle of the night he thought he heard a noise on the stairs, and being in liquor, nothing less id do him but out he must go himself to see what was wrong. Well, after that, all she ever heard of him was himself sayin', 'Oh, God!' and a tumble that shook the very house; and there, sure enough, he was lying on the lower stairs, under the lobby, with his neck smashed double undher him, where he was flung over the banisters."

Then the handmaiden added—

"I'll go down to the lane, and send up Joe Gavvey to pack up the rest of the taythings, and bring all the things across to your new lodgings."

And so we all sallied out together, each of us breathing more freely, I have no doubt, as we crossed that ill-omened threshold for the last time.

Now, I may add thus much, in compliance with the immemorial usage of the realm of fiction, which sees the hero not only through his adventures, but fairly out of the world. You must have perceived that what the flesh, blood, and bone hero of romance proper is to the regular compounder of fiction, this old house of brick, wood, and mortar is to the humble recorder of this true tale. I, therefore, relate, as in duty bound, the catastrophe which ultimately befell it, which was simply this—that about two years subsequently to my story it was taken by a quack doctor, who called himself Baron Duhlstoerf, and filled the parlour windows with bottles of indescribable horrors preserved in brandy, and the newspapers with the usual grandiloquent and mendacious advertisements. This gentleman among his virtues did not reckon sobriety, and one night, being overcome with much wine, he set fire to his bed curtains, partially burned himself, and totally consumed the house. It was afterwards rebuilt, and for a time an undertaker established himself in the premises.

I have now told you my own and Tom's adventures, together with some valuable collateral particulars; and having acquitted myself of my engagement, I wish you a very good night, and pleasant dreams.

CONFESSION

By Algernon Blackwood

THE FOG swirled slowly round him, driven by a heavy movement of its own, for of course there was no wind. It hung in poisonous thick coils and loops; it rose and sank; no light penetrated it directly from street lamp or motorcar, though here and there some big shop window shed a glimmering patch upon its evershifting curtain.

O'Reilly's eyes ached and smarted with the incessant effort to see a foot beyond his face. The optic nerve grew tired, and sight, accordingly, less accurate. He coughed as he shuffled forward cautiously through the choking gloom. Only the stifled rumble of crawling traffic persuaded him he was in a crowded city at all—this, and the vague outlines of groping figures, hugely magnified, emerging suddenly and disappearing again, as they fumbled along inch by inch towards uncertain destinations.

The figures, however, were human beings; they were real. That much he knew. He heard their muffled voices, now close, now distant, strangely smothered always. He also heard the tapping of innumerable sticks, feeling for iron railings or the kerb. These phantom outlines represented living people. He was not alone.

It was the dread of finding himself *quite* alone that haunted him, for he was still unable to cross an open space without assistance. He had the physical strength, it was the mind that failed him. Midway the panic terror might descend upon him, he would shake all over, his will dissolve, he would shriek for help, run wildly—into the traffic probably—or, as they called it in his North Ontario home, "throw a fit" in the street before advancing wheels. He was not yet entirely cured, although under ordinary conditions he was safe enough, as Dr. Henry had assured him.

When he left Regent's Park by Tube an hour ago the air was clear, the November sun shone brightly, the pale blue sky was cloudless, and the assumption that he could manage the journey across London Town alone was justified. The following day he was to leave for Brighton for the week of final convalescence: this little preliminary test of his powers on a bright November afternoon was all to the good. Doctor Henry furnished minute instructions: "You change at Piccadilly Circus—without leaving the underground station, mind—and get out at South Kensington. You know the address of your V.A.D. friend. Have your cup of tea with her, then come back the same way to Regent's Park. Come back before dark—say six o'clock at latest. It's better." He had described exactly what turns to take after leaving the station, so many to the right, so many to the left; it was a little confusing, but the distance was short. "You can always ask. You can't possibly go wrong."

The unexpected fog, however, now blurred these instructions in a confused jumble in his mind. The failure of outer sight reacted upon memory. The V.A.D. besides had warned him that her address was "not easy to find the first time. The house lies in a backwater. But with your 'backwoods' instincts you'll probably manage it better than any Londoner!" She, too, had not calculated upon the fog.

When O'Reilly came up the stairs at South Kensington Station, he emerged into such murky darkness that he thought he was still underground. An impenetrable world lay round him. Only a raw bite in the damp atmosphere told him he stood beneath an open sky. For some little time he stood and stared—a Canadian soldier, his home among clear brilliant spaces, now face to face for the first time in his life with that thing he had so often read about—a bad London fog. With keenest interest and surprise he "enjoyed" the novel spectacle for perhaps ten minutes, watching the people arrive and vanish, and wondering why the station lights stopped dead the instant they touched the street—then, with a sense of adventure—it cost an effort—he left the covered, building and plunged into the opaque sea beyond.

Repeating to himself the directions he had received—first to the right, second to the left, once more to the left, and so forth—he checked each turn, assuring himself it was impossible to go wrong. He made correct if slow progress, until someone blundered into him with an abrupt and startling question: "Is this right, do you know, for South Kensington Station?"

It was the suddenness that startled him; one moment there was no one, the next they were face to face, another, and the stranger had vanished into the gloom with a courteous word of grateful thanks. But the little shock of interruption had put memory out of gear. Had he already turned twice to the right, or had he not? O'Reilly realised sharply he had forgotten his memorised instructions. He stood still, making strenuous efforts at recovery, but each effort left him more uncertain than before. Five minutes later he was lost as hopelessly as any townsman who leaves his tent in the backwoods without blazing the trees to ensure finding his way back again. Even the sense of direction, so strong in him among his native forests, was completely gone. There were no stars, there was no wind, no smell, no sound of running water. There was nothing anywhere to guide him, nothing but occasional dim outlines, groping, shuffling, emerging and disappearing in the eddying fog, but rarely coming within actual speaking, much less touching, distance. He was lost utterly; more, he was alone.

Yet not *quite* alone—the thing he dreaded most. There were figures still in his immediate neighbourhood. They emerged, vanished, reappeared, dissolved. No, he was not quite alone. He saw these thickenings of the fog, he heard their voices, the tapping of their cautious sticks, their shuffling feet as well. They were real. They moved, it seemed, about him in a circle, never coming very close.

"But they're real," he said to himself aloud, betraying the weak point in his armour. "They're human beings right enough. I'm positive of that."

He had never argued with Dr. Henry—he wanted to get

well; he had obeyed implicitly, believing everything the doctor told him—up to a point. But he had always had his own idea about these "figures," because, among them, were often enough his own pals from the Somme, Gallipoli, the Mespot horror, too. And he ought to know his own pals when he saw them! At the same time he knew quite well he had been "shocked," his being dislocated, half dissolved as it were, his system pushed into some lopsided condition that meant inaccurate registration. True. He grasped that perfectly. But, in that shock and dislocation, had he not possibly picked up another gear? Were there not gaps and broken edges, pieces that no longer dovetailed, fitted as usual, interstices, in a word? Yes, that was the word—interstices. Cracks, so to speak, between his perception of the outside world and his inner interpretation of these? Between memory and recognition? Between the various states of consciousness that usually dovetailed so neatly that the joints were normally imperceptible?

His state, he well knew, was abnormal, but were his symptoms on that account unreal? Could not these "interstices" be used by—others? When he saw his "figures," he used to ask himself: "Are not these the real ones, and the others—the human beings—unreal?"

This question now revived in him with a new intensity. Were these figures in the fog real or unreal? The man who had asked the way to the station, was he not, after all, a shadow merely?

By the use of his cane and foot and what of sight was left to him he knew that he was on an island. A lamppost stood up solid and straight beside him, shedding its faint patch of glimmering light. Yet there were railings, however, that puzzled him, for his stick hit the metal rods distinctly in a series. And there should be no railings round an island. Yet he had most certainly crossed a dreadful open space to get where he was. His confusion and bewilderment increased with dangerous rapidity. Panic was not far away.

He was no longer on an omnibus route. A rare taxi crawled past occasionally, a whitish patch at the window indicating an anxious human face; now and again came a van or cart, the driver holding a lantern as he led the stumbling horse. These comforted him, rare though they were. But it was the figures that drew his attention most. He was quite sure they were real. They were human beings like himself.

For all that, he decided he might as well be positive on the point. He tried one accordingly—a big man who rose suddenly before him out of the very earth.

"Can you give me the trail to Morley Place?" he asked.

But his question was drowned by the other's simultaneous inquiry in a voice much louder than his own.

"I say, is this right for the Tube station, d'you know? I'm utterly lost. I want South Ken."

And by the time O'Reilly had pointed the direction whence he himself had just come, the man was gone again, obliterated, swallowed up, not so much as his footsteps audible, almost as if—it seemed again—he never had been there at all.

This left an acute unpleasantness in him, a sense of bewilderment greater than before. He waited five minutes, not daring to move a step, then tried another figure, a woman this time, who, luckily, knew the immediate neighbourhood intimately. She gave him elaborate instructions in the kindest possible way, then vanished with incredible swiftness and case into the sea of gloom beyond. The instantaneous way she vanished was disheartening, upsetting: it was so uncannily abrupt and sudden. Yet she comforted him. Morley Place, according to her version, was not two hundred yards from where he stood. He felt his way forward, step by step, using his cane, crossing a giddy open space, kicking the kerb with each boot alternately, coughing and choking all the time as he did so.

"They were real, I guess, anyway," he said aloud. "They were both real enough all right. And it may lift a bit soon!" He was making a great effort to hold himself in hand. He was already fighting, that is. He realised this perfectly. The only point was—the reality of the figures. "It may lift now any minute," he repeated louder. In spite of the cold, his skin was sweating profusely.

But, of course, it did not lift. The figures, too, became

fewer. No carts were audible. He had followed the woman's directions carefully, but now found himself in some byway, evidently, where pedestrians at the best of times were rare. There was dull silence all about him. His foot lost the kerb, his cane swept the empty air, striking nothing solid, and panic rose upon him with its shuddering, icy grip. He was alone, he knew himself alone, worse still—he was in another open space.

It took him fifteen minutes to cross that open space, most of the way upon his hands and knees, oblivious of the icy slime that stained his trousers, froze his fingers, intent only upon feeling solid support against his back and spine again. It was an endless period. The moment of collapse was close, the shriek already rising in his throat, the shaking of the whole body uncontrollable, when—his outstretched fingers struck a friendly kerb, and he saw a glimmering patch of diffused radiance overhead. With a great, quick effort he stood upright, and an instant later his stick rattled along an area railing. He leaned against it, breathless, panting, his heart beating painfully while the street lamp gave him the further comfort of its feeble gleam, the actual flame, however, invisible. He looked this way and that; the pavement was deserted. He was engulfed in the dark silence of the fog.

But Morley Place, he knew, must be very close by now. He thought of the friendly little V.A.D. he had known in France, of a warm bright fire, a cup of tea and a cigarette. One more effort, he reflected, and all these would be his. He pluckily groped his way forward again, crawling slowly by the area railings. If things got really bad again, he would ring a bell and ask for help, much as he shrank from the idea. Provided he had no more open spaces to cross, provided he saw no more figures emerging and vanishing like creatures born of the fog and dwelling within it as within their native element —it was the figures he now dreaded more than anything else, more than even the loneliness—provided the panic sense—

A faint darkening of the fog beneath the next lamp caught his eye and made him start. He stopped. It was not a figure this time, it was the shadow of the pole grotesquely magnified. No, it moved. It moved towards him. A flame of fire followed by ice flowed through him. It was a figure—close against his face. It was a woman.

The doctor's advice came suddenly back to him, the counsel that had cured him of a hundred phantoms:

"Do not ignore them. Treat them as real. Speak and go with them. You will soon prove their unreality then. And they will leave you . . ."

He made a brave, tremendous effort. He was shaking. One hand clutched the damp and icy area railing.

"Lost your way like myself, haven't you, ma'am?" he said in a voice that trembled. "Do you know where we are at all? Morley Place I'm looking for—"

He stopped dead. The woman moved nearer and for the first time he saw her face clearly. Its ghastly pallor, the bright, frightened eyes that stared with a kind of dazed bewilderment into his own, the beauty, above all, arrested his speech midway. The woman was young, her tall figure wrapped in a dark fur coat.

"Can I help you?" he asked impulsively, forgetting his own terror for the moment. He was more than startled. Her air of distress and pain stirred a peculiar anguish in him. For a moment she made no answer, thrusting her white face closer as if examining him, so close, indeed, that he controlled with difficulty his instinct to shrink back a little.

"Where am I?" she asked at length, searching his eyes intently. "I'm lost—I've lost myself. I can't find my way back." Her voice was low, a curious wailing in it that touched his pity oddly. He felt his own distress merging in one that was greater.

"Same here," he replied more confidently. "I'm terrified of being alone, too. I've had shellshock, you know. Let's go together. We'll find a way together—"

"Who are you?" the woman murmured, still staring at him with her big bright eyes, their distress, however, no whit lessened. She gazed at him as though aware suddenly of his presence.

He told her briefly. "And I'm going to tea with a V.A.D. friend in Morley Place. What's your address? Do you know the name of the street?"

She appeared not to hear him, or not to understand exactly; it was as if she was not listening again.

"I came out so suddenly, so unexpectedly," he heard the low voice with pain in every syllable; "I can't find my way home again. Just when I was expecting him too—" She looked about her with a distraught expression that made O'Reilly long to carry her in his arms to safety then and there. "He may be there now—waiting for me at this very moment—and I can't get back." And so sad was her voice that only by an effort did O'Reilly prevent himself putting out his hand to touch her. More and more he forgot himself in his desire to help her. Her beauty, the wonder of her strange bright eyes in the pallid face, made an immense appeal. He became calmer. This woman was real enough. He asked again the address, the street and number, the distance she thought it was. "Have you any idea of the direction, ma'am, any idea at all? We'll go together and—"

She suddenly cut him short. She turned her head as if to listen, so that he saw her profile a moment, the outline of the slender neck, a glimpse of jewels just below the fur.

"Hark! I hear him calling! I remember . . . !" And she was gone from his side into the swirling fog.

Without an instant's hesitation O'Reilly followed her, not only because he wished to help, but because he dared not be left alone. The presence of this strange, lost woman comforted him; he must not lose sight of her, whatever happened. He had to run, she went so rapidly, ever just in front, moving with confidence and certainty, turning right and left, crossing the street, but never stopping, never hesitating, her companion always at her heels in breathless haste, and with a growing terror that he might lose her any minute. The way she found her direction through the dense fog was marvellous enough, but O'Reilly's only thought was to keep her in sight, lest his own panic redescend upon him with its inevitable collapse in the dark and lonely street. It was a wild and panting pursuit, and he kept her in view with difficulty, a dim fleeting outline always a few yards ahead of him. She did not once turn her head, she uttered no sound, no cry; she hurried forward with unfaltering instinct. Nor did the chase occur to him once as singular; she was his safety, and that was all he realised.

One thing, however, he remembered afterwards, though at the actual time he no more than registered the detail, paying no attention to it—a definite perfume she left upon the atmosphere, one, moreover, that he knew, although he could not find its name as he ran. It was associated vaguely, for him, with something unpleasant, something disagreeable. He connected it with misery and pain. It gave him a feeling of uneasiness. More than that he did not notice at the moment, nor could he remember—he certainly did not try—where he had known this particular scent before.

Then suddenly the woman stopped, opened a gate and passed into a small private garden—so suddenly that O'Reilly, close upon her heels, only just avoided tumbling into her. "You've found it?" he cried. "May I come in a moment with you? Perhaps you'll let me telephone to the doctor?"

She turned instantly. Her face, close against his own, was livid.

"Doctor!" she repeated in an awful whisper. The word meant terror to her. O'Reilly stood amazed. For a second or two neither of them moved. The woman seemed petrified.

"Dr. Henry, you know," he stammered, finding his tongue again. "I'm in his care. He's in Harley Street."

Her face cleared as suddenly as it had darkened, though the original expression of bewilderment and pain still hung in her great eyes. But the terror left them, as though she suddenly forgot some association that had revived it.

"My home," she murmured. "My home is somewhere here. I'm near it. I must get back—in time—for him. I must. He's coming to me." And with these extraordinary words she turned, walked up the narrow path, and stood upon the porch of a two-storey house before her companion had recovered from his astonishment sufficiently to move or utter a syllable in reply. The front door, he saw, was ajar. It had been left open.

For five seconds, perhaps for ten, he hesitated; it was the fear that the door would close and shut him out that brought the decision to his will and muscles. He ran up the steps and

followed the woman into a dark hall where she had already
preceded him, and amid whose blackness she now had finally
vanished. He closed the door, not knowing exactly why he
did so, and knew at once by an instinctive feeling that the
house he now found himself in with this unknown woman
was empty and unoccupied. In a house, however, he felt safe.
It was the open streets that were his danger. He stood waiting, listening a moment before he spoke; and he heard the
woman moving down the passage from door to door, repeating to herself in her low voice of unhappy wailing some
words he could not understand:

"Where is it? Oh, where is it? I must get back . . ."

O'Reilly then found himself abruptly stricken with
dumbness, as though, with these strange words, a haunting
terror came up and breathed against him in the darkness.

"Is she after all a figure?" ran in letters of fire across his
numbed brain. "Is she unreal—or real?"

Seeking relief in action of some kind he put out a hand automatically, feeling along the wall for an electric switch, and
though he found it by some miraculous chance, no answering
glow responded to the click.

And the woman's voice from the darkness: "Ah! Ah! At
last I've found it. I'm home again—at last . . . !" He heard
a door open and close upstairs. He was on the ground floor
now—alone. Complete silence followed.

In the conflict of various emotions—fear for himself lest
his panic should return, fear for the woman who had led him
into this empty house and now deserted him upon some mysterious errand of her own that made him think of madness—
in this conflict that held him a moment spellbound, there
was a yet bigger ingredient demanding instant explanation,
but an explanation that he could not find. Was the woman
real or was she unreal? Was she a human being or a "figure"?
The horror of doubt obsessed him with an acute uneasiness
that betrayed itself in a return of that unwelcome inner trembling he knew was dangerous.

What saved him from a *crise* that must have had most
dangerous results for his mind and nervous system generally,
seems to have been the outstanding fact that he felt more for

the woman than for himself. His sympathy and pity had
been deeply moved; her voice, her beauty, her anguish
and bewilderment, all uncommon, inexplicable, mysterious,
formed together a claim that drove self into the background.
Added to this was the detail that she had left him, gone to
another floor without a word, and now, behind a closed door
in a room upstairs, found herself face to face at last with the
unknown object of her frantic search—with "it," whatever
"it" might be. Real or unreal, figure or human being, the
overmastering impulse of his being was that he must go to
her.

It was this clear impulse that gave him decision and energy
to do what he then did. He struck a match, he found a
stump of candle, he made his way by means of this flickering
light along the passage and up the carpetless stairs. He
moved cautiously, stealthily, though not knowing why he did
so. The house, he now saw, was indeed untenanted; dust-
sheets covered the piled-up furniture; he glimpsed, through
doors ajar, pictures screened upon the walls, brackets draped
to look like hooded heads. He went on slowly, steadily, moving on tiptoe as though conscious of being watched, noting
the well of darkness in the hall below, the grotesque shadows
that his movements cast on walls and ceiling. The silence was
unpleasant, yet, remembering that the woman was "expecting" someone, he did not wish it broken. He reached the
landing and stood still. Closed doors on both sides of a corridor met his sight, as he shaded the candle to examine the
scene. Behind which of these doors, he asked himself, was
the woman, figure or human being, now alone with "it"?

There was nothing to guide him, but an instinct that he
must not delay sent him forward again upon his search. He
tried a door on the right—an empty room, with the furniture
hidden by dust-sheets, and mattress rolled up on the bed. He
tried a second door, leaving the first one open behind him,
and it was, similarly, an empty bedroom. Coming out into the
corridor again he stood a moment waiting, then called aloud
in a low voice that yet woke echoes unpleasantly in the hall
below: "Where are you? I want to help—which room are
you in?"

There was no answer; he was almost glad he heard no sound, for he knew quite well that he was waiting really for another sound—the steps of him who was "expected." And the idea of meeting with this unknown third sent a shudder through him, as though related to an interview he dreaded with his whole heart, and must at all costs avoid. Waiting another moment or two, he noted that his candlestump was burning low, then crossed the landing with a feeling, at once of hesitation and determination, towards a door opposite to him. He opened it; he did not halt on the threshold. Holding the candle at arm's length, he went boldly in.

And instantly his nostrils told him he was right at last, for a whiff of the strange perfume, though this time much stronger than before, greeted him, sending a new quiver along his nerves. He knew now why it was associated with unpleasantness, with pain, with misery, for he recognised it—the odour of a hospital. In this room a powerful anæsthetic had been used—and recently.

Simultaneously with smell, sight brought its message too. On the large double bed behind the door on his right lay, to his amazement, the woman in the dark fur coat. He saw the jewels on the slender neck; but the eyes he did not see, for they were closed—closed too, he grasped at once, in death. The body lay stretched at full length, quite motionless. He approached. A dark thin streak that came from the parted lips and passed downwards over the chin, losing itself then in the fur collar, was a trickle of blood. It was hardly dry. It glistened.

Strange it was perhaps that, while imaginary fears had the power to paralyse him, mind and body, this sight of something real had the effect of restoring confidence. The sight of blood and death, amid conditions often ghastly and even monstrous was no new thing to him. He went up quietly, and with steady hand he felt the woman's cheek, the warmth of recent life still in its softness. The final cold had not yet mastered this empty form whose beauty, in its perfect stillness, had taken on the new strange sweetness of an unearthly bloom. Pallid, silent, untenanted, it lay before him, lit by the flicker of his guttering candle. He lifted the fur coat to feel for the unbeating heart. A couple of hours ago at most, he judged, this heart was working busily, the breath came through those parted lips, the eyes were shining in full beauty. His hand encountered a hard knob—the head of a long steel hat-pin driven through the heart up to its hilt.

He knew then which was the figure—which was the real and which the unreal. He knew also what had been meant by "it."

But before he could think or reflect what action he must take, before he could straighten himself even from his bent position over the body on the bed, there sounded through the empty house below the loud clang of the front door being closed. And instantly rushed over him that other fear he had so long forgotten—fear for himself. The panic of his own shaken nerves descended with irresistible onslaught. He turned, extinguishing the candle in the violent trembling of his hand, and tore headlong from the room.

The following ten minutes seemed a nightmare in which he was not master of himself and knew not exactly what he did. All he realized was that steps already sounded on the stairs, coming quickly nearer. The flicker of an electric torch played on the banisters, whose shadows ran swiftly sideways along the wall as the hand that held the light ascended. He thought in a frenzied second of police, of his presence in the house, of the murdered woman. It was a sinister combination. Whatever happened, he must escape without being so much as even seen. His heart raced madly. He darted across the landing into the room opposite, whose door he had luckily left open. And by some incredible chance, apparently, he was neither seen nor heard by the man who, a moment later, reached the landing, entered the room where the body of the woman lay, and closed the door carefully behind him.

Shaking, scarcely daring to breathe lest his breath be audible, O'Reilly, in the grip of his own personal terror, remnant of his uncured shock of war, had no thought of what duty might demand or not demand of him. He thought only of himself. He realized one clear issue—that he must get out of the house without being heard or seen. Who the newcomer was he did not know, beyond an uncanny assurance that it was *not* he whom the woman had "expected," but the murderer himself, and that it was the murderer, in his turn, who was expecting this third person. In that room with death at his elbow, a death he had himself brought about but an hour or two ago, the murderer now hid in waiting for his second victim. And the door was closed.

Yet any minute it might open again, cutting off retreat.

O'Reilly crept out, stole across the landing, reached the head of the stairs, and began, with the utmost caution, the perilous descent. Each time the bare boards creaked beneath his weight no matter how stealthily this weight was adjusted, his heart missed a beat. He tested each step before he pressed upon it, distributing as much of his weight as he dared upon the banisters. It was a little more than halfway down that, to his horror, his foot caught in a projecting carpet tack; he slipped on the polished wood, and only saved himself from falling headlong by a wild clutch at the railing, making an uproar that seemed to him like the explosion of a hand-grenade in the forgotten trenches. His nerves gave way then, and panic seized him. In the silence that followed the resounding echoes he heard the bedroom door opening on the floor above.

Concealment was now useless. It was impossible, too. He took the last flight of stairs in a series of leaps, four steps at a time, reached the hall, flew across it, and opened the front door, just as his pursuer, electric torch in hand, covered half the stairs behind him. Slamming the door, he plunged headlong into the welcome, all-obscuring fog outside.

The fog had now no terrors for him, he welcomed its concealing mantle; nor did it matter in which direction he ran so long as he put distance between him and the house of death. The pursuer had, of course, not followed him into the street. He crossed open spaces without a tremor. He ran in a circle nevertheless, though without being aware he did so. No people were about, no single groping shadow passed him, no boom of traffic reached his ears, when he paused for breath at length against an area railing. Then for the first time he made the discovery that he had no hat. He remembered now. In examining the body, partly out of respect, partly perhaps unconsciously, he had taken it off and laid it—on the very bed.

It was there, a telltale bit of damning evidence, in the house of death. And a series of probable consequences flashed through his mind like lightning. It was a new hat fortunately; more fortunate still, he had not yet written name or initials in it; but the maker's mark was there for all to read, and the police would go immediately to the shop where he had bought it only two days before. Would the shop-people remember his appearance? Would his visit, the date, the conversation be recalled? He thought it was unlikely; he resembled dozens of men; he had no outstanding peculiarity. He tried to think, but his mind was confused and troubled, his heart was beating dreadfully, he felt desperately ill. He sought vainly for some story to account for his being out in the fog and far from home without a hat. No single idea presented itself. He clung to the icy railings, hardly able to keep upright, collapse very near—when suddenly a figure emerged from the fog, paused a moment to stare at him, put out a hand and caught him, and then spoke.

"You're ill, my dear sir," said a man's kindly voice. "Can I be of any assistance? Come, let me help you." He had seen at once that it was not a case of drunkenness. "Come, take my arm, won't you? I'm a physician. Luckily, too, you are just outside my very house. Come in." And he half dragged, half pushed O'Reilly, now bordering on collapse, up the steps and opened the door with his latchkey.

"Felt ill suddenly—lost in the fog . . . terrified, but be all right soon, thanks awfully—" the Canadian stammered his gratitude, already feeling better. He sank into a chair in the hall, while the other put down a paper parcel he had been carrying, and led him presently into a comfortable room; a fire burned brightly; the electric lamps were pleasantly shaded; a decanter of whisky and a siphon stood on a small table beside a big armchair; and before O'Reilly could find another word to say the other had poured him out a glass and bade him sip it slowly, without troubling to talk till he felt better.

"That will revive you. Better drink it slowly. You should

never have been out a night like this. If you've far to go, better let me put you up—"

"Very kind, very kind, indeed," mumbled O'Reilly, recov-
ering rapidly in the comfort of a presence he already liked
and felt even drawn to.

"No trouble at all," returned the doctor. "I've been at the
front, you know. I can see what your trouble is—shellshock,
I'll be bound."

The Canadian, much impressed by the other's quick diag-
nosis, noted also his tact and kindness. He had made no
reference to the absence of a hat, for instance.

"Quite true," he said. "I'm with Dr. Henry, in Harley
Street," and he added a few words about his case. The
whisky worked its effect, he revived more and more, feeling
better every minute. The other handed him a cigarette; they
began to talk about his symptoms and recovery; confidence
returned in a measure, though he still felt badly frightened.
The doctor's manner and personality did much to help, for
there was strength and gentleness in the face, though the features showed unusual determination, softened occasionally by
a sudden hint as of suffering in the bright, compelling eyes.
It was the face, thought O'Reilly, of a man who had seen
much and probably been through hell, but of a man who was
simple, good, sincere. Yet not a man to trifle with; behind his
gentleness lay something very stern. This effect of character
and personality woke the other's respect in addition to his
gratitude. His sympathy was stirred.

"You encourage me to make another guess," the man was
saying, after a successful reading of the impromptu patient's
state, "that you have had, namely, a severe shock quite
recently, and"—he hesitated for the merest fraction of a
second—"that it would be a relief to you," he went on, the
skilful suggestion in the voice unnoticed by his companion,
"it would be wise as well, if you could unburden yourself to
—someone—who would understand." He looked at O'Reilly
with a kindly and very pleasant smile. "Am I not right, perhaps?" he asked in his gentle tone.

"Someone who would understand," repeated the Canadian. "That's my trouble exactly. You've hit it. It's all so incredible."

The other smiled. "The more incredible," he suggested, "the greater your need for expression. Suppression, as you may know, is dangerous in cases like this. You think you have hidden it, but it bides its time and comes up later, causing a lot of trouble. Confession, you know"—he emphasized the word—"confession is good for the soul!"

"You're dead right," agreed the other.

"Now, if you can, bring yourself to tell it to someone who will listen and believe—to myself, for instance. I am a doctor, familiar with such things. I shall regard all you say as a professional confidence, of course; and, as we are strangers, my belief or disbelief is of no particular consequence. I may tell you in advance of your story, however—I think I can promise it—that I shall believe all you have to say."

O'Reilly told his story without more ado, for the suggestion of the skilled physician had found easy soil to work in. During the recital his host's eyes never once left his own. He moved no single muscle of his body. His interest seemed intense.

"A bit tall, isn't it?" said the Canadian, when his tale was finished. "And the question is—" he continued with a threat of volubility which the other checked instantly.

"Strange, yes, but incredible, no," the doctor interrupted. "I see no reason to disbelieve a single detail of what you have just told me. Things equally remarkable, equally incredible, happen in all large towns, as I know from personal experience. I could give you instances." He paused a moment, but his companion, staring into his eyes with interest and curiosity, made no comment. "Some years ago, in fact," continued the other, "I knew of a very similar case—strangely similar."

"Really! I should be immensely interested—"

"So similar that it seems almost a coincidence. You may find it hard, in your turn, to credit it." He paused again, while O'Reilly sat forward in his chair to listen. "Yes," pursued the doctor slowly, "I think everyone connected with it is now dead. There is no reason why I should not tell it, for one confidence deserves another, you know. It happened during the Boer War—as long ago as that," he added with emphasis. "It is really a very commonplace story in one way, though very dreadful in another, but a man who has served at the front will understand and—I'm sure—will sympathize."

"I'm sure of that," offered the other readily.

"A colleague of mine, now dead, as I mentioned—a surgeon, with a big practice, married a young and charming girl. They lived happily together for several years. His wealth made her very comfortable. His consulting room, I must tell you, was some distance from his house—just as this might be —so that she was never bothered with any of his cases. Then came the war. Like many others, though much over age, he volunteered. He gave up his lucrative practice and went to South Africa. His income, of course, stopped; the big house was closed; his wife found her life of enjoyment considerably curtailed. This she considered a great hardship, it seems. She felt a bitter grievance against him. Devoid of imagination, without any power of sacrifice, a selfish type, she was yet a beautiful, attractive woman—and young. The inevitable lover came upon the scene to console her. They planned to run away together. He was rich. Japan they thought would suit them. Only, by some ill luck, the husband got wind of it and arrived in London just in the nick of time."

"Well rid of her," put in O'Reilly, "I think."

The doctor waited a moment. He sipped his glass. Then his eyes fixed upon his companion's face somewhat sternly.

"Well rid of her, yes," he continued, "only he determined to make that riddance final. He decided to kill her—and her lover. You see, he loved her."

O'Reilly made no comment. In his own country this method with a faithless woman was not unknown. His interest was very concentrated. But he was thinking, too, as he listened, thinking hard.

"He planned the time and place with care," resumed the other in a lower voice, as though he might possibly be overheard. "They met, he knew, in the big house, now closed, the house where he and his young wife had passed such happy years during their prosperity. The plan failed, however, in an important detail—the woman came at the appointed hour, but without her lover. She found death waiting for her —it was a painless death. Then her lover, who was to arrive half an hour later, did not come at all. The door had been left open for him purposely. The house was dark, its rooms shut up, deserted; there was no caretaker even. It was a foggy night—just like this."

"And the other?" asked O'Reilly in a failing voice. "The lover—"

"A man did come in," the doctor went on calmly, "but it was not the lover. It was a stranger."

"A stranger?" the other whispered. "And the surgeon— where was he all the time?"

"Waiting outside to see him enter—concealed in the fog. He saw the man go in. Five minutes later he followed, meaning to complete his vengeance, his act of justice, whatever you like to call it. But the man who had come in was a stranger—he came in by chance—just as you might have done—to shelter from the fog—or—"

O'Reilly, though with a great effort, rose abruptly to his feet. He had an appalling feeling that the man facing him was mad. He had a keen desire to get outside, fog or no fog, to leave this room, to escape from the calm accents of this insistent voice. The effect of the whisky was still in his blood. He felt no lack of confidence. But words came to him with difficulty.

"I think I'd better be pushing off now, doctor," he said clumsily. "But I feel I must thank you very much for all your kindness and help." He turned and looked hard into the keen eyes facing him. "Your friend," he asked in a whisper, "the surgeon—I hope—I mean, was he ever caught?"

"No," was the grave reply, the doctor standing up in front of him, "he was never caught."

O'Reilly waited a moment before he made another remark. "Well," he said at length, but in a louder tone than before, "I think—I'm glad." He went to the door without shaking hands.

"You have no hat," mentioned the voice behind him. "If you'll wait a moment I'll get you one of mine. You need not trouble to return it." And the doctor passed him, going into the hall. There was a sound of tearing paper. O'Reilly left the house a moment later with a hat upon his head, but it was not till he reached the Tube station half an hour afterwards that he realized it was his own.

THE BECKONING FAIR ONE

By Oliver Onions

I

THE THREE or four "To Let" boards had stood within the low paling as long as the inhabitants of the little triangular "Square" could remember, and if they had ever been vertical it was a very long time ago. They now overhung the palings each at its own angle, and resembled nothing so much as a row of wooden choppers, ever in the act of falling upon some passer-by, yet never cutting off a tenant for the old house from the stream of his fellows. Not that there was ever any great "stream" through the square; the stream passed a furlong and more away, beyond the intricacy of tenements and alleys and byways that had sprung up since the old house had been built, hemming it in completely, and probably the house itself was only suffered to stand pending the falling-in of a lease or two, when doubtless a clearance would be made of the whole neighbourhood.

It was of gloomy old red brick, and built into its walls were the crowns and clasped hands and other insignia of insurance companies long since defunct. The children of the secluded square had swung upon the low gate at the end of the entrance alley until little more than the solid top bar of it remained, and the alley itself ran past boarded basement windows on which tramps had chalked their cryptic marks. The path was washed and worn uneven by the spilling of water from the eaves of the encroaching next house, and cats and dogs had made the approach their own. The chances of a tenant did not seem such as to warrant the keeping of the "To Let" boards in a state of legibility and repair, and as a matter of fact they were not so kept.

For six months Oleron had passed the old place twice a day or oftener, on his way from his lodgings to the room, ten minutes' walk away, he had taken to work in; and for six months no hatchet-like notice-board had fallen across his path. This might have been due to the fact that he usually took the other side of the square. But he chanced one morning to take the side that ran past the broken gate and the rain-worn entrance alley, and to pause before one of the inclined boards. The board bore, besides the agent's name, the announcement, written apparently about the time of Oleron's own early youth, that the key was to be had at Number Six.

Now Oleron was already paying, for his separate bedroom and workroom, more than an author who, without private means, habitually disregards his public, can afford; and he was paying in addition a small rent for the storage of the greater part of his grandmother's furniture. Moreover, it invariably happened that the book he wished to read in bed was at his working-quarters half a mile and more away, while the note or letter he had sudden need of during the day was as likely as not to be in the pocket of another coat hanging behind his bedroom door. And there were other inconveniences in having a divided domicile. Therefore Oleron, brought suddenly up by the hatchet-like notice-board, looked first down through some scanty privet bushes at the boarded basement windows, then up at the blank and grimy windows of the first floor, and so up to the second floor and the flat stone coping of the leads. He stood for a minute thumbing his lean and shaven jaw; then, with another glance at the board, he walked slowly across the square to Number Six.

He knocked, and waited for two or three minutes, but, although the door stood open, received no answer. He was knocking again when a long-nosed man in shirt-sleeves appeared.

"I was arsking a blessing on our food," he said in severe explanation.

Oleron asked if he might have the key of the old house; and the long-nosed man withdrew again.

Oleron waited for another five minutes on the step; then

the man, appearing again and masticating some of the food of which he had spoken, announced that the key was lost.

"But you won't want it," he said. "The entrance door isn't closed, and a push'll open any of the others. I'm a agent for it, if you're thinking of taking it—"

Oleron recrossed the square, descended the two steps at the broken gate, passed along the alley, and turned in at the old wide doorway. To the right, immediately within the door, steps descended to the roomy cellars, and the staircase before him had a carved rail, and was broad and handsome and filthy. Oleron ascended it, avoiding contact with the rail and wall, and stopped at the first landing. A door facing him had been boarded up, but he pushed at that on his right hand, and an insecure bolt or staple yielded. He entered the empty first floor.

He spent a quarter of an hour in the place, and then came out again. Without mounting higher, he descended and recrossed the square to the house of the man who had lost the key.

"Can you tell me how much the rent is?" he asked.

The man mentioned a figure, the comparative lowness of which seemed accounted for by the character of the neighbourhood and the abominable state of unrepair of the place.

"Would it be possible to rent a single floor?"

The long-nosed man did not know; they might. . . .

"Who are they?"

The man gave Oleron the name of a firm of lawyers in Lincoln's Inn.

"You might mention my name—Barrett," he added.

Pressure of work prevented Oleron from going down to Lincoln's Inn that afternoon, but he went on the morrow, and was instantly offered the whole house as a purchase for fifty pounds down, the remainder of the purchase money to remain on mortgage. It took him half an hour to disabuse the lawyer's mind of the idea that he wished anything more of the place than to rent a single floor of it. This made certain hums and haws of a difference, and the lawyer was by no means certain that it lay within his power to do as Oleron suggested; but it was finally extracted from him that, provided the notice boards were allowed to remain up, and that, provided it was agreed that in the event of the whole house letting, the arrangement should terminate automatically without further notice, something might be done. That the old place should suddenly be let over his head seemed to Oleron the slightest of risks to take, and he promised a decision within a week. On the morrow he visited the house again, went through it from top to bottom, and then went home to his lodgings to take a bath.

He was immensely taken with that portion of the house he had already determined should be his own. Scraped clean and repainted, and with that old furniture of Oleron's grandmother's, it ought to be entirely charming. He went to the storage warehouse to refresh his memory of his half-forgotten belongings, and to take measurements; and thence he went to a decorator's. He was very busy with his regular work, and could have wished that the notice-board had caught his attention either a few months earlier or else later in the year; but the quickest way would be to suspend work entirely until after his removal. . . .

A fortnight later his first floor was painted throughout in a tender, elder-flower white, the paint was dry, and Oleron was in the middle of his installation. He was animated, delighted; and he rubbed his hands as he polished and made disposals of his grandmother's effects—the tall lattice-paned china cupboard with its Derby and Mason and Spode, the large folding Sheraton table, the long, low bookshelves (he had had two of them "copied"), the chairs, the Sheffield candlesticks, the riveted rosebowls. These things he set against his newly painted elder-white walls—walls of wood panelled in the happiest proportions, and moulded and coffered to the low-seated window recesses in a mood of gaiety and rest that the builders of rooms no longer know. The ceilings were lofty, and faintly painted with an old pattern of stars; even the tapering mouldings of his iron fireplace were as delicately designed as jewellery; and Oleron walked about rubbing his hands, frequently stopping for the mere pleasure of the glimpses from white room to white room. . . .

"Charming, charming!" he said to himself. "I wonder what Elsie Bengough will think of this!"

He bought a bolt and a Yale lock for his door, and shut off his quarters from the rest of the house. If he now wanted to read in bed, his book could be had for stepping into the next room. All the time, he thought how exceedingly lucky he was to get the place. He put up a hatrack in the little square hall, and hung up his hats and caps and coats; and passers through the small triangular square late at night, looking up over the little serried row of wooden "To Let" hatchets, could see the light within Oleron's red blinds, or else the sudden darkening of one blind and the illumination of another, as Oleron, candlestick in hand, passed from room to room, making final settlings of his furniture, or preparing to resume the work that his removal had interrupted.

II

As far as the chief business of his life—his writing—was concerned, Paul Oleron treated the world a good deal better than he was treated by it; but he seldom took the trouble to strike a balance, or to compute how far, at forty-four years of age, he was behind his points on the handicap. To have done so wouldn't have altered matters, and it might have depressed Oleron. He had chosen his path, and was committed to it beyond possibility of withdrawal. Perhaps he had chosen it in the days when he had been easily swayed by something a little disinterested, a little generous, a little noble; and had he ever thought of questioning himself he would still have held to it that a life without nobility and generosity and disinterestedness was no life for him. Only quite recently, and rarely, had he even vaguely suspected that there was more in it than this; but it was no good anticipating the day when, he supposed, he would reach that maximum point of his powers beyond which he must inevitably decline, and be left face to face with the question whether it would not have profited him better to have ruled his life by less exigent ideals.

In the meantime, his removal into the old house with the insurance marks built into its brick merely interrupted *Romilly Bishop* at the fifteenth chapter.

As this tall man with the lean, ascetic face moved about his new abode, arranging, changing, altering, hardly yet into his working stride again, he gave the impression of almost spinster-like precision and nicety. For twenty years past, in a score of lodgings, garrets, flats, and rooms furnished and unfurnished, he had been accustomed to do many things for himself, and he had discovered that it saves time and temper to be methodical. He had arranged with the wife of the long-nosed Barrett, a stout Welsh woman with a falsetto voice, the Merionethshire accent of which long residence in London had not perceptibly modified, to come across the square each morning to prepare his breakfast, and also to "turn the place out" on Saturday mornings; and for the rest, he even welcomed a little housework as a relaxation from the strain of writing.

His kitchen, together with the adjoining strip of an apartment into which a modern bath had been fitted, overlooked the alley at the side of the house; and at one end of it was a large closet with a door, and a square sliding hatch in the upper part of the door. This had been a powder-closet, and through the hatch the elaborately dressed head had been thrust to receive the click and puff of the powder-pistol. Oleron puzzled a little over this closet; then, as its use occurred to him, he smiled faintly, a little moved, he knew not by what. . . . He would have to put it to a very different purpose from its original one; it would probably have to serve as his larder. . . . It was in this closet that he made a discovery. The back of it was shelved, and, rummaging on an upper shelf that ran deeply into the wall, Oleron found a couple of mushroom-shaped old wooden wig-stands. He did not know how they had come to be there. Doubtless the painters had turned them up somewhere or other, and had put them there. But his five rooms, as a whole, were short of cupboard and closet room, and it was only by the exercise of some ingenuity that he was able to find places for the bestowal of his household linen, his boxes, and his seldom-used but not-to-be-destroyed accumulations of papers.

It was in the early spring that Oleron entered on his tenancy, and he was anxious to have *Romilly* ready for publication in the coming autumn. Nevertheless, he did not intend to force its production. Should it demand longer in the doing, so much the worse; he realised its importance, its crucial importance, in his artistic development, and it must have its own length and time. In the workroom he had recently left he had been making excellent progress: *Romilly* had begun, as the saying is, to speak and act of herself; and he did not doubt she would continue to do so the moment the distraction of his removal was over. This distraction was almost over; he told himself it was time he pulled himself together again; and on a March morning he went out, returned again with two great bunches of yellow daffodils, placed one bunch on his mantelpiece between the Sheffield sticks and the other on the table before him, and took out the half-completed manuscript of *Romilly Bishop.*

But before beginning work he went to a small rosewood cabinet and took from a drawer his cheque-book and pass-book. He totted them up, and his monklike face grew thoughtful. His installation had cost him more than he had intended it should, and his balance was rather less than fifty pounds, with no immediate prospect of more.

"Hm! I'd forgotten rugs and chintz curtains and so forth mounted up so," said Oleron. "But it would have been a pity to spoil the place for the want of ten pounds or so. . . . Well, *Romilly* simply *must* be out for the autumn, that's all. So here goes—"

He drew his papers towards him.

But he worked badly; or, rather, he did not work at all. The square outside had its own noises, frequent and new, and Oleron could only hope that he would speedily become accustomed to these. First came hawkers, with their carts and cries; at midday the children, returning from school, trooped into the square and swung on Oleron's gate; and when the children had departed again for afternoon school, an itinerant musician with a mandolin posted himself beneath Oleron's window and began to strum. This was a not unpleasant distraction, and Oleron, pushing up his window, threw the man a penny. Then he returned to his table again. . . .

But it was no good. He came to himself, at long intervals, to find that he had been looking about his room and wondering how it had formerly been furnished—whether a settee in buttercup or petunia satin had stood under the farther window, whether from the centre moulding of the light lofty ceiling had depended a glimmering crystal chandelier, or where the tambour-frame or the picquet-table had stood. . . . No, it was no good; he had far better be frankly doing nothing than getting fruitlessly tired; and he decided that he would take a walk, but, chancing to sit down for a moment, dozed in his chair instead.

"This won't do," he yawned when he awoke at half-past four in the afternoon; "I must do better than this to-morrow—"

And he felt so deliciously lazy that for some minutes he even contemplated the breach of an appointment he had for the evening.

The next morning he sat down to work without even permitting himself to answer one of his three letters—two of them tradesmen's accounts, the third a note from Miss Bengough, forwarded from his old address. It was a jolly day of white and blue, with a gay noisy wind and a subtle turn in the colour of growing things; and over and over again, once or twice a minute, his room became suddenly light and then subdued again, as the shining white clouds rolled north-eastwards over the square. The soft fitful illumination was reflected in the polished surface of the table and even in the footworn old floor; and the morning noises had begun again.

Oleron made a pattern of dots on the paper before him, and then broke off to move the jar of daffodils exactly opposite the centre of a creamy panel. Then he wrote a sentence that ran continuously for a couple of lines, after which it broke off into notes and jottings. For a time he succeeded in persuading himself that in making these memoranda he was really working; and then he rose and began to pace his room. As he did so, he was struck by an idea. It was that the place might possibly be a little better for more positive colour. It was, perhaps, a thought *too* pale—mild and sweet as a kind old face, but a little devitalised, even wan. . . . Yes, decidedly it would bear a robuster note—more and richer flowers, and possibly some warm and gay stuff for cushions for the window seats. . . .

"Of course, I really can't afford it," he muttered, as he went for a two-foot and began to measure the width of the window recesses. . . .

In stooping to measure a recess, his attitude suddenly changed to one of interest and attention. Presently he rose again, rubbing his hands with gentle glee.

"Oho, oho!" he said. "These look to me very much like window boxes, nailed up. We must look into this! Yes, those are boxes, or I'm . . . oho, this is an adventure!"

On that wall of his sitting-room there were two windows (the third was in another corner), and, beyond the open bed-room door, on the same wall, was another. The seats of all had been painted, repainted, and painted again; and Oleron's investigating finger had barely detected the old nailheads be-neath the paint. Under the ledge over which he stooped an old keyhole also had been puttied up. Oleron took out his penknife.

He worked carefully for five minutes, and then went into the kitchen for a hammer and chisel. Driving the chisel cau-tiously under the seat, he started the whole lid slightly. Again using the penknife, he cut along the hinged edge and out-ward along the ends; and then he fetched a wedge and a wooden mallet.

"Now for our little mystery—" he said.

The sound of the mallet on the wedge seemed, in that sweet and pale apartment, somehow a little brutal—nay, even shocking. The panelling rang and rattled and vibrated to the blows like a sounding-board. The whole house seemed to echo; from the roomy cellarage to the garrets above a flock of echoes seemed to awake; and the sound got a little on Oleron's nerves. All at once he paused, fetched a duster, and muffled the mallet. . . . When the edge was sufficiently raised he put his fingers under it and lifted. The paint flaked and starred a little; the rusty old nails squeaked and grunted; and the lid came up, laying open the box beneath. Oleron

looked into it. Save for a couple of inches of scurf and mould
and old cobwebs it was empty.

"No treasure there," said Oleron, a little amused that he
should have fancied there might have been. "*Romilly* will
still have to be out by the autumn. Let's have a look at the
others."

He turned to the second window.

The raising of the two remaining seats occupied him until
well into the afternoon. That of the bedroom, like the first,
was empty; but from the second seat of his sitting-room he
drew out something yielding and folded and furred over an
inch thick with dust. He carried the object into the kitchen,
and having swept it over a bucket, took a duster to it.

It was some sort of a large bag, of an ancient friezelike material, and when unfolded it occupied the greater part of the
small kitchen floor. In shape it was an irregular, a very irregular, triangle, and it had a couple of wide flaps, with the
remains of straps and buckles. The patch that had been up-
permost in the folding was of a faded yellowish brown; but
the rest of it was of shades of crimson that varied according to
the exposure of the parts of it.

"Now whatever can that have been?" Oleron mused as he
stood surveying it. . . . "I give it up. Whatever it is, it's settled my work for to-day, I'm afraid—"

He folded the object up carelessly and thrust it into a
corner of the kitchen; then, taking pans and brushes and an
old knife, he returned to the sitting-room and began to
scrape and to wash and to line with paper his newly discovered receptacles. When he had finished, he put his spare
boots and books and papers into them; and he closed the lids
again, amused with his little adventure, but also a little anxious for the hour to come when he should settle fairly down
to his work again.

III

It piqued Oleron a little that his friend, Miss Bengough,
should dismiss with a glance the place he himself had found
so singularly winning. Indeed she scarcely lifted her eyes to
it. But then she had always been more or less like that—a lit-

tle indifferent to the graces of life, careless of appearances, and perhaps a shade more herself when she ate biscuits from a paper bag than when she dined with greater observance of the convenances. She was an unattached journalist of thirty-four, large, showy, fair as butter, pink as a dog-rose, reminding one of a florist's picked specimen bloom, and given to sudden and ample movements and moist and explosive utterances. She "pulled a better living out of the pool" (as she expressed it) than Oleron did; and by cunningly disguised puffs of drapers and haberdashers she "pulled" also the greater part of her very varied wardrobe. She left small whirlwinds of air behind her when she moved, in which her veils and scarves fluttered and spun.

Oleron heard the flurry of her skirts on his staircase and her single loud knock at his door when he had been a month in his new abode. Her garments brought in the outer air, and she flung a bundle of ladies' journals down on a chair.

"Don't knock off for me," she said across a mouthful of large-headed hatpins as she removed her hat and veil, "I didn't know whether you were straight yet, so I've brought some sandwiches for lunch. You've got coffee, I suppose?— No, don't get up—I'll find the kitchen—"

"Oh, that's all right, I'll clear these things away. To tell the truth, I'm rather glad to be interrupted," said Oleron.

He gathered his work together and put it away. She was already in the kitchen; he heard the running of water into the kettle. He joined her, and ten minutes later followed her back to the sitting-room with the coffee and sandwiches on a tray. They sat down, with the tray on a small table between them.

"Well, what do you think of the new place?" Oleron asked as she poured out coffee.

"Hm! . . . Anybody'd think you were going to get married, Paul."

He laughed.

"Oh, no. But it's an improvement on some of them, isn't it?"

"Is it? I suppose it is; I don't know. I liked the last place, in spite of the black ceiling and no water-tap. How's *Romilly?*"

Oleron thumbed his chin.

"Hm! I'm rather ashamed to tell you. The fact is, I've not got on very well with it. But it will be all right on the night, as you used to say."

"Stuck?"

"Rather stuck."

"Got any of it you care to read to me? . . ."

Oleron had long been in the habit of reading portions of his work to Miss Bengough occasionally. Her comments were always quick and practical, sometimes directly useful, sometimes indirectly suggestive. She, in return for his confidence, always kept all mention of her own work sedulously from him. His, she said, was "real work"; hers merely filled space, not always even grammatically.

"I'm afraid there isn't," Oleron replied, still meditatively dry-shaving his chin. Then he added, with a little burst of candour. "The fact is, Elsie, I've not written—not actually written—very much more of it—*any* more of it, in fact. But, of course, that doesn't mean I haven't progressed. I've progressed, in one sense, rather alarmingly. I'm now thinking of reconstructing the whole thing."

Miss Bengough gave a gasp. "Reconstructing!"

"Making Romilly herself a different type of woman. Somehow, I've begun to feel that I'm not getting the most out of her. As she stands, I've certainly lost interest in her to some extent."

"But—but—" Miss Bengough protested, "you had her so real, so *living*, Paul!"

Oleron smiled faintly. He had been quite prepared for Miss Bengough's disapproval. He wasn't surprised that she liked Romilly as she at present existed; she would. Whether she realised it or not, there was much of herself in his fictitious creation. Naturally Romilly would seem "real," "living," to her. . . .

"But are you really serious, Paul?" Miss Bengough asked presently, with a round-eyed stare.

"Quite serious."

"You're really going to scrap those fifteen chapters?"

"I didn't exactly say that."

"That fine, rich love scene?"

"I should only do it reluctantly, and for the sake of something I thought better."

"And that beautiful, *beautiful* description of Romilly on the shore?"

"It wouldn't necessarily be wasted," he said a little uneasily.

But Miss Bengough made a large and windy gesture, and then let him have it.

"Really, you are *too* trying!" she broke out. "I do wish sometimes you'd remember you're human, and live in a world! You know I'd be the *last* to wish you to lower your standard one inch, but it wouldn't be lowering it to bring it within human comprehension. Oh, you're sometimes altogether too godlike! . . . Why, it would be a wicked, criminal waste of your powers to destroy those fifteen chapters! Look at it reasonably, now. You've been working for nearly twenty years; you've now got what you've been working for almost within your grasp; your affairs are at a most critical stage (oh, don't tell me; I know you're about at the end of your money); and here you are, deliberately proposing to withdraw a thing that will probably make your name, and to substitute for it something that ten to one nobody on earth will ever want to read—and small blame to them! Really, you try my patience!"

Oleron had shaken his head slowly as she had talked. It was an old story between them. The noisy, able, practical journalist was an admirable friend—up to a certain point; beyond that . . . well, each of us knows that point beyond which we stand alone. Elsie Bengough sometimes said that had she had one-tenth part of Oleron's genius there were a few things she could not have done—thus making that genius a quantitatively divisible thing, a sort of ingredient, to be added to or subtracted from in the admixture of his work. That it was a qualitative thing, essential, indivisible, informing, passed her comprehension. Their spirits parted company at that point. Oleron knew it. She did not appear to know it.

"Yes, yes, yes," he said a little wearily, by and by, "practically you're quite right, entirely right, and I haven't a word to say. If I could only turn *Romilly* over to you, you'd make an enormous success of her. But that can't be, and I, for my part, am seriously doubting whether she's worth my while. You know what that means."

"What does it mean?" she demanded bluntly.

"Well," he said, smiling wanly, "what *does* it mean when you're convinced a thing isn't worth doing? You simply don't do it."

Miss Bengough's eyes swept the ceiling for assistance against this impossible man.

"What utter rubbish!" she broke out at last. "Why, when I saw you last you were simply oozing *Romilly*; you were turning her off at the rate of four chapters a week; if you hadn't moved you'd have had her three-parts done by now. What on earth possessed you to move right in the middle of your most important work?"

Oleron tried to put her off with a recital of inconveniences, but she wouldn't have it. Perhaps in her heart she partly suspected the reason. He was simply mortally weary of the narrow circumstances of his life. He had had twenty years of it—twenty years of garrets and roof-chambers and dingy flats and shabby lodgings, and he was tired of dinginess and shabbiness. The reward was as far off as ever—or if it was not, he no longer cared as once he would have cared to put out his hand and take it. It is all very well to tell a man who is at the point of exhaustion that only another effort is required of him; if he cannot make it he is as far off as ever. . . .

"Anyway," Oleron summed up, "I'm happier here than I've been for a long time. That's some sort of a justification."

"And doing no work," said Miss Bengough pointedly.

At that a trifling petulance that had been gathering in Oleron came to a head.

"And why should I do nothing but work?" he demanded. "How much happier am I for it? I don't say I don't love my work—when it's done; but I hate doing it. Sometimes it's an intolerable burden that I simply long to be rid of. Once in many weeks it has a moment, one moment, of glow and thrill for me; I remember the days when it was all glow and thrill; and now I'm forty-four, and it's becoming drudgery. Nobody wants it; I'm ceasing to want it myself; and if any ordinary sensible man were to ask me whether I didn't think I was a fool to go on, I think I should agree that I was."

Miss Bengough's comely pink face was serious.

"But you knew all that, many, many years ago, Paul—and still you chose it," she said in a low voice.

"Well, and how should I have known?" he demanded. "I didn't know. I was told so. My heart, if you like, told me so, and I thought I knew. Youth always thinks it knows; then one day it discovers that it is nearly fifty—"

"Forty-four, Paul—"

"—forty-four, then—and it finds that the glamour isn't in front, but behind. Yes, I knew and chose, if *that's* knowing and choosing . . . but it's a costly choice we're called on to make when we're young!"

Miss Bengough's eyes were on the floor. Without moving them she said, "You're not regretting it, Paul?"

"Am I not?" he took her up. "Upon my word, I've lately thought I am! What *do* I get in return for it all?"

"You know what you get," she replied.

He might have known from her tone what else he could have had for the holding up of a finger—herself. She knew, but could not tell him, that he could have done no better thing for himself. Had he, any time these ten years, asked her to marry him, she would have replied quietly, "Very well; when?" He had never thought of it. . . .

"Yours is the real work," she continued quietly. "Without you we jackals couldn't exist. You and a few like you hold everything upon your shoulders."

For a minute there was a silence. Then it occurred to Olcron that this was common vulgar grumbling. It was not his habit. Suddenly he rose and began to stack cups and plates on the tray.

"Sorry you catch me like this, Elsie," he said, with a little laugh. ". . . No, I'll take them out; then we'll go for a walk if you like. . . ."

He carried out the tray, and then began to show Miss Bengough round his flat. She made few comments. In the kitchen she asked what an old faded square of reddish frieze was, that Mrs. Barrett used as a cushion for her wooden chair.

"That? I should be glad if you could tell *me* what it is," Oleron replied as he unfolded the bag and related the story of its finding in the window seat.

"I think I know what it is," said Miss Bengough. "It's been used to wrap up a harp before putting it into its case."

"By Jove, that's probably just what it was," said Oleron. "I could make neither head nor tail of it. . . ."

They finished the tour of the flat, and returned to the sitting-room.

"And who lives in the rest of the house?" Miss Bengough asked.

"I dare say a tramp sleeps in the cellar occasionally. Nobody else."

"Hm! . . . Well, I'll tell you what I think about it, if you like."

"I should like."

"You'll never work here."

"Oh?" said Oleron quickly. "Why not?"

"You'll never finish *Romilly* here. Why, I don't know, but you won't. I know it. You'll have to leave before you get on with that book."

He mused for a moment, and then said:

"Isn't that a little—prejudiced, Elsie?"

"Perfectly ridiculous. As an argument it hasn't a leg to stand on. But there it is," she replied, her mouth once more full of the large-headed hatpins.

Oleron was reaching down his hat and coat. He laughed.

"I can only hope you're entirely wrong," he said, "for I shall be in a serious mess if *Romilly* isn't out in the autumn."

IV

As Oleron sat by his fire that evening, pondering Miss Bengough's prognostication that difficulties awaited him in his work, he came to the conclusion that it would have been far better had she kept her beliefs to herself. No man does a thing better for having his confidence damped at the outset, and to speak of difficulties is in a sense to make them. Speech itself becomes a deterrent act, to which other discouragements accrete until the very event of which warning is given is as likely as not to come to pass. He heartily confounded her. An influence hostile to the completion of *Romilly* had been born.

And in some illogical, dogmatic way women seem to have, she had attached this antagonistic influence to his new abode. Was ever anything so absurd! "You'll never finish *Romilly* here." . . . Why not? Was this her idea of the luxury that saps the springs of action and brings a man down to indolence and dropping out of the race? The place was well enough—it was entirely charming, for that matter—but it was not so demoralising as all that! No; Elsie had missed her mark that time. . . .

He moved his chair to look round the room that smiled, positively smiled, in the firelight. He too smiled, as if pity was to be entertained for a maligned apartment. Even that slight lack of robust colour he had remarked was not noticeable in the soft glow. The drawn chintz curtains—they had a flowered and trellised pattern, with baskets and oaten pipes—fell in long quiet folds to the window seats; the rows of bindings in old bookcases took the light richly; the last trace of sallowness had gone with the daylight; and, if the truth must be told, it had been Elsie herself who had seemed a little out of the picture.

That reflection struck him a little, and presently he returned to it. Yes, the room had, quite accidently, done Miss Bengough a disservice that afternoon. It had, in some subtle but unmistakable way, placed her, marked a contrast of qualities. Assuming for the sake of argument the slightly ridiculous proposition that the room in which Oleron sat *was* characterised by a certain sparsity and lack of vigour, so much the worse for Miss Bengough; she certainly erred on the side of redundancy and general muchness. And if one must contrast abstract qualities, Oleron inclined to the austere in taste. . . .

Yes, here Oleron had made a distinct discovery; he wondered he had not made it before. He pictured Miss Bengough again as she had appeared that afternoon—large, showy, moistly pink, with that quality of the prize bloom exuding, as it were, from her; and instantly she suffered in his thought. He even recognised now that he had noticed something odd at the time, and that unconsciously his attitude, even while she had been there, had been one of criticism. The mechanism of her was a little obvious; her melting humidity was the result of analysable processes; and behind her there had seemed to lurk some dim shape emblematic of mortality. He had never, during the ten years of their intimacy, dreamed for a moment of asking her to marry him; none the less, he now felt for the first time a thankfulness that he had not done so. . . .

Then, suddenly and swiftly, his face flamed that he should be thinking thus of his friend. What! Elsie Bengough, with whom he had spent weeks and weeks of afternoons—she, the good chum, on whose help he would have counted had all the rest of the world failed him—she, whose loyalty to him would not, he knew, swerve as long as there was breath in her —Elsie to be even in thought dissected thus! He was an ingrate and a cad. . . .

Had she been there in that moment he would have abased himself before her.

For ten minutes and more he sat, still gazing into the fire, with that humiliating red fading slowly from his cheeks. All was still within and without, save for a tiny musical tinkling that came from his kitchen—the dripping of water from an imperfectly turned-off tap into the vessel beneath it. Mechanically he began to beat with his fingers to the faintly heard falling of the drops; the tiny regular movement seemed to hasten that shameful withdrawal from his face. He grew cool once more; and when he resumed his meditation he was all unconscious that he took it up again at the same point. . . .

It was not only her florid superfluity of build that he had approached in the attitude of criticism; he was conscious also of the wide differences between her mind and his own. He felt no thankfulness that up to a certain point their natures

had ever run companionably side by side; he was now full of
questions beyond that point. Their intellects diverged; there
was no denying it; and, looking back, he was inclined to
doubt whether there had been any real coincidence. True, he
had read his writings to her and she had appeared to speak
comprehendingly and to the point; but what can a man do
who, having assumed that another sees as he does, is suddenly brought up sharp by something that falsifies and dis-
credits all that has gone before? He doubted all now. . . . It
did for a moment occur to him that the man who demands
of a friend more than can be given to him is in danger of losing that friend, but he put the thought aside.

Again he ceased to think, and again moved his finger to
the distant dripping of the tap. . . .

And now (he resumed by and by), if these things were
true of Elsie Bengough, they were also true of the creation of
which she was the prototype—Romilly Bishop. And since he
could say of Romilly what for very shame he could not say of
Elsie, he gave his thoughts rein. He did so in that smiling,
fire-lighted room, to the accompaniment of the faintly heard
tap.

There was no longer any doubt about it; he hated the central character of his novel. Even as he had described her
physically she overpowered the senses; she was coarse-fibred,
overcoloured, rank. It became true the moment he form-
ulated his thought; Gulliver had described the Bröbding-
nagian maids-of-honour thus: and mentally and spiritually
she corresponded—was unsensitive, limited, common. The
model (he closed his eyes for a moment)—the model stuck
out through fifteen vulgar and blatant chapters to such a
pitch that, without seeing the reason, he had been unable to
begin the sixteenth. He marvelled that it had only just
dawned upon him.

And *this* was to have been his Beatrice, his vision! As Elsie
she was to have gone into the furnace of his art, and she was
to have come out the Woman all men desire! Her thoughts
were to have been culled from his own finest, her form from
his dearest dreams, and her setting wherever he could find
one fit for her worth. He had brooded long before making

the attempt; then one day he had felt her stir within him as a mother feels a quickening, and he had begun to write, and so he had added chapter to chapter. . . .

And those fifteen sodden chapters were what he had produced!

Again he sat, softly moving his finger. . . .

Then he bestirred himself.

She must go, all fifteen chapters of her. That was settled. For what was to take her place his mind was a blank; but one thing at a time; a man is not excused from taking the wrong course because the right one is not immediately revealed to him. Better would come if it was to come; in the meantime—

He rose, fetched the fifteen chapters, and read them over before he should drop them into the fire.

But instead of putting them into the fire he let them fall from his hand. He became conscious of the dripping of the tap again. It had a tinkling gamut of four or five notes, on which it rang irregular changes, and it was foolishly sweet and dulcimer-like. In his mind Oleron could see the gathering of each drop, its little tremble on the lip of the tap, and the tiny percussion of its fall "Plink—plunk," minimised almost to inaudibility. Following the lowest note there seemed to be a brief phrase, irregularly repeated; and presently Oleron found himself waiting for the recurrence of this phrase. It was quite pretty. . . .

But it did not conduce to wakefulness, and Oleron dozed over his fire.

When he awoke again the fire had burned low and the flames of the candles were licking the rims of the Sheffield sticks. Sluggishly he rose, yawned, went his nightly round of doorlocks and window fastenings, and passed into his bedroom. Soon, he slept soundly.

But a curious little sequel followed on the morrow. Mrs. Barrett usually tapped, not at his door, but at the wooden wall beyond which lay Oleron's bed; and then Oleron rose, put on his dressing-gown, and admitted her. He was not conscious that as he did so that morning he hummed an air;

but Mrs. Barrett lingered with her hand on the doorknob and her face a little averted and smiling.

"De-ar me!" her soft falsetto rose. "But that will be a very o-ald tune, Mr. Oleron! I will not have heard it this for-ty years!"

"What tune?" Oleron asked.

"The tune, indeed, that you was humming, sir."

Oleron had his thumb in the flap of a letter. It remained there.

"I was humming? . . . Sing it, Mrs. Barrett."

Mrs. Barrett prut-prutted.

"I have no voice for singing, Mr. Oleron; it was Ann Pugh was the singer of our family; but the tune will be very o-ald, and it is called 'The Beckoning Fair One.'"

"Try to sing it," said Oleron, his thumb still in the envelope; and Mrs. Barrett, with much dimpling and confusion, hummed the air.

"They do say it was sung to a harp, Mr. Oleron, and it will be very o-ald," she concluded.

"And *I* was singing that?"

"Indeed you wass. I would not be likely to tell you lies."

With a "Very well—let me have breakfast," Oleron opened his letter; but the trifling circumstance struck him as more odd than he would have admitted to himself. The phrase he had hummed had been that which he had associated with the falling from the tap on the evening before.

V

Even more curious than that the commonplace dripping of an ordinary water-tap should have tallied so closely with an actually existing air was another result it had, namely, that it awakened or seemed to awaken, in Oleron an abnormal sensitiveness to other noises of the old house. It has been remarked that silence obtains its fullest and most impressive quality when it is broken by some minute sound; and, truth to tell, the place was never still. Perhaps the mildness of the spring air operated on its torpid old timbers; perhaps Oleron's fires caused it to stretch its old anatomy; and certainly a whole world of insect life bored and burrowed in its baulks and joists. At any rate Oleron had only to sit quiet in his chair and to wait for a minute or two in order to become aware of such a change in the auditory scale as comes upon a man who, conceiving the midsummer woods to be motionless and still, all at once finds his ear sharpened to the crepitation of a myriad insects.

And he smiled to think of man's arbitrary distinction between that which has life and that which has not. Here, quite apart from such recognisable sounds as the scampering of mice, the falling of plaster behind his panelling, and the popping of purses or coffins from his fire, was a whole house talking to him had he but known its language. Beams settled with a tired sigh into their old mortices; creatures ticked in the walls; joints cracked, boards complained; with no palpable stirring of the air, window sashes changed their positions with a soft knock in their frames. And whether the place had life in this sense or not, it had at all events a winsome personality. It needed but an hour of musing for Oleron to conceive the idea that, as his own body stood in friendly relation to his soul, so, by an extension and an attenuation, his habitation might fantastically be supposed to stand in some relation to himself. He even amused himself with the farfetched fancy that he might so identify himself with the place that some future tenant, taking possession, might regard it as in a sense haunted. It would be rather a joke if he, a perfectly harmless author, with nothing on his mind worse than a novel he had discovered he must begin again, should turn out to be laying the foundation of a future ghost! . . .

In proportion, however, as he felt this growing attachment to the fabric of his abode, Elsie Bengough, from being merely unattracted, began to show a dislike of the place that was more and more marked. And she did not scruple to speak of her aversion.

"It doesn't belong to to-day at all, and for you especially it's bad," she said with decision. "You're only too ready to let go your hold on actual things and to slip into apathy; *you* ought to be in a place with concrete floors and a patent gas meter and a tradesmen's lift. And it would do you all the good in the world if you had a job that made you scramble and rub elbows with your fellow-men. Now, if I could get you a job, for, say, two or three days a week, one that would allow you heaps of time for your proper work—would you take it?"

Somehow, Oleron resented a little being diagnosed like this. He thanked Miss Bengough, but without a smile.

"Thank you, but I don't think so. After all, each of us has his own life to live," he could not refrain from adding.

"His own life to live! . . . How long is it since you were out, Paul?"

"About two hours."

"I don't mean to buy stamps or to post a letter. How long is it since you had anything like a stretch?"

"Oh, some little time perhaps. I don't know."

"Since I was here last?"

"I haven't been out much."

"And has *Romilly* progressed much better for your being cooped up?"

"I think she has. I'm laying the foundations of her. I shall begin the actual writing presently."

It seemed as if Miss Bengough had forgotten their tussle about the first *Romilly*. She frowned, turned half away, and then quickly turned again.

"Ah! . . . So you've still got that ridiculous idea in your head?"

"If you mean," said Oleron slowly, "that I've discarded the old *Romilly*, and am at work on a new one, you're right. I have still got that idea in my head."

Something uncordial in his tone struck her; but she was a fighter. His own absurd sensitiveness hardened her. She gave a "Pshaw!" of impatience.

"Where is the old one?" she demanded abruptly.

"Why?" asked Oleron.

"I want to see it. I want to show some of it to you. I want, if you're not wool-gathering entirely, to bring you back to your senses."

This time it was he who turned his back. But when he turned round again he spoke more gently.

"It's no good, Elsie. I'm responsible for the way I go, and

you must allow me to go it—even if it should seem wrong to you. Believe me, I am giving thought to it. . . . The manuscript? I was on the point of burning it, but I didn't. It's in that window seat, if you must see it."

Miss Bengough crossed quickly to the window seat, and lifted the lid. Suddenly she gave a little exclamation, and put the back of her hand to her mouth. She spoke over her shoulder:

"You ought to knock those nails in, Paul," she said.

He strode to her side.

"What? What is it? What's the matter?" he asked. "I did knock them in—or, rather, pulled them out."

"You left enough to scratch with," she replied, showing her hand. From the upper wrist to the knuckle of the little finger a welling red wound showed.

"Good-gracious!" Oleron ejaculated. . . . "Here, come to the bathroom and bathe it quickly—"

He hurried her to the bathroom, turned on warm water, and bathed and cleansed the bad gash. Then, still holding the hand, he turned cold water on it, uttering broken phrases of astonishment and concern.

"Good Lord, how did that happen! As far as I knew I'd . . . is this water too cold? Does that hurt? I can't imagine how on earth . . . there; that'll do—"

"No—one moment longer—I can bear it," she murmured, her eyes closed. . . .

Presently he led her back to the sitting-room and bound the hand in one of his handkerchiefs; but his face did not lose its expression of perplexity. He had spent half a day in opening and making serviceable the three window boxes, and he could not conceive how he had come to leave an inch and a half of rusty nail standing in the wood. He himself had opened the lids of each of them a dozen times and had not noticed any nail; but there it was. . . .

"It shall come out now, at all events," he muttered, as he went for a pair of pincers. And he made no mistake about it that time.

Elsie Bengough had sunk into a chair, and her face was rather white; but in her hand was the manuscript of *Romilly*.

She had not finished with *Romilly* yet. Presently she returned to the charge.

"Oh, Paul, it will be the greatest mistake you ever, *ever* made if you do not publish this!" she said.

He hung his head, genuinely distressed. He couldn't get that incident of the nail out of his head, and *Romilly* occupied a second place in his thoughts for the moment. But still she insisted; and when presently he spoke it was almost as if he asked her pardon for something.

"What can I say, Elsie? I can only hope that when you see the new version, you'll see how right I am. And if in spite of all you *don't* like her, well . . ." he made a hopeless gesture. "Don't you see that I *must* be guided by my own lights?"

She was silent.

"Come, Elsie," he said gently. "We've got along well so far, don't let us split on this."

The last words had hardly passed his lips before he regretted them. She had been nursing her injured hand, with her eyes once more closed; but her lips and lids quivered simultaneously. Her voice shook as she spoke.

"I can't help saying it, Paul, but you are so greatly changed."

"Hush, Elsie," he murmured soothingly; "you've had a shock; rest for a while. How could I change?"

"I don't know, but you are. You've not been yourself ever since you came here. I wish you'd never seen the place. It stopped your work, it's making you into a person I hardly know and it's made me horribly anxious about you. . . . Oh, how my hand is beginning to throb!"

"Poor child!" he murmured. "Will you let me take you to a doctor and have it properly dressed?"

"No—I shall be all right presently—I'll keep it raised—"

She put her elbow on the back of her chair, and the bandaged hand rested lightly on his shoulder.

At that touch an entirely new anxiety stirred suddenly within him. Hundreds of times previously, on their jaunts and excursions, she had slipped her hand within his arm as she might have slipped it into the arm of a brother, and he had accepted the little affectionate gesture as a brother might have accepted it. But now, for the first time, there rushed into his mind a hundred startling questions. Her eyes were still closed, and her head had fallen pathetically back; and there was a lost and ineffable smile on her parted lips. The truth broke in upon him. Good God! . . . And he had never divined it!

And stranger than all was that, now that he did see that she was lost in love of him, there came to him, not sorrow and humility and abasement, but something else that he struggled in vain against—something entirely strange and new, that, had he analysed it, he would have found to be petulance and irritation and resentment and ungentleness. The sudden selfish prompting mastered him before he was aware. He all but gave it words. What was she doing there at all? Why was she not getting on with her own work? Why was she here interfering with his? Who had given her this guardianship over him that lately she had put forward so assertively?—"Changed?" It was she, not himself, who had changed. . . .

But by the time she had opened her eyes again he had overcome his resentment sufficiently to speak gently, albeit with reserve.

"I wish you would let me take you to a doctor."

She rose.

"No, thank you, Paul," she said. "I'll go now. If I need a dressing I'll get one; take the other hand, please. Goodbye—"

He did not attempt to detain her. He walked with her to the foot of the stairs. Halfway along the narrow alley she turned.

"It would be a long way to come if you happened not to be in," she said; "I'll send you a postcard the next time."

At the gate she turned again.

"Leave here, Paul," she said, with a mournful look. "Everything's wrong with this house."

Then she was gone.

Oleron returned to his room. He crossed straight to the window box. He opened the lid and stood long looking at it. Then he closed it again and turned away.

"That's rather frightening," he muttered. "It's simply not possible that I should not have removed that nail. . . ."

VI

Oleron knew very well what Elsie had meant when she had said that her next visit would be preceded by a postcard. She, too, had realised that at last, at last he knew—knew, and didn't want her. It gave him a miserable, pitiful pang, therefore, when she came again within a week, knocking at the door unannounced. She spoke from the landing; she did not intend to stay, she said; and he had to press her before she would so much as enter.

Her excuse for calling was that she had heard of an inquiry for short stories that he might be wise to follow up. He thanked her. Then, her business over, she seemed anxious to get away again. Oleron did not seek to detain her; even he saw through the pretext of the stories; and he accompanied her down the stairs.

But Elsie Bengough had no luck whatever in that house. A second accident befell her. Halfway down the staircase there was the sharp sound of splintering wood, and she checked a loud cry. Oleron knew the woodwork to be old, but he himself had ascended and descended frequently enough without mishap. . . .

Elsie had put her foot through one of the stairs.

He sprang to her side in alarm.

"Oh, I say! My poor girl!"

She laughed hysterically.

"It's my weight—I know I'm getting fat—"

"Keep still—let me clear these splinters away," he muttered between his teeth.

She continued to laugh and sob that it was her weight—she was getting fat—

He thrust downwards at the broken boards. The extrication was no easy matter, and her torn boot showed him how badly the foot and ankle within it must be abraded.

"Good God—good God!" he muttered over and over again.

"I shall be too heavy for anything soon," she sobbed and laughed.

But she refused to reascend and to examine her hurt.

"No, let me go quickly—let me go quickly," she repeated.

"But it's a frightful gash!"

"No—not so bad—let me get away quickly—I'm—I'm not wanted."

At her word, that she was not wanted, his head dropped as if she had given him a buffet.

"Elsie!" he choked, brokenly and shocked.

But she too made a quick gesture, as if she put something violently aside.

"Oh, Paul, not *that*—not *you*—of course I do mean that too in a sense—oh, you know what I mean! . . . But if the other can't be, spare me this now! I—I wouldn't have come, but—but oh, I did, I *did* try to keep away!"

It was intolerable, heartbreaking; but what could he do—what could he say? He did not love her. . . .

"Let me go—I'm not wanted—let me take away what's left of me—"

"Dear Elsie—you are very dear to me—"

But again she made the gesture, as of putting something violently aside.

"No, not that—not anything less—don't offer me anything less—leave me a little pride—"

"Let me get my hat and coat—let me take you to a doctor," he muttered.

But she refused. She refused even the support of his arm. She gave another unsteady laugh.

"I'm sorry I broke your stairs, Paul. . . . You will go and see about the short stories, won't you?"

He groaned.

"Then if you won't see a doctor, will you go across the square and let Mrs. Barrett look at you? Look, there's Barrett passing now—"

The long-nosed Barrett was looking curiously down the alley, but as Oleron was about to call him he made off without a word. Elsie seemed anxious for nothing so much as to be clear of the place, and finally promised to go straight to a doctor, but insisted on going alone.

"Good-bye," she said.

And Oleron watched her until she was past the hatchet-like "To Let" boards, as if he feared that even they might fall upon her and maim her.

That night Oleron did not dine. He had far too much on his mind. He walked from room to room of his flat, as if he could have walked away from Elsie Bengough's haunting cry that still rang in his ears. "I'm not wanted—don't offer me anything less—let me take away what's left of me—"

Oh, if he could only have persuaded himself that he loved her!

He walked until twilight fell; then, without lighting candles, he stirred up the fire and flung himself into a chair.

Poor, poor Elsie! . . .

But even while his heart ached for her, it was out of the question. If only he had known! If only he had used common observation! But those walks, those sisterly takings of the arm—what a fool he had been! . . . Well, it was too late now. It was she, not he, who must now act—act by keeping away. He would help her all he could. He himself would not sit in her presence. If she came, he would hurry her out again as fast as he could. . . . Poor, poor Elsie!

His room grew dark; the fire burned dead; and he continued to sit, wincing from time to time as a fresh tortured phrase rang again in his ears.

Then suddenly, he knew not why, he found himself anxious for her in a new sense—uneasy about her personal safety. A horrible fancy that even then she might be looking over an embankment down into dark water, that she might even now be glancing up at the hook on the door, took him. Women had been known to do those things. . . . Then there would be an inquest, and he himself would be called upon to identify her, and would be asked how she had come by an ill-healed wound on the hand and a bad abrasion of the ankle. Barrett would say that he had seen her leaving his house. . . .

Then he recognised that his thoughts were morbid. By an effort of will he put them aside, and sat for a while listening to the faint creakings and tickings and rappings within his panelling. . . .

If only he could have married her! . . . But he couldn't. Her face had risen before him again as he had seen it on the stairs, drawn with pain and ugly and swollen with tears. Ugly —yes, positively blubbered; if tears were women's weapons, as they were said to be, such tears were weapons turned against themselves . . . suicide again. . . .

Then all at once he found himself attentively considering her two accidents.

Extraordinary they had been, both of them. He *could not* have left that old nail standing in the wood; why, he had fetched tools specially from the kitchen; and he was convinced that that step that had broken beneath her weight had been as sound as the others. It was inexplicable. If these things could happen, anything could happen. There was not a beam nor a jamb in the place that might not fall without warning, not a plank that might not crash inwards, not a nail that might not become a dagger. The whole place was full of life even now; as he sat there in the dark he heard its crowds of noises as if the house had been one great microphone. . . .

Only half conscious that he did so, he had been sitting for some time identifying these noises, attributing to each crack or creak or knock its material cause; but there was one noise which, again not fully conscious of the omission, he had not sought to account for. It had last come some minutes ago; it came again now—a sort of soft sweeping rustle that seemed to hold an almost inaudibly minute crackling. For half a minute or so it had Oleron's attention; then his heavy thoughts were of Elsie Bengough again.

He was nearer to loving her in that moment than he had ever been. He thought how to some men their loved ones were but the dearer for those poor mortal blemishes that tell us we are but sojourners on earth, with a common fate not far distant that makes it hardly worth while to do anything but love for the time remaining. Strangling sobs, blearing tears, bodies buffeted by sickness, hearts and minds callous and hard with the rubs of the world—how little love there would be were these things a barrier to love! In that sense he did love Elsie Bengough. What her happiness had never moved in him her sorrow almost awoke. . . .

Suddenly his meditation went. His ear had once more become conscious of that soft and repeated noise—the long sweep with the almost inaudible crackle in it. Again and again it came, with a curious insistence and urgency. It quickened a little as he became increasingly attentive . . . it seemed to Oleron that it grew louder. . . .

All at once he started bolt upright in his chair, tense and listening. The silky rustle came again; he was trying to attach it to something. . . .

The next moment he had leapt to his feet, unnerved and terrified. His chair hung poised for a moment, and then went over, setting the fire-irons clattering as it fell. There was only one noise in the world like that which had caused him to spring thus to his feet. . . .

The next time it came Oleron felt behind him at the empty air with his hand, and backed slowly until he found himself against the wall.

"God in heaven!" The ejaculation broke from Oleron's lips. The sound had ceased.

The next moment he had given a high cry.

"What is it? What's there? Who's there?"

A sound of scuttling caused his knees to bend under him for a moment; but that, he knew, was a mouse. That was not something that his stomach turned sick and his mind reeled to entertain. That other sound, the like of which was not in the world, had now entirely ceased; and again he called. . . .

He called and continued to call; and then another terror, a terror of the sound of his own voice, seized him. He did not dare to call again. His shaking hand went to his pocket for a match, but found none. He thought there might be matches on the mantelpiece—

He worked his way to the mantelpiece round a little recess, without for a moment leaving the wall. Then his hand encountered the mantelpiece, and groped along it. A box of matches fell to the hearth. He could just see them in the firelight, but his hand could not pick them up until he had cornered them inside the fender.

Then he rose and struck a light.

The room was as usual. He struck a second match. A candle stood on the table. He lighted it, and the flame sank for a moment and then burned up clear. Again he looked round.

There was nothing.

There was nothing; but there had been something, and might still be something. Formerly, Oleron had smiled at the fantastic thought that, by a merging and interplay of identities between himself and his beautiful room, he might be preparing a ghost for the future; it had not occured to him *that there might have been a similar merging and coalescence in the past.* Yet with this staggering impossibility he was now face to face. Something did persist in the house; it had a tenant other than himself; and that tenant, whatsoever or whosoever, had appalled Oleron's soul by producing the sound of a woman brushing her hair.

VII

Without quite knowing how he came to be there Oleron found himself striding over the loose board he had temporarily placed on the step broken by Miss Bengough. He was hatless, and descending the stairs. Not until later did there return to him a hazy memory that he had left the candle burning on the table, had opened the door no wider than was necessary to allow the passage of his body, and had sidled out, closing the door softly behind him. At the foot of the stairs another shock awaited him. Something dashed with a flurry up from the disused cellars and disappeared out of the door. It was only a cat, but Oleron gave a childish sob.

He passed out of the gate, and stood for a moment under the "To Let" boards, plucking foolishly at his lip and looking up at the glimmer of light behind one of his red blinds. Then, still looking over his shoulder, he moved stumblingly up the square. There was a small public house round the corner; Oleron had never entered it; but he entered it now, and put down a shilling that missed the counter by inches.

"B—b—bran—brandy," he said, and then stooped to look for the shilling.

He had the little sawdusted bar to himself; what company there was—carters and labourers and the small tradesmen of the neighbourhood—was gathered in the farther compartment, beyond the space where the white-haired landlady moved among her taps and bottles. Oleron sat down on a hardwood settee with a perforated seat, drank half his brandy and then, thinking he might as well drink it as spill it, finished it.

Then he fell to wondering which of the men whose voices he heard across the public house would undertake the removal of his effects on the morrow.

In the meantime he ordered more brandy.

For he did not intend to go back to that room where he had left the candle burning. Oh no! He couldn't have faced even the entry and the staircase with the broken step—certainly not that pith-white, fascinating room. He would go back for the present to his old arrangement, of workroom and separate sleeping quarters; he would go to his old landlady at once—presently—when he had finished his brandy—and see if she could put him up for the night. His glass was empty now. . . .

He rose, had it refilled, and sat down again.

And if anybody asked his reason for removing again? Oh, he had reason enough—reason enough! Nails that put themselves back into wood again and gashed people's hands, steps that broke when you trod on them, and women who came into a man's place and brushed their hair in the dark were reasons enough! He was querulous and injured about it all. He had taken the place for himself, not for invisible women to brush their hair in; that lawyer fellow in Lincoln's Inn should be told so, too, before many hours were out; it was outrageous, letting people in for agreements like that!

A cut-glass partition divided the compartment where Oleron sat from the space where the white-haired landlady moved; but it stopped seven or eight inches above the level of the counter. There was no partition at the farther bar. Presently Oleron, raising his eyes, saw that faces were watch-

ing him through the aperture. The faces disappeared when
he looked at them.

He moved to a corner where he could not be seen from the
other bar; but this brought him into line with the white-
haired landlady.

She knew him by sight—had doubtless seen him passing
and repassing; and presently she made a remark on the
weather. Oleron did not know what he replied, but it sufficed
to call forth the further remark that the winter had been a
bad one for influenza, but that the spring weather seemed to
be coming at last. . . . Even this slight contact with the
commonplace steadied Oleron a little; an idle, nascent wonder whether the landlady brushed her hair every night, and,
if so, whether it gave out those little electric cracklings, was
shut down with a snap; and Oleron was better. . . .

With his next glass of brandy he was all for going back to
his flat. Not go back? Indeed, he would go back! They should
very soon see whether he was to be turned out of his place
like that! He began to wonder why he was doing the rather
unusual thing he was doing at that moment, unusual for him
—sitting hatless, drinking brandy, in a public house. Suppose
he were to tell the white-haired landlady all about it—to tell
her that a caller had scratched her hand on a nail, had later
had the bad luck to put her foot through a rotten stair,
and that he himself, in an old house full of squeaks and
creaks and whispers, had heard a minute noise and had
bolted from it in fright—what would she think of him? That
he was mad, of course. . . . Pshaw! The real truth of the
matter was that he hadn't been doing enough work to occupy
him. He had been dreaming his days away, filling his head
with a lot of moonshine about a new *Romilly* (as if the old
one was not good enough), and now he was surprised that
the devil should enter an empty head!

Yes, he would go back. He would take a walk in the air first
—he hadn't walked enough lately—and then he would take
himself in hand, settle the hash of that sixteenth chapter of
Romilly (fancy, he had actually been fool enough to think of
destroying fifteen chapters!) and thenceforward he would

remember that he had obligations to his fellow-men and work to do in the world. There was the matter in a nutshell.

He finished his brandy and went out.

He had walked for some time before any other bearing of the matter than that on himself occurred to him. At first, the fresh air had increased the heady effect of the brandy he had drunk; but afterwards his mind grew clearer than it had been since morning. And the clearer it grew, the less final did his boastful self-assurances become, and the firmer his conviction that, when all explanations had been made, there remained something that could not be explained. His hysteria of an hour before had passed; he grew steadily calmer; but the disquieting conviction remained. A deep fear took possession of him. It was a fear for Elsie.

For something in his place was inimical to her safety. Of themselves, her two accidents might not have persuaded him of this; but she herself had said it, *"I'm not wanted here. . . ."* And she had declared that there was something wrong with the place. She had seen it before he had. Well and good. One thing stood out clearly: namely, that if this was so, she must be kept away for quite another reason than that which had so confounded and humiliated Oleron. Luckily she had expressed her intention of staying away; she must be held to that intention. He must see to it.

And he must see to it all the more that he now saw his first impulse, never to set foot in the place again, was absurd. People did not do that kind of thing. With Elsie made secure, he could not with any respect to himself suffer himself to be turned out by a shadow, nor even by a danger merely because it was a danger. He had to live somewhere, and he would live there. He must return.

He mastered the faint chill of fear that came with the decision, and turned in his walk abruptly. Should fear grow on him again he would, perhaps, take one more glass of brandy. . . .

But by the time he reached the short street that led to the square he was too late for more brandy. The little public house was still lighted, but closed, and one or two men were standing talking on the kerb. Oleron noticed that a sudden silence fell on them as he passed, and he noticed further that the long-nosed Barrett, whom he passed a little lower down, did not return his good night. He turned in at the broken gates, hesitated merely an instant in the alley, and then mounted his stairs again.

Only an inch of candle remained in the Sheffield stick, and Oleron did not light another one. Deliberately he forced himself to take it up and to make the tour of his five rooms before retiring. It was as he returned from the kitchen across his little hall that he noticed that a letter lay on the floor. He carried it into his sitting-room and glanced at the envelope before opening it.

It was unstamped, and had been put into the door by hand. Its handwriting was clumsy, and it ran from beginning to end without comma or period. Oleron read the first line, turned to the signature, and then finished the letter.

It was from the man Barrett, and it informed Oleron that he, Barrett, would be obliged if Mr. Oleron would make other arrangements for the preparing of his breakfasts and the cleaning-out of his place. The sting lay in the tail, that is to say, the postscript. This consisted of a text of Scripture. It embodied an allusion that could only be to Elsie Bengough. . . .

A seldom-seen frown had cut deeply into Oleron's brow. So! That was it! Very well; they would see about that on the morrow. . . . For the rest, this seemed merely another reason why Elsie should keep away. . . .

Then his suppressed rage broke out. . . .

The foul-minded lot! The devil himself could not have given a leer at anything that had ever passed between Paul Oleron and Elsie Bengough, yet this nosing rascal must be prying and talking! . . .

Oleron crumpled the paper up, held it in the candle flame, and then ground the ashes under his heel.

One useful purpose, however, the letter had served: it had created in Oleron a wrathful blaze that effectually banished pale shadows. Nevertheless, one other puzzling circumstance was to close the day. As he undressed, he chanced to glance at his bed. The coverlets bore an impress as if somebody had lain on them. Oleron could not remember that he himself had lain down during the day—off-hand, he would have said that certainly he had not; but after all he could not be positive. His indignation for Elsie, acting possibly with the residue of the brandy in him, excluded all other considerations; and he put out his candle, lay down, and passed immediately into a deep and dreamless sleep, which, in the absence of Mrs. Barrett's call, lasted almost once round the clock.

VIII

To the man who pays heed to that voice within him which warns him that twilight and danger are settling over his soul, terror is apt to appear an absolute thing, against which his heart must be safeguarded in a twink unless there is to take place an alteration in the whole range and scale of his nature. Mercifully, he has never far to look for safeguards. Of the immediate and small and common and momentary things of life, of usages and observances and modes and conventions, he builds up fortifications against the powers of darkness. He is even content that not terror only, but joy also, should for working purposes be placed in the category of the absolute things; and the last treason he will commit will be that breaking down of terms and limits that strikes, not at one man, but at the welfare of the souls of all.

In his own person, Oleron began to commit this treason. He began to commit it by admitting the inexplicable and horrible to an increasing familiarity. He did it insensibly, unconsciously, by a neglect of the things that he now regarded it as an impertinence in Elsie Bengough to have prescribed. Two months before, the words "a haunted house," applied to his lovely bemusing dwelling, would have chilled his marrow; now, his scale of sensation becoming depressed, he could ask "Haunted by what?" and remain unconscious that horror, when it can be proved to be relative, by so much loses its proper quality. He was setting aside the landmarks. Mists and confusion had begun to enwrap him.

And he was conscious of nothing so much as of a voracious inquisitiveness. He wanted to *know*. He was resolved to know. Nothing but the knowledge would satisfy him; and craftily he cast about for means whereby he might attain it.

He might have spared his craft. The matter was the easiest imaginable. As in time past he had known, in his writing, moments when his thoughts had seemed to rise of themselves and to embody themselves in words not to be altered afterwards, so now the questions he put himself seemed to be answered even in the moment of their asking. There was exhilaration in the swift, easy processes. He had known no such joy in his own power since the days when his writing had been a daily freshness and a delight to him. It was almost as if the course he must pursue was being dictated to him.

And the first thing he must do, of course, was to define the problem. He defined it in terms of mathematics. Granted that he had not the place to himself; granted that the old house had inexpressibly caught and engaged his spirit; granted that, by virtue of the common denominator of the place, this unknown co-tenant stood in some relation to himself: what next? Clearly, the nature of the other numerator must be ascertained.

And how? Ordinarily this would not have seemed simple, but to Oleron it was now pellucidly clear. The key, *of course*, lay in his half-written novel—or rather, in both *Romillys*, the old and the proposed new one.

A little while before Oleron would have thought himself mad to have embraced such an opinion; now he accepted the dizzying hypothesis without a quiver.

He began to examine the first and second *Romillys*.

From the moment of his doing so the thing advanced by leaps and bounds. Swiftly he reviewed the history of the *Romilly* of the fifteen chapters. He remembered clearly now that he had found her insufficient on the very first morning on which he had sat down to work in his new place. Other instances of his aversion leaped up to confirm his obscure investigation. There had come the night when he had hardly forborne to throw the whole thing into the fire; and the next morning he had begun the planning of the new *Romilly*. It had been on that morning that Mrs. Barrett, overhearing him humming a brief phrase that the dripping of a tap the night before had suggested, had informed him that he was singing some air he had never in his life heard before, called "The Beckoning Fair One." . . .

The Beckoning Fair One! . . .

With scarcely a pause in thought he continued:

The first *Romilly* having been definitely thrown over, the second had instantly fastened herself upon him, clamouring for birth in his brain. He even fancied now, looking back, that there had been something like passion, hate almost, in the supplanting, and that more than once a stray thought given to his discarded creation had—(it was astonishing how credible Oleron found the almost unthinkable idea)—had offended the supplanter.

Yet that a malignancy almost homicidal should be extended to his fiction's poor mortal prototype. . . .

In spite of his inuring to a scale in which the horrible was now a thing to be fingered and turned this way and that, a "Good God!" broke from Oleron.

This intrusion of the first *Romilly's* prototype into his thought again was a factor that for the moment brought his inquiry into the nature of his problem to a termination; the mere thought of Elsie was fatal to anything abstract. For another thing, he could not yet think of that letter of Barrett's, nor of a little scene that had followed it, without a mounting of colour and a quick contraction of the brow. For, wisely or not, he had had that argument out at once. Striding across the square on the following morning, he had bearded Barrett on his own doorstep. Coming back again a few minutes later, he had been strongly of opinion that he had only made matters worse. The man had been vagueness itself. He had not been able to be either challenged or browbeaten into anything more definite than a muttered farrago in which the words "Certain things . . . Mrs. Barrett . . . respectable house . . . if the cap fits . . . proceedings that shall be nameless," had been constantly repeated.

"Not that I make any charge—" he had concluded.

"Charge!" Oleron had cried.

"I 'ave my idears of things, as I don't doubt you 'ave yours—"

"Ideas—mine!" Oleron had cried wrathfully, immediately dropping his voice as heads had appeared at windows of the square. "Look you here, my man; you've an unwholesome mind, which probably you can't help, but a tongue which you can help, and shall! If there is a breath of this repeated . . ."

"I'll not be talked to on my own doorstep like this by anybody . . ." Barrett had blustered. . . .

"You shall, and I'm doing it . . ."

"Don't you forget there's a Gawd above all, Who 'as said . . ."

"You're a low scandalmonger! . . ."

And so forth, continuing badly what was already badly begun. Oleron had returned wrathfully to his own house, and thenceforward, looking out of his windows, had seen Barrett's face at odd times, lifting blinds or peering round curtains, as if he sought to put himself in possession of Heaven knew what evidence, in case it should be required of him.

The unfortunate occurrence made certain minor differences in Oleron's domestic arrangements. Barrett's tongue, he gathered, had already been busy; he was looked at askance by the dwellers of the square; and he judged it better, until he should be able to obtain other help, to make his purchases of provisions a little farther afield rather than at the small shops of the immediate neighbourhood. For the rest, housekeeping was no new thing to him, and he would resume his old bachelor habits. . . .

Besides, he was deep in certain rather abstruse investigations, in which it was better that he should not be disturbed.

He was looking out of his window one midday rather tired, not very well, and glad that it was not very likely he would have to stir out of doors, when he saw Elsie Bengough crossing the square towards his house. The weather had broken; it was a raw and gusty day; and she had to force her way against the wind that set her ample skirts bellying about her opulent figure and her veil spinning and streaming behind her.

Oleron acted swiftly and instinctively. Seizing his hat, he

sprang to the door and descended the stairs at a run. A sort of panic had seized him. She must be prevented from setting foot in the place. As he ran along the alley he was conscious that his eyes went up to the eaves as if something drew them. He did not know that a slate might not accidentally fall. . . .

He met her at the gate, and spoke with curious volubleness.

"This is really too bad, Elsie! Just as I'm urgently called away! I'm afraid it can't be helped though, and that you'll have to think me an inhospitable beast." He poured it out just as it came into his head.

She asked if he was going to town.

"Yes, yes—to town," he replied. "I've got to call on—on Chambers. You know Chambers, don't you? No, I remember you don't; a big man you once saw me with. . . . I ought to have gone yesterday, and"—this he felt to be a brilliant effort —"and he's going out of town this afternoon. To Brighton. I had a letter from him this morning."

He took her arm and led her up the square. She had to remind him that his way to town lay in the other direction.

"Of course—how stupid of me!" he said, with a little loud laugh. "I'm so used to going the other way with you—of course: it's the other way to the bus. Will you come along with me? I am so awfully sorry it's happened like this. . . ."

They took the street to the bus terminus.

This time Elsie bore no signs of having gone through interior struggles. If she detected anything unusual in his manner she made no comment, and he, seeing her calm, began to talk less recklessly through silences. By the time they reached the bus terminus, nobody, seeing the pallid-faced man without an overcoat and the large ample-skirted girl at his side, would have supposed that one of them was ready to sink on his knees for thankfulness that he had, as he believed, saved the other from a wildly unthinkable danger.

They mounted to the top of the bus, Oleron protesting that he should not miss his overcoat, and that he found the day, if anything, rather oppressively hot. They sat down on a front seat.

Now that this meeting was forced upon him, he had something else to say that would make demands upon his tact. It had been on his mind for some time, and was, indeed, peculiarly difficult to put. He revolved it for some minutes, and then, remembering the success of his story of a sudden call to town, cut the knot of his difficulty with another lie.

"I'm thinking of going away for a little while, Elsie," he said.

She merely said, "Oh?"

"Somewhere for a change. I need a change. I think I shall go to-morrow, or the day after. Yes, to-morrow, I think."

"Yes," she replied.

"I don't quite know how long I shall be," he continued. "I shall have to let you know when I am back."

"Yes, let me know," she replied in an even tone.

The tone was, for her, suspiciously even. He was a little uneasy.

"You don't ask me where I'm going," he said, with a little cumbrous effort to rally her.

She was looking straight before her, past the bus-driver.

"I know," she said.

He was startled. "How, you know?"

"You're not going anywhere," she replied.

He found not a word to say. It was a minute or so before she continued, in the same controlled voice she had employed from the start.

"You're not going anywhere. You weren't going out this morning. You only came out because I appeared; don't behave as if we were strangers, Paul."

A flush of pink had mounted to his cheeks. He noticed that the wind had given her the pink of early rhubarb. Still he found nothing to say.

"Of course, you ought to go away," she continued. "I don't know whether you look at yourself often in the glass, but you're rather noticeable. Several people have turned to look at you this morning. So, of course, you ought to go away. But you won't, and I know why."

He shivered, coughed a little, and then broke silence.

"Then if you know, there's no use in continuing this discussion," he said curtly.

"Not for me, perhaps, but there is for you," she replied. "Shall I tell you what I know?"

"No," he said in a voice slightly raised.

"No?" she asked, her round eyes earnestly on him.

"No."

Again he was getting out of patience with her; again he was conscious of the strain. Her devotion and fidelity and love plagued him; she was only humiliating both herself and him. It would have been bad enough had he ever, by word or deed, given her cause for thus fastening herself on him . . . but there; that was the worst of that kind of life for a woman. Women such as she, business women, in and out of offices all the time, always, whether they realised it or not, made comradeship a cover for something else. They accepted the unconventional status, came and went freely, as men did, were honestly taken by men at their own valuation—and then it turned out to be the other thing after all, and they went and fell in love. No wonder there was gossip in shops and squares and public houses! In a sense the gossipers were in the right of it. Independent, yet not efficient with some of womanhood's graces foregone, and yet with all the woman's hunger and need; half sophisticated, yet not wise. Oleron was tired of it all. . . .

And it was time he told her so.

"I suppose," he said tremblingly, looking down between his knees, "I suppose the real trouble is in the life women who earn their own living are obliged to lead."

He could not tell in what sense she took the lame generality; she merely replied, "I suppose so."

"It can't be helped," he continued, "but you do sacrifice a good deal."

She agreed: a good deal; and then she added after a moment, "What, for instance?"

"You may or may not be gradually attaining a new status, but you're in a false position to-day."

"It was very likely," she said; "she hadn't thought of it much in that light—"

"And," he continued desperately, "you're bound to suffer.

Your most innocent acts are misunderstood; motives you
never dreamed of are attributed to you; and in the end it
comes to"—he hesitated a moment and then took the
plunge,—"to the sidelong look and the leer."

She took his meaning with perfect ease. She merely shivered a little as she pronounced the name.

"Barrett?"

His silence told her the rest.

Anything further that was to be said must come from her.
It came as the bus stopped at a stage and fresh passengers
mounted the stairs.

"You'd better get down here and go back, Paul," she said.
"I understand perfectly—perfectly. It isn't Barrett. You'd be
able to deal with Barrett. It's merely convenient for you to
say it's Barrett. I know what it is . . . but you said I wasn't to
tell you that. Very well. But before you go let me tell you
why I came up this morning."

In a dull tone he asked her why. Again she looked straight
before her as she replied:

"I came to force your hand. Things couldn't go on as they
have been going, you know; and now that's all over."

"All over," he repeated stupidly.

"All over. I want you now to consider yourself, as far as
I'm concerned, perfectly free. I make only one reservation."

He hardly had the spirit to ask her what that was.

"If I merely need you," she said, "please don't give that a
thought; that's nothing; I shan't come near for that. But,"
she dropped her voice, "if you're in need of me, Paul—I shall
know if you are, and you will be—then I shall come at no
matter what cost. You understand that?"

He could only groan.

"So that's understood," she concluded. "And I think that's
all. Now go back. I should advise you to walk back, for you're
shivering—good-bye—"

She gave him a cold hand, and he descended. He turned
on the edge of the kerb as the bus started again. For the first
time in all the years he had known her she parted from him
with no smile and no wave of her long arm.

IX

He stood on the kerb plunged in misery, looking after her as long as she remained in sight; but almost instantly with her disappearance he felt the heaviness lift a little from his spirit. She had given him his liberty; true, there was a sense in which he had never parted with it, but now was no time for splitting hairs; he was free to act, and all was clear ahead. Swiftly the sense of lightness grew on him: it became a positive rejoicing in his liberty; and before he was halfway home he had decided what must be done next.

The vicar of the parish in which his dwelling was situated lived within ten minutes of the square. To his house Oleron turned his steps. It was necessary that he should have all the information he could get about this old house with the insurance marks and the sloping "To Let" boards, and the vicar was the person most likely to be able to furnish it. This last preliminary out of the way, and—aha! Oleron chuckled—things might be expected to happen!

But he gained less information than he had hoped for. The house, the vicar said, was old—but there needed no vicar to tell Oleron that; it was reputed (Oleron pricked up his ears) to be haunted—but there were few old houses about which some rumour did not circulate among the ignorant; and the deplorable lack of Faith of the modern world, the vicar thought, did not tend to dissipate these superstitions. For the rest, his manner was the soothing manner of one who prefers not to make statements without knowing how they will be taken by his hearer. Oleron smiled as he perceived this.

"You may leave my nerves out of the question," he said. "How long has the place been empty?"

"A dozen years, I should say," the vicar replied.

"And the last tenant—did you know him—or her?" Oleron was conscious of a tingling of his nerves as he offered the vicar the alternative of sex.

"Him," said the vicar. "A man. If I remember rightly, his name was Madley; an artist. He was a great recluse; seldom went out of the place, and—" the vicar hesitated and then

broke into a little gush of candour "—and since you appear
to have come for this information, and since it is better that
the truth should be told than that garbled versions should get
about, I don't mind saying that this man Madley died there,
under somewhat unusual circumstances. It was ascertained at
the post-mortem that there was not a particle of food in his
stomach, although he was found to be not without money.
And his frame was simply worn out. Suicide was spoken of,
but you'll agree with me that deliberate starvation is, to say
the least, an uncommon form of suicide. An open verdict was
returned."

"Ah!" said Oleron. . . . "Does there happen to be any
comprehensive history of this parish?"

"No; partial ones only. I myself am not guiltless of having
made a number of notes on its purely ecclesiastical history,
its registers and so forth, which I shall be happy to show you
if you would care to see them; but it is a large parish, I have
only one curate, and my leisure, as you will readily understand . . ."

The extent of the parish and the scantiness of the vicar's
leisure occupied the remainder of the interview, and Oleron
thanked the vicar, took his leave, and walked slowly home.

He walked slowly for a reason, twice turning away from the
house within a stone's-throw of the gate and taking another
turn of twenty minutes or so. He had a very ticklish piece of
work now before him; it required the greatest mental concentration; it was nothing less than to bring his mind, if he
might, into such a state of unpreoccupation and receptivity
that he should see the place as he had seen it on that morning when, his removal accomplished, he had sat down to
begin the sixteenth chapter of the first *Romilly*.

For, could he recapture the first impression, he now hoped
for far more from it. Formerly he had carried no end of mental lumber. Before the influence of the place had been able to
find him out at all, it had had the inertia of those dreary
chapters to overcome. No results had shown. The process had
been one of slow saturation, charging, filling up to a brim.
But now he was light, unburdened, rid at last both of that

Romilly and of her prototype. Now for the new unknown, coy, jealous, bewitching Beckoning Fair! . . .

At half-past two of the afternoon he put his key into the Yale lock, entered, and closed the door behind him. . . .

His fantastic attempt was instantly and astonishingly successful. He could have shouted with triumph as he entered the room; it was as if he had *escaped* into it. Once more, as in the days when his writing had had a daily freshness and wonder and promise for him, he was conscious of that new ease and mastery and exhilaration and release. The air of the place seemed to hold more oxygen; as if his own specific gravity had changed, his very tread seemed less ponderable. The flowers in the bowls, the fair proportions of the meadow-sweet-coloured panels and mouldings, the polished floor, and the lofty and faintly starred ceiling, fairly laughed their welcome. Oleron actually laughed back, and spoke aloud.

"Oh, you're pretty, pretty!" he flattered it.

Then he lay down on his couch.

He spent that afternoon as a convalescent who expected a dear visitor might have spent it—in a delicious vacancy, smiling now and then as if in his sleep, and ever lifting drowsy and contented eyes to his alluring surroundings. He lay thus until darkness came, and, with darkness, the nocturnal noises of the old house. . . .

But if he waited for any specific happening, he waited in vain.

He waited similarly in vain on the morrow, maintaining, though with less ease, that sensitised-platelike condition of his mind. Nothing occurred to give it an impression. Whatever it was which he so patiently wooed, it seemed to be both shy and exacting.

Then on the third day he thought he understood. A look of gentle drollery and cunning came into his eyes, and he chuckled.

"Oho, oho! . . . Well, if the wind sits in *that* quarter we must see what else there is to be done. What is there, now? . . . No, I won't send for Elsie; we don't need a wheel to break the butterfly on; we won't go to those lengths, my butterfly. . . ."

He was standing musing, thumbing his lean jaw, looking aslant; suddenly he crossed to his hall, took down his hat, and went out.

"My lady is coquettish, is she? Well, we'll see what a little neglect will do," he chuckled as he went down the stairs.

He sought a railway station, got into a train, and spent the rest of the day in the country. Oh, yes: Oleron thought *he* was the man to deal with Fair Ones who beckoned, and invited, and then took refuge in shyness and hanging back!

He did not return until after eleven that night.

"*Now*, my Fair Beckoner!" he murmured as he walked along the alley and felt in his pocket for his keys. . . .

Inside his flat, he was perfectly composed, perfectly deliberate, exceedingly careful not to give himself away. As if to intimate that he intended to retire immediately, he lighted only a single candle; and as he set out with it on his nightly round he affected to yawn. He went first into his kitchen. There was a full moon, and a lozenge of moonlight, almost peacock-blue by contrast with his candle-flame, lay on the floor. The window was uncurtained, and he could see the reflection of the candle, and, faintly, that of his own face, as he moved about. The door of the powder-closet stood a little ajar, and he closed it before sitting down to remove his boots on the chair with the cushion made of the folded harp-bag. From the kitchen he passed to the bathroom. There, another slant of blue moonlight cut the window sill and lay across the pipes on the wall. He visited his seldom-used study, and stood for a moment gazing at the silvered roofs across the square. Then, walking straight through his sitting-room, his stockinged feet making no noise, he entered his bedroom and put the candle on the chest of drawers. His face all this time wore no expression save that of tiredness. He had never been wilier nor more alert.

His small bedroom fireplace was opposite the chest of drawers on which the mirror stood, and his bed and the window occupied the remaining sides of the room. Oleron drew down his blind, took off his coat, and then stooped to get his slippers from under the bed.

He could have given no reason for the conviction, but that

the manifestation that for two days had been withheld was close at hand he never for an instant doubted. Nor, though he could not for the faintest guess of the shape it might take, did he experience fear. Startling or surprising it might be; he was prepared for that; but that was all; his scale of sensation had become depressed. His hand moved this way and that under the bed in search of his slippers. . . .

But for all his caution and method and preparedness, his heart all at once gave a leap and a pause that was almost horrid. His hand had found the slippers, but he was still on his knees; save for this circumstance he would have fallen. The bed was a low one; the groping for the slippers accounted for the turn of his head to one side; and he was careful to keep the attitude until he had partly recovered his self-possession. When presently he rose there was a drop of blood on his lower lip where he had caught at it with his teeth, and his watch had jerked out of the pocket of his waistcoat and was dangling at the end of its short leather guard. . . .

Then, before the watch had ceased its little oscillation, he was himself again.

In the middle of his mantelpiece there stood a picture, a portrait of his grandmother; he placed himself before this picture, so that he could see in the glass of it the steady flame of the candle that burned behind him on the chest of drawers. He could see also in the picture-glass the little glancings of light from the bevels and facets of the objects about the mirror and candle. But he could see more. These twinklings and reflections and re-reflections did not change their position; but there was one gleam that had motion. It was fainter than the rest, and it moved up and down through the air. It was the reflection of the candle on Oleron's black vulcanite comb, and each of its downward movements was accompanied by a silky and crackling rustle.

Oleron, watching what went on in the glass of his grandmother's portrait, continued to play his part. He felt for his dangling watch and began slowly to wind it up. Then, for a moment ceasing to watch, he began to empty his trousers pockets and to place methodically in a little row on the mantelpiece the pennies and halfpennies he took from them. The sweeping, minutely electric noise filled the whole bedroom, and had Oleron altered his point of observation he could have brought the dim gleam of the moving comb so into position that it would almost have outlined his grandmother's head.

Any other head of which it might have been following the outline was invisible.

Oleron finished the emptying of his pockets; then, under cover of another simulated yawn, not so much summoning his resolution as overmastered by an exorbitant curiosity, he swung suddenly round. That which was being combed was still not to be seen, but the comb did not stop. It had altered its angle a little, and had moved a little to the left. It was passing, in fairly regular sweeps, from a point rather more than five feet from the ground, in a direction roughly vertical, to another point a few inches below the level of the chest of drawers.

Oleron continued to act to admiration. He walked to his little washstand in the corner, poured out water, and began to wash his hands. He removed his waistcoat, and continued his preparations for bed. The combing did not cease, and he stood for a moment in thought. Again his eyes twinkled. The next was very cunning—

"Hm! . . . . I think I'll read for a quarter of an hour," he said aloud. . . . .

He passed out of the room.

He was away a couple of minutes; when he returned again the room was suddenly quiet. He glanced at the chest of drawers: the comb lay still, between the collar he had removed and a pair of gloves. Without hesitation Oleron put out his hand and picked it up. It was an ordinary eighteen-penny comb, taken from a card in a chemist's shop, of a substance of a definite specific gravity, and no more capable of rebellion against the Laws by which it existed than are the worlds that keep their orbits through the void. Oleron put it down again; then he glanced at the bundle of papers he held in his hand. What he had gone to fetch had been the fifteen chapters of the original *Romilly*.

"Hm!" he muttered as he threw the manuscript into a

chair. .... "As I thought. .... She's just blindly, ragingly, murderously jealous."

On the night after that, and on the following night, and for many nights and days, so many that he began to be uncertain about the count of them, Oleron, courting, cajoling, neglecting, threatening, beseeching, eaten out with unappeased curiosity and regardless that his life was becoming one consuming passion and desire, continued his search for the unknown co-numerator of his abode.

X

As time went on, it came to pass that few except the postman mounted Oleron's stairs; and since men who do not write letters receive few, even the postman's tread became so infrequent that it was not heard more than once or twice a week. There came a letter from Oleron's publishers, asking when they might expect to receive the manuscript of his new book; he delayed for some days to answer it, and finally forgot it. A second letter came, which also he failed to answer. He received no third.

The weather grew bright and warm. The privet bushes among the chopperlike notice-boards flowered, and in the streets where Oleron did his shopping the baskets of flower-women lined the kerbs. Oleron purchased flowers daily; his room clamoured for flowers, fresh and continually renewed; and Oleron did not stint its demands. Nevertheless, the necessity for going out to buy them began to irk him more and more, and it was with a greater and ever greater sense of relief that he returned home again. He began to be conscious that again his scale of sensation had suffered a subtle change—a change that was not restoration to its former capacity, but an extension and enlarging that once more included terror. It admitted it in an entirely new form. *Lux orco, tenebræ Jovi.* The name of this terror was agoraphobia. Oleron had begun to dread air and space and the horror that might pounce upon the unguarded back.

Presently he so contrived it that his food and flowers were delivered daily at his door. He rubbed his hands when he had hit upon this expedient. That was better! Now he could please himself whether he went out or not. . . .

Quickly he was confirmed in his choice. It became his pleasure to remain immured.

But he was not happy—or, if he was, his happiness took an extraordinary turn. He fretted discontentedly, could sometimes have wept for mere weakness and misery; and yet he was dimly conscious that he would not have exchanged his sadness for all the noisy mirth of the world outside. And speaking of noise: noise, much noise, now caused him the acutest discomfort. It was hardly more to be endured than that new-born fear that kept him, on the increasingly rare occasions when he did go out, sidling close to walls and feeling friendly railings with his hand. He moved from room to room softly and in slippers, and sometimes stood for many seconds closing a door so gently that not a sound broke the stillness that was in itself a delight. Sunday now became an intolerable day to him, for, since the coming of the fine weather, there had begun to assemble in the square under his windows each Sunday morning certain members of the sect to which the long-nosed Barrett adhered. These came with a great drum and large brass-bellied instruments; men and women uplifted anguished voices, struggling with their God; and Barrett himself, with upraised face and closed eyes and working brows, prayed that the sound of his voice might penetrate the ears of all unbelievers—as it certainly did Oleron's. One day, in the middle of one of these rhapsodies, Oleron sprang to his blind and pulled it down, and heard as he did so his own name made the object of a fresh torrent of outpouring.

And sometimes, but not as expecting a reply, Oleron stood still and called softly. Once or twice he called "Romilly!" and then waited; but more often his whispering did not take the shape of a name.

There was one spot in particular of his abode that he began to haunt with increasing persistency. This was just within the opening of his bedroom door. He had discovered one day that by opening every door in his place (always excepting the outer one, which he only opened unwillingly) and by placing himself on this particular spot, he could actually see to a greater or less extent into each of his five rooms without changing his position. He could see the whole of his sitting-room, all of his bedroom except the part hidden by the open door, and glimpses of his kitchen, bathroom, and of his rarely used study. He was often in this place, breathless and with his finger on his lip. One day, as he stood there, he suddenly found himself wondering whether this Madley, of whom the vicar had spoken, had ever discovered the strategic importance of the bedroom entry.

Light, moreover, now caused him greater disquietude than did darkness. Direct sunlight, of which, as the sun passed daily round the house, each of his rooms had now its share, was like a flame in his brain; and even diffused light was a dull and numbing ache. He began, at successive hours of the day, one after another, to lower his crimson blinds. He made short and daring excursions in order to do this; but he was ever careful to leave his retreat open, in case he should have sudden need of it. Presently this lowering of the blinds had become a daily methodical exercise, and his rooms, when he had been his round, had the blood-red half-light of a photographer's darkroom.

One day, as he drew down the blind of his little study and backed in good order out of the room again, he broke into a soft laugh.

"*That* bilks Mr. Barrett!" he said; and the baffling of Barrett continued to afford him mirth for an hour.

But on another day, soon after, he had a fright that left him trembling also for an hour. He had seized the cord to darken the window over the seat in which he had found the harp-bag, and was standing with his back well protected in the embrasure, when he thought he saw the tail of a black-and-white check skirt disappear round the corner of the house. He could not be sure—had he run to the window of the other wall, which was blinded, the skirt must have been already past—but he was *almost* sure that it was Elsie. He listened in an agony of suspense for her tread on the stairs. . . .

But no tread came, and after three or four minutes he drew a long breath of relief.

"By Jove, but that would have compromised me horribly!"
he muttered. . . .

And he continued to mutter from time to time, "Horribly
compromising . . . *no* woman would stand that . . . not *any*
kind of woman . . . Oh, compromising in the extreme!"

Yet he was not happy. He could not have assigned the
cause of the fits of quiet weeping which took him sometimes;
they came and went, like the fitful illumination of the clouds
that travelled over the square; and perhaps, after all, if he was
not happy, he was not unhappy. Before he could be unhappy
something must have been withdrawn, and nothing had yet
been withdrawn from him, for nothing had been granted. He
was waiting for that granting, in that flower-laden, frightfully
enticing apartment of his, with the pith-white walls tinged
and subdued by the crimson blinds to a bloodlike gloom.

He paid no heed to it that his stock of money was running
perilously low, nor that he had ceased to work. Ceased to
work? He had not ceased to work. They knew very little
about it who supposed that Oleron had ceased to work! He
was in truth only now beginning to work. He was preparing
such a work . . . such a work . . . such a Mistress was a-mak-
ing in the gestation of his Art . . . let him but get this period
of probation and poignant waiting over and men should
see. . . . How *should* men know her, this Fair One of
Oleron's, until Oleron himself knew her? Lovely radiant creations are not thrown off like How-d'ye-do's. The men to
whom it is committed to father them must weep wretched
tears, as Oleron did, must swell with vain presumptuous
hopes, as Oleron did, must pursue, as Oleron pursued, the
capricious, fair, mocking, slippery, eager Spirit that, ever
eluding, ever sees to it that the chase does not slacken. Let
Oleron but hunt this Huntress a little longer . . . he would
have her sparkling and panting in his arms yet. . . . Oh, no:
they were very far from the truth who supposed that Oleron
had ceased to work!

And if all else was falling away from Oleron, gladly he was
letting it go. So do we all when our Fair Ones beckon. Quite
at the beginning we wink, and promise ourselves that we will
put Her Ladyship through her paces, neglect her for a day,

turn her own jealous wiles against her, flout and ignore her when she comes wheedling; perhaps there lurks within us all the time a heartless sprite who is never fooled; but in the end all falls away. She beckons, beckons, and all goes. . . .

And so Oleron kept his strategic post within the frame of his bedroom door, and watched, and waited, and smiled, with his finger on his lips. . . . It was his duteous service, his worship, his troth-plighting, all that he had ever known of Love. And when he found himself, as he now and then did, hating the dead man Madley, and wishing that he had never lived, he felt that that, too, was an acceptable service. . . .

But, as he thus prepared himself, as it were, for a Marriage, and moped and chafed more and more that the Bride made no sign, he made a discovery that he ought to have made weeks before.

It was through a thought of the dead Madley that he made it. Since that night when he had thought in his greenness that a little studied neglect would bring the lovely Beckoner to her knees, and had made use of her own jealousy to banish her, he had not set eyes on those fifteen discarded chapters of *Romilly*. He had thrown them back into the window seat, forgotten their very existence. But his own jealousy of Madley had put him in mind of hers, of her jilted rival of flesh and blood, and he remembered them. . . . Fool that he had been! Had he, then, expected his Desire to manifest herself while there still existed the evidence of his divided allegiance? What, and she with a passion so fierce and centred that it had not hesitated at the destruction, twice attempted, of her rival? Fool that he had been! . . .

But if *that* was all the pledge and sacrifice she required she should have it—ah, yes, and quickly!

He took the manuscript from the window seat, and brought it to the fire.

He kept his fire always burning now; the warmth brought out the last vestige of odour of the flowers with which his room was banked. He did not know what time it was; long since he had allowed his clock to run down—it had seemed a foolish measurer of time in regard to the stupendous things that were happening to Oleron; but he knew it was late. He took the *Romilly* manuscript and knelt before the fire.

But he had not finished removing the fastening that held the sheets together before he suddenly gave a start, turned his head over his shoulder, and listened intently. The sound he had heard had not been loud—it had been, indeed, no more than a tap, twice or thrice repeated—but it had filled Oleron with alarm. His face grew dark as it came again.

He heard a voice outside on his landing.

"Paul! . . . Paul! . . ."

It was Elsie's voice.

"Paul! . . . I know you're in . . . I want to see you. . . ."

He cursed her under his breath, but kept perfectly still. He did not intend to admit her.

"Paul! . . . You're in trouble. . . . I believe you're in danger . . . at least come to the door! . . ."

Oleron smothered a low laugh. It somehow amused him that she, in such danger herself, should talk to him of *his* danger! . . . Well, if she was, serve her right; she knew, or said she knew, all about it.

"Paul! . . . Paul! . . ."

"*Paul! . . . Paul! . . .*" He mimicked her under his breath.

"Oh, Paul, it's *horrible!* . . ."

Horrible, was it? thought Oleron. Then let her get away. . . .

"I only want to help you, Paul. . . . I didn't promise not to come if you needed me. . . ."

He was impervious to the pitiful sob that interrupted the low cry. The devil take the woman! Should he shout to her to go away and not come back? No: let her call and knock and sob. She had a gift for sobbing; she mustn't think her sobs would move him. They irritated him, so that he set his teeth and shook his fist at her, but that was all. Let her sob.

"*Paul! . . . Paul! . . .*"

With his teeth hard set, he dropped the first page of *Romilly* into the fire. Then he began to drop the rest in, sheet by sheet.

For many minutes the calling behind his door continued; then suddenly it ceased. He heard the sound of her feet slowly descending the stairs. He listened for the noise of a fall or a cry or a crash of a piece of the handrail of the upper landing; but none of these things came. She was spared. Apparently her rival suffered her to crawl abject and beaten away. Oleron heard the passing of her steps under his window; then she was gone.

He dropped the last page into the fire, and then, with a low laugh, rose. He looked fondly round his room.

"Lucky to get away like that," he remarked. "She wouldn't have got away if I'd given her as much as a word or a look! What devils these women are! . . . But no; I oughtn't to say that; one of 'em showed forbearance. . . ."

Who showed forbearance? And what was forborne? Ah, Oleron knew! . . . Contempt, no doubt, had been at the bottom of it, but that didn't matter: the pestering creature had been allowed to go unharmed. Yes, she was lucky; Oleron hoped she knew it. . . .

And now, now, now for his reward!

Oleron crossed the room. All his doors were open; his eyes shone as he placed himself within that of his bedroom.

Fool that he had been, not to think of destroying the manuscript sooner! . . .

How, in a houseful of shadows, should he know his own shadow? How, in a houseful of noises, distinguish the summons he felt to be at hand? Ah, trust him! He would know! The place was full of a jugglery of dim lights. The blind at his elbow that allowed the light of a street lamp to struggle vaguely through—the glimpse of greeny blue moonlight seen through the distant kitchen door—the sulky glow of the fire under the black ashes of the burnt manuscript—the glimmering of the tulips and the moon-daisies and narcissi in the bowls and jugs and jars—these did not so trick and bewilder his eyes that he would not know his Own! It was he, not she, who had been delaying the shadowy Bridal; he hung his head for a moment in mute acknowledgment; then he bent his eyes on the deceiving, puzzling gloom again. He would have called her name had he known it—but now he would not ask her to share even a name with the other. . . .

His own face, within the frame of the door, glimmered white as the narcissi in the darkness. . . .

A shadow, light as fleece, seemed to take shape in the kitchen (the time had been when Oleron would have said that a cloud had passed over the unseen moon). The low illumination on the blind at his elbow grew dimmer (the time had been when Oleron would have concluded that the lamplighter going his rounds had turned low the flame of the lamp). The fire settled, letting down the black and charred papers; a flower fell from a bowl, and lay indistinct upon the floor; all was still; and then a stray draught moved through the old house, passing before Oleron's face. . . .

Suddenly, inclining his head, he withdrew a little from the doorjamb. The wandering draught caused the door to move a little on its hinges. Oleron trembled violently, stood for a moment longer, and then, putting his hand out to the knob, softly drew the door to, sat down on the nearest chair, and waited, as a man might await the calling of his name that should summon him to some weighty, high and privy Audience. . . .

XI

One knows not whether there can be human compassion for anæmia of the soul. When the pitch of Life is dropped, and the spirit is so put over and reversed that that is only horrible which before was sweet and worldly and of the day, the human relation disappears. The sane soul turns appalled away, lest not merely itself, but sanity should suffer. We are not gods. We cannot drive out devils. We must see selfishly to it that devils do not enter into ourselves.

And this we must do even though Love so transfuse us that we may well deem our nature to be half divine. We shall but speak of honour and duty in vain. The letter dropped within the dark door will lie unregarded, or, if regarded for a brief instant between two unspeakable lapses, left and forgotten again. The telegram will be undelivered, nor will the whistling messenger (wiselier guided than he knows to whistle) be conscious as he walks away of the drawn blind that is pushed aside an inch by a finger and then fearfully replaced again. No: let the miserable wrestle with his own shadows; let him, if indeed he be so mad, clip and strain and enfold and couch the succubus; but let him do so in a house into which not an air of Heaven penetrates, nor a bright finger of the sun pierces the filthy twilight. The lost must remain lost. Humanity has other business to attend to.

For the handwriting of the two letters that Oleron, stealing noiselessly one June day into his kitchen to rid his sitting-room of an armful of fœtid and decaying flowers, had seen on the floor within his door, had had no more meaning for him than if it had belonged to some dim and far-away dream. And at the beating of the telegraph boy upon the door, within a few feet of the bed where he lay, he had gnashed his teeth and stopped his ears. He had pictured the lad standing there, just beyond his partition, among packets of provisions and bundles of dead and dying flowers. For his outer landing was littered with these. Oleron had feared to open his door to take them in. After a week, the errand lads had reported that there must be some mistake about the order, and had left no more. Inside, in the red twilight, the old flowers turned brown and fell and decayed where they lay.

Gradually his power was draining away. The Abomination fastened on Oleron's power. The steady sapping sometimes left him for many hours of prostration gazing vacantly up at his red-tinged ceiling, idly suffering such fancies as came of themselves to have their way with him. Even the strongest of his memories had no more than a precarious hold upon his attention. Sometimes a flitting half-memory, of a novel to be written, a novel it was important that he should write, tantalised him for a space before vanishing again; and sometimes whole novels, perfect, splendid, established to endure, rose magically before him. And sometimes the memories were absurdly remote and trivial, of garrets he had inhabited and lodgings that had sheltered him, and so forth. Oleron had known a good deal about such things in his time, but all that was now past. He had at last found a place which he did not intend to leave until they fetched him out—a place that some might have considered to be a little on the green-sick side, that others might have considered to be a little too redo-

lent of long-dead and morbid things for a living man to be
mewed up in, but ah, so irresistible, with such an authority of
its own, with such an associate of its own, and a place of such
delights when once a man had ceased to struggle against its
inexorable will! A novel? Somebody ought to write a novel
about a place like that! There must be lots to write about in
a place like that if one could but get to the bottom of it! It
had probably already been painted, by a man called Madley
who had lived there . . . but Oleron had not known this
Madley—had a strong feeling that he wouldn't have liked
him—would rather he had lived somewhere else—really
couldn't stand the fellow—hated him, Madley, in fact. (Aha!
That was a joke!) He seriously doubted whether the man had
led the life he ought; Oleron was in two minds sometimes
whether he wouldn't tell that long-nosed guardian of the
public morals across the way about him; but probably he
knew, and had made his praying hullabaloos for him also.
That was his line. Why, Oleron himself had had a dust-up
with him about something or other . . . some girl or other
. . . Elsie Bengough her name was, he remembered. . . .

Oleron had moments of deep uneasiness about this Elsie
Bengough. Or rather, he was not so much uneasy about her
as restless about the things she did. Chief of these was the
way in which she persisted in thrusting herself into his
thoughts; and, whenever he was quick enough, he sent her
packing the moment she made her appearance there. The
truth was that she was not merely a bore; she had always
been that; it had now come to the pitch when her very presence in his fancy was inimical to the full enjoyment of certain experiences. . . . She had no tact; really ought to have
known that people are not at home to the thoughts of everybody all the time; ought in mere politeness to have allowed
him certain seasons quite to himself; and was monstrously ignorant of things if she did not know, as she appeared not to
know, that there were certain special hours when a man's
veins ran with fire and daring and power, in which . . . well,
in which he had a reasonable right to treat folk as he had
treated that prying Barrett—to shut them out completely. . . . But no: up she popped, the thought of her, and

ruined all. Bright towering fabrics, by the side of which even those perfect, magical novels of which he dreamed were dun and grey, vanished utterly at her intrusion. It was as if a fog should suddenly quench some fair-beaming star, as if at the threshold of some golden portal prepared for Oleron a pit should suddenly gape, as if a batlike shadow should turn the growing dawn to murk and darkness again. . . . Therefore, Oleron strove to stifle even the nascent thought of her.

Nevertheless, there came an occasion on which this woman Bengough absolutely refused to be suppressed. Oleron could not have told exactly when this happened; he only knew by the glimmer of the street lamp on his blind that it was some time during the night, and that for some time she had not presented herself.

He had no warning, none, of her coming; she just came— was there. Strive as he would, he could not shake off the thought of her nor the image of her face. She haunted him.

But for her to come at *that* moment of all moments! . . . Really, it was past belief! How *she* could endure it, Oleron could not conceive! Actually, to look on, as it were, at the triumph of a Rival. . . . Good God! It was monstrous! Tact— reticence—he had never credited her with an overwhelming amount of either: but he had never attributed mere—oh, there was no word for it! Monstrous—monstrous! Did she intend thenceforward. . . . Good God! To look on! . . .

Oleron felt the blood rush up to the roots of his hair with anger against her.

"Damnation take her!" he choked. . . .

But the next moment his heat and resentment had changed to a cold sweat of cowering fear. Panic-stricken, he strove to comprehend what he had done. For though he knew not what, he knew he had done something, something fatal, irreparable, blasting. Anger he had felt, but not *this* blaze of ire that suddenly flooded the twilight of his consciousness with a white infernal light. That appalling flash was not his—not his *that* open rift of bright and searing Hell —not his, not his! His had been the hand of a child, preparing a puny blow; but what was *this other* horrific hand that was drawn back to strike in the same place? Had *he* set that in motion? Had *he* provided the spark that had touched off the whole accumulated power of that formidable and relentless place? He did not know. He only knew that that poor igniting particle in himself was blown out, that—Oh, impossible!—a clinging kiss (how else to express it?) had changed on his very lips to a gnashing and a removal, and that for very pity of the awful odds he must cry out to her against whom he had lately raged to guard herself . . . guard herself. . . .

"*Look out!*" he shrieked aloud. . . .

The revulsion was instant. As if a cold slow billow had broken over him, he came to to find that he was lying in his bed, that the mist and horror that had for so long enwrapped him had departed, that he was Paul Oleron, and that he was sick, naked, helpless, and unutterably abandoned and alone. His faculties, though weak, answered at last to his calls upon them; and he knew that it must have been a hideous nightmare that had left him sweating and shaking thus.

Yes, he was himself, Paul Oleron, a tired novelist, already past the summit of his best work, and slipping downhill again empty-handed from it all. He had struck short in his life's aim. He had tried too much, had overestimated his strength, and was a failure, a failure. . . .

It all came to him in the single word, enwrapped and complete; it needed no sequential thought; he was a failure. He had missed. . . .

And he had missed not one happiness, but two. He had missed the ease of this world, which men love, and he had missed also that other shining prize for which men forego ease, the snatching and holding and triumphant bearing up aloft of which is the only justification of the mad adventurer who hazards the enterprise. And there was no second attempt. Fate has no morrow. Oleron's morrow must be to sit down to profitless, ill-done, unrequired work again, and so on the morrow after that, and the morrow after that, and as many morrows as there might be. . . .

He lay there, weakly yet sanely considering it. . . .

And since the whole attempt had failed, it was hardly

worth while to consider whether a little might not be saved from the general wreck. No good would ever come of that half-finished novel. He had intended that it should appear in the autumn; was under contract that it should appear; no matter; it was better to pay forfeit to his publishers than to waste what days were left. He was spent; age was not far off; and paths of wisdom and sadness were the properest for the remainder of the journey. . . .

If only he had chosen the wife, the child, the faithful friend at the fireside, and let them follow an *ignis fatuus* that list! . . .

In the meantime it began to puzzle him exceedingly why he should be so weak, that his room should smell so overpoweringly of decaying vegetable matter, and that his hand, chancing to stray to his face in the darkness, should encounter a beard.

"Most extraordinary!" he began to mutter to himself. "Have I been ill? Am I ill now? And if so, why have they left me alone? . . . Extraordinary! . . ."

He thought he heard a sound from the kitchen or bathroom. He rose a little on his pillow, and listened. . . . Ah! He was not alone, then! It certainly would have been extraordinary if they had left him ill and alone—Alone? Oh, no. He would be looked after. He wouldn't be left, ill, to shift for himself. If everybody else had forsaken him, he could trust Elsie Bengough, the dearest chum he had, for that . . . bless her faithful heart!

But suddenly a short, stifled, spluttering cry rang sharply out:

"*Paul!*"

It came from the kitchen.

And in the same moment it flashed upon Oleron, he knew not how, that two, three, five, he knew not how many minutes before, another sound, unmarked at the time but suddenly transfixing his attention now, had striven to reach his intelligence. This sound had been the slight touch of metal on metal—just such a sound as Oleron made when he put his key into the lock.

"Hallo! . . . Who's that?" he called sharply from his bed.

He had no answer.

He called again. "Hallo! . . . Who's there? . . . Who is it?"

This time he was sure he heard noises, soft and heavy, in the kitchen.

"This is a queer thing altogether," he muttered. "By Jove, I'm as weak as a kitten too. . . . Hallo, there! Somebody called, didn't they? . . . Elsie! Is that you? . . ."

Then he began to knock with his hand on the wall at the side of his bed.

"Elsie! . . . Elsie! . . . You called, didn't you? . . . Please come here, whoever it is! . . ."

There was a sound as of a closing door, and then silence. Oleron began to get rather alarmed.

"It may be a nurse," he muttered; "Elsie'd have to get me a nurse, of course. She'd sit with me as long as she could spare the time, brave lass, and she'd get a nurse for the rest. . . . But it was awfully like her voice. . . . Elsie, or whoever it is! . . . I can't make this out at all. I must go and see what's the matter. . . ."

He put one leg out of bed. Feeling his feebleness, he reached with his hand for the additional support of the wall. . . .

But before putting out the other leg he stopped and considered, picking at his new-found beard. He was suddenly wondering whether he *dared* go into the kitchen. It was such a frightfully long way; no man knew what horror might not leap and huddle on his shoulders if he went so far; when man has an overmastering impulse to get back into bed he ought to take heed of the warning and obey it. Besides, why should he go? What was there to go for? If it was that Bengough creature again, let her look after herself; Oleron was not going to have things cramp themselves on his defenceless back for the sake of such a spoil-sport as *she!* . . . If she was in, let her let herself out again, and the sooner the better for her! Oleron simply couldn't be bothered. He had his work to do. On the morrow, he must set about the writing of a novel with a heroine so winsome, capricious, adorable, jealous, wicked, beautiful, inflaming, and altogether evil, that men should stand amazed. She was coming over him now; he knew by the alteration of the very air of the room when she was near him; and that soft thrill of bliss that had begun to stir in him never came unless she was beckoning, beckoning. . . .

He let go the wall and fell back into bed again as—oh, unthinkable!—the other half of that kiss that a gnash had interrupted was placed (how else convey it?) on his lips, robbing him of very breath. . . .

XII

In the bright June sunlight a crowd filled the square, and looked up at the windows of the old house with the antique insurance marks in its walls of red brick and the agents' notice boards hanging like wooden choppers over the paling. Two constables stood at the broken gate of the narrow entrance alley, keeping folk back. The women kept to the outskirts of the throng, moving now and then as if to see the drawn red blinds of the old house from a new angle, and talking in whispers. The children were in the houses, behind closed doors.

A long-nosed man had a little group about him, and he was telling some story over and over again; and another man, little and fat and wide-eyed, sought to capture the long-nosed man's audience with some relation in which a key figured.

". . . and it was revealed to me that there'd been something that very afternoon," the long-nosed man was saying. "I was standing there, where Constable Saunders is—or rather, I was passing about my business, when they came out. There was no deceiving me, oh, no deceiving *me! I* saw her face. . . ."

"What was it like, Mr. Barrett?" a man asked.

"It was like hers whom our Lord said to, 'Woman, doth any man accuse thee?'—white as paper, and no mistake! Don't tell *me!* . . . And so I walks straight across to Mrs. Barrett, and 'Jane,' I says, 'this must stop, and stop at once; we are commanded to avoid evil,' I says, 'and it must come to an end now; let him get help elsewhere.' And she says to me, 'John,' she says, 'it's four-an-sixpence a week'—them was her words. 'Jane,' I says, 'if it was forty-six thousand pounds it should stop' . . . and from that day to this she hasn't set foot inside that gate."

There was a short silence: then,

"Did Mrs. Barrett ever . . . *see* anything, like?" somebody vaguely inquired.

Barrett turned austerely on the speaker.

"What Mrs. Barrett saw and Mrs. Barrett didn't see shall not pass these lips; even as it is written, keep thy tongue from speaking evil," he said.

Another man spoke.

"He was pretty near canned up in the *Waggon and Horses* that night, weren't he, Jim?"

"Yes, 'e 'adn't 'alf copped it. . . ."

"Not standing treat much, neither; he was in the bar, all on his own. . . ."

"So 'e was; we talked about it. . . ."

The fat, scared-eyed man made another attempt.

"She got the key off of me—she 'ad the number of it—she come into my shop of a Tuesday evening. . . ."

Nobody heeded him.

"Shut your heads," a heavy labourer commented gruffly, "she hasn't been found yet. 'Ere's the inspectors; we shall know more in a bit."

Two inspectors had come up and were talking to the constables who guarded the gate. The little fat man ran eagerly forward, saying that she had bought the key of him. "I remember the number, because of it's being three one's and three three's—111333!" he exclaimed excitedly.

An inspector put him aside.

"Nobody's been in?" he asked of one of the constables.

"No, sir."

"Then you, Brackley, come with us; you, Smith, keep the gate. There's a squad on its way."

The two inspectors and the constable passed down the alley and entered the house. They mounted the wide carved staircase.

"This don't look as if he'd been out much lately," one of the inspectors muttered as he kicked aside a litter of dead leaves and paper that lay outside Oleron's door. "I don't think we need knock—break a pane, Brackley."

The door had two glazed panels; there was a sound of shattered glass; and Brackley put his hand through the hole his elbow had made and drew back the latch.

"Faugh!" . . . choked one of the inspectors as they entered. "Let some light and air in, quick. It stinks like a hearse—"

The assembly out in the square saw the red blinds go up and the windows of the old house flung open.

"That's better," said one of the inspectors, putting his head out of a window and drawing a deep breath. . . . "That seems to be the bedroom in there; will you go in, Simms, while I look over the rest? . . ."

They had drawn up the bedroom blind also, and the waxy white, emaciated man on the bed had made a blinker of his hand against the torturing flood of brightness. Nor could he believe that his hearing was not playing tricks with him, for there were two policemen in his room, bending over him and asking where "she" was. He shook his head.

"This woman Bengough . . . goes by the name of Miss Elsie Bengough . . . d'ye hear? Where is she? . . . No good, Bradley; get him up; be careful with him; I'll just shove *my* head out of the window, I think. . . ."

The other inspector had been through Oleron's study and had found nothing, and was now in the kitchen, kicking aside an ankle-deep mass of vegetable refuse that cumbered the floor. The kitchen window had no blind, and was overshadowed by the blank end of the house across the alley. The kitchen appeared to be empty.

But the inspector, kicking aside the dead flowers, noticed that a shuffling track that was not of his making had been swept to a cupboard in the corner. In the upper part of the door of the cupboard was a square panel that looked as if it slid on runners. The door itself was closed.

The inspector advanced, put out his hand to the little knob, and slid the hatch along its groove.

Then he took an involuntary step back again.

Framed in the aperture, and falling forward a little before it jammed again in its frame, was something that resembled a large lumpy pudding, done up in a pudding-bag of faded browny red frieze.

"Ah!" said the inspector.

To close the hatch again he would have had to thrust that pudding back with his hand; and somehow he did not quite like the idea of touching it. Instead, he turned the handle of the cupboard itself. There was weight behind it, so much weight that, after opening the door three or four inches and peering inside, he had to put his shoulder to it in order to close it again. In closing it he left sticking out, a few inches from the floor, a triangle of black and white check skirt.

He went into the small hall.

"All right!" he called.

They had got Oleron into his clothes. He still used his hands as blinkers, and his brain was very confused. A number of things were happening that he couldn't understand. He couldn't understand the extraordinary mess of dead flowers there seemed to be everywhere; he couldn't understand why there should be police officers in his room; he couldn't understand why one of these should be sent for a four-wheeler and a stretcher; and he couldn't understand what heavy article they seemed to be moving about in the kitchen—his kitchen. . . .

"What's the matter?" he muttered sleepily. . . .

Then he heard a murmur in the square, and the stopping of a four-wheeler outside. A police officer was at his elbow again, and Oleron wondered why, when he whispered something to him, he should run off a string of words—something about "used in evidence against you." They had lifted him to his feet, and were assisting him towards the door. . . .

No, Oleron couldn't understand it at all.

They got him down the stairs and along the alley. Oleron was aware of confused angry shoutings; he gathered that a number of people wanted to lynch somebody or other. Then his attention became fixed on a little fat frightened-eyed man who appeared to be making a statement that an officer was taking down in a notebook.

"I'd seen her with him . . . they was often together . . . she came into my shop and said it was for him . . . I thought it was all right . . . 111333 the number was," the man was saying.

The people seemed to be very angry; many police were keeping them back; but one of the inspectors had a voice that Oleron thought quite kind and friendly. He was telling somebody to get somebody else into the cab before something or other was brought out; and Oleron noticed that a four-wheeler was drawn up at the gate. It appeared that it was himself who was to be put into it; and as they lifted him up he saw that the inspector tried to stand between him and something that stood behind the cab but was not quick enough to prevent Oleron seeing that this something was a hooded stretcher. The angry voices sounded like a sea; something hard, like a stone, hit the back of the cab and the inspector followed Oleron in and stood with his back to the window nearer the side where the people were. The door they had put Oleron in at remained open, apparently till the other inspector should come; and through the opening Oleron had a glimpse of the hatchet-like "To Let" boards among the privet trees. One of them said that the key was at Number Six. . . .

Suddenly the raging of voices was hushed. Along the entrance alley shuffling steps were heard, and the other inspector appeared at the cab door.

"Right away," he said to the driver.

He entered, fastened the door after him, and blocked up the second window with his back. Between the two inspectors Oleron slept peacefully. The cab moved down the square, the other vehicle went up the hill. The mortuary lay that way.

OH, WHISTLE, AND I'LL COME TO YOU, MY LAD

By M. R. James

"I SUPPOSE you will be getting away pretty soon, now Full term is over, Professor," said a person not in the story to the Professor of Ontography, soon after they had sat down next to each other at a feast in the hospitable hall of St. James's College.

The Professor was young, neat, and precise in speech.

"Yes," he said; "my friends have been making me take up golf this term, and I mean to go to the East Coast—in point of fact to Burnstow—(I dare say you know it) for a week or ten days, to improve my game. I hope to get off to-morrow."

"Oh, Parkins," said his neighbour on the other side, "if you are going to Burnstow, I wish you would look at the site of the Templars' preceptory, and let me know if you think it would be any good to have a dig there in the summer."

It was, as you might suppose, a person of antiquarian pursuits who said this, but, since he merely appears in this prologue, there is no need to give his entitlements.

"Certainly," said Parkins, the Professor: "if you will describe to me whereabouts the site is, I will do my best to give you an idea of the lie of the land when I get back; or I could write to you about it, if you would tell me where you are likely to be."

"Don't trouble to do that, thanks. It's only that I'm thinking of taking my family in that direction in the Long, and it occurred to me that, as very few of the English preceptories have ever been properly planned, I might have an opportunity of doing something useful on off-days."

The Professor rather sniffed at the idea that planning

out a preceptory could be described as useful. His neighbour continued:

"The site—I doubt if there is anything showing above ground—must be down quite close to the beach now. The sea has encroached tremendously, as you know, all along that bit of coast. I should think, from the map, that it must be about three-quarters of a mile from the Globe Inn, at the north end of the town. Where are you going to stay?"

"Well, *at* the Globe Inn, as a matter of fact," said Parkins; "I have engaged a room there. I couldn't get in anywhere else; most of the lodging-houses are shut up in winter, it seems; and, as it is, they tell me that the only room of any size I can have is really a double-bedded one, and that they haven't a corner in which to store the other bed; and so on. But I must have a fairly large room, for I am taking some books down, and mean to do a bit of work; and though I don't quite fancy having an empty bed—not to speak of two —in what I may call for the time being my study, I suppose I can manage to rough it for the short time I shall be there."

"Do you call having an extra bed in your room roughing it, Parkins?" said a bluff person opposite. "Look here, I shall come down and occupy it for a bit; it'll be company for you."

The Professor quivered, but managed to laugh in a courteous manner.

"By all means, Rogers; there's nothing I should like better. But I'm afraid you would find it rather dull; you don't play golf, do you?"

"No, thank Heaven!" said rude Mr. Rogers.

"Well, you see, when I'm not writing I shall most likely be out on the links, and that, as I say, would be rather dull for you, I'm afraid."

"Oh, I don't know! There's certain to be somebody I know in the place; but, of course, if you don't want me, speak the word, Parkins; I shan't be offended. Truth, as you always tell us, is never offensive."

Parkins was, indeed, scrupulously polite and strictly truthful. It is to be feared that Mr. Rogers sometimes practised upon his knowledge of these characteristics. In Parkins's breast there was a conflict now raging, which for a moment or two did not allow him to answer. That interval being over, he said:

"Well, if you want the exact truth, Rogers, I was considering whether the room I speak of would really be large enough to accommodate us both comfortably; and also whether (mind, I shouldn't have said this if you hadn't pressed me) you would not constitute something in the nature of a hindrance to my work."

Rogers laughed loudly.

"Well done, Parkins!" he said. "It's all right. I promise not to interrupt your work; don't you disturb yourself about that. No, I won't come if you don't want me; but I thought I should do so nicely to keep the ghosts off." Here he might have been seen to wink and to nudge his next neighbour. Parkins might also have been seen to become pink. "I beg pardon, Parkins," Rogers continued; "I oughtn't to have said that. I forgot you didn't like levity on these topics."

"Well," Parkins said, "as you have mentioned the matter, I freely own that I do *not* like careless talk about what you call ghosts. A man in my position," he went on, raising his voice a little, "cannot, I find, be too careful about appearing to sanction the current beliefs on such subjects. As you know, Rogers, or as you ought to know; for I think I have never concealed my views—"

"No, you certainly have not, old man," put in Rogers *sotto voce*.

"—I hold that any semblance, any appearance of concession to the view that such things might exist is equivalent to a renunciation of all that I hold most sacred. But I'm afraid I have not succeeded in securing your attention."

"Your *undivided* attention, was what Dr. Blimber actually said,"[1] Rogers interrupted, with every appearance of an earnest desire for accuracy. "But I beg your pardon, Parkins: I'm stopping you."

"No, not at all," said Parkins. "I don't remember Blimber; perhaps he was before my time. But I needn't go on. I'm sure you know what I mean."

[1] Mr. Rogers was wrong, *vide Dombey and Son*, chapter xii.

"Yes, yes," said Rogers, rather hastily—"just so. We'll go into it fully at Burnstow, or somewhere."

In repeating the above dialogue I have tried to give the impression which it made on me, that Parkins was something of an old woman—rather henlike, perhaps, in his little ways; totally destitute, alas! of the sense of humour, but at the same time dauntless and sincere in his convictions, and a man deserving of the greatest respect. Whether or not the reader has gathered so much, that was the character which Parkins had.

On the following day Parkins did, as he had hoped, succeed in getting away from his college, and in arriving at Burnstow. He was made welcome at the Globe Inn, was safely installed in the large double-bedded room of which we have heard, and was able before retiring to rest to arrange his materials for work in apple-pie order upon a commodious table which occupied the outer end of the room, and was surrounded on three sides by windows looking out seaward; that is to say, the central window looked straight out to sea, and those on the left and right commanded prospects along the shore to the north and south respectively. On the south you saw the village of Burnstow. On the north no houses were to be seen, but only the beach and the low cliff backing it. Immediately in front was a strip—not considerable—of rough grass, dotted with old anchors, capstans, and so forth; then a broad path; then the beach. Whatever may have been the original distance between the Globe Inn and the sea, not more than sixty yards now separated them.

The rest of the population of the inn was, of course, a golfing one, and included few elements that call for a special description. The most conspicuous figure was, perhaps, that of an *ancien militaire*, secretary of a London club, and possessed of a voice of incredible strength, and of views of a pronouncedly Protestant type. These were apt to find utterance after his attendance upon the ministrations of the Vicar, an estimable man with inclinations towards a picturesque ritual, which he gallantly kept down as far as he could out of deference to East Anglian tradition.

Professor Parkins, one of whose principal characteristics was pluck, spent the greater part of the day following his arrival at Burnstow in what he had called improving his game, in company with this Colonel Wilson: and during the afternoon—whether the process of improvement were to blame or not, I am not sure—the Colonel's demeanour assumed a colouring so lurid that even Parkins jibbed at the thought of walking home with him from the links. He determined, after a short and furtive look at that bristling moustache and those incarnadined features, that it would be wiser to allow the influences of tea and tobacco to do what they could with the Colonel before the dinner hour should render a meeting inevitable.

"I might walk home to-night along the beach," he reflected —"yes, and take a look—there will be light enough for that —at the ruins of which Disney was talking. I don't exactly know where they are, by the way; but I expect I can hardly help stumbling on them."

This he accomplished, I may say, in the most literal sense, for in picking his way from the links to the shingle beach his foot caught, partly in a gorse root and partly in a biggish stone, and over he went. When he got up and surveyed his surroundings, he found himself in a patch of somewhat broken ground covered with small depressions and mounds. These latter, when he came to examine them, proved to be simply masses of flints embedded in mortar and grown over with turf. He must, he quite rightly concluded, be on the site of the preceptory he had promised to look at. It seemed not unlikely to reward the spade of the explorer; enough of the foundations was probably left at no great depth to throw a good deal of light on the general plan. He remembered vaguely that the Templars, to whom this site had belonged, were in the habit of building round churches, and he thought a particular series of the humps or mounds near him did appear to be arranged in something of a circular form. Few people can resist the temptation to try a little amateur research in a department quite outside their own, if only for the satis-

faction of showing how successful they would have been had
they only taken it up seriously. Our Professor, however, if he
felt something of this mean desire, was also truly anxious to
oblige Mr. Disney. So he paced with care the circular area he
had noticed, and wrote down its rough dimensions in his
pocketbook. Then he proceeded to examine an oblong eminence which lay east of the centre of the circle, and seemed
to his thinking likely to be the base of a platform or altar. At
one end of it, the northern, a patch of the turf was gone—
removed by some boy or other creature *ferae naturae*. It
might, he thought, be as well to probe the soil here for evidences of masonry, and he took out his knife and began
scraping away the earth. And now followed another little discovery: a portion of soil fell inward as he scraped, and
disclosed a small cavity. He lighted one match after another
to help him to see of what nature the hole was, but the wind
was too strong for them all. By tapping and scratching the
sides with his knife, however, he was able to make out that it
must be an artificial hole in masonry. It was rectangular, and
the sides, top, and bottom, if not actually plastered, were
smooth and regular. Of course it was empty. No! As he withdrew the knife he heard a metallic clink, and when he introduced his hand it met with a cylindrical object lying on the
floor of the hole. Naturally enough, he picked it up, and
when he brought it into the light, now fast fading, he could
see that it, too, was of man's making—a metal tube about
four inches long, and evidently of some considerable age.

By the time Parkins had made sure that there was nothing else in this odd receptacle, it was too late and too dark
for him to think of undertaking any further search. What he
had done had proved so unexpectedly interesting that he determined to sacrifice a little more of the daylight on the morrow to archæology. The object which he now had safe in his
pocket was bound to be of some slight value at least, he felt
sure.

Bleak and solemn was the view on which he took a last
look before starting homeward. A faint yellow light in the
west showed the links, on which a few figures moving to-

wards the clubhouse were still visible, the squat martello tower, the lights of Aldsey village, the pale ribbon of sands intersected at intervals by black wooden groynings, the dim and murmuring sea. The wind was bitter from the north, but was at his back when he set out for the Globe. He quickly rattled and clashed through the shingle and gained the sand, upon which, but for the groyning which had to be got over every few yards, the going was both good and quiet. One last look behind, to measure the distance he had made since leaving the ruined Templars' church, showed him a prospect of company on his walk, in the shape of a rather indistinct personage, who seemed to be making great efforts to catch up with him, but made little, if any, progress. I mean that there was an appearance of running about his movements, but that the distance between him and Parkins did not seem materially to lessen. So, at least, Parkins thought, and decided that he almost certainly did not know him, and that it would be absurd to wait until he came up. For all that, company, he began to think, would really be very welcome on that lonely shore, if only you could choose your companion. In his unenlightened days he had read of meetings in such places which even now would hardly bear thinking of. He went on thinking of them, however, until he reached home, and particularly of one which catches most people's fancy at some time of their childhood. "Now I saw in my dream that Christian had gone but a very little way when he saw a foul fiend coming over the field to meet him." "What should I do now," he thought, "if I looked back and caught sight of a black figure sharply defined against the yellow sky, and saw that it had horns and wings? I wonder whether I should stand or run for it. Luckily, the gentleman behind is not of that kind, and he seems to be about as far off now as when I saw him first. Well, at this rate, he won't get his dinner as soon as I shall; and, dear me! it's within a quarter of an hour of the time now. I must run!"

Parkins had, in fact, very little time for dressing. When he met the Colonel at dinner, Peace—or as much of her as that

gentleman could manage—reigned once more in the military
bosom; nor was she put to flight in the hours of bridge that
followed dinner, for Parkins was a more than respectable
player. When, therefore, he retired towards twelve o'clock,
he felt that he had spent his evening in quite a satisfactory
way, and that, even for so long as a fortnight or three weeks,
life at the Globe would be supportable under similar conditions—"especially," thought he, "if I go on improving my
game."

As he went along the passages he met the boots of the
Globe, who stopped and said:

"Beg your pardon, sir, but as I was abrushing your coat just
now there was something fell out of the pocket. I put it on
your chest of drawers, sir, in your room, sir—a piece of a pipe
or somethink of that, sir. Thank you, sir. You'll find it on
your chest of drawers, sir—yes, sir. Good night, sir."

The speech served to remind Parkins of his little discovery
of that afternoon. It was with some considerable curiosity
that he turned it over by the light of his candles. It was of
bronze, he now saw, and was shaped very much after the
manner of the modern dog whistle; in fact it was—yes, certainly it was—actually no more nor less than a whistle. He
put it to his lips, but it was quite full of a fine, caked-up sand
or earth, which would not yield to knocking, but must be
loosened with a knife. Tidy as ever in his habits, Parkins
cleared out the earth onto a piece of paper, and took the latter to the window to empty it out. The night was clear and
bright, as he saw when he had opened the casement, and he
stopped for an instant to look at the sea and note a belated
wanderer stationed on the shore in front of the inn. Then he
shut the window, a little surprised at the late hours people
kept at Burnstow, and took his whistle to the light again.
Why, surely there were marks on it, and not merely marks,
but letters! A very little rubbing rendered the deeply cut inscription quite legible, but the Professor had to confess, after
some earnest thought, that the meaning of it was as obscure
to him as the writing on the wall to Belshazzar. There were
legends both on the front and on the back of the whistle.

The one read thus:

$$\mathfrak{FLA}$$

$$\mathfrak{FUR} \qquad \mathfrak{BIS}$$

$$\mathfrak{FLE}$$

The other:

QUIS EST ISTE QUI VENIT

"I ought to be able to make it out," he thought; "but I suppose I am a little rusty in my Latin. When I come to think of it, I don't believe I even know the word for a whistle. The long one does seem simple enough. It ought to mean: 'Who is this who is coming?' Well the best way to find out is evidently to whistle for him."

He blew tentatively and stopped suddenly, startled and yet pleased at the note he had elicited. It had a quality of infinite distance in it, and, soft as it was, he somehow felt it must be audible for miles round. It was a sound, too, that seemed to have the power (which many scents possess) of forming pictures in the brain. He saw quite clearly for a moment a vision of a wide, dark expanse at night, with a fresh wind blowing, and in the midst a lonely figure—how employed, he could not tell. Perhaps he would have seen more had not the picture been broken by the sudden surge of a gust of wind against his casement, so sudden that it made him look up, just in time to see the white glint of a seabird's wing somewhere outside the dark panes.

The sound of the whistle had so fascinated him that he could not help trying it once more, this time more boldly. The note was little, if at all, louder than before, and repetition broke the illusion—no picture followed, as he had half hoped it might. "But what is this? Goodness! what force the wind can get up in a few minutes! What a tremendous gust! There! I knew that window-fastening was no use! Ah! I thought so—both candles out. It is enough to tear the room to pieces."

The first thing was to get the window shut. While you might count twenty Parkins was struggling with the small casement, and felt almost as if he were pushing back a sturdy burglar, so strong was the pressure. It slackened all at once, and the window banged to and latched itself. Now to relight the candles and see what damage, if any, had been done. No, nothing seemed amiss; no glass even was broken in the casement. But the noise had evidently roused at least one member of the household: the Colonel was to be heard stumping in his stockinged feet on the floor above, and growling.

Quickly as it had risen, the wind did not fall at once. On it went, moaning and rushing past the house, at times rising to a cry so desolate that, as Parkins disinterestedly said, it might have made fanciful people feel quite uncomfortable; even the unimaginative, he thought after a quarter of an hour, might be happier without it.

Whether it was the wind, or the excitement of golf or of the researches in the preceptory that kept Parkins awake, he was not sure. Awake he remained, in any case, long enough to fancy (as I am afraid I often do myself under such conditions) that he was the victim of all manner of fatal disorders: he would lie counting the beats of his heart, convinced that it was going to stop work every moment, and would entertain grave suspicions of his lungs, brain, liver, etc.—suspicions which he was sure would be dispelled by the return of daylight, but which until then refused to be put aside. He found a little vicarious comfort in the idea that someone else was in the same boat. A near neighbour (in the darkness it was not easy to tell his direction) was tossing and rustling in his bed, too.

The next stage was that Parkins shut his eyes and determined to give sleep every chance. Here again overexcitement asserted itself in another form—that of making pictures. *Experto crede*, pictures do come to the closed eyes of one trying to sleep, and are often so little to his taste that he must open his eyes and disperse them.

Parkins's experience on this occasion was a very distressing one. He found that the picture which presented itself to him was continuous. When he opened his eyes, of course, it went; but when he shut them once more it framed itself afresh, and acted itself out again, neither quicker nor slower than before. What he saw was this:

A long stretch of shore—shingle edged by sand, and intersected at short intervals with black groynes running down to the water—a scene, in fact, so like that of his afternoon's walk that, in the absence of any landmark, it could not be distinguished therefrom. The light was obscure, conveying an impression of gathering storm, late winter evening, and slight cold rain. On this bleak stage at first no actor was visible. Then, in the distance, a bobbing black object appeared; a moment more, and it was a man running, jumping, clambering over the groynes, and every few seconds looking eagerly back. The nearer he came the more obvious it was that he was not only anxious, but even terribly frightened, though his face was not to be distinguished. He was, moreover, almost at the end of his strength. On he came; each successive obstacle seemed to cause him more difficulty than the last. "Will he get over this next one?" thought Parkins; "it seems a little higher than the others." Yes; half climbing, half throwing himself, he did get over, and fell all in a heap on the other side (the side nearest to the spectator). There, as if really unable to get up again, he remained crouching under the groyne, looking up in an attitude of painful anxiety.

So far no cause whatever for the fear of the runner had been shown; but now there began to be seen, far up the shore, a little flicker of something light-coloured moving to and fro with great swiftness and irregularity. Rapidly growing larger, it, too, declared itself as a figure in pale, fluttering draperies, ill-defined. There was something about its motion which made Parkins very unwilling to see it at close quarters. It would stop, raise arms, bow itself toward the sand, then run stooping across the beach to the water's edge and back again; and then, rising upright, once more continue its course forward at a speed that was startling and terrifying. The moment came when the pursuer was hovering about from left to right only a few yards beyond the groyne where the runner lay in hiding. After two or three ineffectual castings hither and thither it came to a stop, stood upright, with arms raised high, and then darted straight forward towards the groyne.

It was at this point that Parkins always failed in his resolution to keep his eyes shut. With many misgivings as to incipient failure of eyesight, overworked brain, excessive smoking, and so on, he finally resigned himself to light his candle, get out a book, and pass the night waking, rather than be tormented by this persistent panorama, which he saw clearly enough could only be a morbid reflection of his walk and his thoughts on that very day.

The scraping of the match on box and the glare of light must have startled some creatures of the night—rats or what not—which he heard scurry across the floor from the side of his bed with much rustling. Dear, dear! the match is out! Fool that it is! But the second one burnt better, and a candle and book were duly procured, over which Parkins pored till sleep of a wholesome kind came upon him, and that in no long space. For about the first time in his orderly and prudent life he forgot to blow out the candle, and when he was called next morning at eight there was still a flicker in the socket and a sad mess of guttered grease on the top of the little table.

After breakfast he was in his room, putting the finishing touches to his golfing costume—fortune had again allotted the Colonel to him for a partner—when one of the maids came in.

"Oh, if you please," she said, "would you like any extra blankets on your bed, sir?"

"Ah! thank you," said Parkins. "Yes, I think I should like one. It seems likely to turn rather colder."

In a very short time the maid was back with the blanket.

"Which bed should I put it on, sir?" she asked.

"What? Why, that one—the one I slept in last night," he said, pointing to it.

"Oh yes! I beg your pardon, sir, but you seemed to have tried both of 'em; leastways, we had to make 'em both up this morning."

"Really? How very absurd!" said Parkins. "I certainly never

touched the other, except to lay some things on it. Did it actually seem to have been slept in?"

"Oh yes, sir!" said the maid. "Why, all the things was crumpled and throwed about all ways, if you'll excuse me, sir —quite as if anyone 'adn't passed but a very poor night, sir."

"Dear me," said Parkins. "Well, I may have disordered it more than I thought when I unpacked my things. I'm very sorry to have given you the extra trouble, I'm sure. I expect a friend of mine soon, by the way—a gentleman from Cambridge—to come and occupy it for a night or two. That will be all right, I suppose, won't it?"

"Oh yes, to be sure, sir. Thank you, sir. It's no trouble, sir, I'm sure," said the maid, and departed to giggle with her colleagues.

Parkins set forth, with a stern determination to improve his game.

I am glad to be able to report that he succeeded so far in this enterprise that the Colonel, who had been rather repining at the prospect of a second day's play in his company, became quite chatty as the morning advanced; and his voice boomed out over the flats, as certain also of our own minor poets have said, "like some great bourdon in a minster tower."

"Extraordinary wind, that, we had last night," he said. "In my old home we should have said someone had been whistling for it."

"Should you, indeed!" said Parkins. "Is there a superstition of that kind still current in your part of the country?"

"I don't know about superstition," said the Colonel. "They believe in it all over Denmark and Norway, as well as on the Yorkshire coast; and my experience is, mind you, that there's generally something at the bottom of what these countryfolk hold to, and have held to for generations. But it's your drive" (or whatever it might have been: the golfing reader will have to imagine appropriate digressions at the proper intervals).

When conversation was resumed, Parkins said, with a slight hesitancy:

"Apropos of what you were saying just now, Colonel, I

think I ought to tell you that my own views on such subjects are very strong. I am, in fact, a convinced disbeliever in what is called the 'supernatural.'"

"What!" said the Colonel, "do you mean to tell me you don't believe in second sight, or ghosts, or anything of that kind?"

"In nothing whatever of that kind," returned Parkins firmly.

"Well," said the Colonel, "but it appears to me at that rate, sir, that you must be little better than a Sadducee."

Parkins was on the point of answering that, in his opinion, the Sadducees were the most sensible persons he had ever read of in the Old Testament; but, feeling some doubt as to whether such mention of them was to be found in that work, he preferred to laugh the accusation off.

"Perhaps I am," he said; "but— Here, give me my cleek, boy!—Excuse me one moment, Colonel." A short interval. "Now, as to whistling for the wind, let me give you my theory about it. The laws which govern winds are really not at all perfectly known—to fisherfolk and such, of course, not known at all. A man or woman of eccentric habits, perhaps, or a stranger, is seen repeatedly on the beach at some unusual hour, and is heard whistling. Soon afterwards a violent wind rises; a man who could read the sky perfectly or who possessed a barometer could have foretold that it would. The simple people of a fishing village have no barometers, and only a few rough rules for prophesying weather. What more natural than that the eccentric personage I postulated should be regarded as having raised the wind, or that he or she should clutch eagerly at the reputation of being able to do so? Now, take last night's wind: as it happens, I myself was whistling. I blew a whistle twice, and the wind seemed to come absolutely in answer to my call. If anyone had seen me—"

The audience had been a little restive under this harangue, and Parkins had, I fear, fallen somewhat into the tone of a lecturer; but at the last sentence the Colonel stopped.

"Whistling, were you?" he said. "And what sort of whistle did you use? Play this stroke first." Interval.

"About that whistle you were asking, Colonel. It's rather a curious one. I have it in my— No; I see I've left it in my room. As a matter of fact, I found it yesterday."

And then Parkins narrated the manner of his discovery of the whistle, upon hearing which the Colonel grunted, and opined that, in Parkins's place, he should himself be careful about using a thing that had belonged to a set of Papists, of whom, speaking generally, it might be affirmed that you never knew what they might not have been up to. From this topic he diverged to the enormities of the Vicar, who had given notice on the previous Sunday that Friday would be the Feast of St. Thomas the Apostle, and that there would be service at eleven o'clock in the church. This and other similar proceedings constituted in the Colonel's view a strong presumption that the Vicar was a concealed Papist, if not a Jesuit; and Parkins, who could not very readily follow the Colonel in this region, did not disagree with him. In fact, they got on so well together in the morning that there was no talk on either side of their separating after lunch.

Both continued to play well during the afternoon, or at least, well enough to make them forget everything else until the light began to fail them. Not until then did Parkins remember that he had meant to do some more investigating at the preceptory; but it was of no great importance, he reflected. One day was as good as another; he might as well go home with the Colonel.

As they turned the corner of the house, the Colonel was almost knocked down by a boy who rushed into him at the very top of his speed, and then, instead of running away, remained hanging on to him and panting. The first words of the warrior were naturally those of reproof and objurgation, but he very quickly discerned that the boy was almost speechless with fright. Inquiries were useless at first. When the boy got his breath he began to howl, and still clung to the Colonel's legs. He was at last detached, but continued to howl.

"What in the world *is* the matter with you? What have you been up to? What have you seen?" said the two men.

"Ow, I seen it wive at me out of the winder," wailed the boy, "and I don't like it."

"What window?" said the irritated Colonel. "Come pull yourself together, my boy."

"The front winder it was, at the 'otel," said the boy.

At this point Parkins was in favour of sending the boy home, but the Colonel refused; he wanted to get to the bottom of it, he said; it was most dangerous to give a boy such a fright as this one had had, and if it turned out that people had been playing jokes, they should suffer for it in some way. And by a series of questions he made out this story: The boy had been playing about on the grass in front of the Globe with some others; then they had gone home to their teas, and he was just going, when he happened to look up at the front winder and see it a-wiving at him. *It* seemed to be a figure of some sort, in white as far as he knew—couldn't see its face; but it wived at him, and it warn't a right thing—not to say not a right person. Was there a light in the room? No, he didn't think to look if there was a light. Which was the window? Was it the top one or the second one? The seckind one it was—the big winder what got two little uns at the sides.

"Very well, my boy," said the Colonel, after a few more questions. "You run away home now. I expect it was some person trying to give you a start. Another time, like a brave English boy, you just throw a stone—well, no, not that exactly, but you go and speak to the waiter, or to Mr. Simpson, the landlord, and—yes—and say that I advised you to do so."

The boy's face expressed some of the doubt he felt as to the likelihood of Mr. Simpson's lending a favourable ear to his complaint, but the Colonel did not appear to perceive this, and went on:

"And here's a sixpence—no, I see it's a shilling—and you be off home, and don't think any more about it."

The youth hurried off with agitated thanks, and the Colonel and Parkins went round to the front of the Globe and reconnoitred. There was only one window answering to the description they had been hearing.

"Well, that's curious," said Parkins; "it's evidently my window the lad was talking about. Will you come up for a moment, Colonel Wilson? We ought to be able to see if anyone has been taking liberties in my room."

They were soon in the passage, and Parkins made as if to open the door. Then he stopped and felt in his pockets.

"This is more serious than I thought," was his next remark. "I remember now that before I started this morning I locked the door. It is locked now, and, what is more, here is the key." And he held it up. "Now," he went on, "if the servants are in the habit of going into one's room during the day when one is away, I can only say that—well, that I don't approve of it at all." Conscious of a somewhat weak climax, he busied himself in opening the door (which was indeed locked) and in lighting candles. "No," he said, "nothing seems disturbed."

"Except your bed," put in the Colonel.

"Excuse me, that isn't my bed," said Parkins. "I don't use that one. But it does look as if someone had been playing tricks with it."

It certainly did: the clothes were bundled up and twisted together in a most tortuous confusion. Parkins pondered.

"That must be it," he said at last. "I disordered the clothes last night in unpacking, and they haven't made it since. Perhaps they came in to make it, and that boy saw them through the window; and then they were called away and locked the door after them. Yes, I think that must be it."

"Well, ring and ask," said the Colonel, and this appealed to Parkins as practical.

The maid appeared, and, to make a long story short, deposed that she had made the bed in the morning when the gentleman was in the room, and hadn't been there since. No, she hadn't no other key. Mr. Simpson, he kep' the keys; he'd be able to tell the gentleman if anyone had been up.

This was a puzzle. Investigation showed that nothing of value has been taken, and Parkins remembered the disposition of the small objects on tables and so forth well enough to be pretty sure that no pranks had been played with them. Mr. and Mrs. Simpson furthermore agreed that neither of them had given the duplicate key of the room to any person whatever during the day. Nor could Parkins, fair-minded man as he was, detect anything in the demeanour of master, mistress or maid that indicated guilt. He was much more inclined to think that the boy had been imposing on the Colonel.

The latter was unwontedly silent and pensive at dinner and throughout the evening. When he bade good night to Parkins, he murmured in a gruff undertone:

"You know where I am if you want me during the night."

"Why, yes, thank you, Colonel Wilson, I think I do; but there isn't much prospect of my disturbing you, I hope. By the way," he added, "did I show you that old whistle I spoke of? I think not. Well, here it is."

The Colonel turned it over gingerly in the light of the candle.

"Can you make anything of the inscription?" asked Parkins, as he took it back.

"No, not in this light. What do you mean to do with it?"

"Oh, well, when I get back to Cambridge I shall submit it to some of the archæologists there, and see what they think of it; and very likely, if they consider it worth having, I may present it to one of the museums."

"'M!" said the Colonel. "Well, you may be right. All I know is that, if it were mine, I should chuck it straight into the sea. It's no use talking, I'm well aware, but I expect that with you it's a case of live and learn. I hope so, I'm sure, and I wish you a good night."

He turned away, leaving Parkins in act to speak at the bottom of the stair, and soon each was in his own bedroom.

By some unfortunate accident, there were neither blinds nor curtains to the windows of the Professor's room. The previous night he had thought little of this, but to-night there seemed every prospect of a bright moon rising to shine directly on his bed, and probably wake him later on. When he noticed this he was a good deal annoyed, but, with an ingenuity which I can only envy, he succeeded in rigging up, with the help of a railway rug, some safety pins, and a stick and umbrella, a screen which, if it only held together, would completely keep the moonlight off his bed. And shortly afterwards he was comfortably in that bed. When he had read a somewhat solid work long enough to produce a decided wish for sleep, he cast a drowsy glance round the room, blew out the candle, and fell back upon the pillow.

He must have slept soundly for an hour or more, when a sudden clatter shook him up in a most unwelcome manner. In a moment he realized what had happened: his carefully constructed screen had given way, and a very bright frosty moon was shining directly on his face. This was highly annoying. Could he possibly get up and reconstruct the screen? or could he manage to sleep if he did not?

For some minutes he lay and pondered over the possibilities; then he turned over sharply, and with all his eyes open lay breathlessly listening. There had been a movement, he was sure, in the empty bed on the opposite side of the room. To-morrow he would have it moved, for there must be rats or something playing about in it. It was quiet now. No! the commotion began again. There was a rustling and shaking: surely more than any rat could cause.

I can figure to myself something of the Professor's bewilderment and horror, for I have in a dream thirty years back seen the same thing happen; but the reader will hardly, perhaps, imagine how dreadful it was to him to see a figure suddenly sit up in what he had known was an empty bed. He was out of his own bed in one bound, and made a dash towards the window, where lay his only weapon, the stick with which he had propped his screen. This was, as it turned out, the worst thing he could have done, because the personage in the empty bed, with a sudden smooth motion, slipped from the bed and took up a position, with outspread arms, between the two beds, and in front of the door. Parkins watched it in a horrid perplexity. Somehow, the idea of getting past it and escaping through the door was intolerable to him; he could not have borne—he didn't know why—to touch it; and as for its touching him, he would sooner dash himself through the window than have that happen. It stood for the moment in a band of dark shadow, and he had not seen what its face was like. Now it began to move, in a stooping posture, and all at once the spectator realized, with some horror and some relief, that it must be blind, for it seemed to feel about it with its muffled arms in a groping and random fashion. Turning half away from him, it became suddenly conscious of the bed he had just left, and darted towards it, and bent and felt over the pillows in a way which made Parkins shudder as he had never in his life thought it possible. In a very few moments it seemed to know that the bed was empty, and then, moving forward into the area of light and facing the window, it showed for the first time what manner of thing it was.

Parkins, who very much dislikes being questioned about it, did once describe something of it in my hearing, and I gathered that what he chiefly remembers about it is a horrible, an intensely horrible, face *of crumpled linen*. What expression he read upon it he could not or would not tell, but that the fear of it went nigh to maddening him is certain.

But he was not at leisure to watch it for long. With formidable quickness it moved into the middle of the room, and, as it groped and waved, one corner of its draperies swept across Parkins's face. He could not, though he knew how perilous a sound was—he could not keep back a cry of disgust, and this gave the searcher an instant clue. It leapt towards him upon the instant, and the next moment he was halfway through the window backwards, uttering cry upon cry at the utmost pitch of his voice, and the linen face was thrust close into his own. At this, almost the last possible second, deliverance came, as you will have guessed: the Colonel burst the door open, and was just in time to see the dreadful group at the window. When he reached the figures only one was left. Parkins sank forward into the room in a faint, and before him on the floor lay a tumbled heap of bedclothes.

Colonel Wilson asked no questions, but busied himself in keeping everyone else out of the room and in getting Parkins back to his bed; and himself, wrapped in a rug, occupied the other bed for the rest of the night. Early on the next day Rogers arrived, more welcome than he would have been a day before, and the three of them held a very long consultation in the Professor's room. At the end of it the Colonel left the hotel door carrying a small object between his finger and thumb, which he cast as far into the sea as a very brawny arm could send it. Later on the smoke of a burning ascended from the back premises of the Globe.

Exactly what explanation was patched up for the staff and visitors at the hotel I must confess I do not recollect. The Professor was somehow cleared of the ready suspicion of delirium tremens, and the hotel of the reputation of a troubled house.

There is not much question as to what would have happened to Parkins if the Colonel had not intervened when he did. He would either have fallen out of the window or else lost his wits. But it is not so evident what more the creature that came in answer to the whistle could have done than frighten. There seemed to be absolutely nothing material about it save the bedclothes of which it had made itself a body. The Colonel, who remembered a not very dissimilar occurrence in India, was of opinion that if Parkins had closed with it, it could really have done very little, and that its one power was that of frightening. The whole thing, he said, served to confirm his opinion of the Church of Rome.

There is really nothing more to tell, but, as you may imagine, the Professor's views on certain points are less clear-cut than they used to be. His nerves, too, have suffered: he cannot even now see a surplice hanging on a door quite unmoved, and the spectacle of a scarecrow in a field late on a winter afternoon has cost him more than one sleepless night.

COME LADY DEATH

By Peter S. Beagle

THIS ALL happened in England a long time ago, when that George who spoke English with a heavy German accent and hated his sons was King. At that time there lived in London a lady who had nothing to do but give parties. Her name was Flora, Lady Neville, and she was a widow and very old. She lived in a great house not far from Buckingham Palace, and she had so many servants that she could not possibly remember all their names; indeed, there were some she had never even seen. She had more food than she could eat, more gowns than she could ever wear; she had wine in her cellars that no one would drink in her lifetime, and her private vaults were filled with great works of art that she did not know she owned. She spent the last years of her life giving parties and balls to which the greatest lords of England—and sometimes the King himself—came, and she was known as the wisest and wittiest woman in all London.

But in time her own parties began to bore her, and though she invited the most famous people in the land and hired the greatest jugglers and acrobats and dancers and magicians to entertain them, still she found her parties duller and duller. Listening to court gossip, which she had always loved, made her yawn. The most marvelous music, the most exciting feats of magic put her to sleep. Watching a beautiful young couple dance by her made her feel sad, and she hated to feel sad.

And so, one summer afternoon she called her closest friends around her and said to them, "More and more I find that my parties entertain everyone but me. The secret of my long life is that nothing has ever been dull for me. For all my life, I have been interested in everything I saw and been anxious to see more. But I cannot stand to be bored, and I will not go to parties at which I expect to be bored, especially if they are my own. Therefore, to my next ball I shall invite the one guest I am sure no one, not even myself, could possibly find boring. My friends, the guest of honor at my next party shall be Death himself!"

A young poet thought that this was a wonderful idea, but the rest of her friends were terrified and drew back from her. They did not want to die, they pleaded with her. Death would come for them when he was ready; why should she invite him before the appointed hour, which would arrive soon enough? But Lady Neville said, "Precisely. If Death has planned to take any of us on the night of my party, he will come whether he is invited or not. But if none of us are to die, then I think it would be charming to have Death among us—perhaps even to perform some little trick if he is in a good humor. And think of being able to say that we had been to a party with Death! All of London will envy us, all of England!"

The idea began to please her friends, but a young lord, very new to London, suggested timidly, "Death is so busy. Suppose he has work to do and cannot accept your invitation?"

"No one has ever refused an invitation of mine," said Lady Neville, "not even the King." And the young lord was not invited to her party.

She sat down then and there and wrote out the invitation. There was some dispute among her friends as to how they should address Death. "His Lordship Death" seemed to place him only on the level of a viscount or a baron. "His Grace Death" met with more acceptance, but Lady Neville said it sounded hypocritical. And to refer to Death as "His Majesty" was to make him the equal of the King of England, which even Lady Neville would not dare to do. It was finally decided that all should speak of him as "His Eminence Death," which pleased nearly everyone.

Captain Compson, known both as England's most dashing

cavalry officer and most elegant rake, remarked next, "That's all very well, but how is the invitation to reach Death? Does anyone here know where he lives?"

"Death undoubtedly lives in London," said Lady Neville, "like everyone else of any importance, though he probably goes to Deauville for the summer. Actually, Death must live fairly near my own house. This is much the best section of London, and you could hardly expect a person of Death's importance to live anywhere else. When I stop to think of it, it's really rather strange that we haven't met before now, on the street."

Most of her friends agreed with her, but the poet, whose name was David Lorimond, cried out, "No, my lady, you are wrong! Death lives among the poor. Death lives in the foulest, darkest alleys of this city, in some vile, rat-ridden hovel that smells of—" He stopped here, partly because Lady Neville had indicated her displeasure, and partly because he had never been inside such a hut or thought of wondering what it smelled like. "Death lives among the poor," he went on, "and comes to visit them every day, for he is their only friend."

Lady Neville answered him as coldly as she had spoken to the young lord. "He may be forced to deal with them, David, but I hardly think that he seeks them out as companions. I am certain that it is as difficult for him to think of the poor as individuals as it is for me. Death is, after all, a nobleman."

There was no real argument among the lords and ladies that Death lived in a neighborhood at least as good as their own, but none of them seemed to know the name of Death's street, and no one had ever seen Death's house.

"If there were a war," Captain Compson said, "Death would be easy to find. I have seen him, you know, even spoken to him, but he has never answered me."

"Quite proper," said Lady Neville. "Death must always speak first. You are not a very correct person, Captain." But she smiled at him, as all women did.

Then an idea came to her. "My hairdresser has a sick child, I understand," she said. "He was telling me about it yesterday, sounding most dull and hopeless. I will send for

him and give him the invitation, and he in his turn can give
it to Death when he comes to take the brat. A bit unconventional, I admit, but I see no other way."

"If he refuses?" asked a lord who had just been married.

"Why should he?" asked Lady Neville.

Again it was the poet who exclaimed amidst the general
approval that this was a cruel and wicked thing to do. But he
fell silent when Lady Neville innocently asked him, "Why,
David?"

So the hairdresser was sent for, and when he stood before
them, smiling nervously and twisting his hands to be in the
same room with so many great lords, Lady Neville told him
the errand that was required of him. And she was right, as
she usually was, for he made no refusal. He merely took the
invitation in his hand and asked to be excused.

He did not return for two days, but when he did he
presented himself to Lady Neville without being sent for and
handed her a small white envelope. Saying, "How very nice
of you, thank you very much," she opened it and found
therein a plain calling card with nothing on it except these
words: *Death will be pleased to attend Lady Neville's ball.*

"Death gave you this?" she asked the hairdresser eagerly.
"What was he like?" But the hairdresser stood still, looking
past her, and said nothing, and she, not really waiting for an
answer, called a dozen servants to her and told them to run
and summon her friends. As she paced up and down the
room waiting for them, she asked again, "What is Death
like?" The hairdresser did not reply.

When her friends came they passed the little card excitedly from hand to hand, until it had gotten quite smudged
and bent from their fingers. But they all admitted that, beyond its message, there was nothing particularly unusual
about it. It was neither hot nor cold to the touch, and what
little odor clung to it was rather pleasant. Everyone said that
it was a very familiar smell, but no one could give it a name.
The poet said that it reminded him of lilacs but not exactly.

It was Captain Compson, however, who pointed out the
one thing that no one else had noticed. "Look at the hand-

writing itself," he said. "Have you ever seen anything more graceful? The letters seem as light as birds. I think we have wasted our time speaking of Death as His This and His That. A woman wrote this note."

Then there was an uproar and a great babble, and the card had to be handed around again so that everyone could exclaim, "Yes, by God!" over it. The voice of the poet rose out of the hubbub saying, "It is very natural, when you come to think of it. After all, the French say *la mort*. Lady Death. I should much prefer Death to be a woman."

"Death rides a great black horse," said Captain Compson firmly, "and wears armor of the same color. Death is very tall, taller than anyone. It was no woman I saw on the battlefield, striking right and left like any soldier. Perhaps the hairdresser wrote it himself, or the hairdresser's wife."

But the hairdresser refused to speak, though they gathered around him and begged him to say who had given him the note. At first they promised him all sorts of rewards, and later they threatened to do terrible things to him. "Did you write this card?" he was asked, and "Who wrote it, then? Was it a living woman? Was it really Death? Did Death say anything to you? How did you know it was Death? Is Death a woman? Are you trying to make fools of us all?"

Not a word from the hairdresser, not one word, and finally Lady Neville called her servants to have him whipped and thrown into the street. He did not look at her as they took him away, or utter a sound.

Silencing her friends with a wave of her hand, Lady Neville said, "The ball will take place two weeks from tonight. Let Death come as Death pleases, whether as man or woman or strange, sexless creature." She smiled calmly. "Death may well be a woman," she said. "I am less certain of Death's form than I was, but I am also less frightened of Death. I am too old to be afraid of anything that can use a quill pen to write me a letter. Go home now, and as you make your preparations for the ball see that you speak of it to your servants, that they may spread the news all over London. Let it be known that on this one night no one in the world will die, for Death will be dancing at Lady Neville's ball."

For the next two weeks Lady Neville's great house shook and groaned and creaked like an old tree in a gale as the servants hammered and scrubbed, polished and painted, making ready for the ball. Lady Neville had always been very proud of her house, but as the ball drew near she began to be afraid that it would not be nearly grand enough for Death, who was surely accustomed to visiting in the homes of richer, mightier people than herself. Fearing the scorn of Death, she worked night and day supervising her servants' preparations. Curtains and carpets had to be cleaned, goldwork and silverware polished until they gleamed by themselves in the dark. The grand staircase that rushed down into the ballroom like a waterfall was washed and rubbed so often that it was almost impossible to walk on it without slipping. As for the ballroom itself, it took thirty-two servants working at once to clean it properly, not counting those who were polishing the glass chandelier that was taller than a man and the fourteen smaller lamps. And when they were done she made them do it all over, not because she saw any dust or dirt anywhere, but because she was sure that Death would.

As for herself, she chose her finest gown and saw to its laundering personally. She called in another hairdresser and had him put up her hair in the style of an earlier time, wanting to show Death that she was a woman who enjoyed her age and did not find it necessary to ape the young and beautiful. All the day of the ball she sat before her mirror, not making herself up much beyond the normal touches of rouge and eye shadow and fine rice powder, but staring at the lean old face she had been born with, wondering how it would appear to Death. Her steward asked her to approve his wine selection, but she sent him away and stayed at her mirror until it was time to dress and go downstairs to meet her guests.

Everyone arrived early. When she looked out of a window, Lady Neville saw that the driveway of her home was choked with carriages and fine horses. "It all looks like a great funeral procession," she said. The footman cried the names of her guests to the echoing ballroom. "Captain Henry Compson, His Majesty's Household Cavalry! Mr. David Lorimond! Lord and Lady Torrance!" (They were the youngest couple there, having been married only three months before.) "Sir Roger Harbison! The Contessa della Candini!" Lady Neville permitted them all to kiss her hand and made them welcome.

She engaged the finest musicians she could find to play for the dancing, but though they began to play at her signal not one couple stepped out on the floor, nor did one young lord approach her to request the honor of the first dance, as was proper. They milled together, shining and murmuring, their eyes fixed on the ballroom door. Every time they heard a carriage clatter up the driveway they seemed to flinch a little and draw closer together; every time the footman announced the arrival of another guest, they all sighed softly and swayed a little on their feet with relief.

"Why did they come to my party if they were afraid?" Lady Neville muttered scornfully to herself. "I am not afraid of meeting Death. I ask only that Death may be impressed by the magnificence of my house and the flavor of my wines. I will die sooner than anyone here, but I am not afraid."

Certain that Death would not arrive until midnight, she moved among her guests, attempting to calm them, not with her words, which she knew they would not hear, but with the tone of her voice, as if they were so many frightened horses. But little by little, she herself was infected by their nervousness: whenever she sat down she stood up again immediately, she tasted a dozen glasses of wine without finishing any of them, and she glanced constantly at her jeweled watch, at first wanting to hurry the midnight along and end the waiting, later scratching at the watch face with her forefinger, as if she would push away the night and drag the sun backward into the sky. When midnight came, she was standing with the rest of them, breathing through her mouth, shifting from foot to foot, listening for the sound of carriage wheels turning in gravel.

When the clock began to strike midnight, everyone, even Lady Neville and the brave Captain Compson, gave one startled little cry and then was silent again, listening to the tolling of the clock. The smaller clocks upstairs began to chime. Lady Neville's ears hurt. She caught sight of herself in the ballroom mirror, one gray face turned up toward the ceiling as if she were gasping for air, and she thought, "Death will be a woman, a hideous, filthy old crone as tall and strong as a man. And the most terrible thing of all will be that she will have my face." All the clocks stopped striking, and Lady Neville closed her eyes.

She opened them again only when she heard the whispering around her take on a different tone, one in which fear was fused with relief and a certain chagrin. For no new carriage stood in the driveway. Death had not come.

The noise grew slowly louder; here and there people were beginning to laugh. Near her, Lady Neville heard young Lord Torrance say to his wife, "There, my darling, I told you there was nothing to be afraid of. It was all a joke."

"I am ruined," Lady Neville thought. The laughter was increasing; it pounded against her ears in strokes, like the chiming of the clocks. "I wanted to give a ball so grand that those who were not invited would be shamed in front of the whole city, and this is my reward. I am ruined, and I deserve it."

Turning to the poet Lorimond, she said, "Dance with me, David." She signaled to the musicians, who at once began to play. When Lorimond hesitated, she said, "Dance with me now. You will not have another chance. I shall never give a party again."

Lorimond bowed and led her out onto the dance floor. The guests parted for them, and the laughter died down for a moment, but Lady Neville knew that it would soon begin again. "Well, let them laugh," she thought. "I did not fear Death when they were all trembling. Why should I fear their laughter?" But she could feel a stinging at the thin lids of her eyes, and she closed them once more as she began to dance with Lorimond.

And then, quite suddenly, all the carriage horses outside

the house whinnied loudly, just once, as the guests had cried out at midnight. There were a great many horses, and their one salute was so loud that everyone in the room became instantly silent. They heard the heavy steps of the footman as he went to open the door, and they shivered as if they felt the cool breeze that drifted into the house. Then they heard a light voice saying, "Am I late? Oh, I am so sorry. The horses were tired," and before the footman could re-enter to announce her, a lovely young girl in a white dress stepped gracefully into the ballroom doorway and stood there smiling.

She could not have been more than nineteen. Her hair was yellow, and she wore it long. It fell thickly upon her bare shoulders that gleamed warmly through it, two limestone islands rising out of a dark golden sea. Her face was wide at the forehead and cheekbones, and narrow at the chin, and her skin was so clear that many of the ladies there—Lady Neville among them—touched their own faces wonderingly, and instantly drew their hands away as though their own skin had rasped their fingers. Her mouth was pale, where the mouths of the other women were red and orange and even purple. Her eyebrows, thicker and straighter than was fashionable, met over dark, calm eyes that were set so deep in her young face and were so black, so uncompromisingly black, that the middle-aged wife of a middle-aged lord murmured, "Touch of the gypsy there, I think."

"Or something worse," suggested her husband's mistress.

"Be silent!" Lady Neville spoke louder than she had intended, and the girl turned to look at her. She smiled, and Lady Neville tried to smile back, but her mouth seemed very stiff. "Welcome," she said. "Welcome, my lady Death."

A sigh rustled among the lords and ladies as the girl took the old woman's hand and curtsied to her, sinking and rising in one motion, like a wave. "You are Lady Neville," she said. "Thank you so much for inviting me." Her accent was as faint and as almost familiar as her perfume.

"Please excuse me for being late," she said earnestly. "I had to come from a long way off, and my horses are so tired."

"The groom will rub them down," Lady Neville said, "and feed them if you wish."

"Oh, no," the girl answered quickly. "Tell him not to go near the horses, please. They are not really horses, and they are very fierce."

She accepted a glass of wine from a servant and drank it slowly, sighing softly and contentedly. "What good wine," she said. "And what a beautiful house you have."

"Thank you," said Lady Neville. Without turning, she could feel every woman in the room envying her, sensing it as she could always sense the approach of rain.

"I wish I lived here," Death said in her low, sweet voice. "I will, one day."

Then, seeing Lady Neville become as still as if she had turned to ice, she put her hand on the old woman's arm and said, "Oh, I'm sorry, I'm so sorry. I am so cruel, but I never mean to be. Please forgive me, Lady Neville. I am not used to company, and I do such stupid things. Please forgive me."

Her hand felt as light and warm on Lady Neville's arm as the hand of any other young girl, and her eyes were so appealing that Lady Neville replied, "You have said nothing wrong. While you are my guest, my house is yours."

"Thank you," said Death, and she smiled so radiantly that the musicians began to play quite by themselves, with no sign from Lady Neville. She would have stopped them, but Death said, "Oh, what lovely music! Let them play, please."

So the musicians played a gavotte, and Death, unabashed by eyes that stared at her in greedy terror, sang softly to herself without words, lifted her white gown slightly with both hands, and made hesitant little patting steps with her small feet. "I have not danced in so long," she said wistfully. "I'm quite sure I've forgotten how."

She was shy; she would not look up to embarrass the young lords, not one of whom stepped forward to dance with her. Lady Neville felt a flood of shame and sympathy, emotions she thought had withered in her years ago. "Is she to be humiliated at my own ball?" she thought angrily. "It is because she is Death; if she were the ugliest, foulest hag in all the world they would clamor to dance with her, because they are gentlemen and they know what is expected of them. But no gentleman will dance with Death, no matter how beautiful she is." She glanced sideways at David Lorimond. His face was flushed, and his hands were clasped so tightly as he stared at Death that his fingers were like glass, but when Lady Neville touched his arm he did not turn, and when she hissed, "David!" he pretended not to hear her.

Then Captain Compson, gray-haired and handsome in his uniform, stepped out of the crowd and bowed gracefully before Death. "If I may have the honor," he said.

"Captain Compson," said Death, smiling. She put her arm in his. "I was hoping you would ask me."

This brought a frown from the older women, who did not consider it a proper thing to say, but for that Death cared not a rap. Captain Compson led her to the center of the floor, and there they danced. Death was curiously graceless at first—she was too anxious to please her partner, and she seemed to have no notion of rhythm. The Captain himself moved with the mixture of dignity and humor that Lady Neville had never seen in another man, but when he looked at her over Death's shoulder, she saw something that no one else appeared to notice: that his face and eyes were immobile with fear, and that, though he offered Death his hand with easy gallantry, he flinched slightly when she took it. And yet he danced as well as Lady Neville had ever seen him.

"Ah, that's what comes of having a reputation to maintain," she thought. "Captain Compson too must do what is expected of him. I hope someone else will dance with her soon."

But no one did. Little by little, other couples overcame their fear and slipped hurriedly out on the floor when Death was looking the other way, but nobody sought to relieve Captain Compson of his beautiful partner. They danced every dance together. In time, some of the men present began to look at her with more appreciation than terror, but when she returned their glances and smiled at them, they clung to their partners as if a cold wind were threatening to blow them away.

One of the few who stared at her frankly and with pleasure

was young Lord Torrance, who usually danced only with his wife. Another was the poet Lorimond. Dancing with Lady Neville, he remarked to her, "If she is Death, what do these frightened fools think they are? If she is ugliness, what must they be? I hate their fear. It is obscene."

Death and the Captain danced past them at that moment, and they heard him say to her, "But if that was truly you that I saw in the battle, how can you have changed so? How can you have become so lovely?"

Death's laughter was gay and soft. "I thought that among so many beautiful people it might be better to be beautiful. I was afraid of frightening everyone and spoiling the party."

"They all thought she would be ugly," said Lorimond to Lady Neville. "I—I knew she would be beautiful."

"Then why have you not danced with her?" Lady Neville asked him. "Are you also afraid?"

"No, oh, no," the poet answered quickly and passionately. "I will ask her to dance very soon. I only want to look at her a little longer."

The musicians played on and on. The dancing wore away the night as slowly as falling water wears down a cliff. It seemed to Lady Neville that no night had ever endured longer, and yet she was neither tired nor bored. She danced with every man there, except with Lord Torrance, who was dancing with his wife as if they had just met that night, and, of course, with Captain Compson. Once he lifted his hand and touched Death's golden hair very lightly. He was a striking man still, a fit partner for so beautiful a girl, but Lady Neville looked at his face each time she passed him and realized that he was older than anyone knew.

Death herself seemed younger than the youngest there. No woman at the ball danced better than she now, though it was hard for Lady Neville to remember at what point her awkwardness had given way to the liquid sweetness of her movements. She smiled and called to everyone who caught her eye —and she knew them all by name; she sang constantly, making up words to the dance tunes, nonsense words, sounds without meaning, and yet everyone strained to hear her soft voice without knowing why. And when, during a waltz, she caught up the trailing end of her gown to give her more freedom as she danced, she seemed to Lady Neville to move like a little sailing boat over a still evening sea.

Lady Neville heard Lady Torrance arguing angrily with the Contessa della Candini. "I don't care if she is Death, she's no older than I am, she can't be!"

"Nonsense," said the Contessa, who could not afford to be generous to any other woman. "She is twenty-eight, thirty, if she is an hour. And that dress, that bridal gown she wears—really!"

"Vile," said the woman who had come to the ball as Captain Compson's freely acknowledged mistress. "Tasteless. But one should know better than to expect taste from Death, I suppose." Lady Torrance looked as if she were going to cry.

"They are jealous of Death," Lady Neville said to herself. "How strange. I am not jealous of her, not in the least. And I do not fear her at all." She was very proud of herself.

Then, as unbiddenly as they had begun to play, the musicians stopped. They began to put away their instruments. In the sudden shrill silence, Death pulled away from Captain Compson and ran to look out of one of the tall windows, pushing the curtains apart with both hands. "Look!" she said, with her back turned to them. "Come and look. The night is almost gone."

The summer sky was still dark, and the eastern horizon was only a shade lighter than the rest of the sky, but the stars had vanished and the trees near the house were gradually becoming distinct. Death pressed her face against the window and said, so softly that the other guests could barely hear her, "I must go now."

"No," Lady Neville said, and was not immediately aware that she had spoken. "You must stay a while longer. The ball was in your honor. Please stay."

Death held out both hands to her, and Lady Neville came and took them in her own. "I've had a wonderful time," she said gently. "You cannot possibly imagine how it feels to be actually invited to such a ball as this, because you have given them and gone to them all your life. One is like another to you, but for me it is different. Do you understand me?" Lady Neville nodded silently. "I will remember this night forever," Death said.

"Stay," Captain Compson said. "Stay just a little longer." He put his hand on Death's shoulder, and she smiled and leaned her cheek against it. "Dear Captain Compson," she said. "My first real gallant. Aren't you tired of me yet?"

"Never," he said. "Please stay."

"Stay," said Lorimond, and he too seemed about to touch her. "Stay. I want to talk to you. I want to look at you. I will dance with you if you stay."

"How many followers I have," Death said in wonder. She stretched one hand toward Lorimond, but he drew back from her and then flushed in shame. "A soldier and a poet. How wonderful it is to be a woman. But why did you not speak to me earlier, both of you? Now it is too late. I must go."

"Please stay," Lady Torrance whispered. She held on to her husband's hand for courage. "We think you are so beautiful, both of us do."

"Gracious Lady Torrance," the girl said kindly. She turned back to the window, touched it lightly, and it flew open. The cool dawn air rushed into the ballroom, fresh with rain but already smelling faintly of the London streets over which it had passed. They heard birdsong and the strange, harsh nickering of Death's horses.

"Do you want me to stay?" she asked. The question was put, not to Lady Neville, nor to Captain Compson, nor to any of her admirers, but to the Contessa della Candini, who stood well back from them all, hugging her flowers to herself and humming a little song of irritation. She did not in the least want Death to stay, but she was afraid that all the other women would think her envious of Death's beauty, and so she said, "Yes. Of course I do."

"Ah," said Death. She was almost whispering. "And you," she said to another woman, "do you want me to stay? Do you want me to be one of your friends?"

"Yes," said the woman, "because you are beautiful and a true lady."

"And you," said Death to a man, "and you," to a woman,

"and you," to another man, "do you want me to stay?" And they all answered, "Yes, Lady Death, we do."

"Do you want me, then?" she cried at last to all of them. "Do you want me to live among you and to be one of you, and not to be Death anymore? Do you want me to visit your houses and come to all your parties? Do you want me to ride horses like yours instead of mine, do you want me to wear the kind of dresses you wear, and say the things you would say? Would one of you marry me, and would the rest of you dance at my wedding and bring gifts to my children? Is that what you want?"

"Yes," said Lady Neville. "Stay here, stay with me, stay with us."

Death's voice, without becoming louder, had become clearer and older; too old a voice, thought Lady Neville, for such a young girl. "Be sure," said Death. "Be sure of what you want, be very sure. Do all of you want me to stay? For if one of you says to me, no, go away, then I must leave at once and never return. Be sure. Do you all want me?"

And everyone there cried with one voice, "Yes! Yes, you must stay with us. You are so beautiful that we cannot let you go."

"We are tired," said Captain Compson.

"We are blind," said Lorimond, adding, "especially to poetry."

"We are afraid," said Lord Torrance quietly, and his wife took his arm and said, "Both of us."

"We are dull and stupid," said Lady Neville, "and growing old uselessly. Stay with us, Lady Death."

And then Death smiled sweetly and radiantly and took a step forward, and it was as though she had come down among them from a great height. "Very well," she said. "I will stay with you. I will be Death no more. I will be a woman."

The room was full of a deep sigh, although no one was seen to open his mouth. No one moved, for the golden-haired girl was Death still, and her horses still whinnied for

her outside. No one could look at her for long, although she
was the most beautiful girl anyone there had ever seen.

"There is a price to pay," she said. "There is always a
price. Some one of you must become Death in my place, for
there must forever be Death in the world. Will anyone
choose? Will anyone here become Death of his own free
will? For only thus can I become a human girl."

No one spoke, no one spoke at all. But they backed slowly
away from her, like waves slipping back down a beach to the
sea when you try to catch them. The Contessa della Candini
and her friends would have crept quietly out of the door, but
Death smiled at them and they stood where they were. Captain Compson opened his mouth as though he were going to
declare himself, but he said nothing. Lady Neville did not
move.

"No one," said Death. She touched a flower with her finger,
and it seemed to crouch and flex itself like a pleased cat. "No
one at all," she said. "Then I must choose, and that is just,
for that is the way that I became Death. I never wanted to
be Death, and it makes me so happy that you want me to become one of yourselves. I have searched a long time for people who would want me. Now I have only to choose someone
to replace me and it is done. I will choose very carefully."

"Oh, we were so foolish," Lady Neville said to herself.
"We were so foolish." But she said nothing aloud; she
merely clasped her hands and stared at the young girl, thinking vaguely that if she had had a daughter she would have
been greatly pleased if she resembled the lady Death.

"The Contessa della Candini," said Death thoughtfully,
and that woman gave a little squeak of terror because she
could not draw her breath for a scream. But Death laughed
and said, "No, that would be silly." She said nothing more,
but for a long time after that the Contessa burned with hu-
miliation at not having been chosen to be Death.

"Not Captain Compson," murmured Death, "because he
is too kind to become Death, and because it would be too
cruel to him. He wants to die so badly." The expression on
the Captain's face did not change, but his hands began to
tremble.

"Not Lorimond," the girl continued, "because he knows so little about life, and because I like him." The poet flushed, and turned white, and then turned pink again. He made as if to kneel clumsily on one knee, but instead he pulled himself erect and stood as much like Captain Compson as he could.

"Not the Torrances," said Death, "never Lord and Lady Torrance, for both of them care too much about another person to take any pride in being Death." But she hesitated over Lady Torrance for a while, staring at her out of her dark and curious eyes. "I was your age when I became Death," she said at last. "I wonder what it will be like to be your age again. I have been Death for so long," Lady Torrance shivered and did not speak.

And at last Death said quietly, "Lady Neville."

"I am here," Lady Neville answered.

"I think you are the only one," said Death. "I choose you, Lady Neville."

Again Lady Neville heard every guest sigh softly, and although her back was to them all she knew that they were sighing in relief that neither themselves nor anyone dear to themselves had been chosen. Lady Torrance gave a little cry of protest, but Lady Neville knew that she would have cried out at whatever choice Death made. She heard herself say calmly, "I am honored. But was there no one more worthy than I?"

"Not one," said Death. "There is no one quite so weary of being human, no one who knows better how meaningless it is to be alive. And there is no one else here with the power to treat life"—and she smiled sweetly and cruelly—"the life of your hairdresser's child, for instance, as the meaningless thing it is. Death has a heart, but it is forever an empty heart, and I think, Lady Neville, that your heart is like a dry riverbed, like a seashell. You will be very content as Death, more so than I, for I was very young when I became Death."

She came toward Lady Neville, light and swaying, her deep eyes wide and full of the light of the red morning sun that was beginning to rise. The guests at the ball moved back from her, although she did not look at them, but Lady Neville clenched her hands tightly and watched Death come toward her with her little dancing steps. "We must kiss each other," Death said. "That is the way I became Death." She shook her head delightedly, so that her soft hair swirled about her shoulders. "Quickly, quickly," she said. "Oh, I cannot wait to be human again."

"You may not like it," Lady Neville said. She felt very calm, though she could hear her old heart pounding in her chest and feel it in the tips of her fingers. "You may not like it after a while," she said.

"Perhaps not." Death's smile was very close to her now. "I will not be as beautiful as I am, and perhaps people will not love me as much as they do now. But I will be human for a while, and at last I will die. I have done my penance."

"What penance?" the old woman asked the beautiful girl. "What was it you did? Why did you become Death?"

"I don't remember," said the lady Death. "And you too will forget in time." She was smaller than Lady Neville, and so much younger. In her white dress she might have been the daughter that Lady Neville had never had, who would have been with her always and held her mother's head lightly in the crook of her arm when she felt old and sad. Now she lifted her head to kiss Lady Neville's cheek, and as she did so she whispered in her ear, "You will still be beautiful when I am ugly. Be kind to me then."

Behind Lady Neville the handsome gentlemen and ladies murmured and sighed, fluttering like moths in their evening dress, in their elegant gowns. "I promise," she said, and then she pursed her dry lips to kiss the soft, sweet-smelling cheek of the young lady Death.

THREE MILES UP

By Elizabeth Jane Howard

THERE WAS absolutely nothing like it.

An unoriginal conclusion, and one that he had drawn a hundred times during the last fortnight. Clifford would make some subtle and intelligent comparison, but he, John, could only continue to repeat that it was quite unlike anything else. It had been Clifford's idea, which, considering Clifford, was surprising. When you looked at him, you would not suppose him capable of it. However, John reflected, he had been ill, some sort of breakdown these clever people went in for, and that might account for his uncharacteristic idea of hiring a boat and travelling on canals. On the whole, John had to admit, it was a good idea. He had never been on a canal in his life, although he had been in almost every kind of boat, and thought he knew a good deal about them; so much, indeed, that he had embarked on the venture in a light-hearted, almost a patronizing manner. But it was not nearly as simple as he had imagined. Clifford, of course, knew nothing about boats; but he had admitted that almost everything had gone wrong with a kind of devilish versatility which had almost frightened him. However, that was all over, and John, who had learned painfully all about the boat and her engine, felt that the former at least had run her gamut of disaster. They had run out of food, out of petrol, and out of water; had dropped their windlass into the deepest lock, and, more humiliating, their boathook into the side-pond. The head had come off the hammer. They had been disturbed for one whole night by a curious rustling in the cabin, like a rat in a paper bag, when there was no paper, and, so far as they knew, no rat. The battery had failed and had had to be

recharged. Clifford had put his elbow through an already
cracked window in the cabin. A large piece of rope had
wound itself round the propeller with a malignant intensity
which required three men and half a morning to unravel.
And so on, until now there was really nothing left to go
wrong, unless one of them drowned, and surely it was impossible to drown in a canal.

"I suppose one might easily drown in a lock?" he asked
aloud.

"We must be careful not to fall into one," Clifford replied.

"What?" John steered with fierce concentration, and never
heard anything people said to him for the first time, almost
on principle.

"I said we must be careful not to fall *into* a lock."

"Oh. Well there aren't any more now until after the Junction. Anyway, we haven't yet, so there's really no reason why
we should start now. I only wanted to know whether we'd
drown if we did."

"Sharon might."

"What?"

"Sharon might."

"Better warn her then. She seems agile enough." His concentrated frown returned, and he settled down again to the
wheel. John didn't mind where they went, or what happened,
so long as he handled the boat, and all things considered, he
handled her remarkably well. Clifford planned and John
steered: and until two days ago they had both quarrelled and
argued over a smoking and unusually temperamental primus.
Which reminded Clifford of Sharon. Her advent and the
weather were really their two unadulterated strokes of good
fortune. There had been no rain, and Sharon had, as it were,
dropped from the blue on to the boat, where she speedily restored domestic order, stimulated evening conversation, and
touched the whole venture with her attractive being: the req-
uisite number of miles each day were achieved, the boat
behaved herself, and admirable meals were steadily and
regularly prepared. She had, in fact, identified herself with
the journey, without making the slightest effort to control it:
a talent which many women were supposed in theory to pos-

sess, when, in fact, Clifford reflected gloomily, most of them were bored with the whole thing, or tried to dominate it.

Her advent was a remarkable, almost a miraculous, piece of luck. He had, after a particularly ill-fed day, and their failure to dine at a small hotel, desperately telephoned all the women he knew who seemed in the least suitable (and they were surprisingly few), with no success. They had spent a miserable evening, John determined to argue about everything, and he, Clifford, refusing to speak; until, both in a fine state of emotional tension, they had turned in for the night. While John snored, Clifford had lain distraught, his resentment and despair circling round John and then touching his own smallest and most random thoughts; until his mind found no refuge and he was left, divided from it, hostile and afraid, watching it in terror racing on in the dark like some malignant machine utterly out of his control.

The next day things had proved no better between them, and they had continued throughout the morning in a silence which was only occasionally and elaborately broken. They had tied up for lunch beside a wood, which hung heavy and magnificent over the canal. There was a small clearing beside which John then proposed to moor, but Clifford failed to achieve the considerable leap necessary to stop the boat; and they had drifted helplessly past it. John flung him a line, but it was not until the boat was secured, and they were safely in the cabin, that the storm had broken. John, in attempting to light the primus, spilt a quantity of paraffin on Clifford's bunk. Instantly all his despair of the previous evening had contracted. He hated John so much that he could have murdered him. They both lost their tempers, and for the ensuing hour and a half had conducted a blazing quarrel which, even at the time, secretly horrified them both in its intensity.

It had finally ended with John striding out of the cabin, there being no more to say. He had returned almost at once, however.

"I say, Clifford. Come and look at this."

"At what?"

"Outside, on the bank."

For some unknown reason Clifford did get up and did

look. Lying face downwards quite still on the ground, with her arms clasping the trunk of a large tree, was a girl.

"How long has she been there?"

"She's asleep."

"She can't have been asleep all the time. She must have heard some of what we said."

"Anyway, who is she? What is she doing here?"

Clifford looked at her again. She was wearing a dark twill shirt and dark trousers, and her hair hung over her face, so that it was almost invisible. "I don't know. I suppose she's alive?"

John jumped cautiously ashore. "Yes, she's alive all right. Funny way to lie."

"Well, it's none of our business anyway. Anyone can lie on a bank if they want to."

"Yes, but she must have come in the middle of our row, and it does seem queer to stay, and then go to sleep."

"Extraordinary," said Clifford wearily. Nothing was really extraordinary, he felt, nothing. "Are we moving on?"

"Let's eat first. I'll do it."

"Oh, I'll do it."

The girl stirred, unclasped her arms, and sat up. They had all stared at each other for a moment, the girl slowly pushing the hair from her forehead. Then she had said: "If you will give me a meal, I'll cook it."

Afterwards they had left her to wash up, and had walked about the wood, while Clifford suggested to John that they ask the girl to join them. "I'm sure she'd come," he said. "She didn't seem at all clear about what she was doing."

"We can't just pick somebody up out of a wood," said John, scandalized.

"Where do you suggest we pick them up? If we don't have someone, this holiday will be a failure."

"We don't know anything about her."

"I can't see that that matters very much. She seems to cook well. We can at least ask her."

"All right. Ask her then. She won't come."

When they returned to the boat, she had finished the washing-up, and was sitting on the floor of the cockpit, with her arms stretched behind her head. Clifford asked her; and she accepted as though she had known them a long time and they were simply inviting her to tea.

"Well, but look here," said John, thoroughly taken aback. "What about your things?"

"My things?" she looked inquiringly and a little defensively from one to the other.

"Clothes and so on. Or haven't you got any? Are you a gypsy or something? Where do you come from?"

"I am not a gypsy," she began patiently; when Clifford, thoroughly embarrassed and ashamed, interrupted her.

"Really, it's none of our business who you are, and there is absolutely no need for us to ask you anything. I'm very glad you will come with us, although I feel we should warn you that we are new to this life, and anything might happen."

"No need to warn me," she said, and smiled gratefully at him.

After that, they both felt bound to ask her nothing; John because he was afraid of being made to look foolish by Clifford, and Clifford because he had stopped John.

"Good Lord, we shall never get rid of her; and she'll fuss about condensation," John had muttered aggressively as he started the engine. But she was very young, and did not fuss about anything. She had told them her name, and settled down, immediately and easily: gentle, assured and unselfconscious to a degree remarkable in one so young. They were never sure how much she had overheard them, for she gave no sign of having heard anything. A friendly but uncommunicative creature.

The map on the engine box started to flap, and immediately John asked, "Where are we?"

"I haven't been watching, I'm afraid. Wait a minute."

"We just passed under a railway bridge," John said helpfully.

"Right. Yes. About four miles from the Junction, I think. What's the time?"

"Five-thirty."

"Which way are we going when we get to the Junction?"

"We haven't time for the big loop. I must be back in London by the fifteenth."

"The alternative is to go up as far as the basin, and then simply turn round and come back, and who wants to do that?"

"Well, we'll know the route then. It'll be much easier coming back."

Clifford did not reply. He was not attracted by the route being easier, and he wanted to complete his original plan.

"Let us wait till we get there." Sharon appeared with tea and marmalade sandwiches.

"All right, let's wait." Clifford was relieved.

"It'll be almost dark by five-thirty. I think we ought to have a plan," John said. "Thank you, Sharon."

"Have tea first." She curled herself on to the floor with her back to the cabin doors and a mug in her hands.

They were passing rows of little houses with gardens that backed on to the canal. They were long narrow strips, streaked with cinder paths, and crowded with vegetables and chicken-huts, fruit trees and perambulators; sometimes ending with fat white ducks, and sometimes in a tiny patch of grass with a bench on it.

"Would you rather keep ducks or sit on a bench?" asked Clifford.

"Keep ducks," said John promptly. "More useful. Sharon wouldn't mind which she did. Would you, Sharon?" He liked saying her name, Clifford noticed. "You could be happy anywhere, couldn't you?" He seemed to be presenting her with the widest possible choice.

"I might *be* anywhere," she answered after a moment's thought.

"Well you happen to be on a canal, and very nice for us."

"In a wood, and then on a canal," she replied contentedly, bending her smooth dark head over her mug.

"Going to be fine tomorrow," said John. He was always a little embarrassed at any mention of how they found her and his subsequent rudeness.

"Yes, I like it when the whole sky is so red and burning and it begins to be cold."

"*Are* you cold?" said John, wanting to worry about it: but she tucked her dark shirt into her trousers and answered composedly:

"Oh no. I am never cold."

They drank their tea in a comfortable silence. Clifford started to read his map, and then said they were almost on to another sheet. "New country," he said with satisfaction. "I've never been here before."

"You make it sound like an exploration; doesn't he, Sharon?" said John.

"Is that a bad thing?" She collected the mugs. "I am going to put these away. You will call me if I am wanted for anything." And she went into the cabin again.

There was a second's pause, a minute tribute to her departure; and, lighting cigarettes, they settled down to stare at the long silent stretch of water ahead.

John thought about Sharon. He thought rather desperately that really they still knew nothing about her, and that when they went back to London they would in all probability never see her again. Perhaps Clifford would fall in love with her, and she would naturally reciprocate, because she was so young and Clifford was reputed to be so fascinating and intelligent, and because women were always foolish and loved the wrong man. He thought all these things with equal intensity, glanced cautiously at Clifford, and supposed he was thinking about her; then wondered what she would be like in London, clad in anything else but her dark trousers and shirt. The engine coughed; and he turned to it in relief.

Clifford was making frantic calculations of time and distance; stretching their time, and diminishing the distance, and groaning that with the utmost optimism they could not be made to fit. He was interrupted by John swearing at the engine, and then for no particular reason he remembered Sharon, and reflected with pleasure how easily she left the mind when she was not present, how she neither obsessed nor possessed one in her absence, but was charming to see.

The sun had almost set when they reached the Junction, and John slowed down to neutral while they made up their minds. To the left was the straight cut which involved the longer journey originally planned; and curving away to the right was the short arm which John advocated. The canal was fringed with rushes, and there was one small cottage with no light in it. Clifford went into the cabin to tell Sharon where they were, and then, as they drifted slowly in the middle of the Junction, John suddenly shouted: "Clifford! What's the third turning?"

"There are only two." Clifford reappeared. "Sharon is busy with dinner."

"No, look. Surely that is another cut."

Clifford stared ahead. "Can't see it."

"Just to the right of the cottage. Look. It's not so dark as all that."

Then Clifford saw it very plainly. It seemed to wind away from the cottage on a fairly steep curve, and the rushes shrouding it from anything but the closest view were taller than the rest.

"Have another look at the map. I'll reverse for a bit."

"Found it. It's just another arm. Probably been abandoned," said Clifford eventually.

The boat had swung round; and now they could see the continuance of the curve dully gleaming ahead, and banked by reeds.

"Well, what shall we do?"

"Getting dark. Let's go up a little way, and moor. Nice quiet mooring."

"With some nice quiet mudbanks," said John grimly. "Nobody uses that."

"How do you know?"

"Well look at it. All those rushes, and it's sure to be thick with weed."

"Don't go up it then. But we shall go aground if we drift about like this."

"I don't mind going up it," said John doggedly. "What about Sharon?"

"What about her?"

"Tell her about it."

"We've found a third turning," Clifford called above the noise of the primus through the cabin door.

"One you had not expected?"

"Yes. It looks very wild. We were thinking of going up it."

"Didn't you say you wanted to explore?" she smiled at him.

"You are quite ready to try it? I warn you we shall probably run hard aground. Look out for bumps with the primus."

"I am quite ready, and I am quite sure we shan't run aground," she answered with charming confidence in their skill.

They moved slowly forward in the dusk. Why they didn't run aground, Clifford could not imagine: John really was damned good at it. The canal wound and wound, and the reeds grew not only thick on each bank, but in clumps across the canal. The light drained out of the sky into the water and slowly drowned there; the trees and the banks became heavy and black.

Clifford began to clear things away from the heavy dew which had begun to rise. After two journeys he remained in the cabin, while John crawled on, alone. Once, on a bend, John thought he saw a range of hills ahead with lights on them, but when he was round the curve and had time to look again he could see no hills: only a dark indeterminate waste of country stretched ahead.

He was beginning to consider the necessity of mooring, when they came to a bridge; and shortly after he saw a dark mass which he took to be houses. When the boat had crawled for another fifty yards or so, he stopped the engine, and drifted in absolute silence to the bank. The houses, about half a dozen of them, were much nearer than he had at first imagined, but there were no lights to be seen. Distance is always deceptive in the dark, he thought, and jumped ashore with a bow line. When, a few minutes later, he took a sounding with the boathook, the water proved unexpectedly deep; and he concluded that by incredible good fortune they had moored at the village wharf. He made everything fast, and joined the others in the cabin with mixed feelings of pride and resentment; that he should have achieved so much under such difficult conditions, and that they (by "they" he meant Clifford), should have contributed so little towards the

achievement. He found Clifford reading *Bradshaw's Guide to
the Canals and Navigable Rivers* in one corner and Sharon,
with her hair pushed back behind her ears, bending over the
primus with a knife. Her ears are pale, exactly the colour of
her face, he thought; wanted to touch them; then felt horribly ashamed, and hated Clifford.

"Let's have a look at Bradshaw," he said, as though he had
not noticed Clifford reading it.

But Clifford handed him the book in the most friendly
manner, remarking that he couldn't see where they were. "In
fact you have surpassed yourself with your brilliant navigation. We seem to be miles from anywhere."

"What about your famous ordnance?"

"It's not on any sheet I have. The new one I thought we
should use only covers the loop we planned. There is precisely three-quarters of a mile of this canal shown on the present sheet and then we run off the map. I suppose there must
once have been trade here, but I cannot imagine what, or
where."

"I expect things change," said Sharon. "Here is the meal."

"How can you see to cook?" asked John, eyeing his plate
ravenously.

"There is a candle."

"Yes, but we've selfishly appropriated that."

"Should I need more light?" she asked, and looked troubled.

"There's no should about it. I just don't know how you do
it, that's all. Chips exactly the right colour, and you never
drop anything. It's marvellous."

She smiled a little uncertainly at him and lit another candle. "Luck, probably," she said, and set it on the table.

They ate their meal, and John told them about the mooring. "Some sort of village. I think we're moored at the wharf,
I couldn't find any rings without the torch, so I've used the
anchor." This small shaft was intended for Clifford, who had
dropped the spare torch-battery in the washing-up bowl, and
forgotten to buy another. But it was only a small shaft, and
immediately afterwards John felt much better. His aggression

slowly left him, and he felt nothing but a peaceful and well-fed affection for the other two.

"Extraordinarily cut off this is," he remarked over coffee.

"It's very pleasant in here. Warm, and extremely full of us."

"Yes. I know. A quiet village, though, you must admit."

"I shall believe in your village when I see it."

"Then you would believe it?"

"No he wouldn't, Sharon. Not if he didn't want to, and couldn't find it on the map. That map!"

The conversation turned again to their remoteness, and to how cut off one liked to be and at what point it ceased to be desirable; to boats, telephones, and finally, canals: which, Clifford maintained, possessed the perfect proportions of urbanity and solitude.

Hours later, when they had turned in for the night, Clifford reviewed the conversation, together with others they had had, and remembered with surprise how little Sharon had actually said. She listened to everything and occasionally, when they appealed to her, made some small composed remark which was oddly at variance with their passionate interest. "She has an elusive quality of freshness about her," he thought, "which is neither naïve nor stupid nor dull, and she invokes no responsibility. She does not want us to know what she was, or why we found her as we did, and curiously, I, at least, do not want to know. She is what women ought to be," he concluded with sudden pleasure; and slept.

He woke the next morning to find it very late, and stretched out his hand to wake John.

"We've all overslept. Look at the time."

"Good Lord! Better wake Sharon."

Sharon lay between them on the floor, which they had ceded her because, oddly enough, it was the widest and most comfortable bed. She seemed profoundly asleep, but at the mention of her name sat up immediately, and rose, almost as though she had not been asleep at all.

The morning routine, which, involving the clothing of three people and shaving of two of them, was necessarily a long and complicated business, began. Sharon boiled water, and Clifford, grumbling gently, hoisted himself out of his bunk and repaired with a steaming jug to the cockpit. He put the jug on a seat, lifted the canvas awning, and leaned out. It was absolutely grey and still; a little white mist hung over the canal, and the country stretched out desolate and unkempt on every side with no sign of a living creature. The village, he thought suddenly: John's village: and was possessed of a perilous uncertainty and fear. I am getting worse, he thought, this holiday is doing me no good. I am mad. I imagined that he said we moored by a village wharf. For several seconds he stood gripping the gunwale, and searching desperately for anything, huts, a clump of trees, which could in the darkness have been mistaken for a village. But there was nothing near the boat except tall rank rushes which did not move at all. Then, when his suspense was becoming unbearable, John joined him with another steaming jug of water.

"We shan't get anywhere at this rate," he began; and then . . . "Hullo! Where's my village?"

"I was wondering that," said Clifford. He could almost have wept with relief, and quickly began to shave, deeply ashamed of his private panic.

"Can't understand it," John was saying. It was no joke, Clifford decided, as he listened to his hearty puzzled ruminations.

At breakfast John continued to speculate upon what he had or had not seen, and Sharon listened intently while she filled the coffee-pot and cut bread. Once or twice she met Clifford's eye with a glance of discreet amusement.

"I must be mad, or else the whole place is haunted," finished John comfortably. These two possibilities seemed to relieve him of any further anxiety in the matter, as he ate a huge breakfast and set about greasing the engine.

"Well," said Clifford, when he was alone with Sharon. "What do you make of that?"

"It is easy to be deceived in such matters," she answered perfunctorily.

"Evidently. Still, John is an unlikely candidate, you must admit. Here, I'll help you dry."

"Oh no. It is what I am here for."

"Not entirely, I hope."

"Not entirely." She smiled and relinquished the cloth.

John eventually announced that they were ready to start. Clifford, who had assumed that they were to retrace their journey, was surprised, and a little alarmed, to find John intent upon continuing it. He seemed undeterred by the state of the canal, which, as Clifford immediately pointed out, rendered navigation both arduous and unrewarding. He announced that the harder it was, the more he liked it, adding very firmly, "Anyway we must see what happens."

"We shan't have time to do anything else."

"Thought you wanted to explore."

"I do, but . . . What do you think, Sharon?"

"I think John will have to be a very good navigator to manage that." She indicated the rush- and weed-ridden reach before them. "Do you think it's possible?"

"Of course it's possible. I'll probably need some help though."

"I'll help you," she said.

So on they went.

They made incredibly slow progress. John enjoys showing off his powers to her, thought Clifford, half amused, half exasperated, as he struggled for the fourth time in an hour to scrape weeds off the propeller.

Sharon eventually retired to cook lunch.

"Surprising amount of water here," John said suddenly.

"Oh?"

"Well, I mean, with all this weed and stuff, you'd expect the canal to have silted up. I'm sure nobody uses it."

"The whole thing is extraordinary."

"Is it too late in the year for birds?" asked Clifford later.

"No, I don't think so. Why?"

"I haven't heard one, have you?"

"Haven't noticed, I'm afraid. There's someone anyway. First sign of life."

An old man stood near the bank watching them. He was dressed in corduroy and wore a straw hat.

"Good morning," shouted John, as they drew nearer.

He made no reply, but inclined his head slightly. He seemed very old. He was leaning on a scythe, and as they

drew almost level with him, he turned away and began slowly
cutting rushes. A pile of them lay neatly stacked beside him.

"Where does this canal go? Is there a village further on?"
Clifford and John asked simultaneously. He seemed not to
hear, and as they chugged steadily past, Clifford was about to
suggest that they stop and ask again, when he called after
them: "Three miles up you'll find the village. Three miles up
that is," and turned away to his rushes again.

"Well now we know something, anyway," said John.

"We don't even know what the village is called."

"Soon find out. Only three miles."

"Three miles!" said Clifford darkly. "That might mean
anything."

"Do you want to turn back?"

"Oh no, not now. I want to see this village now. My curiosity is thoroughly aroused."

"Shouldn't think there'll be anything to see. Never been in
such a wild spot. Look at it."

Clifford looked at it. Half wilderness, half marsh, dank and
grey and still, with single trees bare of their leaves; clumps of
hawthorn that might once have been hedge, sparse and sharp
with berries; and, in the distance, hills and an occasional
wood: these were all one could see, beyond the lines of
rushes which edged the canal winding ahead.

They stopped for a lengthy meal, which Sharon described
as lunch and tea together, it being so late; and then, appalled
at how little daylight was left, continued.

"We've hardly been any distance at all," said John for-
lornly. "Good thing there were no locks. I shouldn't think
they'd have worked if there were."

"*Much* more than three miles," he said, about two hours
later. Darkness was descending and it was becoming very
cold.

"Better stop," said Clifford.

"Not yet. I'm determined to reach that village."

"Dinner is ready," said Sharon sadly. "It will be cold."

"Let's stop."

"You have your meal. I'll call if I want you."

Sharon looked at them, and Clifford shrugged his shoulders. "Come on. I will. I'm tired of this."

They shut the cabin doors. John could hear the pleasant clatter of their meal, and just as he was coming to the end of the decent interval which he felt must elapse before he gave in, they passed under a bridge, the first of the day, and, clutching at any straw, he immediately assumed that it prefaced the village. "I think we're nearly there," he called.

Clifford opened the door. "The village?"

"No, a bridge. Can't be far now."

"You're mad, John. It's pitch dark."

"You can see the bridge though."

"Yes. Why not moor under it?"

"Too late. Can't turn round in this light, and she's not good at reversing. Must be nearly there. You go back, I don't need you."

Clifford shut the door again. He was beginning to feel irritated with John behaving in this childish manner and showing off to impress Sharon. It was amusing in the morning, but really he was carrying it a bit far. Let him manage the thing himself then. When, a few minutes later, John shouted that they had reached the sought-after village, Clifford merely pulled back the little curtain over a cabin window, rubbed the condensation, and remarked that he could see nothing. "No light at least."

"He is happy anyhow," said Sharon peaceably.

"Going to have a look around," said John, slamming the cabin doors and blowing his nose.

"Surely you'll eat first?"

"If you've left anything. My God it's cold! It's *unnaturally* cold."

"We won't be held responsible if he dies of exposure will we?" said Clifford.

She looked at him, hesitated a moment, but did not reply, and placed a steaming plate in front of John. She doesn't want us to quarrel, Clifford thought, and with an effort of friendliness he asked: "What does tonight's village look like?"

"Much the same. Only one or two houses you know. But

the old man called it a village." He seemed uncommunicative; Clifford thought he was sulking. But after eating the meal, he suddenly announced, almost apologetically, "I don't think I shall walk round. I'm absolutely worn out. You go if you like. I shall start turning in."

"All right. I'll have a look. You've had a hard day."

Clifford pulled on a coat and went outside. It was as John said, incredibly cold and almost overwhelmingly silent. The clouds hung very low over the boat, and mist was rising everywhere from the ground, but he could dimly discern the black huddle of cottages lying on a little slope above the bank against which the boat was moored. He did actually set foot on shore, but his shoe sank immediately into a marshy hole. He withdrew it, and changed his mind. The prospect of groping round those dark and silent houses became suddenly distasteful, and he joined the others with the excuse that it was too cold and that he also was tired.

A little later, he lay half-conscious in a kind of restless trance, with John sleeping heavily opposite him. His mind seemed full of foreboding, fear of something unknown and intangible: he thought of them lying in warmth on the cold secret canal with desolate miles of water behind and probably beyond; the old man and the silent houses; John, cut off and asleep, and Sharon, who lay on the floor beside him. Immediately he was filled with a sudden and most violent desire for her, even to touch her, for her to know that he was awake.

"Sharon," he whispered; "Sharon, Sharon," and stretched down his fingers to her in the dark.

Instantly her hand was in his, each smooth and separate finger warmly clasped. She did not move or speak, but his relief was indescribable and for a long while he lay in an ecstasy of delight and peace, until his mind slipped imperceptibly with her fingers into oblivion.

When he woke he found John absent and Sharon standing over the primus. "He's outside," she said.

"Have I overslept again?"

"It is late. I am boiling water for you now."

"We'd better try and get some supplies this morning."

"There is no village," she said, in a matter-of-fact tone.

"What?"

"John says not. But we have enough food, if you don't mind this queer milk from a tin."

"No, I don't mind," he replied, watching her affectionately. "It doesn't really surprise me," he added after a moment.

"The village?"

"No village. Yesterday I should have minded awfully. Is that you, do you think?"

"Perhaps."

"It doesn't surprise you about the village at all, does it? Do you love me?"

She glanced at him quickly, a little shocked, and said quietly: "Don't you know?" then added: "It doesn't surprise me."

John seemed very disturbed. "I don't like it," he kept saying as they shaved. "Can't understand it at all. I could have sworn there were houses last night. You saw them didn't you?"

"Yes."

"Well, don't you think it's very odd?"

"I do."

"Everything looks the same as yesterday morning. I don't like it."

"It's an adventure, you must admit."

"Yes, but I've had enough of it. I suggest we turn back."

Sharon suddenly appeared, and, seeing her, Clifford knew that he did not want to go back. He remembered her saying: "Didn't you say you wanted to explore?" She would think him weak-hearted if they turned back all those dreary miles with nothing to show for it. At breakfast, he exerted himself in persuading John to the same opinion. John finally agreed to one more day, but, in turn, extracted a promise that they would then go back whatever happened. Clifford agreed to this, and Sharon for some inexplicable reason laughed at them both. So that eventually they prepared to set off in an atmosphere of general good humour.

Sharon began to fill the water-tank with their four-gallon

can. It seemed too heavy for her, and John dropped the
starter and leapt to her assistance.

She let him take the can and held the funnel for him. Together they watched the rich, even stream of water disappear.

"You shouldn't try to do that," he said. "You'll hurt yourself."

"Gypsies do it," she said.

"I'm awfully sorry about that. You know I am."

"I shouldn't have minded if you had thought I was a
gypsy."

"I do like you," he said, not looking at her. "I do like you.
You won't disappear altogether when this is over, will you?"

"You probably won't find I'll disappear for good," she
replied comfortingly.

"Come on," shouted Clifford.

It's all right for *him* to talk to her, John thought, as he
struggled to swing the starter. He just doesn't like me doing
it; and he wished, as he had often begun to do, that Clifford
was not there.

They had spasmodic engine trouble in the morning, which
slowed them down; and the consequent halts, with the
difficulty they experienced of mooring anywhere (the banks
seemed nothing but marsh), were depressing and cold. Their
good spirits evaporated: by lunch-time John was plainly irrita-
ble and frightened, and Clifford had begun to hate the grey
silent land on either side, with the woods and hills which
remained so consistently distant. They both wanted to give it
up by then, but John felt bound to stick to his promise, and
Clifford was secretly sure that Sharon wished to continue.

While she was preparing another late lunch, they saw a
small boy who stood on what once had been the towpath
watching them. He was bare-headed, wore corduroy, and had
no shoes. He held a long reed, the end of which he chewed
as he stared at them.

"Ask him where we are," said John; and Clifford asked.

He took the reed out of his mouth, but did not reply.

"Where do you live then?" asked Clifford as they drew almost level with him.

"I told you. Three miles up," he said; and then gave a sudden little shriek of fear, dropped the reed, and turned to run down the bank the way they had come. Once he looked back, stumbled and fell, picked himself up sobbing, and ran faster. Sharon had appeared with lunch a moment before, and together they listened to his gasping cries growing fainter and fainter, until he had run himself out of their sight.

"What on earth frightened him?" said Clifford.

"I don't know. Unless it was Sharon popping out of the cabin like that."

"Nonsense. But he was a very frightened little boy. And, I say, do you realize . . ."

"He was a very foolish little boy," Sharon interrupted. She was angry, Clifford noticed with surprise, really angry, white and trembling, and with a curious expression which he did not like.

"We might have got something out of him," said John sadly.

"Too late now," Sharon said. She had quite recovered herself.

They saw no one else. They journeyed on throughout the afternoon; it grew colder, and at the same time more and more airless and still. When the light began to fail, Sharon disappeared as usual to the cabin. The canal became more tortuous, and John asked Clifford to help him with the turns. Clifford complied unwillingly: he did not want to leave Sharon, but as it had been he who had insisted on their continuing, he could hardly refuse. The turns were nerve-racking, as the canal was very narrow and the light grew worse and worse.

"All right if we stop soon?" asked John eventually.

"Stop now if you like."

"Well, we'll try and find a tree to tie up to. This swamp is awful. Can't think how that child ran."

"That child . . ." began Clifford anxiously; but John, who had been equally unnerved by the incident, and did not want to think about it, interrupted. "Is there a tree ahead anywhere?"

"Can't see one. There's a hell of a bend coming though. Almost back on itself. Better slow a bit more."

"Can't. We're right down as it is."

They crawled round, clinging to the outside bank, which seemed always to approach them, its rushes to rub against their bows, although the wheel was hard over. John grunted with relief, and they both stared ahead for the next turn.

They were presented with the most terrible spectacle. The canal immediately broadened, until no longer a canal but a sheet, an infinity, of water stretched ahead; oily, silent, and still, as far as the eye could see, with no country edging it, nothing but water to the low grey sky above it. John had almost immediately cut out the engine, and now he tried desperately to start it again, in order to turn round. Clifford instinctively glanced behind them. He saw no canal at all, no inlet, but grasping and close to the stern of the boat, the reeds and rushes of a marshy waste closing in behind them. He stumbled to the cabin doors and pulled them open. It was very neat and tidy in there, but empty. Only one stern door of the cabin was free of its catch, and it flapped irregularly backwards and forwards with their movements in the boat.

There was no sign of Sharon at all.

BENSON WATTS IS DEAD
AND IN VIRGINIA

By Doris Betts

AFTER I died, I woke up here.

Or so it seems. Perhaps I am actually still dying, locked in that darkness between one breath and the next, still wearing tubes which leak from my nostrils and drain that long incision. My wife may even yet continue to bend over the high bed to catch the next beat of my heart while the blood jar is ticking down, like a water clock, into my veins. Perhaps that last hospital scene is the only scene and all the rest is a dream in passage.

But the room and her melting face clicked off, I think. Then the smells went. She was saying something; I could still hear that—I stopped hearing it. I unbloated and the queer whistle in my breathing stopped. I could no longer tell the pain from cold. All my circuit breakers opened and sensations blurred. Someone set fire to my hand but it barely tickled.

Through all this, my mind was clearer and more finely tuned than it had ever been. I treasured that clarity, though it had less and less raw material to think with now. I thought: I must withdraw into my brain and hide—there's nothing left outside.

So I did. I backed into my brain farther and farther and got smaller and smaller the deeper I went, until I fell out the other side.

And woke up prone in this yellow grass. The color is important. When they rolled me back from surgery, it was May.

At first I didn't dare move. If I lifted my hand, it might fall through the air and drop back onto a starched sheet. I could not tell what was still attached to me and might clatter if I stirred.

The place where I lay was so . . . so ordinary. A sky as blue as a postcard. Between it and me, one tree limb: oak. White oak, I thought. The grass felt like all grass. When a cricket bounced over my head, I knew for sure we were a long way from the recovery room; they would not recover me. I sat up. I was on a sloping postcard meadow. At the bottom, a narrow stream. Willows. I touched my abdomen, which should have been hot and painful. Dacron trousers instead of gauze. Not mine, though. These were new.

Around my wrist hung a small bracelet and a yellowish tag which looked like the ivory sliver off a piano key. On it, carved, was the following:

TO AVOID G.B.——

1. Dwell, then travel
2. Join forces
3. Disremember

Very carefully, I got to my feet. It had been a long time since I could move without pain. The cool wind was a shock and made me clap both hands to my head. Bald as an egg! Not even a prickle, a wisp, a whisker. Otherwise I was myself as I had been before the intestinal cancer, even a little younger. I tried to guess by flexing muscles, checking where pounds were gone, feeling my smoother face. A little beard starting down the cheeks. I thought I might be forty again, or maybe less. I tried out my voice. Normal. For practice, I said aloud, "Well, it sure as hell isn't Heaven," and my laugh was normal, too—forced, but even that was normal. I took a few steps, then ran downhill and splashed into the water in a pair of shoes I had never owned. Everything normal. A bright September day and I was alive in it.

Yet there was something. There was something wrong with my mind. Too quiet up there, not enough panic, too small a load of bewilderment, not even enough curiosity. Earlier I said of the tree limb, "White oak, I thought," and that wasn't right. I didn't *quite* think. This was spooky. It was more as if Something thought in me. I felt the words were moving by their own choice through my head the way air bubbles slide down the bowel.

I began walking along the stream bank waiting for—I don't know. For my head to clear? I felt aged forty from the neck down. I waited for that age to rise and cover me like water.

I was in Texas when I died. These hills and fields and meadows looked more to me like—what should I guess?— like Virginia. I said this over and over, aloud, "I'm dead and in Virginia," trying to make the sentence taste like mine. It never quite did.

Now and then, beside the stream, I would spot hoofprints. Cattle? Or deer? I saw nothing else alive except me, that cricket, and dozens of yellow birds on quick and nervous flights. Rice-birds in Virginia? They fed off tall stems and some stunted bush with brown catkins on its twigs. I jangled my wrist tag. I'd worn a bracelet there in the hospital, too, with my name spelled out in beads like an infant's. WATTS. Benson Watts. Ben.

I got the first pain, under one ear. Ben Watts. 226 Tracy Avenue . . .

I got the second pain, a needle, higher. I rattled the tag. *Disremember*, it said.

Crossing the stream, I noticed for the first time I was traveling in the direction it flowed—there! You see how my brain was? Unobservant. Unconcerned. At the water's edge was a stretch of pale sand. Beyond that the mud was like milk chocolate. More yellow grass grew on both sides to the edge of trees just turning from solid green to red maples and yellow hickories. The scattered pines were thinning their needles for fall.

I rounded a bend. To my right the land dipped off, and the water turned and ran downhill faster to empty into a long lake I could not see the end of, maybe half a mile wide. Its surface was very still with a skim of reflections. As I got closer, I knew what was wrong with this scenery, so ordinary and yet so unreal; and it came from absence. Everything I expected to see did not appear. No boats or motors, no fishermen, dogs, garbage, foam, signs, fences. No plastic bottles drifting near the shore. My head was aching. The sun was too harsh on my peeled scalp.

Near the water I glimpsed a small house, almost a hut. *Déjà vu*. I spun to the southwest to see if the Fitchburg Railroad skirted the lake. No. Yet it was his house or nearly like it, built beside a pond a hundred years ago for less than thirty dollars. Built yesterday. I began to run through the ripening grass. If I was back in time, was Thoreau inside? Writing in his journal? Or was it possible that each of us died away into our own personal image of serenity and would be tucked there forever like something in a pocket?

Running made my head worse. But that gut I had cursed for a year was now so new and strong I thought it might be turned to gold or silver, and I ran with both palms pressed there to feel each strand of muscle move.

The wooden door was half open, heavy on its leather hinges. I jumped a low stone wall and ran up the path.

One room with an earthen floor, a smaller one beyond in which I could see strings of onions, peppers, and bean pods. I touched the table, chair, bunk, saw that high shelves on both sides of a fieldstone hearth reached over my head. They held a set of books, maybe a hundred, all with the same green binding. I called out "Hello!" to more absence. Nobody answered; though there were ashes in the fireplace, not quite cold, and the charred spine of a book which seemed to match the others.

There was no dust. Under the bunk I found a stack of empty picture frames, white canvases, a wood box of paints and brushes, and I could see the clean squares on one wall where somebody's pictures had hung. There were no titles on the books, and when I pulled one out I found each page was lined but blank—the other books were the same. This time something happened that I expected; I found pen and ink on the bottom shelf.

To enter the back room I had to stoop. It was a pantry with a board floor. Cured hams were hanging from the ceiling over a flour bin. Crocks of meal and dried beans in sacks were under a table on which apples, potatoes, yams, pears, green tomatoes lay in neat rows. One high shelf held what looked like scuppernong wine in gallon jars. The woodbin was behind the door, full of oak logs, with a sack of cedar kindling nailed outside. The pantry was dim and its odors thick as fog.

I laid the wood over the andirons. Matches had been left in a tin by the hearth, and after I lit the lightwood I rummaged in a second strongbox where small jars of spices were jumbled, some without labels. I read once that if a man eats nutmeg his urine will smell like violets. Perhaps I will try it.

Slowly the oak bark caught fire underneath, curled off, till the log smoked and finally burned. Beautiful was the fire. Its colors moved and changed. I sat before it, watching for the sudden lick of blue which would reappear in a new place. So long as I stared into the flames, my head did not hurt. When there were coals, I slid three sweet potatoes in to roast and sat on, dreaming, sometimes tapping the log with a poker so sparks would leap off and shower onto the dirt floor. I must have sat that way for hours.

But the potato hearts were still raw when I peeled and ate them. I rolled the thickest log across the floor and heaved it into place. Then I went to bed though it was barely dark.

In the night I woke to hear rustling beyond me, something large scraping its hide between a bush and the wall of my house. There were no windows. In the red firelight I found the poker and carried it with me and swung open the heavy door. A large deer moved down the path, stepping as carefully as if he had made it, so heavily antlered that he seemed to be holding up an iron grille by stiffening his neck. He bent and drank from the lake, snuffled lightly, moved off along the water's edge. As soon as he passed, the frogs that he left would sing out again, so I could follow him through the dark long after he was lost to sight.

It was the same deer. I put the poker under my bunk with the paints and brushes. Only when I was settled and warm again and had closed my eyes against the glow of the fireside did I wonder: What does that mean? *Same* deer?

I knew suddenly it must be very dangerous to sleep. I might slide back. My gut would reopen; some bastard in a white coat would whisper, "He's coming out of it." I could almost see my wife hunched in her chair, the brown rubber tubes in her hands, waiting for me. And there was a drop of borrowed blood, halfway down, hung there till my arm would be under it.

But in spite of my fear I went to sleep and when I woke up, I was still here.

2

In the morning I could not remember the deer. I could remember getting out of bed in the dark, but not why. I ate an apple, found coffee beans and an old-fashioned hand grinder, and at last boiled the grounds in a cooking pot. The brew was thick and scummy, but its smell was magnificent. I remembered I'd had no cigarettes for two weeks, no solid food for longer than that. When I picked up the apple, saliva ran down my throat in a flood, and I felt my nose was twitching like a dog's.

I had dreamed about a deer. That's it. In the dream, an old stag came into this house and offered to carry me across the lake on his back. He spoke in rather a high voice for so large an animal. He told me that when many deer swam the lake, each rested his head on the haunches of the one in front, and since the one behind did the same, they suffered no trouble from the weight. He said the whole line swam for the far shore with all speed in this linked position, to reach land before being befouled. He would be lead deer on this trip, he said, and would carry me himself.

No. The headache started.

No, there had been a real deer, outside. I saw him by the lake. It was hard to remember the simplest details. Was it a doe, a fawn? I had never seen a deer this close before—that much was certain.

I grabbed one of the green ledgers and began to write down who I was and how I got here and that the deer was real. It was hard to write. My head felt as if something had come loose inside and was banging the bone. I read the entry twice, until I had it all straight and in order. Every day I would do this; every morning I would set down the previous day and read all the earlier entries. This would be good training for my mind, which, I now thought, had suffered oxygen deprivation there at the end. At the beginning? Whichever it was.

My name is Benson Watts and when I died in Houston, Texas, I was sixty-five and had grandchildren—none of whom I liked very much. I also had thick gray hair and brushy eyebrows. When I told my namesake grandson I looked like John L. Lewis, he didn't know who Lewis was. Now I'm twenty-five years younger, in Virginia, and my scalp is like orange rind, nothing but skin and pores; and I don't remember Lewis too well myself except for the eyebrows.

He might have been a principal in some school where I taught. He had the face for the job. For years I taught U.S. and world history in high schools all over Texas, for peanuts, because that left my summers free. Summers I read books, collected stamps, built halves of sailboats in the back yard, took auto trips, sold Fuller brushes (once), and encyclopedias (four times), coached Little League, tried pottery and built my own kiln, got divorced and remarried, and made notes for the book I would someday write on the Cherokee Indian in North Carolina. Here I am at last, dead and in Virginia, with a pen and inkpot and one wall of blank paper handy, and all I can remember is Tsali and the Trail of Tears. Some joke.

Once, too, I thought I might go to graduate school and write a book on the Dark Ages, on the flickers of light in the Dark Ages. By 1969, I thought we might be edging into the shadow of some new darkness, and without a Church to persevere. I taught myself Latin so I could read illuminated manuscripts at Oxford instead of translations in Texas libraries. *Illuminated* manuscripts. What a good phrase! But I did not write that book, either, and now I cannot call up a single Latin root.

All I can easily remember are random facts about myself, which don't amount to much. Trivia. The substance is missing. Let me write down the details.

Texas is bigger than France. There are four or five Texases to be born in—mine happened to be Beaumont, four years after the Spindletop oil gusher blew in. There might have been 10,000 people there then; the city multiplied itself by twelve in my lifetime. I stopped liking Beaumont when it passed 20,000, finished at Baylor, and started teaching history to conceited teen-agers who—if they owned the world and Texas—would rent out the world and live in Texas. That may be why Lyndon Johnson went to Washington, to see for himself how unlucky everybody else was. He stayed gone a long time.

Most summers I escaped from Texas, and once in the Notre Dame library I read the twelfth-century bestiaries and made notes, later lost in a Southern Railway boxcar. In the thirties I jumped freights and thumbed and left my wives (there were three in all) to go discuss me with their mothers.

The third wife, Grace, sat with me in the Houston Hospital while I died. She didn't shed a tear. Grace came late in my life; she never expected much, so was never disappointed. When I loaded up the car, she'd stand in the yard with her arms folded and just say, "Okay, Sunnybitch, don't leave me no dirty laundry." Grace had Indian blood. I miss her calm ways and her slow talking in an alto voice. I've seen her make a face at a coming tornado and then go inside and forget about it. Nothing affected her much. Even sex. She was a challenge. If Grace had cried—even once—in that sterile hospital room, I might have stuck out a finger; I might have blotted that tear and sucked it off and gotten well, just from the novelty of the thing.

She didn't cry, though, and I had not died off into a medieval abbey or a Cherokee camp. You'd think there'd be some choice. They even claim to give you that in the army.

Outside the hut I sat with my book and pen by the lake in the warm sun, reminding myself how the deer had stood and blown the water. Yes, it felt like September here. Indian summer. And for all I knew some real Indian, even a Cherokee with strings of hickory bark around his waist, might step out of these woods. Wonderful!

Might shoot me with his locust bow strung with bear entrails. Not so good. Could I die twice? Re-die? All that was . . . metaphysics. I could not think about it yet.

Could not. The landscape would not allow me. Virginia was opposed to thinking. While I sat in the brightness, empty as a sack, a praying mantis climbed up a weed stalk and lay along its blade. I bent my face beside that green swaying. Red knobby eyes. The only insect, I'm told, that can look over its shoulder. Maybe when this one died of winter, she would be raised up to my scale; as maybe I—shrunken—was now living on the tip of some weed and my lake was a dewdrop in the morning sun.

Yet none of this interested me. The four spread legs, two bent prayer claws, wings folded in layers on her back—I could have watched these tiny things all day, as I had waited for a blue flick on a burning log the night before.

Once I would have touched the mantis to see where she would spring. It was not necessary. I had been let out of thinking as if thinking were a jail. Nothing expected me to connect it with anything else. Not to anticipate—delicious. I felt that first morning the way a baby feels. *I am here.* Nothing else.

Some days went by. My ledger notes are sketchy. Like Thoreau, I gave time to birds and anthills. One afternoon—feeling so far from my other world that I mistook distance for wisdom—I analyzed completely how Western culture fell apart after World War II, and wrote down how this might have been prevented. My words lacked urgency. Nobody would read them. I bored myself.

After burning that, I tried to put on canvas my nighttime deer bent over a floating picture of himself in the black water. My painting was squat and clumsy, a hog at a wallow.

The fifth morning I was sitting on a log by the lake, watching the mist rise. Every morning it lay over the lake like cloud, then slowly churned to blow up the shore and fade among the tree trunks. I watched it begin to thin itself over the land. Down the lake, the mist suddenly shook like a curtain and I had a glimpse of someone walking by the water's edge.

I ran forward a few steps. Like gauze, the air blew shut. I saw it again. If not a man, a bear, upright and moving toward me.

My eye fixed on the fog, I walked in that direction. Fear? I could not remember how it felt to be afraid. In the thinning haze I saw again a—a polar bear? Impossible. White but too small. We could hear each other now. Crackling brush, dry stems breaking underfoot. I moved faster but those other noises stayed unhurried and regular. The mist was waist-high. I walked beyond it into a field of broom sedge and she, at the same moment, worked out of a wispy alder thicket and stared at me. She had on a white uniform, like a nurse.

I called, "Hello!"

She kept one bent alder limb taut in her hand. She was in her late twenties, red-haired, and pregnant. I saw that not only in her shape but the way she stood, bare feet spread wide, her spine tilted. She stepped forward and the branch twanged behind her. "Who are you?"

"My name is Benson Watts. I live . . ." That verb wasn't right. I jerked a thumb over one shoulder. "I've been staying in a little house by the lake."

"Good," she said. "I've not had anything to eat but persimmons. My mouth has shrunk down to zero." She gave me a normal-sized smile as she passed. "This way?"

"Just follow my track. What are you doing here?"

"Eating persimmons is all so far." Flatfooted, she walked along the swath I had made in the ripe weeds. I could not think of a way to ask a pregnant woman if she were dead. I thought about it, but the question sounded impolite. I followed. She was no more than five feet tall. Her short hair was full of beggar's-lice and sticktights.

I said, "Have you been here long?"

"Don't remember."

Her white skirt was streaked with mud and resin. "What's the last thing you do remember?"

"Spending the night in the woods. Oh. There it is." She made for my cabin in that stride which, from behind, looked bowlegged and clumsy. "What's the last thing you remember?"

I decided to say, "A hospital room."

"You're not contagious, are you? TB or anything?" She looked back and I saw how thickly her face was freckled.

"You can see why I've got to ask." She patted her belly with her left hand on which she wasn't wearing a single ring. There was a bracelet, though, like mine. I pulled at her tag and turned it over. *Dwell, then travel. Join forces, Disremember.*

"Where'd you get this?"

"The fairies brought it," she said. "And the baby, too." She led the way into my house, stroked the earth floor with the sole of her foot. "This is nice." The tops of her feet were scratched, some of the marks white, some bloodied. I pointed to the pantry. Quickly she ran up to a dangling ham and laid her face on its salty mold. I said I'd slice and fry some. She poked among the pears until she found one mellow enough to eat.

While I chopped off some meat and set the pan in the fireplace, she finished the pear and bit into a cucumber, peeling and all. "What's in this sack?" she called. I was trying to keep the ham from catching fire. "Peanuts!" She crowed, "Oh, glory! Peanuts!" I heard them rattle in a pot. "Let's parch some." She pushed the pan onto a bed of coals and a little grease popped into and speckled their hulls. "Smell that ham, honey!" she said—not to me, but to the lump at her middle.

I sat back on the dirt floor and let her tend the skillet. "What's your name?"

"Olena."

I had her spell it. I'd never heard that name before. I think she made it up.

"There's flour but no bread," I said. She didn't offer to make biscuits but sat back with her legs crossed wide under the round bulk of her unborn child. I thought through several questions before I chose, "Is your home around here?"

Olena said, "It never was before. Where's yours?"

"Texas." She plucked the fork from my hand and turned over the ham. I took a long breath and blew out a statement on it, watching her. "I was sick in a hospital and then I woke up here."

Olena said matter-of-factly, "I fell down a flight of stairs and this place was at the bottom."

We stared at each other, then quickly looked away. Each

of us stole a glance at the pale tag strung to the other's wrist. With a grunt, Olena got to her feet and went to the pantry to find a plate and cutlery. I warned her pork needed to cook longer than that, but she was already spearing an oily slice. "I don't think you can get worms here," she said, staring at the ham.

"I see plenty of regular insects."

Chewing, she didn't care. "Oh, glory, that's good!" she said, with a sigh. I brought her a salt shaker and a tomato with the top cut off; she buried half her freckled face until its juice ran down her chin. "Can I sleep here tonight?" she asked, swiping a forearm over her mouth. I said she could.

Watching her chew the ham and pull its pink shreds from between her teeth, I tried to decide what accident had sent us both here, what kink in orderly process, whether there was some link between our lives or some similarity in our natures which made us candidates for transport to this place. I asked about the location of the stairs where she fell, and Olena said, "Florida. Fort Lauderdale." All I got out of that was a vague sense of regional districts, but it made me walk to the door and search the edges of the lake for some other Southerner. The mist had cleared.

"What you looking for?"

"Just looking." Somebody else would be coming soon. I felt certain of it. "Olena, is there someplace you're supposed to be? Or be going?"

She finished the ham and raked a pile of peanuts onto the floor to cool. "I guess not."

"We'll wait here a few days, then."

3

The fire kept me awake. Even with my eyes closed, its pattern of light and shadow on my face was a physical touch and moved like warm water across my skin. I rolled in my blanket farther across the floor and turned my back to the blaze. Above me, in the bunk, Olena lay, spread-legged, bulging. The covers seemed draped on an overturned chair. Behind me, the fire crackled. Rain had begun in late afternoon, so we kept the fire going against a wet chill rising through the dirt floor. Olena's snore was soft as a cat's purr.

I dozed, then leaped alert. What had wakened me? Perhaps that deer, passing my door, had ground his teeth? I threw back the blanket and sat up, listening. It must have been nearly dawn, since mocking birds were taking turns, each song intensely sweet and swelling higher than the last. Barefoot, I crossed the damp floor and stepped onto the path. Raindrops on the weeds looked solid, like tacks or metal pellets, but the sky was full of fading stars. Far down the lake, something large and dark bent in the mist to drink, too wide and bulky to be a stag. My naked scalp prickled, for there had flared through my head the leaves of those old Latin bestiaries, page after page of winged quadrupeds and dromedaries, each fact of natural history bent to reflect an atribute of Christ. Just from Olena's presence, this landscape had become a dream we both were having and, like those books, took on some quality of concealment and mystery.

I started through the wet grasses to surprise the drinking animal, but it melted through the brush and downhill into the woods, looking odd and fictional. The woods were, at the same time, dark and translucent. It seemed to me even the tree trunks were spelling words I could nearly read. I rested my hand on the bark of one, and tried in its cracks and lichen crusts to make out the Braille. Not since I was a child had I felt this expectancy, as if at last I were on the verge of seeing everything unveiled. Most of my life I'd been certain there was nothing *to* unveil. A bit of lichen, like tough lace, came loose in my fingers.

Quietly, I walked inside the hut, dried my feet, and slid again into my blanket roll. Olena had turned her face to the wall and her back took on a woman's curves. I was fearful of desiring her. I slept and dreamed that my mother was lying on her deathbed and the doctor took a large white bird out of his satchel and wrapped its claws on the brass bedstead. "If the bird turns to face her," he said, "this is not a mortal illness, but if he keeps his back turned there'll be nothing I can do." The bird unfolded extra wings and feathers after being cramped in the leather bag and seemed to grow larger and larger. One at a time, he uncurled his feet and shook them, then flapped once around the room. Each wingbeat sounded like an oar slammed flat against the water. At last the bird lit facing away from my mother, who gave a great cry. I ran forward to beat at the big bird but I could not make it move or even look at me, and its yellow talons were wrapped on the metal rail as if molded there.

At daylight, we were wakened by loud thumps on the wooden door. Olena sprang half out of bed, one of her feet touching the floor.

"Don't worry," I said. "It's another one."

She whispered, "Another what?"

"Another one of us." I jangled my bracelet in the air between us and stepped into my shoes. I dragged open the heavy door.

He was ugly. Malformed—not deformed but *mal*formed—six feet tall and the parts of his body mismatched. Hips like a woman and a head flattened on both sides. I could not see a bracelet under the black sleeve of his suit. I pictured him yanked from his mother's womb, not by forceps, but with a pair of cymbals clapped over both ears. His face, driven together by the blow, was long and its features crowded. The nose, buckteeth, popeyes had all pushed forward when the doctor first compressed his skull. "Come in?" he asked softly.

"Of course." Another Southerner—Georgia Cracker by his drawl. "Are you hungry?"

Thinking about it, he rubbed his temples with both thumbs. "I think I just ate," he finally said, and spotted Olena waiting by the bed. "Good morning, Ma'am."

I introduced Olena and myself. He wasn't curious. "Melvin Drum," he said, and wrapped my hand in a long set of fingers. He was too thin for his black suit and the pale bow tie made his Adam's apple look red and malignant. He said politely, "Hate to wake you up."

"We've been expecting you." That puzzled him. He took a seat and stared at his knuckles while he popped each one.

"This is a funny thing," he said mildly. "It might be amnesia. But look here." He leaned his head forward and his longish tan hair divided into two hanks. "You see a knot there? Anything?"

I felt his scalp. "Nothing."

He leaned back and his eyes—which I had thought were blue—glowed green as a cat's. "Maybe I've gone crazy," he said, obviously pleased. "They say religious people do."

Dryly I said I thought Mr. Drum would find he had passed beyond all need for religion now.

He did not hear me. "It's hard to tell nuts from saints," he explained to Olena, "except for God, of course. He can divide them up left and right in the twinkling of an eye. The twinkling. Of one eye." Smiling, he tilted his chair onto two back legs and I grabbed for his sleeve where something gleamed.

"Can you explain this?" I said, shaking my own tag.

"I can accept it," he said. He pulled his cuff over the third bracelet. "We've all passed on and these are our instructions."

"Passed *on?*" said Olena. She crossed to the pantry, carried back a skirtful of yellow apples, and sat on the floor to share them. "Are you certain you're dead, then, Mr. Drum?"

"That was the last promise I heard." His rabbit teeth bit out a sharp triangle and he talked over the sloshing noise of apple in his mouth. "I turned down an alley—there were three men bent over somebody. I tried to run. They grabbed me; one of them put a flashlight on my face and said, Oh, Lord, it was Willy and Willy had a big mouth. The one I couldn't see said, 'Willy's a dead man, then.'"

"Who's Willy?" I asked.

"God only knows." He read the carving softly: "'To avoid going back—dwell, then travel. Join forces. Disremember.' Anybody want to go back?"

I pictured myself hooked up to tubes, pumps, catheters, filling and emptying at the nurses' convenience. No.

But Olena had pressed two freckled hands on her abdomen and was staring at them while her eyes filled. She sounded hoarse. "How did you die, then, Mr. Drum? After that promise?"

Tire iron, lead pipe, he wasn't sure.

"But you were cured of your final . . . condition. Your head wound. And you, Mr. Watts, of yours. Does that mean? Do you think I?"

We tried not to look at what her hands were cupping. Melvin Drum leaned forward and his face shifted in some way I could not see; his tone dropped down an octave and he got older and almost dignified as he laid his thin hand on Olena's red hair. "Sister," he said, nearly rumbling, "leave it to God."

Water ran down her nose and hung there. "This baby's alive," she burst out. "You hear me? When the time comes, you'll have to help me birth. I won't leave that to God." She shook her head loose from under his hand.

"Yes, you will," he said, but I told her we'd both help and maybe by then we'd find a doctor, too.

Melvin Drum tapped his bracelet. "We've joined forces, then," he said. "When does the travel start?"

Tomorrow, we decided. We'd pack food and bottle water. Olena would rest today and we'd swim, clean our clothes. I wrote these things down in my green-bound book. "Which direction shall we take?"

Melvin said east seemed appropriate. I wrote that down.

In the afternoon, he and I floated on our backs in the lake while Olena hung our clothes on the sunlit bushes. My younger body was a joy to me, moving easily, stroking well. Melvin had a large genital and as we drifted I could sometimes see it shift in the water like a pale fish. "Were you married, Melvin?"

He said no. I thought he must be over thirty. "Were you queer?"

Laughing, he had to gargle out some water. "Very," he said.

I don't think he meant for boys.

4

"I'm already tired," Olena complained. "Why must you walk so fast?" On her short legs, she had to make three steps for every one of Melvin Drum's. I was winded, too, and the sun stood directly overhead. "Why hurry?" she puffed, pushing swags of honeysuckle to one side, "when we have no destination and no deadline?"

"None that we *know* of," said Drum, leading the way like the major of a band.

Over her shoulder to me, Olena said, "This is silly. There's no time in this place." Overhearing, Drum pointed straight up at the blazing sun and kept marching. She poked him in the spine above his belt. "Disremember," she said.

We walked noisily, single file, through woods which were thick and shady, their fallen leaves ankle-deep; and the sun slid with us, shooting a ray through a thin branch now and then.

Olena carried the lightest pack—raisins, dried beans and figs, the peanuts she brought over our objections. Drum and I had mostly ham and wine and water jars. The kitchen knife I'd strung at my waist had pricked me half a dozen times climbing uphill from the lake. The land was level forest now, with no sign of paths or trails.

We rested by a shallow spring with a frog in it. I asked Drum, "You hear a river?" He said it might be. Olena stuck her red hair backward into the spring, so the ends uncurled and hung wetly down her back and dripped on the leaves in front of me when we walked on again.

"I'm ready to unstrap this blanket and leave it on some tree."

Drum told her for the third time we'd need blankets later.

"He thinks we'll still be hiking in December," she grumbled. "He's got a new think coming." She passed me a pocketful of peanuts to crack and eat as we walked. She wouldn't give Drum any.

The river still sounded far away when we saw it flowing low between walls of thicket and vines which had briers under their heart-shaped leaves. Drum stopped, and we stepped to either side of him and looked downhill. The water was brown and sluggish, with small sandbars in the middle. "Want to camp here?"

"Won't there be snakes?" But Olena let us lead the way and reach our hands back for her when the slope grew slip-

pery or jagged. Rows of black willows kept us from the
water's edge, but upstream Melvin Drum broke through to a
slab of gray rock which jutted into the current and had built
behind it a sandy pool. Olena unlaced my borrowed shoes
and slid her feet into it. "Glory, that's cool!" she said and
slipped forward until her white hem turned gray in the water.

"It's a good place to build a fire," Drum said, "but we
might want to sleep on higher ground."

"I'm so tired all I'd ask a water moccasin is not to snore,"
she said, lying back and letting her toes float into sight.

Melvin and I dropped our packs to gather firewood and
haul it to the rock. I nudged Olena's shoulder once with my
toe. "All right?"

"Sleepy," she said. I climbed uphill for another load,
thinking that was Drum who thrashed ahead of me through
the bushes in the gathering dusk. I squatted to rip lightwood
from a rotted stump. Suddenly, from behind, he spoke my
name and I jumped up, pointing uphill at the moving underbrush. We watched the dark leaves stir.

"There?" said Drum softly. I saw only a dim trunk of a
thick shrub; then it moved and grew a snout. I could make
out between twigs the animal's long outline, lean and low to
the ground, with a tail curved around its hindquarters. He
whispered, "Dog?"

"Wolf," I said. Lupus. Very still, like a carving or a piece
of statuary. In slow motion the wolf began to back away
uphill, and at one point I could see the whole arch of his
back and curve of his tucked-in tail. Once he stepped on a
twig which snapped, and he punished his own paw with a
nip. I saw the sharp flash of teeth. He turned then, and went
up the slope in three long bounds.

Drum's breath blew out on the back of my neck. "A real
wolf? Here?"

I didn't think it was a real wolf. More like an animated art-
work I had seen drawn somewhere, and I said so. "Didn't
you see how the shape was exaggerated? It looked so . . . so
stylized."

Drum sniffed at his armpit. "Well, I'm real enough. I'm
organic and I stink and there's a blister on my foot."

I wanted to tell him about a pictured Lupus who could only copulate twelve days in the whole year and whose female could not whelp except in May and then when it thundered; but that was like saying a twelfth-century picture book had come alive before our eyes, and the Psalter or Apocalypse might be next. For all I knew, Melvin Drum had dream beasts in his own head to which I had yet to be subjected.

We carried down the remaining firewood, pulled the small bag of white beans out of its river soak, and boiled them slowly with a chunk of ham fat in our only pot. While they were cooking, I asked Melvin just how religious he had been.

"The last five years I thought of nothing else." He stretched out on the rock. "It's a shame I'm dead," he said, "because someday I would have finished the stealing and had it all."

"Stealing what?" asked Olena, stirring a peeled stick through the beans.

"Religion. I went in every church I could. Catechisms, hymnals, prayer books, rosaries, creeds—I stole them all. Went on field trips to the Mormons and Christian Scientists. I stacked all that stuff in my room. You could hardly walk for candles and books and shawls." Olena speared a bean for him but he shook his head that it was too hard to eat. "I was in Los Angeles at the end," he said. "On the way to visit the Rosicrucians."

She snapped, "What on earth was it for?"

He smiled at the rising moon. "You ever seen a big set of railroad scales? Where you keep adding weights till the arm is perfectly balanced? When I got all the stuff together, when I had collected the right balance . . . weight . . ." Suddenly he giggled toward the darkening sky. "It sounds dumber now than it did then."

I leaned toward him on both my gritty palms. "Doesn't your head hurt when you remember things like that?"

"No. Does yours?"

Olena said hers hurt, too, just behind both eyebrows. She spoke in a fast singsong: "So I've quit remembering I was a beautician and having a baby and he was already married and I didn't care and one day I fell down the steps of my apartment building all the way to the washing machines in the basement and the woman folding towels just stood there and hollered all the time I came rolling down and all I could see looking up was her open mouth and fillings in every tooth in her head." She grabbed her forehead. "Whew! That's the last time, damn it." She turned away and for a while the three of us lay flat on our backs on the hard rock, not saying anything, while the sky got darker behind the stars.

The beans took a long time to soften. We got our spoons out of our pockets and tried them and lay down again.

I was almost asleep when Drum said, "Why don't we use the river?"

"Use it for what? To travel, you mean?"

"Beats walking," Olena said.

"If we knew anything about boats or canoes," said Drum.

I sat up. "It happens I know a little." I told them how the Indians would burn down a big tree or find one struck low by a storm, and put pine resin and tree gum on one side and set fire to that, chopping out the charred wood and repeating the blazing gum, until they had burned the log hollow. "Some of their dugouts would carry twenty men."

"Won't that take a long time?" One of Olena's hands climbed up by itself and rubbed her belly.

"We have a rock, water, matches, trees . . ."

Olena pointed her finger at me. "Hah! Why didn't your head hurt? Talking about the Indians, why didn't your head hurt then?"

"I think," said Drum thoughtfully, "it must not hurt if the things you recall are useful to you. Useful now, I mean."

Which, in view of his vague religion, made us stare at him.

It was late when we spooned our mushy beans in the dark and rolled up in our blankets, tired enough to sleep on solid stone. If snakes crawled up at night, we never noticed. The last thing I thought was that any serpent I saw in this place would be like the one Pepys claimed could feed on larks by spitting its poison into the air, and for that one I would send forth a weasel, since—as the monks wrote in their illuminated manuscripts—God never makes anything without a remedy.

For all I knew, somewhere in Melvin Drum's last rented room there were stacks of medieval books full of viper-worms and amphisbaenae, and perhaps even stories of the Cherokee Thunders, who lived up in Galunlati, close to that great Apportioner, the Sun.

And Drum was right—thinking of all these things, my head never hurt at all.

5

After that come repeated entries in my ledger: "Worked on boat today."

I don't know how long it took. We had one hatchet and we used sharp rocks. My knuckles bled, made scabs, and bled again.

I slipped into a way of life I seemed to know from the bone out. Squatted in the woods, wiped with a leaf, covered my shit. I peed on tree trunks like a hound—it's instinct, I think. We're meant to give back our excrement to plants. We washed in the river. Even Olena, after a while, bathed with us and I stopped staring at her stretched white skin and the brown mat of hair below. My beard grew out itchy; there were welts across my chest and the beans made gas growl inside us all. One night I spotted the wolf's eyes shining near the rock and I called to him, but the lights stayed where they were. When the ham got moldier, we lived off fish. My fingernails smelled like fertilizer.

Olena kept saying the boat was done, but I wanted the shell thinner, lighter, and we chopped through the heartwood and sanded the inside down with stones. We pointed the stern and rounded the bow. Even after dark, we'd sit scrubbing her surface absently with rocks until she felt smoother than our calloused hands.

"She's ready," Melvin Drum said at last. "Admit it, Ben. We can go on."

I did not want to stop. It seemed to me there was grace in the log we had not yet freed, shape that was still unrefined. But finally I gave in. I crushed pokeberries in my palm and wrote on her side with a finger, *"Escarius."*

They made me explain. A labrus fish, thick-lipped, called

by Sylvester "Golden-Eye." The monks had thought the Scar clever, since, when it was trapped in a fish pot—they wrote— it would not dash forward but would turn around and undo the gate with frequent blows of its tail and escape backward. Other Scars, if they saw him struggle, were said to seize their brother's tail with their teeth and help him back loose to freedom.

We loaded *Escarius*, even filling our water bottles, though we would be afloat in water. We still had beans and damp peanuts, and we opened a jar of grape wine on the rock and poured some on the boat and each spat a swallow into the river—I don't remember why.

Pushing off from the gray rock, we started down the river, Drum and I trying our new poles and paddles. Olena sat amidships and let her fingers trail. She was singing. "Shall we gather at the river? The beautiful, the beautiful river? Gather with the Saints at the river that flows by the throne of God?"

Into the current we moved and skirted the sandbars, slipped silently past the drooping willows, and began an easy drift. The knobs of turtle heads dropped below the water as we drifted by, and floated up again when we had passed. We may have looked majestic, moving downstream in a boat so much longer than we needed. *Escarius* tended to wallow to this side and that, but we learned how to balance with our oars. Our rock went out of sight and the water seemed thick and reluctant and bore us without interest, slowly, while the river spread wider and showed us floodplains and sycamores with watching squirrels.

I felt like a man on a color calendar, poised with my oar level, going off the page and out of sight.

"She's all right," called Melvin Drum. "She rides fine."

Sometimes a snake would drop limp off a low limb and lie on the water like a black ribbon. Olena stopped worrying, since they seemed to fear us and would at the last glide toward the shallow edge and blend with tree roots there. "We're dreaming," she said, turning her face to me. "Even the snakes are dreaming."

The first set of rapids was shallow and we bumped down it like a sledge. Late in the afternoon we pulled up to a low bank under pines and slid the hull over brown needles and braced her ashore with stones. Olena found a tick on her ankle but said it was still a fair place to sleep. My shoulders ached. I walked up the small creek to relieve myself, and on its far side saw the bent tail and stiff fur of the same gray wolf as he slunk away. He could not be the same wolf, yet I was sure he was.

With darkness, the air turned cool and rain spattered overhead. We huddled together under our three blankets but slowly the wool soaked through. Then we just pressed together to outlast the rain, Olena with her back against a pine trunk, Drum and I on either side. Her knees were up, her face down. "I hate it here," she suddenly said. We leaned closer. "I hate it." Putting an arm about her shoulders, Drum and I got tangled with each other, and once I slapped at the wet shreds of his sleeve. "I could have been married by now," she said between her knees. "And had regular customers on my sun porch and bought myself a dishwashing machine." Rain poured over us. "I could have joined the Eastern Star," she wailed.

Trying to rub our foreheads on her soaked hair, Drum and I bumped skulls, and he said angrily, "You let me do all the work today!" Which wasn't so.

When at last the rain stopped, what could we do? We went on sitting there while the moon started down. We were soggy and chilled and had wet wool in our lungs.

In the morning nobody spoke. We spread our clothes to dry and tried to nap but the bugs were too bad.

"We might as well go on," I finally said. I felt resigned. There was nothing at the end of this river but a sea waiting to drown us. It would pull us home like caught fish on a line.

In silence, Drum wadded our wet blankets into the boat. Olena waded out and hoisted herself aboard, and without a word we pushed loose into the current. I was lonely and the river seemed hypnotic, just fast enough not to need our thrust. For a long time we sat with our oars laid in our laps. If Drum watched one bank, I stared at the other, and when his attention shifted I crossed mine over, too.

Once Olena said we should capture the next snake, lift

him into the boat, just to see what would happen. Maybe, she said, if one of us was bitten he would move on another layer to someplace else. "We might wake up in the pyramids."

Or Bethlehem, she hoped. I stroked the water hard. Drum grabbed at blackberries hanging from the bank until his hands were purple. I said, "Am I using my paddle enough today? Are you satisfied?"

He said, "It was raining, Ben." We drifted on.

By night we had passed into drier land and could build a fire and string our clothes nearby. We heated a cup of wine apiece. I asked him, "Is there a God? Now? What do you think now?"

"It's hard to think here."

"You can remember, though, better than we can."

The tin cup covered half his face. "I'm like every other expert," he said. "In time, I got interested in the smaller sects. I specialized. Osiris or the voodoo drums. I went to the Hutterites and Shakers. Once I met Frank Buchman and I couldn't see anything special about him. A man had the Psychiana lessons, all twenty-four. It had cost him twenty-six dollars during the Depression; I won't tell you the price he wanted. I didn't pay, of course. I stole the set and hid it in my mattress." He finished the wine. "If a snake bit me, I'd wake up in Moscow, Idaho, asking about Frank Robinson." He said to Olena, "I'd just as soon be here. You feeling better?"

She had fallen asleep, mouth open, the edge of her teeth in view. I knew that I wanted to put my tongue there. I jumped when Drum said, "One thing we mustn't do is fight."

Swallowing, I nodded. He rinsed his cup in the river, stared across its lighted surface. "My brother used to have dizzy fits and he said he dreamed like this. Always of journeys and trips. Mostly he rode on a train that went very fast and roared. He was always on top of the engine, holding to the bells, and the whistle would go right through him, he said. If a tunnel could feel a train go through it, he said he could feel the sound of that whistle, boring, passing." Away from the fire, Drum looked taller. "The dream was always dark except for the engine lamps."

"Where did he go?"

"He woke up too soon."

"Is your brother dead now?"

Melvin Drum laughed coming back into the firelight. He couldn't stop laughing. Even after we had curled up in the damp blankets, I heard him laughing in the dark.

6

How was it possible to dream in that place? Yet I went on dreaming, every night, inventing an overlap of worlds which spun out from me without end. I dreamed of a life in an Indian village ringed by sharpened stakes, where my job was to be watchman over the fields of corn and pumpkins and to run forth with screams and rattles to drive off crows or animals. I dreamed of being alone on a sandy plain, lost, staying alive by eating fly larvae scraped from the surface of alkaline pools.

Drum said he never dreamed. Olena did; she tossed and grunted in her sleep but claimed she could not remember why in the morning.

We blundered on down the river, shipping water, overturning once in white froth when *Escarius* scraped a jagged rock.

"If we took turns sleeping, we could travel at night, too," Drum said; but what was the point now that time did not rush from left to right? Only the river moved—for all we knew, moved forever.

Finally the banks began to withdraw and the wider current slowed. We seldom had to use oars or poles. Early one morning, the shores were suddenly flung outward and we were afloat in a wrinkled lake which seemed without end. Drum said it might be an ocean sound at low tide, since the waves were light but regular. We turned south to keep a shore in view. Soon Drum thrust down with our longest poplar pole and struck no bottom. It flew under the water like a spear and bobbed up far away, beating slowly and steadily toward the sandy bank. Under the hot sun my brain cooked like stew in a pot.

Olena had been silent for a long time. Suddenly she burst out, "You two might be dead but I'm not." Perhaps the child had moved in her, or she imagined that it moved.

Over her head, Drum said to me, "Shall we keep on?" For the first time, he sounded tired.

"Olena?"

She jerked her face away from the disappointing shoreline, so plainly empty of other people like ourselves. Her freckles were wet and her sweaty forehead flamed. "There's nothing here," she said, almost whining. We stroked the water. "You, Melvin Drum, you made us leave that house too soon. Somebody else might have come if we had just waited awhile."

Or, by now, why hadn't we caught up with whoever had burned his books in that fireplace? Yet, I thought, Old Lobo might be the fourth one in our group, and I eyed the shore as if I might spot his gray head sliding through the water, parallel.

The sun had started down the sky when we landed on a small and wooded island pocked with crab tunnels. Drum built a fire and dropped a dozen crabs into boiling water. We carried them in cloths, like hot spiders, up the beach and into the shade of high bushes.

"I'll fix yours," Drum said, breaking off claws, throwing the flippers downhill on the sand. He separated back from body, then gouged down to a paper-thin shell. "Hand me your knife, Ben." He scraped out white meat for Olena and offered it in his palm. She ate bits with her fingers. I cleaned my own. In case there should be some later use for them, we scrubbed the pink shells with sand and set them to dry in the sun. Then, while Olena lay resting under a tree, Drum and I explored the narrow island. There were so many loud birds inland that every tree seemed to scream. We found one pool of brackish water and wild grapevines which still had late fruit, although some had fermented on the stem. We could barely see the shore from which our river had issued, but on the island's far side there was only water and some shadows which might be other islands.

Before dark, the waves grew higher and crabs at their foaming edges carried off the claws and flippers we had thrown. Olena felt pain during the night. Her heavy breathing woke us. She sprang up and began walking on the damp sand, hunched over.

"She's aborting," Drum said, watching her pace.

Olena heard him and screamed that she was not.

"It isn't her time. She's not big enough for that," he added.

I called to her, "When were you due? What month?" But she would not answer.

Drum asked, "How long have we been here, anyway?" I looked back through these moonlit pages trying to count days, but it was hard to estimate. I kept glancing at Olena. Drum jerked impatiently at my book. "Is it forty-nine days? Is it close to that?" I didn't know. He said something about people in Tibet once thinking it took forty-nine days for the passage between death and further life; then he clapped both hands to his head. I stared, for at last there was some piece of remembering that made Drum's head hurt. Good, I thought. I wanted his jaw-teeth roots to burn like fire.

I left him and crossed the sand to Olena. "I'll stay with you." The moonlight turned her hair black and skin gray and sank her eyes into pits. Together we marched on the cool sand. When the pain eased, we dragged her blanket closer to mine and I could feel the knob of her bent knee low in my back like something growing on my spine.

She had rolled to the other side when I woke at sunrise. I turned also, and fitted myself to her back. She only murmured as my arm dropped over her. Our parts were sweetly matched as if she were sitting in my lap; under the curve of her hips I could feel my stiffening heat. My fingers slid past her collar to her loose breast until they could play on her nipple like tongues.

Drum coughed. Over Olena's red curls I saw him watching my busy hand, staring at the cloth where it was moving. I pulled on her skin till the breast budded, all the while letting him watch. Olena was awake now. The cells in her body came alive and caused my own skin to prickle.

Now I yanked my blanket and threw it over both of us,

taking care that Drum could see, and that he knew I saw him see.

Under the blanket, creating bulges for his following eye, I ran my long arm over the swell of Olena's child until my thumb was centered low in her body hair and my fingertips pressed on. She moved to help me. I heard her breath. Her leg slid wide and dropped back over mine until I was touching her at last. The hot grasp was too much for me and my spasm came while she was simply widening and making ready for hers. I kept on until she made noises and threw herself on her back, knees up and shivering. Instantly, so Drum could not see her taut face, she jerked up the blanket and pulled it to her eyebrows.

Drum never moved. I gave him a long look, but he never moved. I fell asleep with my hand on Olena's thigh and she must have slept also.

In the morning Drum was gone, and the boat *Escarius* was gone, and half our possessions were neatly laid out by the dried crab shells on the beach. There was a moving speck near the mouth of the river, but I could not tell for sure if it was man or animal and, when the sun got higher, could not find it at all in the glare.

7

Sweet days! Long, languid, poured out like syrup.

Olena slept in my arms. No sex in the regular way—because of her coming child—so, like curious children ourselves, we played touching games on each other's bodies.

Our clothes were very worn. I made a loin wrapping from my torn shirt; she sawed my pants off with a butcher knife for herself and left her breasts naked to the sun. We might have been Polynesian lovers from another age except for our bracelets, which, without ever discussing it, we did not discard.

Maybe ten days, two weeks went by. The nights were cooling but our afternoons were still part of summer. For many meals we dug clams from an inland mudbank, steamed them in salty water.

"Wouldn't you give anything for butter?" Olena said. She

had persuaded herself the sea waters were supplying her baby rich brain food and protein. She would watch me slide a knife along a fish's backbone as if each filet were preordained to become some tender organ inside her unborn child. Maybe, she sometimes said half seriously, we should powder the fishbones since she had no milk to drink?

In spite of the sweet days and sweeter nights, I began gathering wood, poles, stakes, and lashing them together with strings of our ragged clothes or strips of bark. Olena didn't like the raft.

"Where will we go? Not out to sea, and there's nothing ashore but wilderness." She ran a freckled hand around my waist, spun a fingertip in my navel. "You'll help me when the baby comes, Ben. Things will be fine."

But I could hear, in the night wind, winter draw closer than her child. How cold might it get? Which of the fish would stay and what shelter did we have?

She pounded sea oats into flour, mixed that with water, and baked patties in an oven of stones. They were bitter but we ate them for the sake of the different texture. "Now stop working on the raft and let's go swimming," she said. Sometimes I did.

"Isn't it good," she'd whisper to me in the dark, "not to be planning ahead? Saving money? Paying insurance?"

I held her tightly and watched the perpetual sea. "What do you think happened to Melvin Drum?"

Her whole body shrugged. "Who knows?"

Who-knows tormented me more than What-happened. "Maybe," I said, "Drum's found the place by now."

"What place?"

The place it ended. The sweeter Olena felt and tasted, the more certain I was that this was an interlude we would both forget. Our stay on the island was timeless, so I felt certain it could not possibly last. I had even begun to feel homesick for endings, arrivals. Finality.

"Ooh," breathed Olena, grabbing my hand, "Ooh, glory, feel that!" I laid my palm under her ribs. "Feel him move!"

I held my own breath in case there should be some faint shifting at last below her tight skin. "I feel it," I lied.

She rubbed my chest with her forehead so her long red hair tickled. "When Eve had a son, do you think she worried about who he would marry? We're married, Ben. In a way."

"In a way," I said, kissing the peak of her ear.

"Really, you'll be the baby's father."

The word was not real to me, not in this place. I tested it over and over in my head. Fatherfatherfather until the sound was mixed meaninglessness and prayer. Fatherfather.

"We should have asked Melvin to marry us."

I said, "He wasn't a preacher."

"Never did think that mattered much."

What *had* mattered, after all? Damn headache.

"Surely I'll not get much bigger," said Olena, stroking herself. I thought she was the same size as the first time I saw her walking through the mist. We were both browner, though. Her legs were hairier; on my face grew a broad beard, still not a hair on my scalp. We cleaned our teeth by wrapping wet sand in wads of cloth, or chewing twigs into brushes. Nails on our toes and fingers were long and tough; my foot sole felt like canvas. Sea bathing had hardened our skin and crusted the smallest scratch into a quick scar. My forearms looked almost tattooed.

Yes, we had changed. But Olena was the same size.

One morning there washed on our beach an assortment of trash which made me shout for Olena. Empty blue bottles, finger-length. A warped black piece of a nameless book cover . . . the foot of a celluloid doll. She grabbed for that—a toy for the baby, she said. I followed the tidemark of seaweed, stirring it with my toes. Rubber tubing. A piece of comb with the teeth sealed by barnacles. A length of wood which had once been fluted, part of a carved chair or table. Olena traced its design with awe, like some archaeologist.

But I was afraid. While she scanned the horizon for sails or a smokestack, I thought of a rent in the membrane between worlds, perhaps the great suck of a filling vacuum which would sweep Olena down more stairs and drop me under another scalpel. When the wind blew, even lightly, it raised goose bumps under my tan. "I've got to finish the raft," I said firmly. All day I watched, while pretending not to watch, for some vessel to follow its trash ashore. The raft grew wide enough for one person. Olena watched openly for a boat. The raft was wide enough for one person and a half. I worked on it constantly. Olena was bored with the building and bracing of its parts, and no longer sat nearby or carried me cooked fish in crab-shell dishes; but sat at a distance on the beach where the flotsam had washed, crooning to the doll's foot and waiting for something to rear up on the line between sea and sky. Some days she did not cook at all. At sundown I would carry food to her. Often she was sitting in an unnatural, stiff position, and kept her hand poised like an eyeshade longer than she should have been able to keep it there.

One evening she used the doll's foot to mash her fish meat into white gruel, then lapped it up with her tongue. I was disgusted and struck her under one eye. I watched tears spill on her reddening cheekbone.

"I'm sorry, Olena. Forget it. Come sleep now."

She shook her head.

"I want you to put your hands on me."

Her eyes were sliding off my face, across the streak of moonlight on the water.

"I'll put mine on you, then," I wheedled.

No. She shrank away on the darkening sand.

When the raft was done, Olena would not climb on. "We're leaving," I said, "even if it is dark." I held the platform still on the water. She would not come and I threatened to hit her again as I had on that other night.

In the moonlight, then, we walked the raft past the low waves till I hoisted her on board and heaved myself beside. Olena wrapped her body and head in a blanket and sat in the middle, a lump, a cargo bale.

"We can cross most of the water in the cool of the evening," I said. All I could see of her was the roundness of one pale heel showing at the blanket's base. I tried to be cheerful. "We might even see Melvin Drum. I bet he made camp on the shore below the river's mouth, and that's right where we'll land." I paddled with wood, with my hands. The raft was slow and awkward and zigzagged on the black water.

"Even if Drum moved on, he may have left some clue behind for us. Some message. Why don't you answer me?"

"I don't feel good," said the lump.

We moved very slowly across the wide bay, as if the thick moonlight were an impediment. The edges of the dark water beat luminous on our island and the landfall.

In a loud voice I said, "I couldn't stand just waiting like that. I couldn't keep doing that."

Olena would not move but rode on my labors like a keg under a tarpaulin.

At first light we landed on the same inland shore from which we had come, although the river was out of sight. No sign of Drum—no old campfires, no heaped shells or stones. The sand piled quickly into low dunes, stubby grass, underbrush.

"Why don't you sleep now?"

"I still don't feel good." Olena tottered up the beach and lay down in her damp blanket while I dragged the raft high from the water. There were shallow paw prints in the wet sand, some in a circle, as if the animal had paced.

I squatted by Olena. "Are you hurting?"

"No." On her back, she stared beyond me. The last stars looked like flecks of paper stuck on the blueing sky. "I feel funny, though."

"It's from leaving. I'm sorry I forced you, Olena."

"Doesn't matter," she said. "But it's colder on this side of the water."

I asked if she wanted a fire, but she said no. I curled up with my head laid on her thighs and went to sleep.

The sun was high and warm when I woke, feeling sticky. Again, Olena was too rigid, with one arm raised off the sand and her palm spread open to the sky. I felt for her knee and squeezed it. "Move around some." Her skin felt cool and dry.

I sat up, staring. Overnight her pregnancy had collapsed like a balloon which had leaked out its air. Without even thinking, I patted the blankets in case there should be a loose baby lying there. No. Nothing at all—no baby, no stains.

"Olena?" I got a good look at her face. She was—what else to call it?—she was dead, her eyelids halfway down. I kissed her cold mouth, which felt hard as a buckle. Then again I kissed her, frantic, blowing my breath deep and pinching her nostrils shut. I was trying to cry without losing the rhythm of the breath and my body shook. I thought my forced air might inflate Olena anywhere, blow up her abdomen or toes, because I did not understand how anything functioned in this place; but nothing happened except that my heart beat got louder and throbbed in my head until even the sight of Olena lying there pulsated to my eye.

She was dead. I walked away on the beach. I covered her with the blanket and sat there, holding her uplifted hand. I walked some more. I took off every stitch of her clothes and, sure enough, her stomach was flat now as a young girl's. She looked younger, too, fourteen at most, but her face was tired.

I dressed her body again and tried wrapping her hand around the pink doll's foot but there was no grip.

Finally, because I could not bear to put her into this ground, to bury her in Virginia, I laid her on the raft in the blanket and spread her red hair, and combed it with my fingers dipped in water. The bracelet looked tarnished and there was rust in the links of the chain. I placed on her eyes the prettiest coquinas I could find, and she seemed to be staring at the sun with a gaze part pink, purple, pearly. Then I saw I could not push her out to sea without crying, so I wrote in the ledger book awhile, until I could stand to do that.

8

Now it is dark again, and I think I can bear to push Olena off into the waters and let the current carry her down this coast. There have been noises from the thickets at my back. I think the wolf is there.

In a minute I am going to close up this ledger book and wrap it in a strip of wool I have torn off my blanket and put it under Olena's arm, and then I am going to walk waist-deep into the water and watch them both ride away. Who knows where this sea will end, or where Olena will carry the doll's foot and the book? Maybe somewhere there'll be someone to read the words, or someone who dreams he has read them.